Homemaker

ALSO BY
RUTHIE KNOX AND ANNIE MARE

Big Name Fan

Everyone I Kissed Since You Got Famous (writing as Mae Marvel)

If I Told You, I'd Have to Kiss You (writing as Mae Marvel)

Cosmic Love at the Multiverse Hair Salon (by Annie Mare)

Homemaker

A Prairie Nightingale Mystery

RUTHIE KNOX and
ANNIE MARE

THOMAS & MERCER

This is a work of fiction. Names, characters, organizations, places, events, and incidents are either products of the author's imagination or are used fictitiously. Otherwise, any resemblance to actual persons, living or dead, is purely coincidental.

Text copyright © 2025 by Ruthie Knox and Annie Mare
All rights reserved.

No part of this book may be reproduced, or stored in a retrieval system, or transmitted in any form or by any means, electronic, mechanical, photocopying, recording, or otherwise, without express written permission of the publisher.

Published by Thomas & Mercer, Seattle

www.apub.com

Amazon, the Amazon logo, and Thomas & Mercer are trademarks of Amazon.com, Inc., or its affiliates.

EU product safety contact:
Amazon Media EU S. à r.l.
38, avenue John F. Kennedy, L-1855 Luxembourg
amazonpublishing-gpsr@amazon.com

ISBN-13: 9781662530906 (paperback)
ISBN-13: 9781662529795 (digital)

Cover design and illustration by Jarrod Taylor

Printed in the United States of America

*This one is for Annie's therapist, Kate, who quieted
every voice except the one that wanted to tell stories.
Thank you for the joy that found Prairie Nightingale.*

Chapter 1

Prairie Nightingale stood on her tiptoes, ignoring the incessant buzz of her phone in the back pocket of her jeans and craning for a better look at Amber Jenkins.

"What do you think of Mrs. Jenkins's handbag?" she asked her daughter Anabel.

Prairie and Anabel were part of a loose congregation of parents and family members milling around on the paved playground of the K–8 gifted school, waiting for the final release bell. Prairie hated moments like these, when there was a measurable stretch of time but nothing happening and no way to get anything done. An article she'd once read called it "garbage time." When she was going through her divorce, she'd found a lot of articles like that—about how women's time was wasted and their labor undervalued—as she tried to understand why the world believed she'd spent her seventeen years as a wife and mother doing essentially nothing.

"I don't think of Mrs. Jenkins's handbag." Anabel looked away from her phone long enough to flick her eyes over to the purse in question. "But if you're asking me how much it cost, that's a seven-hundred-dollar bag. Nine, if it's from this year."

"Huh." Prairie watched Amber, whose gaze was fixed in the middle distance as she arranged her ripple of blond hair over one shoulder. Bearing up under her own garbage time. Amber had two kids, like Prairie. She was sharp and irreverent, with a slightly faded tattoo of koi circling a lotus blossom on her shoulder. Once, she'd been Prairie's favorite among a group of women who went for coffee after school drop-off and got together to make swag bags for the teachers. Prairie had always thought she and Amber had a genuine connection as the two moms in the group without a prestigious education. Both of them knew how to keep track of the drink orders from a ten top.

"Remember a couple of weeks ago when Mrs. Jenkins backed into that Dodge Ram and smashed her taillight?" Prairie asked Anabel.

"No. I have no idea what you're talking about." Her daughter's dry tone failed to disguise a hint of interest. She was not immune to what some called Prairie's nosiness and what Prairie called her talent at vital pattern recognition.

"Well, that happened. And look." Prairie angled her head at a dirty black Escalade illegally parked across from the school. "The taillight is still busted."

"So?"

"Who spends nine hundred dollars on a new handbag and doesn't get their taillight fixed?"

"I don't know. Why would I know that?" Anabel squinted in Amber's direction. "Didn't she used to carry a Kitty Blue purse?"

"That's right! The metallic blue crossbody bag with the cat ears. And Kitty Blue is not high dollar." Prairie had never bought anything from the faddish direct-to-consumer brand, but she was familiar from seeing it hyped on the social media channels of practically every woman she'd ever met. "An upgrade like that begs a lot of questions."

"Not really. Lots of things could explain it. Maybe someone bought her this new purse because her Kitty Blue one started getting ratty. Or the people who fix cars are too busy. Why do you even care?"

"It's just something to keep me occupied while we wait for your sister," Prairie said. "I don't really *care*."

This was a lie. Prairie did care, in the way that you couldn't help caring about people you'd known for your children's entire lives who didn't talk to you anymore and had blocked you from the group chat for reasons you understood but didn't agree with.

It wasn't Prairie's fault. At least, *she* didn't think so. She blamed Dr. Carmichael. Nathan Carmichael had been a popular local ob-gyn until Prairie found out—via an investigation that began when he failed to deliver an anticipated donation to the PTO the year she was fundraising chair—that the doctor was serially abusing his patients. She couldn't let it go, and didn't let it go, until there was nowhere for Nathan Carmichael to go but prison.

It caused a scandal. Green Bay was not a big town, in population or in generosity of spirit. The doctor's wife, who had been part of Prairie's friend group, had to resign her seat as a state senator and move away with her kids to weather the gossip. Prairie's role in the unpleasantness did not go unnoticed.

She was shunned. Cast out. Politely, Midwest-nice ghosted.

Although, in truth, she had never been completely clear on whether she lost almost all her friends because she was a dog with a bone about Nathan Carmichael or because she'd pulled the trigger on her divorce. Everyone liked Greg, her ex. In fact, Prairie liked Greg, her ex. He was, as the women in her life had never failed to remind her, one of the *good ones.*

But she could have approval, or she could live free and do as she liked. When Prairie felt sad about the friends she'd lost getting to the bottom of the mystery, she looked at the picture she'd saved on her phone of Nathan Carmichael crying in a courtroom. When she felt sad about the friends she'd lost because of her divorce, she let herself feel sad.

Her conscience was clear.

"Will you deal with your phone already, Mom? The sound of your notifications literally gives me nausea."

"I'm going to go talk to her." Prairie adjusted the well-worn messenger bag on her hip and grabbed her daughter's forearm. "Come with me."

"Oh my God." Anabel squared her shoulders and bent her knees. "Please don't make your nemesis talk to you."

Prairie ignored the inaccurate label. "Nemesis" was a rarefied and mutual relationship of jealous hostility, whereas Prairie had nothing against Amber Jenkins. If she *did* have a nemesis, it would be her US congressional representative, who'd once called her "hysterical" in response to a letter she sent him about his abysmal comments on gay marriage.

"It will only take a minute," she told Anabel. "We can't just stand here waiting for your sister. Maelynn's always the last one out."

"If you make me do this, you have to drive us through Firetta's for breakfast tomorrow."

Prairie narrowed her eyes at Anabel. "Deal."

"And you'll turn off the monitoring app on my socials."

"Never."

Now Anabel narrowed her eyes. "One day a week, you let me wear slippers as shoes to school."

Prairie sighed. "Fine. But you have to participate in the conversation."

With Anabel close behind her, Prairie dodged and wove her way through the other school-pickup parents—the lone dads and grandmothers with their heads bent over their phones, the clumps of moms complaining about the parking situation and enjoying the anemic sunlight of a forty-five-degree afternoon that everyone could agree was "pretty good for April in Wisconsin."

"It's not too late to not do this," Anabel said as they drew close. "I'll even take our deal off the table. I do love you, and I'm invested in your long-term survival."

Prairie lifted an arm in a friendly wave. "Amber!"

The other woman mostly succeeded in hiding her surprise at Prairie's approach. It was a social convention that every mom had to at least pretend to be friends with all the other moms, and Prairie was

Homemaker

using that convention to her advantage. Amber seemed to know this, given how she was frozen in place and her smile was close lipped.

"Prairie," Amber said once it was obvious she could not escape. "How tall is Anabel getting? Sophomore?"

"Freshman," Anabel answered dutifully.

Amber smiled genuinely at Prairie's daughter. She wasn't a bad person, just hampered by Prairie's status as a pariah. "You look just like your mom these days. All that shiny brown hair and dimples—I bet everyone tells you that."

Anabel smoothed her palms over the shiny brown hair in question. Even if she buzzed it off, she couldn't avoid being told she looked like her mother's copy-paste. In addition to her hair, Prairie had given Anabel her dimples, an excellent nose, and expressive eyebrows that made Anabel's desire to lightly maim her mother for making her talk to Amber Jenkins more than clear.

"Did you end up at Ashwaubenon for high school?" Amber asked.

"No, East."

"Really? How's the transition going?"

Prairie stepped forward, playing defense against Amber's attempt to make this conversation all about Anabel. "Listen, I was thinking about you the other day, because wasn't it you who told me about a great garage where you take your car? Some under-the-radar place, super reasonable on prices?"

The school bell rang. Amber shook her head, pretending to focus her attention beyond Prairie to where kids were beginning to emerge from the double side doors. "That must have been someone else."

"I could've sworn it was you."

Amber's son broke away from the scrum of children in his usual disarray, his coat dangling from one elbow, the sleeve dragging in the dirty slush. Her mouth compressed a fraction. "No, it couldn't have been," she said. "We're leasing, so we have to take it to the dealership." She adjusted her purse strap in preparation to escape. "Anyway, there's Grayson, so—"

5

"Amber!" Prairie chirped in false surprise. "Dang, girl! Look at your purse!" Beside her, Anabel stiffened in horror.

Prairie understood. She was internally wincing herself, because she was not, even with a few drinks in her, someone who could pull off a *Dang, girl!* Opposite. She was a white woman who'd grown up in a cohousing community outside of Portland, Oregon, in the nineties. But she was also running out of time, and Amber needed to accept this olive branch quickly and answer her questions. "I'm dead of jealousy. Where did you buy it?"

Amber folded her arm protectively over the buttery soft, ostrich-embossed leather of her new purse. "To be honest, I didn't. I went to one of those swap nights with friends. I had a few Coach bags I hadn't used in forever, so I traded up."

The hairs on the back of Prairie's neck stood on end. *Nope.* She ignored Anabel's sharp elbow nudge and how Amber's son was circling her, trying to shove some paper in her face to sign. "That's so lucky! I have literally never been that lucky at a swap. You must feel so smug."

Amber gave her a half smile and a half shrug that obviously meant *Oh my God, go away, Prairie.* She took the paper her son was trying to give her, ran her eyes over it, and pulled her phone out of her impossible purse.

Amber's phone was at least three models out of date and had a cracked screen.

She and Amber had once compared the new phones they'd both purchased the first moment they became available, eager to learn all their ways. Prairie's current phone, humming softly with incoming notifications in her back pocket, was three weeks old, had cost as much as a full mortgage payment, and came equipped with a protection plan that would replace the screen overnight even if she deliberately smashed it just to feel her own power.

Amber hovered her phone over the paper, swiped the screen a few times, and handed the note back to her son. "Go run that over to recycling. I just e-signed it and turned it in." She slid the phone back into her purse. Prairie watched it notch into a well-appointed purse organizer before Amber closed the flap.

"There's Maelynn," Anabel practically shouted. She pulled at Prairie's arm.

"Oh, you better go. It looks like Maelynn needs a hand. It was nice catching up with you."

Prairie glanced over at her younger daughter, exiting the school doors with her backpack, trumpet, and a Sterilite of supplies for her science project. Not a strand of Maelynn's wavy auburn hair was out of place. She wouldn't have let Prairie carry or touch any of her stuff if a hurricane blew in. "Listen—"

But Amber had already started to scurry away, the wind ruffling her hair just enough to show off the stoplight-red streaks at her nape.

"Wait!" Prairie called, out of chances but unable to help herself. "You didn't tell me, and I'm dying to know. Who brought that fabulous bag to the swap? I might pester her for deets."

"Jesus, Mom. *Jesus.*" Anabel didn't even try to keep that under her breath.

"Um, Lisa. It was Lisa's."

"Lisa Radcliffe or Lisa Preet? Or did you mean Lisa Van Der Perren?"

Five feet away now, Amber looked fully panicked. "Radcliffe. Lisa Radcliffe. I really have to run. See you!" She turned and waved over her shoulder, but she didn't look back.

Prairie poked Anabel's upper arm as they turned to meet Maelynn. "No. No way."

"Mom. Stop."

She did stop, but only because her eleven-year-old daughter had completed a mincing circuit of a puddle and come to a stop at Prairie's elbow. "Hey, Mom. Hey, Anabel." Maelynn had zipped her black puffer coat all the way to the top, which made her skin look like skim milk and brought out the freckles across the bridge of her nose.

"Hey, Peanut. You have a good day?"

"Yeah. Can we go by a craft store on the way home? I need poster board. I'm supposed to make a presentation for my special education teacher about strategies to overcome sensory overwhelm. It's a terrible assignment. What if I told *you* to overcome being cold when it's freezing outside? What is your strategy for overcoming the need to breathe in those jeans you made me help you zip up that you can't even sit down in?"

"They had just come out of the dryer, and they still fit, but carry on," Prairie said.

"I'm changing the assignment. I'm going to make a poster about how sensory differences in autistic people cause trauma if they're not accommodated. So will you stop at the craft store?"

Prairie smiled at Maelynn, whose fierce, stormy expression melted her heart like it always had. "I have poster board. White, black, and I think there's still a blue and a couple hot pink. Stick-on letters in black and gold."

Maelynn nodded. "Okay. We can go home, then."

Prairie caught Anabel's eye and arched one brow. "There is zero possibility she got that bag from Lisa Radcliffe at a swap night. You know I'm right."

Maelynn looked around until she located the car. She began walking in that direction. Anabel trailed after her, sliding her finger over the screen of her phone and navigating by peripheral vision.

"The phone and the taillight don't add up," Prairie mused. "They don't go with a nine-hundred-dollar purse."

"That she traded for at a mom flea market."

Prairie waved her hand in dismissal. "Everybody brings trash to those swap meets. If they have anything good, they sell it on Facebook Marketplace or put it out on consignment. Also, you have to stop trying to make things sound unimportant by adjectifying them with the word 'mom.' It's sexist."

"'Adjectifying' is not a word." Maelynn was carefully placing her trumpet case in the trunk of the car in a foam box she had ordered on the internet with her children's Mastercard. Anabel threw herself into the front seat.

Prairie's phone started to ring. She slid it out of her jeans pocket as she dropped into the driver's seat of her zippy little Honda. "I need a few minutes for work."

They knew the drill. Anabel pulled out her AirPods. Maelynn situated herself in the back, unzipping her schoolbag and retrieving her lap desk from the back seat organizer. Prairie unlocked her phone, reveling in the pleasant tingles that sluiced from the top of her scalp down to her lower back.

It hadn't always been like this. Before the divorce, when Greg was constantly working and often forgot to come home for dinner—when he was too tired to help with the housework but nonetheless relied on Prairie to gently midwife him through the labor of processing his day—it got to the point where she didn't want to look at her phone lest she discover one more thing to keep track of. One more job to do.

But all that had changed. Not because she'd gotten a divorce, but because now she earned a salary.

When Prairie asked for a separation five years ago, after she and Greg had tried both couples therapy and marriage counseling, their shared therapist had advised Prairie to start thinking about "next steps." What she meant was that Prairie hadn't gone to college. She'd left the cohousing community where she grew up for Seattle, supporting herself by working a string of unskilled service jobs. Then Anabel was born, and she'd abandoned the workforce entirely. Regardless of the financial agreements that came with the divorce, in the long term, Prairie would require an income, and finding someone willing to hire her wouldn't be easy. She'd need a plan.

At first, Prairie had acknowledged the therapist's point. This was something she should think about.

Then she thought about it and got angrier than she'd ever been in her life.

Greg Ozmanski, her ex-husband, whom she'd met when he was a poor graduate student who sometimes put on two different shoes in the morning, was, at present, the founder and co-owner of an embarrassingly lucrative institutional software development firm that had started in a two-hundred-square-foot office that smelled like mouse.

Prairie was *not* the other co-owner.

She was not, even though she was the one who'd coaxed and cozened him through his dissertation work. Even though it was Prairie who took on extra shifts as a barista and a waitress so Greg could focus on internships and a string of poorly paid jobs at start-ups, and Prairie whose tips covered the rent and utilities so Greg could funnel his salary into buying ground-floor tech stock. She picked out his snappy wardrobe for interviews. She went with him to investor events and fluently conversed with rich white men about rounds of financing and what the digital future anticipated for business and how it was that her husband was uniquely positioned to meet those needs.

When Prairie was pregnant and Greg moved them across the country to his hometown for a job he'd accepted over the phone without telling her first, she was the one who pretended it was fine, even as she'd been reluctant to move so far from her parents. Even as she missed the Olympic Mountains and Pacific Ocean and felt like a literal fish out of water in the Midwest.

She provided twenty-four-hour, seven-days-a-week care for Anabel and, later, for Maelynn. She couldn't earn more than childcare cost, and Greg worked eighteen-hour days, so she made a home for him and their children. She entertained his colleagues and clients. She made everything work.

Prairie gave Greg Ozmanski the patina of a brilliant family man, and he used her skills, her intuition, and her emotional intelligence. He used her flexibility, her organization, and her detail orientation. He used her labor, her time, her ideas, her support, her patience, her *body*, turning them into reputation and work that paid *him* money and paid *other people* money but paid Prairie nothing.

Because the work Greg did was work.

The work Prairie did was not.

That was when Prairie had decided she didn't want alimony and a document splitting their marital assets. She had been working for seventeen years gaining complex and monetizable experience alongside breathtakingly refined soft skills. She wanted what she'd earned.

She wanted the *credit*.

And so, instead of a traditional division of assets when they finalized their divorce a little more than two years ago, Prairie had instructed their lawyer to establish a trust, in which she and Greg *were* partners, though she had all the day-to-day decision-making power. With the trust's money, she hired a staff, who were paid fair and equitable wages to handle everything that had always gone into her successful household—and Prairie was the CEO.

She could admit it was an experiment, or, really, a statement. It wasn't forever. But she liked her life so much better as CEO of the 724 Maple Project. She even had business cards. PRAIRIE NIGHTINGALE, HOMEMAKER.

Prairie fucking loved those business cards.

She tackled her notifications in the order of their arrival. First, an email from Greg with the figure she needed to complete his tax interview. She pulled up the interview doc, filled in the number, and submitted it electronically to the accountant's firm through its online portal.

Next, three news notifications, which she whipped through quickly. The zoo had started offering themed parties and overnight experiences for kids. She set a reminder to look at the website later in case it might be something Maelynn would want to do for her next birthday.

The president's chief of staff had forced an aide to sign an NDA. Sex monster. File under *Men Are Trash*.

The Green Bay chief of police would be giving a statement asking for the public's assistance with an urgent matter at four thirty. File under *Please and Thank You and Bookmark*.

Greg had left a voicemail and sent a text to let her know he'd sent her the email. She texted him back, This kind of behavior is why we got divorced.

He replied, Whatever it takes to get your attention. Followed by a praise-hands emoji. Followed by the smiley face with hearts for eyes.

Prairie's lips twitched, and the dimple in her right cheek started to sink.

You're trying not to smile, he wrote. Send me a selfie so I can see.

She lifted her stylus, let it hover over the screen for a moment, and blocked him.

Was she completely immune to Greg Ozmanski's geeky charms? No. She had built a life with him and made two perfect daughters. She'd had her reasons for falling in love with him when she was a mere dimpled, shiny-haired child.

But when her heart had broken at the end of their marriage, it hadn't gone back together the same way. There were pieces of it that would always belong to Greg. The rest had mended themselves for some unknown something else that she hadn't put her finger on yet.

Whatever it was, it was going to be big, important, and challenging and would make the world better for her children.

Prairie was reviewing a list of substitutions the grocery shopper had made when Anabel took out one AirPod. "Did you just block Dad?"

"Maybe."

"He says to unblock him because he wants to tell you something."

Prairie started the car. "Tell him I'll think about it."

"You know, this is what that one divorce movie said you weren't supposed to do. I believe it was in the part called 'Don't Make Your Kid a Messenger for Your Bullshit.'"

"It was called *Kids in the Middle*," Maelynn said from the back seat. "And you're not supposed to say 'bullshit.'"

"According to Mom, there are no bad words, only strong words," Anabel replied. "Dad says he'll see you soon."

Homemaker

"He's coming for dinner?" Prairie signaled left and turned onto the broad two-lane toward home.

"He's already at the house."

Prairie sighed, pulling away into traffic. "Fuck."

But she mouthed the strong word. Because she was a good mother.

Chapter 2

Greg met her in the driveway.

He must have received Prairie's telepathic message that they needed to talk out of range of their children. Less because they would fight—it had been a long time since they'd had passion to spare for that—and more because they had the kind of daughters who would have listened to everything they said, mentally recording it in the event it became useful to turn against them in the future.

"How's Tuesday treating you?" Greg asked. He needed a haircut. Maelynn had the same auburn hair, though Greg's was darker and starting to go salt and pepper at the temples.

"You parked in the driveway again. Now I'm going to have to move my car so you can move your car. You know how I feel about that."

"I do." Greg nodded at his BMW. "In my defense, I was thinking about a work thing when I pulled up, and I can't even remember doing that."

He wore dark, casually expensive jeans and a fitted concert T-shirt that looked vintage but was really reproduction vintage for the barely Gen-Xer who hadn't been cool enough to buy the real band T-shirt when the band was actually touring. It was tucked in, because Greg was a software engineer and could never quite remember the cool thing to do.

And he had two fingers hooked around a beer. *Her* beer, which he'd taken from the section of the refrigerator he knew perfectly well belonged only to Prairie. On Greg's nights with the girls, he stayed over in a downstairs en suite bedroom with its own separate entrance that they called "the Annex." Tonight was not Greg's night.

Prairie crossed her arms. If he was going to drink her beer, he could pay for it with information. "What do you know about Noah Jenkins?"

Greg's eyebrows immediately forked into a frown. "Why? I thought you didn't like him."

Prairie took a deep breath. "I don't want to *date* him, Greg. Jesus. I just need to know more than I know about him."

Greg's eyebrows were now fully crossing. "You need to."

"Look, that is my beer, and you're not supposed to be in my house tonight. You parked in my spot. There is a spot of barbecue sauce on your chin, so I know you scammed an early dinner from my larder, and you're out here in the driveway talking to me, not parenting. Unless you're interested in having a long conversation where I unnecessarily make an issue out of every single one of those things, yes. I need to."

Greg rubbed his chin, but he wasn't *not* smiling. "Prairie."

She made an *out with it* gesture with her hand.

"Okay. It's not much. He used to come to those Dads, Doughnuts, and Dunks mornings at the school, and he was usually on my team."

Dads, Doughnuts, and Dunks had been a short-lived, dubious community-building effort initiated by the school board, wherein kids would come to school early on the designated morning, eat doughnuts, and cheer on their dads while they played three-on-three basketball against each other in the schoolyard. The brevity of its lifespan was largely due to the fact the dads kept getting into verbal and sometimes physical altercations in full view of the children.

"And?"

Greg leaned his shoulder against the side of the house. "You know, it's never a good sign when guys take more than five seconds and three words to explain what they do for a living. Noah Jenkins talking about his job is a lot of words. Like, crypto stuff. AI-bots-farming-server-rigs stuff. The kind of thing where you have to spend money to make money."

"You mean the kind of thing where you lease cars you can only afford eight payments on and don't fix your wife's phone, leaving her with little choice but to hang on, month by month, keeping everything together with her bare and ridiculously capable hands after you insisted she stay home and raise 'your kids' because that's how your mom did it when she failed to raise you and left it to your wife to give it a go?"

"Sure. Yes. Something like that." Greg sipped the beer. "I feel like there's an undercurrent here you're not saying."

"I don't know if there is an undercurrent yet or not. Anything else?"

Greg gave Prairie a long look. Then he looked at his car, trapped by hers. After that, he looked to the sky—Prairie assumed for divine support. "I suppose, in the category of what predicaments Noah may or may not have led his family into, I heard he tried to short-sell his house in that development of Chris Radcliffe's. Bay Glen."

Prairie raised a finger and pulled out her phone, then navigated to the latest parent contact list from the PTO at Maelynn's school. She scrolled through to *Jenkins*, eyeballed the address, and typed it into her navigation app.

Huh.

"Where'd you go, Prayer?"

"They did move. Amber and Noah."

Prairie had been to the Jenkinses' old address at Bay Glen plenty of times. It was on the same street as Lisa Radcliffe's house—the same Lisa Radcliffe who had *allegedly* given up her high-dollar purse to Amber at one of the swap nights that Prairie wasn't invited to anymore. Prairie had been to Lisa's house, too. It was enormous, as befitted the property developer's family. Prairie had gone there mostly for PTO planning, but sometimes for a get-together, because Lisa was the de facto leader of the mom friends. She'd introduced Prairie to a lot of people, brewing strong mugs of tea and serving honest-to-God scones in her bright, marble-clad kitchen with shiny stainless appliances.

But Amber and Noah Jenkins didn't live in that neighborhood anymore. Now they lived on the other side of town, on the "wrong" side of Gray Street.

If one of Prairie's friends were dealing with a bad husband who desperately needed divorcing, Prairie wouldn't think twice about giving her anything she wanted, even if what she wanted was something expensive and frivolous. In fact, it would probably be easier to give a friend something frivolous during a hard time, especially if your friend was proud.

Lisa Radcliffe was a genuinely wonderful person and a close friend of Amber's. Maybe the purse really had come from Lisa, just as a gift, not from a swap. And maybe Amber had been too embarrassed to say so, especially to Prairie.

"This is getting awkward." Greg broke into her thoughts. "You and me, standing here under the motion-activated side-door light, soaking in the atmosphere of our long acquaintance."

Prairie looked up from her phone fast enough to catch him trying to do an amused eye-twinkle thing at her that used to be a prelude to him getting flirty.

She wished someone had told her five years ago that there was no such thing as asking your husband for a divorce *once*. You had to do it over and over again, in big ways and small ones, like drawing a boundary in the dirt and having to redraw it every time he scuffed his foot over it.

If you didn't redraw the line, it disappeared. She had learned this the hard way.

"I've told you not to drink my beer," she said. "I have to pick that up myself because the grocery delivery won't let you put alcohol on your order, and I am very busy running everyone's lives, raising your children, and providing companionship to your mother." Prairie could hear the tone of amusement in her lecture, which they both knew was not serious.

Greg smiled, but it was teasing her now. "What I hear you saying is, next time, don't call you from the house to ask for an invitation to dinner."

"I would appreciate it."

"Noted."

When Prairie moved to get past him, he backed up and put his hand on the doorframe, blocking her way in with his newly muscly arm. She remembered when his arms were just pale broomsticks, good only for keyboard jockeying in front of his three-monitor computer—before kids, before all this—but give a man money and fear of mortality, and he hits the gym as if sculpted forearms will save his life.

"These little tête-à-têtes are fun, is what I also hear you saying." His eyes were still twinkling at her.

Prairie sighed. She did wish Greg would stop testing out the "moves" she assumed he was bringing out of storage for the dating scene on her, just because she was handy and required by law to answer his phone calls.

Smiling, Greg handed her his nearly full beer. "Tell the girls good night for me," he said. "Truly, the reason I stopped by was to say hi to Mom, since she's back from her conference and I was done with work early."

Prairie adjusted the strap of her messenger bag. She could admit that there was a time after they separated when she wouldn't have been immune to him. They'd both traveled a long way since then, and she knew very well that his continued mothlike attraction to the lights of 724 Maple *was* about the girls. And his mother, Joyce, whom Prairie had retained in the divorce, and who lived in a separate mother-in-law apartment connected by a breezeway to the home that Prairie had also retained.

Also Greg's cat, who still lived with Prairie because Gingernut hated the loft apartment Greg rented.

It would've been easier to stay married. That had been her preference. She'd simply reached a point in her life where easy wasn't a choice she could make anymore.

"I get that," she said. "And thanks for the info about Noah Jenkins."

"Sure. But, hey." He pointed a finger at her. "Be careful. Not just because Noah's a dick, but because I wouldn't want something to get out of hand and you're caught in the middle."

Like last time. That was what he meant. *With Nathan Carmichael, MD.*

"Good night, Greg."

He grinned. "You can't go in yet. You have to move your car so I can move my car."

"You owe me takeout for this."

Prairie moved her car. She circled the block and bumped over the low spot at the end of her driveway before pulling into the garage. Inside the house, she kicked Anabel's shoes out of the doorway and hung up her jacket, savoring the welcome smell of a dinner she hadn't had to cook.

Joyce—her ex-mother-in-law, wonderful grandmother, current housemate, and dear friend—sat at the table in the dining area talking to both girls. Greg had inherited his good looks from Joyce, who had a pleasantly curvaceous figure and big hair highlighted in improbable shades of blond over a version of the auburn she was born with. She liked a lot of bling, which she'd earned many times over. Joyce had retired from a forty-year career at the Department of Natural Resources, where she'd risen through the ranks to the highest levels of leadership. She'd only just returned from a forensic genealogy conference, a field she'd become passionate about after dabbling in family genealogy for years.

Maelynn turned around and saw Prairie. "Mom."

"Maelynn."

"Grayson's shoes are too small."

"What?"

Anabel pulled a scrunchie off her wrist and used it to ball her hair up on top of her head. "When we put our bags in our rooms, we heard you and Dad talking through Maelynn's window."

"Maelynn's window is closed," Prairie said. "It's forty degrees outside."

"Yeah, but it's, like, right over the driveway."

"We saw you through the window talking, and then we opened the window," Maelynn clarified. "And then we could hear you, so we listened. It reminded me of what I wanted to tell you after school when you were talking to Anabel about Mrs. Jenkins."

"That Grayson's shoes are too small." Prairie tried to organize her thoughts enough to keep up with her scheming children, who, unlike her, were public school–educated and could be ruthless.

"Yes. But that's unusual, because Grayson always has the newest sneakers. Only he doesn't anymore. He takes them off when we're at our desk clump in class because they're hurting his toes."

Now Prairie hoped Lisa *had* given Amber that purse stuffed with money and the phone number of a lawyer.

"Perfect," she said. "Thank you, Maelynn. I appreciate your attention to my interests."

"This is where I interject that the girls have filled me in on your observations about Grayson's mother." Joyce's blue eyes did her own version of Greg's twinkle, except hers meant *They are just like you, so you can't be mad at my perfect grandbabies.*

"I see." Prairie walked into the kitchen, which opened onto the dining area, in order to turn on the oven. Beth, the woman who cooked for her family five nights a week, had texted instructions for warming up dinner. Prairie lifted the lid on the casserole dish and observed a portion missing. Greg had indeed stolen her food. "And I assume they also told you that Maelynn has a poster to make for special education and Anabel has a video meeting with her algebra tutor in ten minutes."

Homemaker

"What is even your goal with Mrs. Jenkins?" Anabel backed up to slump against the counter on the dining room side of the breakfast bar. "I'm with Dad. I'm not sure I like where this is going."

Prairie took a moment to remind herself how hard it was to be not-quite-fifteen so she didn't lunge across the breakfast bar and, in a fit of petty retaliation, snatch the scrunchie that Anabel was fidgeting with. "I don't know enough to have a goal yet."

"None of this stuff is yours to know. It never is. Ninety-five percent of the time, when you get obsessed about somebody else's business, it turns out to be nothing."

"You seemed just as interested when you ran in here and told me all about it, Ms. Anabel." This came from Joyce, who liked to keep the peace as much as was possible between three Nightingale women.

Anabel rolled her eyes. Joyce missed it, and Prairie almost told on her daughter, but she decided, again, to go high.

No one informed you before getting pregnant that your kids would hurt your feelings, and the most important thing you could do was suck it up and think clearly about what you wanted to teach them.

Prairie walked out of the kitchen and grabbed a dining chair and sat down, turning her body to face Anabel. "It could be true that ninety-five percent of what I'm interested in is nothing. I don't think so, but I'm not infallible. But if it *is* true, that still means the other five percent of the time, it's Nathan Carmichael. Getting involved in that wasn't comfortable, either. Not at all. But without me saying something, how many more women would that peeling anus wart have hurt?"

"Your mom lost a lot to report that man," Joyce said softly. "At the time, I wasn't sure about it, either. But I just got back from a conference where it came up over and over again that sometimes all it takes for justice to win is for someone to step forward and tell the truth. What your mother did was very brave."

Anabel's expression was sullen now. "I just don't think that some mom who treated herself to a fancy purse is embroiled in scandal. And I don't think that there's something going on all over again."

21

"Here's the thing, sweetpea," Prairie said. "I don't necessarily think so, either. I don't know what the reason is for Amber's purse and the other things I noticed, because I don't have a very good imagination, and in this case I wouldn't want one. If I made up a story for why Amber Jenkins has a busted car, a cracked phone, a poorly shod kid, and a rich lady's purse that she did *not* trade for a few outlet Coach bags, I might miss the real answers right in front of my face. But if I set out to know everything, then I know when one little thing doesn't fit. And the things that don't fit matter."

Anabel picked at her nail polish. "You were embarrassing, though. At Maelynn's school. I get it, there's obviously something going on in Mrs. Jenkins's life, but she had nowhere to run away from you."

Prairie had heard more than one version of Anabel's argument from nearly everyone in her life. That she was embarrassing. That she meddled. That she asked the wrong kinds of questions and cared about the wrong kinds of things. She had grown up in a very different place from her daughters. A "cohousing community" was just a "commune" by another name, and the only way to keep a commune from turning into a cult was for everyone to talk about everything and take care of everyone. It had to really *be* a community.

She wouldn't want to raise her family the way her parents had raised her, but some of the values she grew up with had stuck.

"I'm sorry to have embarrassed you," she said to Anabel. "But every now and then, knowing what the real story is means I can help someone. And the question you might think about asking yourself, Anabel, whenever me being curious starts to seem too embarrassing for you to survive, is whose interest does it serve for me to shut up and stick to my lane?"

Anabel pulled the scrunchie out of her hair, letting it fall around her face. Her cheeks were a little pink.

Prairie gentled her tone. "And, look, it could be that the only thing any of this adds up to is that I'll have to ask Mrs. Jenkins if she's okay, if she and her kids are safe, and if she needs anything. If I had to do that, you're right, she'd hate it, and it would be embarrassing. But if I noticed enough about her situation to be worried, wouldn't it be worth it to ask?"

Anabel put her palms on her cheeks. "This is a lot of lecture to accept that you're nosy."

"Says the young woman I thought was missing for the worst two hours of my life when you were seven years old," Joyce said. "You remember? I went to pick you up from school, but you had followed a second grade teacher home on your bike, convinced she was a voice actor on *Dinosaur Train*, and you wanted proof."

"I'm still not sure I was wrong," Anabel said. "They sound exactly the same. And why was my teacher obsessed with PBS? What was the deal with all the fossils in her classroom?"

Prairie said nothing.

"Fine," Anabel said. "I surrender."

The rest of the evening raced to its finish in the way it always did, with a homework crisis, an unexpected and disgusting cat mess, dinner dishes, interrupting phone calls, and, tonight, helping Joyce try to organize the files and papers that had taken over her apartment after her conference. But later, once the chaos settled down and Prairie walked around the neighborhood with her overgrown baby of a goldendoodle, Zipper, she had time to think about the afternoon's conversations, and she hoped the lecture she'd given Anabel was right. She hoped her interest *was* kind, and that Amber was safe.

This time, she wanted the little hairs on the back of her neck to be wrong.

When she got home, she locked up and set the alarm system. The hush that had settled over the house was so utter, she jumped when her phone buzzed.

Then she looked at it, and her hope broke into pieces.

It was a notification from the *Green Bay Gazette* of a news story posted after the police chief's press conference. When Prairie opened the link to read the story, it punched the breath from her lungs.

23

Lisa Radcliffe was missing.

Amber's close friend, who'd given her the expensive purse, who had hosted countless get-togethers and knew everyone in Prairie's former group of mom friends, was *missing*, gone, whereabouts unknown since last night.

Once, Prairie would have known about it yesterday, when it happened. When Lisa didn't come home last night, Prairie would have been in whatever group chat was alerting and organizing a response. She would have driven around Lisa's neighborhood with Greg, looking for Lisa's car, or called a list of people Lisa's husband had given her.

Prairie *liked* Lisa Radcliffe. They'd been friends, and it was clear—standing here in the dark, her heart racing—that her body still believed they were, even though Prairie had broken the rules. Even though she hadn't really talked to Lisa in years.

And Amber had known. When Prairie asked her about the purse, Amber *must* have known Lisa was gone. That her husband and kids were talking to the police.

Amber had been alone in the schoolyard, staring at nothing, when she was usually in a talkative group of other moms.

The police had held the press conference to ask the community for "information" about what had happened to Lisa Radcliffe. Prairie knew only one thing—that Amber Jenkins had Lisa Radcliffe's brand-new, fancy purse.

It wasn't much.

But given that she knew this one thing, how hard would it be to find out another thing, and then one more? All it took was asking the questions everyone else was too uncomfortable to raise. Prairie didn't even have a reputation to protect anymore.

She held her phone against her chest, thinking about what she'd said to Anabel about how much people had failed to see about Dr. Carmichael. What they hadn't noticed.

What she really believed, but hadn't said, was that she noticed things *because* she was a mom. Because a mom had to notice everything about the entire world, every single day, and question those things, every single day, so that nothing bad would happen.

Something bad had happened to Lisa. Even if she'd simply left for her own reasons, or to escape her own pain—suddenly abandoning three children she adored—that was a nuclear option for a mother.

Who was in a better position to find stuff out about a missing mom, Prairie or the police?

Give her twenty-four hours.

Prairie would have information.

Chapter 3

The school's message came through at 6:30 a.m.

It lit up Prairie's phone with email, text, and voicemail notifications, all pointing toward a PDF letter from Maelynn's principal requesting sensitivity and patience, as well as respect for the Radcliffe family, and offering counseling to students who were upset or worried.

The letter turned morning drop-off at Maelynn's school into ground zero.

Ordinarily, Prairie would drop off Maelynn using the car line—the preference of most middle schoolers—but there was an option to park in the remote lot and walk your child to the front doors. That was the option Prairie had decided to go with this morning.

She signaled and turned into the remote lot.

"What are you doing?"

No one could infuse their voice with more suspicion than Maelynn. It was something Prairie admired about her.

"Oh, I just thought because it's a tough day, I'd walk you to the building."

Maelynn sighed, annoyed at the change in her routine. She sounded just like Greg.

They didn't even get fifteen feet from the car before Prairie overheard two women talking. "I heard she took off right after dinner. Like, put everything away, started the kids on homework, got into her car

Homemaker

to pick up milk for breakfast, and hasn't answered her phone or been seen since."

When Prairie rounded the back end of an SUV, the women came into view, one with her son's cello case in one hand, the other with her daughter's winter boots dangling from her fingertips. She recognized the moms from the school pickup yard, but she didn't know their names.

They both looked at her at the same time, making it clear they knew who Prairie was by reputation. Now that Prairie got a better look at the woman with the cello case, she recognized her as the sister-in-law of one of her former friends.

Now Prairie sighed.

But she kept her ears open.

"Lisa doesn't do milk." Cello Case turned back to her conversation, having thoroughly dismissed Prairie.

"You know what I mean, though. She just didn't come back." This was the second woman, the one carrying her kid's winter boots.

"God knows how many times I've wanted to disappear after dinner. Maybe Lisa just went to her sister's and turned her phone off. Mini breakdown. I had one after Jim's promotion when he had to fly to Chicago every weekend and I went twelve weeks with the kids and no help. I holed myself up at my mom's for three days."

"Maybe, but I don't think the police get involved for a mini breakdown."

"I can't imagine Lisa's younger two will be at school." Cello Case glanced behind her, checking that her kids were still coming but not close enough to hear, and her eyes widened at the sight of Prairie so close. She turned back around and dropped her voice so that Prairie had to strain to hear. "Davey Radcliffe's at Creighton with my Jonathan, and he reminded me that this weekend Davey and Lisa were supposed to be going on a big trip to Chicago, because Davey's a finalist for that mock UN thing at Northwestern. It was in the Creighton newsletter. Davey told Jonathan that he and his mom had behind-the-scenes tickets at the Field Museum. Lisa wouldn't miss any of that on purpose. She was so proud."

Prairie felt a little guilty for listening in, but she had a right to be worried about Lisa. Even when Prairie's phone had stopped ringing after everything went down with the Carmichaels and she was getting a divorce, Lisa had never given her the cut direct. It had been more of a soft fade.

Now approaching the crossing guard, Prairie and the women intersected with Alison Greene, who was waving at her eighth grader, already safe on the other side of the busy intersection. Alison had never seemed to approve or disapprove of Prairie, but Prairie hadn't heard from her in years, either. She was a woman who had been on the periphery of the core group of mom friends, given that she owned an interior design business.

"Hey, Alison," said Cello Case. "I love Piper's unicorn hair. You guys are so artistic."

"Couldn't have stopped her if I tried. But I do kind of like it."

Alison watched her daughter make it to the door while Prairie and the other moms hugged their kids and sent them on their way.

Prairie whispered in Maelynn's ear, "Thanks."

Maelynn shrugged. "Behave," she said.

The women started walking slowly back to their cars. Prairie was grateful for Alison's presence, which justified—barely—her inclusion in the group.

"You must be so worried," Prairie began. "Haven't you worked closely with Lisa before on some of her home-decorating projects?"

Alison nodded. "I don't mind saying that I'm really worked up." She pressed her fingertips under her eyes. "It's so awful, I could scream. I talked to her Sunday afternoon. I needed to check that my courier had delivered a wallpaper sample book because I hadn't heard from her."

"That's right, you're doing her and Chris's new house," Winter Boots said.

Cello Case gave a theatrical gasp. "I forgot about that!"

Prairie sent up a small prayer of thanks that Alison had never been in the loop enough to truly commit to snubbing her. If Alison was working with Lisa again, it meant that she would be likely to have accurate information about how Lisa had been doing recently.

Alison shook her head. "I'm supposed to have it move-in ready right around when school lets out in June, although I doubt they were going to make that, even without this happening. They were still pouring footers last time I was at the site. The thing is"—Alison was fighting tears—"Lisa sounded *fine*. You know she has such a great sense of humor. We were just acquaintances before she hired me for her house, but we'd been getting closer, and she's been the first person who can really make me laugh since my mom died in September." Tears were falling on Alison's face. "I'm *worried* about her."

"Do you have any idea at all what could have happened?" Prairie's heart rate had tripled.

"None," Alison replied. "Like I said, the builders weren't meeting their deadlines, and Chris was working long hours and replacing the site manager with someone he felt like he could trust more. He has a big stake in that development, and it doesn't look good when there's any kind of hang-up. But I've worked on a lot of new builds, and it's always stressful. If anything, Lisa thrives when things get tough." Alison stopped walking beside a red Fiat. "This is me."

Everyone said their goodbyes.

Prairie slid into her car and started the engine, then watched in the rearview mirror as the other women's backup lights came on and they pulled out of the lot. She checked the time on her phone. A few minutes to eight.

Lisa had vanished on Monday after dinner. Call it thirty-six hours ago.

Her husband, Chris, would have called her people sometime late on Monday night. Early Tuesday at the outside. *Have you seen Lisa? She's not answering her phone.*

Prairie closed her eyes. Mentally, she backed up.

First, Chris would have called Lisa. Probably, he'd called her more than once after she didn't come back within an hour, worried something happened to her car, hoping the delay was nothing major, maybe a flat tire or she ran into a friend at the store and her phone battery died.

Either he figured out her phone was dead because his texts weren't delivering and his calls were going straight to voicemail, or else her phone seemed fine and the texts were delivering but she wasn't picking up. Or maybe Lisa didn't have her phone with her at all—although that would be strange, because Prairie didn't know anyone who didn't take their phone everywhere they went.

If Chris and Lisa were the type to track each other's locations and the locations of their kids, Chris might have checked that next. But he hadn't been able to locate her, and so Chris would have called other people. Lisa's family. Lisa's friends. He would have put his kids to bed, and he would have told them something about their mom, probably some softer version of the truth. Maybe he'd had someone come to stay at his house so he could drive to the grocery store and look for his wife.

At some point, either that night or the next morning, he'd called the police. And by the afternoon of the same day, the police had asked the community for help. That meant the police must have ruled out the easy stuff already. They couldn't find Lisa with her phone. She hadn't gone to her mother's or her sister's. She hadn't contacted her friends. She didn't check into a hotel anywhere in town, probably not anywhere in the county, maybe not anywhere in the state of Wisconsin.

Lisa was gone.

Monday night, after dinner, sometime after the sun dropped below the horizon and the temperature started to fall, she'd backed out of her driveway and disappeared from her own life. Her kids had spent Monday night without her, and all day Tuesday, and now it was Wednesday morning, and there was still no news.

Prairie checked the time again, then sent a text. While she waited for a response, she thought about the next right thing to do.

Homemaker

It had been a long time since she'd been in Lisa's neighborhood. After it became clear she wasn't welcome among her old friends, she'd lost track of the details of their lives and how they were changing—Amber going through a hard time, Lisa and Chris building a new house, children growing up and starting to head out into the world.

Maybe she should dip her toe in and reacquaint herself with her old haunts. Chris Radcliffe was one of those Green Bay driveway dads, always fussing with something in the garage. It was possible that to distract himself from Lisa's absence, he would be in his drive, willing to receive a wave and have a brief chat with one of his wife's old friends. That was a good thing to do, wasn't it? A right thing?

Prairie's phone buzzed with the return text she'd been waiting for, which made it clear she had a little time to kill. She pulled out of the lot as the school bell rang through the emptying yard.

🦋

Less than ten minutes later, she was turning left past the tasteful stone-clad sign that marked the entrance to the housing development where Lisa Radcliffe lived.

Bay Glen Estates.

The "estates" sat on several acres of what must have been farmland once, though Chris Radcliffe's development company had made some attempt to reshape the landscape, bulldozing dirt into small hills and contours to wrap the road around—a sign that money had been put into the project on the front end.

The development was one big horseshoe loop of off-white, cream, sand, greige, gray, and the occasional cheeky pale sage. Most of the houses sat far back on double lots, their "architectural character" limited to the front of the house and ordinary vinyl siding wrapped around the parts no one could see from the road.

There was a model home at the entrance. Prairie spotted three different realty agency signs in the windows, probably because they were actively selling phase two. The new part of the development was sited just on the other side of the woodlot, a collection of smaller, more affordable homes, townhomes, and apartment buildings.

She passed Amber Jenkins's old house and spotted a tasteful real estate sign at the top of the brick drive. Prairie made a mental note to take a peek at the listing later. Amber and Noah's place had been one of the smaller homes, closer to the street, with a fenced backyard and overgrown landscaping that Prairie guessed dated to when it was built, around fifteen years ago.

The larger houses were along the U-shape of the horseshoe with their backyards butted up against a patch of woods that had probably once been the property line windbreak between farms. The Radcliffes' was the biggest house on the street. They would have moved here when Lisa's kids were little and this was Chris's flagship project. Stone-faced, beige-sided, with Greek columns on either side of a bright-red front door, it must have been the definition of Green Bay fancy when they built it.

A police cruiser and a black, unmarked sedan sat at the curb. Both were empty. Custom pleated blinds covered the front windows. Those windows let in so much light that Lisa kept them half-closed most of the time. Prairie imagined the dim hush of the front room and wondered who was in there with Chris. The circular drive terminated at the back of the house, where the garage was, so there was no way for her to tell.

She was driving along at less than five miles an hour, taking it in, when she saw a shadow move past the sidelites in the front door. Without thinking, she stepped on the gas, crunching the transmission. In her rearview, she saw a man in a suit and a uniformed police officer come onto the front step, watching her drive away.

She forced herself to assume a residential speed while checking the mirrors, certain she'd spot the officer flagging her, running to his car to chase her, or possibly a black helicopter circling overhead, picking out her car in its spotlight.

Homemaker

"You deserved that scare, Prairie," she whispered to herself.

She listened to music for the rest of her drive to her destination and tried not to wonder if they'd written down her plate number or how many black Honda Accords there were with her particular trim package in the greater Green Bay area.

They couldn't arrest her for aggravated curiosity.

🦋

Megan Storch met Prairie at the door of her townhome with a mug of coffee in one hand and giant Ugg boots on her feet. Her curly hair was darker than its usual honey blond, still damp from her morning shower. Prairie guessed she hadn't had time for self-care until after she got her kids to school.

Whenever she could, Prairie liked to check in with her best friend in the mornings after drop-off to see if there was time for even a short chat. "You know what I was just thinking?" she asked now without preamble. "Chris Radcliffe is home today, it looks like, and that means they don't have him down at the station. I only saw one officer at his house. There was also an unmarked black car, which suggests some other sort of law enforcement, or a lawyer. But surely if the cops thought Chris had something to do with Lisa's disappearance, they would have him sequestered in an interview room, deep into hour six of a help-me-understand-type interrogation. Why are you working from home?"

Megan handed Prairie the mug and walked into the townhome she'd moved into after she got divorced. It sat opposite a cleaned-up city park and represented the kind of medium-size city growth that made Prairie wonder if the development was actually gentrification or just hubris. "They're spraying the center for bedbugs again."

"Nightmare." Prairie flopped into Megan's son's gaming recliner. It looked like something Darth Vader would install in the Death Star, but it was freakishly comfortable. "Isn't this the third time?"

The community center that Megan had founded and now ran consolidated a variety of programs for women and girls under one roof. Unfortunately, that roof was over a building whose owner leased the attached storage area to a used clothing and home goods drop-off, and bedbugs, mice, and other pests were a problem.

"It's the fourth time, and I swear, if the cannery space doesn't open up soon, I'm going to lose my mind. Whenever this happens, I spend a whole day running everything in the house through a hot-water wash and ripping the beds apart with my freaking heart in my throat, and I cannot." Megan took a long drink of coffee from her perch at the breakfast bar. "Logan scratched at an itch on his head at breakfast, and I wanted to throw him into the shower and fumigate him like he was E.T. at the end of the movie."

Megan's youngest had started 4K in the fall. "Yikes."

Megan smiled. "You're not here to listen to my boring shit, though," she said. "If I'm understanding you correctly, you just did a psycho drive-by of Lisa's house. Catch me up."

Prairie did, giving Megan a blow-by-blow of the drama over Amber Jenkins's purse, the scoop from the moms at drop-off, and her ill-advised side trip on the way over. By the end, Megan was sitting across from her on an ottoman, serious.

"Okay, but all of this could still be nothing. The cops could be raising the alarm because she's a rich white lady and Chris is a big deal in this city. His company has a luxury suite at Lambeau Field that comes with staff and a plaque. One of the nonprofit directors I work with got invited with her husband." Megan rubbed her fingers together in the universal gesture for *they've got money*.

"I hear you. But let me ask you this: What was the first thing you thought when you heard Lisa was missing?"

"The first thing I thought was, 'She's dead.' But I'm cynical. You know that."

"You have more reason to be than most people I know."

Homemaker

Megan squared her shoulders almost imperceptibly. She had once been part of Lisa's social circle, too, a woman who'd gone from a liberal arts degree at Wellesley to the role of wife and mother without a single worry about the future.

Five years ago, when Prairie agreed to be appointed the PTO's fundraising chair at Anabel's school, the principal had told her the position was basically a courtesy title because the Carmichael family funded the entire PTO budget with one check every fall. Dr. Nathan Carmichael and his wife were ultra-rich. They sent their kids to public school for the optics, but they bankrolled the PTO to make sure the school wanted for nothing.

Which, yes, Prairie had opinions about, but those opinions would not have prevented her from accepting a pretty, pretty check from Dr. Carmichael's private-equity-funded women's health clinic had the check ever actually arrived.

It did not.

Prairie called Jennifer Carmichael first, of course. And of course, Jennifer said she'd have Nathan's office send the check right over, because, of course, they were donating again that year.

When Prairie had to call Jennifer a second time, Jennifer was sure it was just some problem with the admin staff at the clinic. She'd look into it.

And so on, until Jennifer stopped returning Prairie's calls, and then Nathan's office did the same, and then Prairie's emails started to bounce.

She dropped by the clinic to angle for a quick meeting with the doctor. The receptionist blocked her, but Prairie noticed deep divots in the waiting area's carpet where furniture used to be. The chairs and sofas and end tables were arranged in a way that looked like there used to be more of them. She counted four cars in the staff area of the parking lot, which had a dozen spaces.

Prairie's mother-in-law, Joyce, had a friend whose daughter had been a nurse at the Carmichael clinic. Prairie met the daughter for coffee over at the Catholic hospital, where the daughter now worked nights

35

on the medical-surgical floor. She told Prairie she'd been given four months' severance when she was laid off from the clinic, in exchange for which she'd signed a nondisclosure agreement—which she recalled the purpose of seemingly at the same moment she mentioned it, because then she turned pink, claimed she had to finish charting, and hustled off with the rest of her latte in a to-go cup.

After that, Prairie couldn't get off it.

Greg told her it was probably that the clinic was going under, and the Carmichaels were circumspect about the situation.

Prairie both agreed and didn't know for sure. It was the not knowing for sure that meant she kept going.

She read websites and reviews and ratings. The new moms loved Dr. Carmichael, and they adored the amenities at his clinic—which Prairie had known already, because Megan was a regular at the same Wednesday morning coffee shop meetup that Prairie went to, and she'd said she picked the Carmichael clinic for her prenatal appointments after the other moms in the group couldn't stop telling her how fantastic it was.

One Wednesday morning, Jennifer Carmichael caught up to Prairie before she got into her car after the meetup. Right there in the parking lot of the coffee shop, Jennifer told Prairie to back off or she'd have her removed from the PTO.

In response, Prairie did something she had never done before. She paid for background checks on the Carmichaels. She learned they'd moved to Green Bay from Illinois ten years earlier. She picked through their social media, but she couldn't find a whiff of secret gambling or shopping addiction or anything to explain why they seemed to be bleeding money.

Then, one day at school pickup, she spotted Nathan Carmichael, who *never* picked up his kids, in serious conversation with a short man in an expensive suit who was there to pick up a kindergartener who Prairie knew for a fact got picked up by Grandma on Monday-Wednesday-Friday and took the after-school program bus on Tuesday-Thursday.

Homemaker

She experienced the closest thing she'd ever had to an orgasm without touching when she remembered that the short man in the expensive suit was a partner in the fanciest criminal law firm in the Fox Valley. What the fuck had Nathan Carmichael done that he was—perhaps—arranging clandestine meetings with a criminal attorney and running out of money?

More research. More expensive background checks, and Carmichael's name popped up for a complaint to the Illinois medical board. The complaint had been withdrawn, which meant Prairie couldn't get her hands on it, but the hearing had been scheduled for a date just three months before the Carmichaels packed up their belongings and left the great state of Illinois.

A few days later, Prairie was scrolling one of her social media feeds when she noticed that Megan's first new-baby pictures had not been taken inside one of the Carmichael clinic's birth rooms. They were from the maternity ward at the Catholic hospital. Prairie recognized the color scheme and wallpaper from her own births. But she also knew, due to all her snooping, that Dr. Carmichael didn't deliver babies at the Catholic hospital. He didn't have privileges there, only at the newer hospital close to his clinic. Megan had changed practices at the end of her pregnancy. Why?

Prairie hustled down to her basement, packed a plastic tub full of baby clothes that she'd been keeping around for the third kid she and Greg never had, and drove herself straight to Megan's.

What had surprised her the most, reflecting on it later, was that Megan *wanted* to tell someone her story. Prairie just happened to be the first person who asked. *Why did you leave Dr. Carmichael?*

Or maybe she'd been the first person who listened when Megan answered, and who asked gentle questions when she went quiet.

It was easy to find the others. Megan made a private Facebook group for the women to talk. They found dozens—dozens he had drugged, dozens he'd touched without consent, dozens he'd violated with his hands and his pills and his camera. Nathan Carmichael had been hurting girls and women for almost as long as he'd been breathing, and locking them up tight with payoffs and nondisclosure agreements. He kept doing it until he couldn't keep up with the payoffs anymore because his appetite for being a predator had exceeded the limits of his bank account, and he failed to cut Prairie her PTO check.

It was Megan's decision to go to the police. Prairie drove her there and waited in her car all day at the curb. When Megan finally walked out the front door, her hat pulled down tight over her ears, her hands shoved deep into the pockets of her winter coat, she looked like a mom. Like she could have been any mom in a lineup of anonymous moms. But Prairie thought she was probably the bravest, coolest, most beautiful woman she'd ever met, and she told her so.

That was how Dr. Carmichael lost his medical license and ended up serving a federal sentence at a prison near the Wisconsin Dells, and Megan Storch became Prairie's ride-or-die.

"Whatever went down with Lisa Radcliffe," Megan said, "it's probably not a happy story. I mean, we're talking, what? She got stranger-abducted on her way to the grocery store"—she ticked off the possibility on one finger—"which is wildly unlikely, or she ran away with some dude she met on the internet and doesn't want to be found, or she hurt herself deliberately or by accident, or her husband killed her."

Four fingers. Four possibilities. "Chilling."

"Yes. But there's another thing that makes me think this situation could be more complicated."

"What's that?"

"Lisa sold Kitty Blue."

"Everyone sells Kitty Blue. Or it seems like they do. I don't, but I think that's mainly due to my mom's rants in the nineties about how Avon wasn't selling lipsticks, it was selling a lie to women."

"Wait, are you telling me you haven't fallen down the delicious schadenfreude-laced rabbit hole that is following long-form media articles about the downfall of Kitty Blue? I can't believe it, actually. It's probably my only hobby right now, given that it's grant-writing season."

"No. But tell me everything."

Megan leaned toward Prairie with excitement. "Well, it's an MLM, as you know. Everyone who sells Kitty Blue gets into it through somebody else who sells it, and the person who gets them in is their 'upline.' Then they have to recruit other people to sell it—that's the 'downline.' The whole idea is you make cash selling what you bought from Kitty Blue wholesale, and you make commissions on any sales that your downline makes or buys wholesale from Kitty Blue."

"Sure. Kitty Blue's just the athleisure-wear version of makeup, candles, or dip seasoning, bent on separating women from their money."

"Yes. For most women. But Lisa Radcliffe got in early. All those moms around here you see selling Kitty Blue on social media? Every one of them is in her downline. I know women at the center who are so many levels down in her downline, they've never even met her. And the ladies in this town can't get off those tights and jackets with the mesh panels and the zippers and shit. That little logo with the cat ears is everywhere."

"And why do you think Kitty Blue is worth looking at when it comes to Lisa?"

"Because if she's left her husband, then it's just like what happened when you got divorced, or when I did. Her social group is going to leave her behind. And her social group these days is her downline."

"That means if she leaves her husband, she may lose her business."

"Yes. But also, if I had to guess, Chris didn't give a single fuck about Lisa's involvement with Kitty Blue until two things happened. One, she was bringing in lots and lots and lots of money."

"Money often is what makes a woman's activity real, yes. What's the other thing?"

"The other thing is whatever might have happened in that marriage after the FBI got involved in the slow but certain unraveling of Kitty

Blue corporate, given that Lisa Radcliffe was the number-one seller in the state of Wisconsin."

Prairie thought of the unmarked black sedan parked in front of Lisa's house. "Surely the FBI isn't interested in Lisa's disappearance?"

"I wouldn't think so, at least not at this stage. But definitely, for sure, Kitty Blue is imploding. We're talking multiple states filing lawsuits claiming they're operating a pyramid scheme, misrepresenting income, and encouraging their consultants to focus on getting more women buying more wholesale product from the company instead of selling clothes to make money for themselves. There's a confirmed federal investigation of what might be multistate fraud. More than ninety-eight percent of Kitty Blue sellers lose money. If the FBI has asked her questions, surely Chris wouldn't like that, given his stature in the community. And if the FBI did talk to her and then she disappeared, I imagine the FBI would want to know where she went."

Prairie's brain was racing too fast, running far ahead of anything she could pin down.

"The other thing," Megan continued, "is we know for a fact that Lisa has money of her own, but she's also surrounded herself with women and friends who've lost money—a *lot* of money—in a scheme she got them into. Women like Amber Jenkins, for example."

"I mean, that is highly provocative. I'm provoked. But it tells me nothing about what happened to Lisa."

"No," Megan said. "If I knew that, I'd be calling the number the chief of police published in the newspaper. But I've handed you the ball. Where are you going to run with it?"

"I'm not sure. Maybe nowhere. I would be wise not to chase wild hairs without thinking."

"That doesn't sound like something you'd be worried about."

Prairie smiled over the sting of Megan's comment. She didn't like to think of herself as careless. "It's more that I'm not sure yet if this is the work in front of me to do. I felt like Carmichael was my work. They owed me a check, they lied about why they couldn't give it to me, and following those lies led me right to why, and to you. But this?"

Megan leaned back, her body relaxed, but something in her eyes reminded Prairie that her best friend was frighteningly insightful. "You could be right. No one is going to want you to ask questions, especially since the police are already involved. But you started asking questions anyway, all on your own, as soon as you noticed Amber's purse. You already drove by Lisa's house. You *are* involved. Maybe the question for you, Prairie, is what if *Carmichael* was the thing that was put in front of you so you would know what you wanted to do next? Haven't you been trying to figure that out?"

Oof. "I don't even know what . . . like, do I want to be in the police? No. God. Journalism? I think I'm too old to be a spy. How old was Julia Child when she started spying?"

"Maybe, for now, it's that you're finding out that you're never going to leave a sister behind on the battlefield, and the next right thing for you to do is follow your God-given instinct to connect the dots."

"I just came here for coffee." Prairie tried the joke, but it didn't break the tension.

"No, you didn't," Megan said. "You staked out Lisa's house before you came here, and you haven't even asked me what's new with me." She raised her eyebrows.

"God, I'm sorry." Prairie winced. "What *is* new with you?"

Megan laughed. "Get out of here. You'll be late for your staff meeting, and then I'll get a call from your assistant wondering why you're not there because you're the only one who can get your metaphysical babysitter to stop diffusing essential oils in the conference room."

"I'll have you know that my metaphysical babysitter has transitioned to setting up crystal grids on the table before the meeting instead. They're very pretty." She smiled at her friend. "Besides, Maelynn likes her. She says Deirdre's scientific agnosticism challenges her to think outside the box. And you know Dierdre is the only babysitter I can get to consistently show up on Thursday nights."

41

"For the man auditions."

Last year, Prairie had put herself on the apps and opened up Thursday for dates. She kept a spreadsheet to keep track of the results of her experiments in dating—something her friend never tired of mocking her for.

"Anyone come close to getting a callback recently?" Megan asked.

"I was tempted by the guy who offered me fifteen pounds of frozen venison he never got around to eating last season, but wasn't sure I was in it for the duration of getting through fifteen pounds of venison. I didn't want to lead him on."

Megan rolled her eyes.

Back in her car, Prairie turned the music up loud to keep herself from following any wild hairs on the way home.

Chapter 4

An hour later, Prairie sat at the big shiny conference table in her former main bedroom on the first floor of her home.

Her staff meeting had just ended, and she was staring at the square of morning light from the skylight centered on the table, thinking about how, years ago, she and Greg had taken advantage of the lack of a second story over this suite of rooms and put in the skylight so they could snuggle in bed and look at the stars.

That hadn't ever happened. Instead, they'd gotten divorced and become founding partners in the business of homemaking. But the light was beautiful in the mornings when she had her staff meetings for 724 Maple.

Prairie had discovered that hosting in-person gatherings was the most efficient way to keep all the people who contributed to the upkeep of her household on the same page—childcare, chef, lawn and garden, accountant, and handywoman. No one complained so long as she paid them to attend, and in fact some of the employees of the 724 Maple Project had come to enjoy eating pastry in a social setting once a week. Even now, her handywoman, Barb Diaz, lingered over coffee at the other end of the table. Marian Banks sat beside Prairie, annotating the minutes from the meeting that had just ended on her laptop. Officially, Marian was Prairie's executive assistant, but her role encompassed much more than that.

"You're thinking too much." Marian wound her long, dark hair into a bun on top of her head and stabbed a pencil through it. She wore a fire-engine-red wrap top from her sister's plus-size clothing line that was taking Marian's spectacular cleavage seriously. "For real," Marian said. "I can feel the heat coming off you from over here. It's a little scary."

"What do you know about Kitty Blue?" Prairie asked her.

Marian closed her laptop. "Why? You're not thinking of selling, are you?"

"You should see your beautiful face. No. I'm just trying to figure something out."

Marian leaned back in her office chair, a frown between her eyebrows. "As a matter of fact, I heard that. Asking questions in the schoolyard? Risky."

"How did you hear?" Marian's family was old-school Green Bay, deeply embedded in the community, and therefore Marian knew everyone and everything there was to know. Still, Prairie was impressed.

"I have mixed feelings." Marian ignored Prairie's question. "Lisa Radcliffe is a big deal. I can understand why you're interested because I know she was a friend of yours at one time, but I'm sure every cop in Brown County is on it. I'm also sure that her husband and her friends would not be happy if they thought *you* were on it."

Down at the end of the table, Barb sipped her coffee, then shook her head. "Sad. I was at that woman's place just last year, doing a job to convert her dining room. She was fussy, I tell you, but real nice, and she hired my cousin to paint after I was done building her shelves and installing a bunch of track lighting."

"What was she converting it into?" Prairie asked.

"Some kind of little boutique to sell clothes to other ladies. She had me put in glass shelves she ordered custom. The shelves were primo, but for as nice as that house should be, for what it must have cost, the build was shit. I had to go behind every wall to reinforce the flimsiest studs I've ever seen so all that glass wouldn't come crashing down."

"How did she seem to you?"

Homemaker

Barb's eyes narrowed. "It was last year, like I said."

Prairie held up her hands in surrender. "I swear I'm not trying to get you to violate your client-handywoman privilege. I'm just worried."

"Well, she didn't seem like someone who'd take off on her kids, I can say that. Her kids impressed me, too. The older one would come in and help me after he got home from school. Made me think she was doing something right with them."

Prairie remembered what she'd heard this morning about how Lisa and her oldest, Davey, had plans to go to Chicago. Lisa had gone out of her way to get special tickets to the museum.

"You're thinking again," Marian said to Prairie in a voice with not a little warning.

"Because you implied that Chris Radcliffe doesn't like me. Which is true. I could never figure out why. I was always warm to him."

Marian laughed. "You couldn't figure that out? Chris is never going to like anyone like you."

"Is it how good my ass is? Because I've been told I could model jeans, and that can intimidate people."

Marian cast her eyes toward the skylight. "Women who think for themselves. Women who don't stand around with their own matches waiting for a guy to come light the candles."

Prairie startled and took a breath. *Candles.*

What she did most as a mom of middle school– and high school–aged girls was drive. Back and forth, in every cardinal direction, across Green Bay. It was boring, so to entertain herself, she looked around and asked questions. *How is it possible that diner downtown is still in business? Do they sell weed out of the back?*

What is that windowless cinder block building between the Walgreens and the old Smythe mansion, and why is it so well maintained? Do the people living across the street from the crematorium mind?

Which was why she suddenly remembered that, halfway between the new grocery store and that struggling art gallery and framing business, there was a religious-supply store with a hand-lettered sign in the window. Candlelight service supplies, printed bulletins, pew bibles.

She looked at Marian. "Do you have an extra hour or two you can put in this afternoon?"

"Always. But I'm not loving the light bulb going off over your head."

"You know that religious-supply place on the corner of Fourteenth and Macon?"

"No, but I'm sure I can find it."

"I need you to go there and pick up, let's say, two hundred and fifty service candles, the ones with the paper wax catchers around them. Also, I'll send you a document with information on it to use to design a flyer. You can get them color printed with my account at FedEx. Three hundred of those. And we're going to need a picture of Lisa to blow up really big and put on a foam board with an easel."

Marian stared at Prairie. One eyebrow slowly lifted. "You're serious?"

"I haven't heard of anyone else who's organized a vigil, have you? How are people supposed to process their feelings? How are the police supposed to continue to share information and receive tips from the public?"

"How are you supposed to be able to stand in one place and get a good long look at every single person in Lisa Radcliffe's life?"

Marian's tone was not exactly supportive, but Prairie had to consider that she'd hired Marian at a low moment in the period when her divorce was at peak turbulence. Marian had seen some things. Prairie could always count on her support, but Marian weighed Prairie's individual actions on the scales of her own personal judgment, and this had always been a very good system for both of them.

"Getting a look at all the players is only a secondary bonus to what is a very necessary event." Prairie said this solemnly, then batted her eyelashes at Marian.

"I'd go to a vigil," Barb said. "People will like it."

Prairie pointed at her handywoman. "See? Listen to Barb. People will like it."

Marian tapped a finger on the table, looking at Prairie. "Better make it three hundred candles."

Prairie smiled.

🦋

By dinnertime, the Facebook event page Prairie had set up for the vigil had a list of nearly two hundred people planning to attend, and the event's agenda had snowballed entirely beyond her control.

She didn't mind. Her interest in this gathering did not require her to be in charge of it. Better if she wasn't, all things considered.

When she got to the green field in the middle of the park, Marian was there with the easel and boxes, talking to a cop who looked too young to shave. The officer turned to Prairie when she approached. "Are you the organizer?"

He rested his fingertips on his utility belt. His name badge read PRYZEWSKI, which Prairie hoped she would not be pressed into pronouncing.

"That's me."

"This lady said you should have the permit."

"Right here." Prairie pulled the paper Marian had secured for her out of her messenger bag.

"Thanks. We've spoken with the family, and they're going to say a few words before the chief does. If you would, please let us direct traffic, give directions, and end the event. The media will be here, but we'd appreciate it if no one made a special effort to talk to them, since we'd like to keep their focus on Mrs. Radcliffe. Are these the candles and pictures?"

Prairie had been looking at the corner of the park, where another cop was putting down a black-painted plywood platform and a small speaker. She watched a van from the local news station pull in nearby.

"Yep. Do you want me to arrange to pass those out, or . . . ?"

"We'll take care of it."

"Great. There's a big picture of Lisa and a stand to set it up on. Use it however you'd like. It's a good picture, from the spring carnival last month. We had a photo booth with a professional photographer. The flyer has everything on it, and I have no problem getting out of your way."

The officer clearly had no problem with it, either. He picked up the reusable tote bags of candles and flyers, tucked the foam-mounted photo and collapsed easel under his arm, and walked away. Prairie thanked Marian and dismissed her to her evening off.

Over the next half hour, the park gradually filled as the daylight faded.

When Prairie had told Greg about her plan for the evening, his only objection was that on TV, the bad guy always showed up for the vigil. He joked they'd have to keep a close eye on the girls, but he wasn't really kidding. He'd be five feet from Maelynn, max, with an eye on Anabel, who was hanging out with her best friend and a new person from school who Prairie hadn't met yet.

There was no real reason to worry about her daughters. The park was filled mostly with moms and kids, with cops around the edges and a handful of dads and grandpa-aged men. Prairie couldn't turn her head without seeing someone she knew, including quite a few of the teachers from Maelynn's school. There were so many people, she couldn't even figure out a way over to Megan, who she spotted under a big maple tree holding her tired four-year-old on her hip while her middle boy stabbed dramatically at the air with a stick in wild battle circles and her oldest sat in the wood chips with his phone. Megan gave her an exhausted wave.

Prairie waved back before she returned to scanning the crowd, taking mental notes on all the people she *didn't* know.

There were a lot of women wearing Kitty Blue's tastefully zany take on activewear. She supposed it was a kind of tribute to Lisa. Prairie's brain had gained the ability to spot the cheerful cat-ears logo from fifty paces. She had to give credit to Kitty Blue where it was due—every piece obviously came in every size, the clothes were very cool, and no one looked uncomfortable. She needed to take a close look at Lisa's social media, focusing on the Kitty Blue content. She wasn't convinced by Megan's argument that it was something to look at, but it had been important to Lisa, which was enough to make it worthy of consideration.

Without any obvious signal, Prairie started to notice lit candles—first just a few, then more as the crowd hushed. Someone turned to her and held out their own flame, and she fumbled her candle out of her pocket and touched the wick to the light.

The candlelight made the faces that had seemed familiar just moments ago indistinct and somber. The enormity of why everyone was here, quiet and still, rushed through her, and she felt her eyes sting and her nose burn along with a sudden regret she hadn't found her kids before everything started so she could give them an extra hug.

Near where the speaker had been set up, beside Lisa's picture on its easel, a man dressed in black with a priest's collar accepted the microphone. He introduced himself as being from Lisa's church and thanked everyone for coming to hold space for Lisa and her family in their hearts. Prairie hadn't spoken to him or invited him. It filled her with wonder how any of this had happened—how just by doing a few things, buying candles and poking at her laptop, she'd put in motion something so much bigger than herself.

But it wasn't her who'd done this. It was Lisa. The way Lisa lived her life had brought these people together. Just like Prairie, Lisa would know most of the people here, and just like Prairie, she would rally around any family here who was suffering.

It was what moms did.

Prairie bowed her head and prayed with the crowd, asking for Lisa's safe return.

The media had been milling around the microphone, running cameras, popping flashes, and holding up fuzzy-covered boom mics, but their activity intensified when an older officer in a dress uniform stepped up on the small wooden platform. He was small and wiry, with a surprisingly deep voice. Prairie recognized him as the police chief from photos she'd seen in the newspaper.

He introduced himself and quickly got down to business. "This is an active search, and we do have an announcement we'd like to make. There's a bulletin going out this evening. What I'm able to say at this time is that we've located Ms. Radcliffe's vehicle, a gray Chrysler Pacifica, near the bay on the west side, on Tuesday night."

Prairie held her breath. She was intimate on a cellular level with the kid-hauling magic that was Lisa's Chrysler Red S Edition Pacifica in Granite Crystal. She listened closely, but the police chief didn't say anything more specific about the location or the condition of the van—if it looked like Lisa had been abducted or she was in an accident or had simply parked it.

Maddening.

"If any member of the public observed this vehicle anytime Monday evening or the early-morning hours on Tuesday, please reach out to us right away. We've also shared a description of what Ms. Radcliffe was wearing. There's a photograph in the press release that will be in the paper and on our social media."

Prairie already had her phone out, pulling up her tab for the police department's social media feed. Right on top, she spotted the new post showing Lisa in deep-purple Kitty Blue running tights and a matching warm-up jacket. Her layered blond hair was blowing across her face, and she was laughing.

"If you saw something, please reach out with any information you have, even if it seems trivial," the chief said. "At this time, we are concerned about the safety of Lisa Radcliffe. We have no reason to believe there is any imminent danger to the public or to the members of her family. Thank you."

He stepped off the platform. A murmur passed through the crowd—people reacting to the news he'd shared, wondering what it meant. Prairie scanned over the assembly until she saw Joyce, leaning her head toward a man about her age in a work jacket, who was talking close to her ear as they both kept their eyes forward.

Oh, good job, Joyce.

"Near the bay on the west side" didn't mean anything much to Prairie, who had always lived east of the river that divided the city down its middle, but Joyce had connections who might be able to tell her more. As a lifelong Green Bay resident and a forty-year employee of the DNR, Joyce knew everyone who was anyone in the city bureaucracy. Even better, everybody liked her. She'd promised Prairie that she would keep her ear to the ground and see what she could find out tonight.

The crowd got quiet again as it became clear that the next person getting ready to speak was Chris Radcliffe.

He was a big man. Taller than Greg, with shoulders a third again as wide and a celebrity superhero build. Prairie had heard Lisa's friends tease her at school pickup about the difference in their height and build. Lisa was legit tiny, someone who would have to get even the daintiest of vintage couture taken in and hemmed, whereas Chris looked more like the Packers players Prairie saw sometimes at the restaurants near the stadium—proportionally the same as normal men, until you blinked and realized they were 30 percent bigger in every dimension.

He had one of those hip, barbered cuts that faded artfully into designer stubble, and expensive-looking wire-framed glasses. Objectively, he was hot, and not just dad-hot. She guessed he could afford to keep himself looking that way. The green-and-gold sailboat logo of his company, Bay View Development, was on at least half of the signs in front of commercial and residential development projects around town, including the new multimillion-dollar project by the football stadium.

He leaned over and hugged his daughter, who was a year behind Maelynn and had inherited her dad's height and build. The middle son was a year ahead of Maelynn, a small kid who Prairie had heard was some kind of genuine science genius. He was scrubbing tears off his chin with the palms of his hands.

"Hi, everyone," Chris began. He didn't step onto the wooden platform, she guessed because he didn't need to. His voice broke heartrendingly on *everyone*, and he cleared his throat and looked down at the ground. Prairie swallowed over the tears rising in her own throat.

"It's real difficult right now. I'm sorry." He reached into his jacket pocket and pulled out a piece of folded paper. "I forgot I wrote something down." While he painstakingly opened the paper, his big hands shaking, the media pressed almost imperceptibly closer.

Prairie let her eyes drift as paper rustled before the microphone. At the edge of the crowd, in the darkest spot beside the stage, she saw a man who wasn't looking at Chris. He could pass for a spectator, except he was facing the wrong way, watching the people rather than the proceedings.

"I want to thank the police department and the city workers. Father"—Chris turned to the priest who had spoken—"thank you so much for being here for Lisa and me and the kids. Lisa's friends, I know, have been real helpful to the police, too. Thank you."

Chris had a broad Wisconsin accent that stumbled over his words and the emotion in his voice. It was hard to witness. She darted her eyes back to the man she'd noticed. He didn't spare a single look at Chris, who was still trying to get through his list of people to thank.

The cops were looking at the crowd, too, and she'd already assumed, like Greg had said, that they were watching for a bad guy gloating over his crime. The man who Prairie had noticed wasn't in uniform, though. He wore a dark suit so jarringly well tailored he stood out in the Midwestern crowd. He was probably about her age, with short hair and a square jaw. *He's been in the military,* Prairie thought.

If he'd had a trench coat on, she'd have been able to peg him right away as a detective, but his suit matched the late-model black sedan she'd seen in front of Lisa's house.

FBI.

If he *was* an FBI agent, it would mean this wasn't just a search. It was an investigation.

The very moment Prairie figured all that out, the man looked right at her.

Chapter 5

Yikes. Prairie turned her attention quickly back to the missing woman's husband. Her neck was hot. She wanted to glance at the probably-FBI-agent again but could absolutely tell he was still staring at her, and she needed him to believe that she hadn't been staring at him and was simply an obedient, somber participant, absorbed by Chris Radcliffe's painful verbal stumbling.

"So if anyone can help find Lisa. My wife, Lisa. The kids really miss her. We're kind of lost without her, I mean. Lisa, I—" Chris looked up, and his Adam's apple bobbed. "If you're out there, please. Help us get you home, please." Chris fixed his gaze in the general direction of the crowd, which was silent except for the sounds of sniffing and a few moms hushing younger kids. He then looked over at the police chief.

This seemed to be the cue for a self-assured teenage girl in a puffer coat with a messy pixie cut to go up to the mic. She smiled at Lisa's oldest son. "All of us at Creighton have got your back, Davey." Then she took a deep breath and began singing the most beautiful version of "Amazing Grace" Prairie had ever heard.

Kids. They could be pretty great.

When the song ended, the girl blew out her candle, and everyone else followed suit. The crowd started to break up, the mass of people spreading out into clumps, moms taking their kids' hands or picking up fractious younger children to carry them to the car.

Homemaker

Prairie drifted closer to the platform. She kept the maybe-agent in her peripheral vision but didn't allow herself to look at him directly. Too risky. He was talking to someone in uniform whose face Prairie couldn't see. Could have been the police chief. She ran into Joyce.

"Well, that was beautiful," Joyce said.

"It really was."

"It's the saddest thing."

"It is." They stood together for a moment. Prairie could see Lisa's mom over Joyce's shoulder. She stood with her arms wrapped tightly around herself, staring at nothing.

"Can you take the girls home?" Prairie asked.

"I was going to. I'll just round them up."

"Give them a big hug for me, okay?"

Suddenly, she was wrapped in Joyce's arms, the scent of her ex-mother-in-law's Emeraude perfume all around her. Prairie hung on tight. She let her forehead rest against Joyce's shoulder.

After a long moment, Joyce dropped her arms. "All right," she said. "See you at home."

Prairie watched her walk into the remains of the crowd. She followed her with her eyes across the park to the swings, where a streetlight silhouetted Greg's shape and the shape of Maelynn on a swing, her legs reaching for the sky. Anabel stood a few feet off in a cluster of adolescent bodies.

When Prairie turned away, she collided with Alison Greene, who she'd last seen this morning in the gifted school's remote parking lot.

"Oh! Prairie." Alison sniffed. The interior decorator's cheeks were chapped pink, and she held a handkerchief clutched in one fist at the center of her chest. She looked as though she'd spent most of the evening in a heap of tears. "This was so great. I'm so glad you organized this."

She glanced past Alison. The agent was ten feet away, staring at her again. *Ach.* "How are *you?*"

55

Alison shook her head. "I was doing okay until I heard they found her van."

"I understand. It's genuinely a lot."

"Yeah. One minute I'm fine, and then I'll get a shipping notice on custom wallpaper samples I ordered for Lisa, and part of me's thinking I don't even know if this is still a job, right? I was supposed to meet with her on Tuesday morning, a time-sensitive meeting that was originally Friday, but she wanted to move it until Chris got back from his conference that went through Monday. I was even thinking I would talk to Chris, too, when I saw him picking the kids up at the school Monday afternoon, but he was in and out before I had a chance. Now I just wish I'd seen her Friday like we'd planned, because maybe, I don't know, something would have turned out different and we wouldn't be here, doing this."

Prairie made a note of the timeline Alison had just shared, especially since it overlapped with the timeline of Lisa's disappearance. "Well, if you ever need to talk, just text me," she tried, not knowing where she was at with Alison. "My number's the same. We can go out for coffee."

"I might do that." Alison was still gripping her elbow. "I really might."

Her eyes drifted over Alison's shoulder again. The agent had disappeared. "I'm so sorry, but I wanted to see if I could say hello to Lisa's kids before they leave." Prairie internally pinched herself for the lie.

Alison's eyes widened. "Of course." She took a step back and released Prairie's arm. "Well, thank you again for everything."

"It's nothing, Alison. I was glad to do it." Prairie impulsively leaned over and gave Alison a hug. Though they had not previously been hugging friends, Alison's face was just too broken. Alison squeezed her back.

Homemaker

She turned around, determined to find the agent, if only to get another look at him, and she found herself unable to take another step forward, because if she did, she'd slam right into the man.

She stepped back quickly, putting herself well outside his bubble.

"You're the organizer," he said.

It wasn't a question exactly, but Prairie decided the best course of action was to treat it as such. She mentally mastered her insides and outsides to assume helpful, cheerful mom form.

"I am! Though honestly all I did was create the invitation and print up the flyers." *Nothing to see here, I am merely the handmaiden of men with better ideas.* It was typically a safe initial tack to take with an unknown male. "You must be the FBI agent everyone's talking about," she added. *But I am not an unobservant twit, either, because no one is talking about an FBI agent.*

He raised an eyebrow.

"The suit," she clarified. "Your military officer haircut. If you were hoping to blend in, they always have a discount on Carhartt jackets at Fleet Farm."

He looked at her for two beats longer than was socially normal. She pretended like it was an entirely standard-length pause and focused on a scar that bisected his right eyebrow.

"I was hoping my gutsy tie print would throw off the government-man vibe," he finally said.

Prairie glanced at his tie. Lavender, with gold bees. It *was* a kicky print. And this man, this suit-wearing man, had just told her a joke. Two problems. Prairie's third problem was her secret, painful, and right-now-unacceptable weakness for a clean haircut and a square jaw in sharp menswear. Her first crush had been Clark Kent. She kept the men's Lands' End catalog on her bedside table.

She locked it down.

"Can I help you, Agent?" Back to mom mode.

He looked at her like he'd seen something in her face. Or read her mind. Maybe the FBI could do that. "That depends on if you're a friend of Lisa's."

"I'm not, but our kids go to school together. I just decided to step up to organize this because I thought Lisa's close friends and family would be too overwhelmed."

"You're the kind of person who does that. Just decides to step up."

"Yep." That would have to be a complete sentence.

He unbuttoned one button of his suit, reached into the inner pocket, took out a box of Tic Tacs, and shook one into the palm of his hand while scanning the remainder of the crowd.

Prairie was starting to get annoyed with this taciturn man, regardless of how the cuff links she'd spotted made her feel, so she tapped the gas. "You're an ex-smoker, huh?"

"What makes you say that." Again, not a question.

"Grown men who keep candy in their pockets are either ex-smokers or smokers who think it's rude to smoke where they are. You don't smell like smoke, so you must have quit."

"You're right, Ms. Holmes. Ten years."

"That's a lot of Tic Tacs."

He didn't comment. He was looking at the other people again. She followed his gaze with a bit of a tingle at her lower back. Who would interest an FBI agent? She could sort the crowd into people she knew and people she didn't know, but whoever he was looking at would be people she should actually *talk* to.

She waited until his methodical scan settled. He was focused on a young woman—not right-out-of-college young, but not too many years beyond that. Thirty? She was very short, trim, and a bit curvy, with lots of wavy brown hair in one of those cool, messy bobs that Prairie wished her thick, straight hair could pull off. She wore some kind of ModCloth-acquired work outfit, a little funky but safe. She was talking to the person Prairie had guessed was Lisa's sister.

"Who is she?"

Homemaker

He closed his eyes. "Okay, Nancy Drew, I—"

"I prefer Harriet the Spy, actually. Also, are you a hundred years old? No one even knows who Nancy Drew is anymore."

He honest-to-God *scoffed*. She was surprised he didn't have an old-timey North Atlantic accent, like in the movies. "That's not true. Nancy Drew is in graphic novels now. My nieces love them." He turned away from the woman to look at Prairie. "She's Mr. Radcliffe's office manager, Dawn Mitchell. You didn't know."

"I mean, ask me a question or don't. Is it cooler? To ask a question as a statement?" She kept her tone light. He probably could take her into custody, even in a suit. She wanted to get home to her kids at a reasonable hour.

"It is cooler, actually. You don't learn that in FBI school, more like at the FBI school parties."

His sense of humor was excellent. She didn't laugh, but she did have a tell, because she couldn't control her dimples. "I don't know her. Do you think it's interesting that she's here? I wouldn't, really. There weren't very many men here tonight, but the ones that came all looked like either school dads—most of whom I know or have seen around—or guys who are obviously in construction. A couple in suits who probably know Chris professionally. Chris likely got a lot of calls this afternoon from more of the suit guys expressing their regret they couldn't come because of work stuff, because men. But I don't think it's weird at all that Chris's work people would be here."

"Stop."

Prairie startled. His *stop* was a bit authoritative, and she had just gotten used to his dry sense of humor and the mostly easy back-and-forth. "Stop what?"

"Detecting. Spying. Whatever you call it."

"I'm just making conversation." She smiled, giving him her fullest, breeziest grin, complete with dimples. *Nothing to see here on any level. No matter what anyone's told you.*

"You're not. You were looking for me after the vigil was over. Maybe you have information to share about the investigation."

"So it's an investigation." Two could play at the statement-as-question game. "The police chief said it was a search. Unless you're not talking about *that* investigation and referring to something more federal and follow-the-money-like."

He closed his eyes again. Twice in as many minutes. It had been a long time since Prairie had so frequently forced a man to go into the quiet space inside his head to escape her. "Do you have any information."

"I have lots of information. The problem is, it's not the kind of information that you guys will think is important."

"The chief made it clear that even the most trivial information may be important."

"It's not trivial, at least not to me, and I don't mean the chief, anyway." She waited for one of his nonquestions.

He just raised his eyebrows.

Fine. "I mean men. Dudes. Guys. You guys. You men. You dudes."

"Let me make a couple of things clear."

"Okey-doke." Prairie said this in her best man voice.

"First, I am a feminist."

Well. She had not been expecting that. "Are you *from* here?"

He held up a finger. "Second, I want to find these kids' mom. Be assured that if I am willing to spend this very long day sorting through tips from people whose time would be better spent working in reality television, I am also willing to listen to whatever you think might help. Third, whether it is an investigation or not, it is not your investigation. A woman is missing, a woman who fits your profile at least in the sense that she's a mom. What I do is dangerous. And no, I'm not from here. I grew up in White Plains, New York, but I've lived a lot of places because of the military."

She pointed at him. She *knew* it. "Military. What was your branch and rank?"

He said nothing.

"Okay. Fine. You weren't looking at Lisa's husband," she said. "When he was talking."

"You mean that I didn't seem to be trying to figure out if he was a genuinely worried husband or a good actor."

She nodded.

"This is why you've got to limit yourself to passing on any actual information you have, or think you have, and leave it to us to see if it helps. I've been doing this for a long time. The books and TV shows have it wrong. There is no real thing called a hunch. I've seen guys who cried like the world was ending get convicted, and I've seen guys who act seriously weird or scary have nothing to do with it. I don't know anything until I know it. One verifiable fact after the next. It's not exciting. It takes too long. It involves a lot of paperwork, and even then, if the prosecutor doesn't like it or it doesn't find someone or bring justice to a victim, it can seem like it didn't matter."

I don't know anything until I know it. Prairie liked that.

"But facts are hard to come by," he said, "if I'm distracted by the public involving themselves in ways that make them unsafe. And it takes me longer to figure out what's going on. Plus, there's a fancy legal term, 'obstruction.' The plain word for it is 'pissing everyone off.'"

"That's three words."

He sighed.

Sure.

"I promise, I'm not messing up your case," she said. "Or wasting your time. I am familiar with what it is to piss everyone off. As you gathered, I'm a mother. I have to ask, though, does the FBI have an office *here*? Like, in this town? Because this is the first I'm hearing about it. Or do they put you up in a hotel when you fly in from the J. Edgar Hoover Building?"

He shook another Tic Tac into his palm. "Let me spool something out for you. You drive a black Honda Accord."

Oh, motherlover. Consequences were the worst.

"This morning, you took a drive by Lisa Radcliffe's house. Real slow. Slow enough to get our attention, so we come out on the step, but by this time you're speeding off. The patrolman logged your car. He didn't get your plate. Then on my list of things to do, way down at the bottom, I have to add looking for black Accords with Wisconsin tags and I'M A PROUD BAND PARENT bumper stickers at the vigil and everywhere else I go. One of your kids must be in the band."

"Maelynn. She plays trumpet."

"She any good."

"Let's just say it's not her holy mission."

He raised his eyebrow again. "Look me in the eye and tell me you didn't organize this vigil so you could find something out for yourself about what happened to Lisa Radcliffe."

She looked him in the eyes. They were gray. They'd seem a little softer if he let his dark hair grow out a titch. "I did not organize this vigil to find out, myself, what happened to Lisa Radcliffe. Also, you're welcome for the publicity."

"See, right there. If I just went by what people said, I'd never get any facts. Please, it is not safe for you, or anyone else who is not law enforcement, to play detective."

"Well, it's interesting you would say that. Because you know, statistically, the one thing that makes women less safe than anything else they could do is get married to a man. Which, I've already done that. And the second, even more dangerous, thing they can do is get divorced. I did that, too. I can't imagine there's any way investigating Lisa Radcliffe's disappearance could put me in more danger than I already am. Statistically."

He looked away again, and then he surprised her.

He laughed.

Homemaker

He had an easy laugh. She would have thought laughter would have to muscle its way out of his throat like it was escaping prison, but he laughed like someone who laughed often and enjoyed it.

No wedding ring. She checked.

"Why don't you tell me your name, for the official record," he said.

She pulled open the flap on her messenger bag, took out a small aluminum case, flicked up a card, and gave it to him.

"Prairie Nightingale. Homemaker." The scar-bisected eyebrow lifted a fraction. "There's a story there."

"See, if that had been a question, I might have answered it. But it wasn't." She held out her hand. "You have a card?"

He kept his gray eyes on her and reached back into his interior suit pocket, pulling out a slim black wallet. Handed over a card.

"Foster Rosemare. There is nothing else on this card. Not even a phone number. I guess I'll try holding a flame over it later to see if there's invisible ink. Your name means 'pink horse.'"

"I think it probably means a roan mare, but I'll tell my nieces, they'll like that."

"You on the apps?"

He blinked. She was satisfied by this evidence that she'd surprised him. She had been starting to think she'd lost her magic.

"There is no possible way I can answer that question."

"Well, if you *were* on the apps, and you happened to match with me, I'd be happy to meet up with you somewhere tomorrow night and answer some questions. I keep Thursday evening open for dates. Really more like a screening audition. The rest of my life is extraordinarily busy, and my time is booked. Who knows? Maybe it will turn out I have information that's pertinent to your interests."

He got out his phone and spent a bit of time swiping.

Her back pocket buzzed.

She held up a finger. Pulled out her phone. Tried desperately to tell her brain to paralyze her dimple muscles, but probably failed.

"Would you look at that? I have matched with a 'Foster,' no last name. Thankfully, the picture is not a selfie with sunglasses in the driver's seat of a car, nor are you holding up dead wildlife to show the camera, so I can accept with dignity."

He glanced at his phone and smiled with his lips compressed tight. "Your picture is a good one."

"My daughter Anabel took it. It's possible she Lightroomed me, but I prefer to assume it was just a good angle."

"I could pick you out of a lineup with it." He put his phone back in his pocket. "Promise me this. You'll stay out of anything but homemaking until we have a chance to talk tomorrow, let's say six at Kettle's."

"Kettle's is an old person's coffee shop. They decorate with Hummels, and it smells like Lysol."

His expression was definitely amused. She was still charming. "That's less than twenty-four hours away. Try to keep your notebook with 'Private!' emblazoned on the cover out of it until then."

"You've read it. *Harriet the Spy*."

"Sure. Who hasn't."

She saluted him. "I promise. Only homemaking."

He pinned her with one last look and walked back across the park. She waited until he was out of earshot before she said, "Possibly my definition of 'homemaking' isn't the same as yours, however."

"Your definition of 'homemaking' isn't the same as anyone's." Greg appeared at her right shoulder. "He looked official. Are you getting arrested?"

She bumped him with her hip and tried not to be annoyed that he had waited for her so he could walk her to her car. His secret worry about bad men wouldn't only extend to their girls. "Not today."

"Who is he?"

"Agent Pink Horse. Pretty boring guy."

"Boring, huh? I guess you're over a good suit, then." Greg snorted at his own joke.

"Shush." Prairie looked around at the quiet park. The police officers were packing up cones and picking up discarded flyers. Lisa smiled from the easel. The back of Foster Rosemare's exquisitely tailored jacket receded in the distance. "I hope all of this will have a happy ending."

Greg didn't warn her off a second time or ask her to elaborate. He just walked her across the grass to the parking lot.

She hated that neither one of them could reassure the other it would be okay.

Chapter 6

Prairie set down her mug on the only clear spot on Joyce's desk and leaned closer. Joyce liked to be able to "visualize her own thinking," and she'd crammed her sitting area with a pleasant assortment of stacked papers, books, filing cabinets, and boxes. The room was flooded with light, hushed in the wake of the girls' departure for school, even the dog blessedly quiet at Prairie's feet. It was the best part of the day for catching up with Joyce, before she got absorbed in her genealogy work.

"Okay, so here's where the city yard waste drop is on the west side," Joyce said, pointing the tip of her pen to the paper where she was drawing Prairie a map, using as a reference the satellite Google map of the bay of Green Bay that she had open on her giant curved computer monitor. "Remember, Adam took you to the one on this side of town last summer so you could see if you liked the look of their free mulch."

Adam was Prairie's lawn and garden guy. His enthusiasm for free mulch was inspirational. "Right. Can you put an X where Lisa's house is?"

"Sure." Joyce sketched a tiny house icon instead, complete with a few trees to show the back of the Radcliffes' lot. She was an excellent artist. Prairie marveled at her ability to quickly fill in little landmarks and symbols as she talked. Joyce had always hoped Greg would be an artist, too, but she'd lost him to computers early on. Lately, Joyce had been working on Anabel after going to her freshman art class show.

Homemaker

"North and west of the yard waste site is an old landfill. It's a few strides from the edge of the water." Joyce drew it in, even making a few bars with labeled measurements to show scale. "It's been filled and flooded, so it's more like a rectangular pond. All that is city land. They keep it maintained with fencing and signs warning people not to dump anything, plus a security camera for when they inevitably do." Joyce drew a camera icon in the corner of the parking lot next to the landfill.

"That parking lot goes right up to the water." Prairie tried to compare Joyce's drawing to what was on the screen. She understood Joyce's drawing better. Prairie had never had the greatest sense of direction. She was a big fan of landmarks.

"Yes, it does. Now, the road to get to the parking lot is just a bumpy gravel access road, but it's the terminus of Marine Drive, which obviously gets big as it runs south and is a major west-side road. Here, though, it ends, but if you don't turn west into the parking lot, and you keep going straightish"—Joyce dog-legged her road—"you can technically drive on a narrow track that's probably more suited to a utility truck or ATV, all the way out on a jetty that goes about two hundred feet into the bay."

Prairie watched Joyce's pencil fill in the width and length of the jetty. "Okay."

"And right here, at the end of the jetty, halfway into the water, is where Lisa's van was found." Joyce drew a vehicle and labeled it, then pointed on the screen at the satellite image.

Prairie sipped her coffee, glancing back and forth between the two views. "Okay. The camera in the parking lot—she would have had to drive right past it. If the police say there's no danger to the public, do you think they know that because they saw video showing Lisa driving the van? But then you'd think they would know one way or the other, right? If she drove her own van into the water, that's not 'missing' anymore."

"It's a digital CCTV camera, fairly high-definition black and white, mounted on the same pole as a solar-powered light that comes on at sundown. It can see about 220 degrees"—she sketched in faint arc lines on her map to show the camera's range—"but it's pointed at the landfill with a fish-eye lens, so anything toward the outside of its range is going to be somewhat distorted. You could see most of a vehicle that drove past it on the other side, but they'd disappear out of view once they were on this track on the jetty. There's no city CCTV on that road. I don't know if the coast guard puts anything out there."

Joyce dragged her mouse across the screen and zoomed in on an area that included the camera and the jetty. "As far as what they'd capture at night? No idea. It's under the light, which would suggest the video should be pretty good, but it's capturing a black-and-white image of a car that's in the dark. If there were headlights on, it would be worse, because cameras focus on light."

"Someone would check, though. The footage exists."

"That camera records a couple of weeks, then starts recording back over, starting with the oldest footage. What you're able to pull depends on where it's at in that cycle. Even if the van was recorded at the very end of the two weeks and they didn't pull the footage, it's still there. They should have something."

"But no bodies."

Joyce shook her head. "Darrell was operating the tow to ease the van out of the water. I guess it was a slow operation because they wanted to preserve any evidence in the van and load it up on the crime scene unit's truck bed. He said they had techs gridding the area at the end of the jetty, but no dive team yet when he was out there. Just some cops getting a visual of the water right around where the van was."

Darrell was the man Joyce had been talking to at the vigil. He was in charge of the local vehicle fleet for the Department of Natural Resources. They'd known each other for years, and it turned out he had been eager to talk. The scene made him very emotional. Everyone wanted to find Lisa. No one had wanted to find her van in the ice-cold water of the bay.

Homemaker

"They must have found it as soon as they started seriously searching in places other than store parking lots and along the highways."

Joyce nodded. "Oh yeah. This isn't some isolated spot up in the North Woods. It's not public per se, but the public can access it because part of this site by the landfill is a nature preserve."

"It is?"

"Not a very big one. Nobody hikes there except in the summer, but this time of year the birders like it, especially the older ones who need a place to park and well-packed trails. There's several access roads back and forth, some just for city vehicles, but even those, a private citizen could find themselves driving on. There's nothing to tell them not to."

"I've driven on Marine Drive lots of times, and I had no idea this was here. How would Lisa? I don't think she was a birder."

Joyce put her pencil down and spun around in her computer chair. "You know, Darrell said the same thing. *What was she doing out there?* If you're looking for a place to drive your car into the water, I can think of a bunch that are going to be more the kind of place someone like Lisa would go. Up by the amusement park, for starters. She would know it from taking her kids."

"That leaves it more open that she wasn't the one driving the van. I wish we knew whether they got anything on that camera."

"Like I said, it would depend on a lot of factors what kind of image they got, but they did say they don't believe there's any danger to the public. I've been a bureaucrat long enough to hear that as 'someone did something to themselves.' If someone drove her up there, it begs the question what kind of plan they had. What would they do next, walk back into town? It's true it's less than a mile from busy roads and shops, but it's a mile of a lot of nothing. More likely they'd find somewhere else to take her where they had their own transportation to get out."

"How far is it from Lisa's house to where her van is?"

Joyce pointed at Lisa's house on the map and traced her finger. "Via well-traveled county roads, almost eight miles. And most of those roads will have cameras for the police to look back at and trace her route."

Prairie pressed her fingers against her mouth, looking from the monitor to the map Joyce had drawn. She felt a heaviness through her body, like she should be crying but couldn't.

"I think your point's a good one, though." Joyce rested her finger on her chin. "I wouldn't expect you or one of your friends to be too familiar with areas like this, or to think of them first in a time of crisis. That doesn't mean she didn't, of course. Lisa's lived here her whole life."

"Would—" Prairie tried to find the words. "I mean, I don't know what would happen to . . . *her*."

"Her body?"

Prairie nodded.

"Well. I've been a part of dealing with a bit of that. People fall in, or they swim where they shouldn't. Boats capsize or get in trouble, and fishermen and hunters have accidents on or around the water. It depends a lot on if she was injured. Darrell said there were skid marks in the mud like she'd accelerated, though the airbag wasn't deployed. The driver's-side door was open. He couldn't make himself look to see if there was blood. It would depend on if she was drunk or under the influence of something. If she used a gun. I've been expecting an announcement that they found her, and I'm very surprised they haven't. I've actually never known of someone who went into the water in that kind of area, in my forty years, that didn't come out pretty soon after. The bay there isn't like the open shores of Lake Michigan farther south. It's calm, highly managed, quite shallow in places. There's still some ice, so possibly someone could get caught up under that, but these dive teams are thorough."

Prairie made herself look at the bay on the satellite map. The photo had obviously been taken in the summer, with the trees leafed out, but even then the lake appeared as a rippled expanse of blackness. She couldn't even really imagine what it must have been like when Lisa's van went into the water.

The impact. The darkness. The rush of cold.

And then what? Lisa opening her door, clawing her way out but unable to make it to shore?

Or maybe it wasn't like that. Maybe she'd meant for the car to go all the way in. When it didn't, she'd let herself out and started swimming farther into the bay. Maybe she'd gone as far as she could go and then let the cold take her.

This was why Prairie was glad she didn't have a wild imagination.

"I know what you're thinking," Joyce said. "It feels unkind to stick your nose into something where there's just going to be a lot of pain, and pain that's not yours. But I also understand your drive to figure out what you can. Look at all this." She gestured around at the bursting mess of files and books. "I'm interested in what people got up to who've been dead for decades. Generations. You either have that thing that makes you want to understand and do something or you don't, I guess. Or you have just enough to gossip. But I think you can trust yourself."

"I'm not a cop, though," Prairie said, remembering what Foster, the FBI agent, had said last night. "I don't have experience to always know what I'm looking at or if my looking at something is getting in the way."

Joyce waved her hand sharply, as if knocking a mosquito away from her face. "Pish. Those cops are going to overlook all kinds of things. Why do you think they ask for tips from the public? They need a place to start. We're all on this giant spaceship together."

Prairie felt the tension in her shoulders melt a little. She stood and dropped a kiss on top of Joyce's head. "I'll leave you to it. Thanks."

She wandered down the breezeway that connected Joyce's apartment to the house, Zipper at her heels. She poked a few treats into her goldendoodle's puzzle ball, made him sit, and tossed it to him. He merrily carried it off to his dog bed by the heating vent in the living room.

Prairie's phone buzzed. She woke it up and took a look. There were a few notifications on the 724 Maple Slack channel, which she used between meetings to keep the household organized and solve problems as they cropped up. The notifications weren't time sensitive, so she swiped them closed. Marian would probably take care of them before

Prairie even got around to it. What had just popped up, though, were a couple of Facebook messages from Lisa's decorator, Alison Greene.

> Hi, Prairie. I realized I don't still have your number, so hoping you check here.

> I'm a little at loose ends & wonder if you're free to grab that coffee you mentioned.

Prairie set her phone down and leaned against the kitchen counter.

She closed her eyes, and the sunlight made the space behind her eyelids a deep red-orange. She ran herself through half a dozen square breaths, waiting until she felt centered and calm.

Then she opened her eyes and looked at the messages from Alison again.

She wasn't a cop, but Alison needed someone to talk to, and reaching out to listen to a woman who needed to talk was always the right thing to do.

Chapter 7

"Wait, what?"

Prairie sat across from Alison in the most crowded part of Delco, regretting her choice of meeting venue. The downtown coffee shop always bustled, but she'd forgotten how truly hive-like it could get in late morning, particularly in the front part of the shop, where Alison had snagged a tiny two-seater. The back of Prairie's chair butted against the back of the chair of the dude sitting right behind her, who kept luxuriously stretching and smacking various parts of her body. The volume level was high enough that Prairie couldn't entirely believe she'd heard Alison correctly. "You said Lisa didn't want the new house?"

Alison shrugged, which made Prairie notice how chic her burgundy leather jacket looked with her salon-layered silver hair. Prairie loved it when women leaned into the gray. "She never said outright. It was Chris who hired me. He was my client, officially, not Lisa, but he told me to run everything we talked about past Lisa to make sure she liked it, and to get her final approval on everything. But then I would play phone tag with Lisa endlessly."

"That sounds frustrating."

"It was," Alison agreed. "I was off my pins at first. This house could be my first shot at a little bit of national attention, but I can't design for sixty-five hundred square feet of space for a client who won't call me back."

"Holy Toledo. That's a legit mansion. Why do you think she didn't want it?"

Alison drummed her fingers on the table. She wore a fabulous statement ring on her right hand, a big chunk of polished smoky quartz with three offset rose-cut diamonds that flashed in the light. It made Prairie think Alison's interior decorating boutique must be doing really well. Her husband was a psychology professor at the Green Bay branch of the University of Wisconsin.

"At first, it was just that she wouldn't commit to a vision. You know, did she want something European and formal, or relaxed and upscale country, spare and modern? Nothing. And I'm not a celebrity designer with a signature look who has carte blanche to come in and leave the client with an 'Alison Greene' space. Don't get me wrong, I'd love to get to there, but there's not a lot of call for it in Green Bay. My job is to carry out the ideas of the client and understand them, source the materials and furnishings and finishes that will make their ideas shine and be even better than they thought. But she had nothing, even though I know she has taste and a very well-developed aesthetic. She did the house they live in now by herself, and it's beautiful."

"Was it money? I don't mean to pry."

Alison didn't even seem to register Prairie's last comment. "No, absolutely not money. Chris made it clear that the budget didn't have a ceiling until he said so. Actually, someone from the police department called me this morning and asked if I had any unpaid bills or invoices from the Radcliffes, and I had to tell them that I haven't even finished spending the down payment." Alison looked down and turned her coffee cup in a complete circle on the table. "It was awful to get that call," she said. "It made it so real. I know they're doing their job. I'm sure they have to look into finances whenever something like this happens, but I just hated the idea that Lisa's life will be under that kind of microscope."

Prairie was dying to ask Alison to give her a word-by-word replay of the call from the police, but she could sense this wouldn't be well received.

Homemaker

"Plus, and this *is* terrible, I worked really hard to, well, drag Lisa to the point where she was finally opening up. Sharing some ideas, looking at samples, giving me feedback on my renderings, and those conversations led to us really enjoying each other as friends, too. A lot of people don't know, I think, that she's smart, and really funny, even irreverent. I hadn't had a friend like that since college."

Alison's description matched Prairie's memories of Lisa and made her throat thicken with emotion. "She had come around to it? To the house?"

"In a way. I don't think, if I'm going by my instincts, that it felt like something that would be *hers*. And not because Chris wasn't willing to make that happen. It was a lot more like she was doing it for me, to give me a chance to show off my skills. You know, she told me once that before Chris started planning the house, she'd mentioned to him that with their kids getting older, she'd like to take a look at the new penthouse apartments that just got redeveloped above that city office building downtown—you know the historic one near the library, with all the gorgeous gray stone?"

"Yeah." The dude behind Prairie bumped his knuckles into her shoulder.

"She said she thought it would be kind of nice to live downtown and be able to walk places and be close to things. But Chris thought she was kidding."

Prairie recalled the map Joyce had made her this morning, and her rogue drive-by of Lisa's house. Alison had mentioned at school drop-off that the new house was going to be in the Oneida area, probably in one of those nearly rural alcoves with the kind of multiacre lots a big house would make sense on.

Both places were pretty far off the beaten path.

That wasn't unusual for Green Bay. When Prairie had first moved here with Greg from the busy and iconic Capitol Hill neighborhood in Seattle, after spending her childhood surrounded by neighbors and sharing communal space in cohousing, she couldn't get over how much *room* everyone seemed to want around themselves. She'd limited her and Greg's house search to places on the more populated east side, in older neighborhoods from the fifties and sixties, to make sure she wouldn't end up somewhere she felt isolated.

"Do you think Lisa was lonely?"

The question felt almost taboo, and Prairie knew it was because she was driving at unspoken things. *Was Lisa lonely? Lonely enough to want to disappear? Lonely enough to drive her car to the end of a remote track and into the water? Did she secretly know she would never live in that house?*

Alison's gaze unfocused, and she twisted the quartz ring around her finger. "You know, what surprised me the most at the vigil last night was how emotional Chris got. He's always polite. Friendly, even. I don't have any reason to think he doesn't take good care of Lisa and the kids in his own way. But he's a little reserved, I guess."

"I can see that," Prairie said.

"And Lisa is very social. She's a big personality in a small package, but yeah, I think it's possible Lisa was lonely. It's always possible. She was a mom with three kids."

Prairie let that sit for a minute. She liked—a lot—that Alison had answered her question.

She felt obligated to give Alison the opportunity to steer the conversation somewhere else. She pointed at the ring. "That's pretty."

Alison made a noise in her throat, not quite choking, not quite laughing. "Lisa gave it to me." She twisted it off and set it on the table, where she and Prairie regarded it. The band was wide. It looked like a lot of high-karat gold. "I didn't feel right about taking it, but when Lisa insisted on something, you couldn't tell her no. Her excuse was that she couldn't really wear it in good taste, given that she had such a big rock on her ring finger already."

Prairie couldn't argue with Lisa's logic. The woman's wedding set was legendary. The central princess-cut diamond in its three-diamond design must have been six carats, and the two diamonds on each side weren't shrinking violets, either. The whole thing was cantilevered on a setting embedded with sapphires. Prairie swore she'd seen angels sing around it with harps and trumpets when the sun hit. Chris must have wanted astronauts on the space station to know he'd married Lisa. "It's a beautiful gift."

"I don't think it's ever a great idea to second-guess generosity." Alison's expression clouded over.

"What is it?"

"Lisa was taking antidepressants." She glanced at Prairie. "It came up organically, because Piper takes them. And Piper takes them because half her brain came from me, and I've been taking them since college, so the last thing I would ever claim is that taking antidepressants is necessarily a sign of anything, really, except that an expert decided someone's mental health could be improved."

Alison looked at the ring again.

A generous gift given to a friend before disappearing. It made Prairie think of Amber's purse in an entirely new way.

Alison looked out the window at the streets, and Prairie gave her a moment to compose herself. Before she could do that, though, her phone rang on the table with an incoming call.

"Please take it if you want to," Prairie said. "I can go get a refill and give you a moment." She stood up with her mug. The dude at the next table took the opportunity for a truly luxurious, full-body stretch in his chair. He gave her a lazy grin. Prairie returned his serve with the look she'd perfected on Greg, which she delivered each and every time he left coffee mugs littered throughout the downstairs.

The dude turned away.

That's right.

While the barista pumped fresh coffee, Prairie watched Alison on the phone, glad to see it was someone she obviously enjoyed talking to. Alison was saying goodbye and laughing by the time Prairie returned to the table.

"That was Monty, my work husband. He kills me." Alison swiped a few times on her phone and put it down.

"Your work husband?"

"You know, the person you share all this professional intimacy with, and count on to have your back and know your weird workplace preferences, like who to always let go to voicemail and which brand of creamer to pick up, and you both hate the same people at work. A work spouse is very important, because otherwise you go home to your spouse-spouse and talk about nothing but work, and then you crush each other with mutual grumpiness."

Prairie laughed. "I like that."

Alison stood up. "Okay. This was good. I know I talked and talked, but I promise if we do this again, I want to hear more about you and figure out what's true and what's just rumors." She laughed at Prairie's hairline-level eyebrows. "Oh, you know you get tongues wagging with your unconventional setup and your seemingly perfectly perfect amicable divorce. Don't make a face, though. I've always thought you're great and that you have the right idea, but I'd love the chance to get the details."

Prairie watched her go. It was an odd feeling to have made a friend—*remade* a friend?—in these circumstances.

She checked the time. It wasn't eleven yet. Still three and a half precious hours before she had to meet Anabel at the bus stop and pick Maelynn up from school. It might be nice to eat lunch here. Delco had the kind of pasta salad that people ordered as an excuse to have a cookie, but the cookies were worth eating.

She scooped up her messenger bag, shoved her chair back a little harder than she needed to in order to make a point with Mr. No Personal Space, and picked up her mug to move to the quieter room in the back.

The back was empty save for one of the larger tables filled with women. She didn't know any of them except Rachel Norton, who'd taken over the PTO fundraiser position at Anabel's school after Prairie moved on. Prairie hadn't talked to her in years, so she thought she'd probably be safe to slide into a table along the wall and not be pulled into any small talk.

It's just so incredibly sad. I keep having to tell my kids that Mister Rogers thing about looking for the helpers. Cora crawled into my bed last night and asked me if I would ever disappear.

Prairie stopped rustling through her bag and went still, trying to force her ears to amplify the conversation at the table over the din at the front of the coffee shop.

—don't know. Lisa was such—

Right? I can't even—and Chris looked—

You know I was just at her place last week. I had ordered more Kitty Blue inventory and had it shipped to Lisa because they're doing all that work on my street, and the mail's being held at the post office. We had such a great time talking about the kids. You guys know what a crack-up she is.

The voice Prairie was picking up distinctly was Rachel's, who sat closest to Prairie's table. *Kitty Blue.* Rachel must have been recruited by Lisa and was maybe even a friend.

It didn't surprise Prairie that a bunch of moms were talking about Lisa at the very coffee shop Prairie was currently stationed at. Delco was a favorite lunch spot, and this was a big story in a small city. But running into a mom she had known who definitely knew Lisa well *and* knew about Kitty Blue was an irresistible opportunity.

What she didn't know is if Rachel would talk to her.

She glanced over at the table. They seemed pretty settled in. One of the moms was nursing her baby, and they were all less than halfway through their lunch plates. They'd probably be there awhile—maybe long enough for Prairie to figure out the right approach. She woke up her phone.

"Hey."

"Why are you whispering?" Megan's voice was distracted, and Prairie could hear a keyboard in the background.

"Are you typing?"

The typing stopped. "No. What's up?" Megan's voice wasn't just distracted, it was maybe the very littlest bit annoyed. And she had just lied. *Hm.*

Prairie made a mental note to have a real talk with her best friend soon, one where she wasn't using her as a personal sounding board.

"I'm at Delco."

"Why? Were you running low on bumping into people you didn't want to talk to?"

"I was meeting up with Alison. About Lisa."

There was another brief flurry of keyboard noise. "Okay."

Prairie forced down her impulse to ask Megan what was going on. She was on a short timeline. "I'll tell you later. The reason I'm calling is that I need some excuse to talk about Kitty Blue stuff with Rachel. She's friends with Lisa, but is probably also in her downline. I want to see if you're onto something with Kitty Blue, but I don't know how to bring it up so it won't be weird."

"You need a story lie."

"What?"

"It's like a lie you tell because you want to get someone to tell you something without asking them directly. When I suspected Mason was watching porn in the middle of the night and scrubbing his browser history, I knew that no matter how I brought it up, he was going to lie. So what I did was tell him that I was planning to buy more bandwidth from the cable internet company, but that they would have to run a report with the household's entire browsing history to show me what we used so I could choose the best package, and then he confessed in an explosion of red-faced stuttering."

"That's diabolical."

"That's a story lie. They're efficient."

"But don't you think it would be really shitty to lie in this situation?"

"If it gets you information that might help, no one is going to care. If it doesn't, no one is going to know."

Homemaker

"I don't suppose you have a good story lie for me off the top of your head?"

"No. My whole head is for me today. But good luck. Also, your whisper voice is like nails on a chalkboard. Don't ever do ASMR."

Prairie snorted, and they said goodbye.

She looked over at the table again. The women had barely made any more headway into lunch. Prairie decided she had a quick minute to do some research.

She started with Rachel Norton's Instagram. It didn't take long to confirm that Rachel was indeed selling Kitty Blue, although her posts of stylish outfits laid out on plush comforters were a bit uninspired—and sparsely sprinkled in her feed—compared to others Prairie had seen. She scrolled quickly, looking for pictures of her with Lisa, and hit a jackpot: Rachel and Lisa, arms around each other's shoulders, grinning and wearing head-to-toe Kitty Blue, with a caption that announced Rachel's excitement that she'd just become a Kitty Blue distributor.

Two minutes of scrolling on Lisa's linked account told her that Lisa Radcliffe was not simply making good money selling Kitty Blue. She was making high six figures, low seven figures, if the photos of her holding giant checks were anything to go by. And, link by link, Prairie quickly pieced it together. The women who were passing Lisa the giant checks, hugging her on the decks of Kitty Blue cruise ships, and beaming with their cheeks snuggled up to Lisa's in tightly framed selfies? They were Kitty Blue royalty, including the Chicago-based founder of the company and her sister-in-law.

A news notification popped up on her screen. It was the *Green Bay Gazette* with an article about the vigil.

The story was brief, the accompanying photos affecting. The remaining paragraphs confirmed what Joyce had told her. Lisa's van had been found partway in the water. There was a blurry picture of the crime scene techs working the area and another of the van itself, mostly hidden under a tarp. A grid search was being organized with law enforcement from several nearby counties to comb over acres of land near the bay. The police chief confirmed that at this time there were no persons of interest in the case.

Prairie let her phone drop into her lap.

Her head was spinning.

She needed a cookie.

And she was pretty sure she'd figured out her story lie.

Chapter 8

Prairie discovered a long line snaking through the space between Delco's entrance and the cash register. She queued up at the back of it, thinking about the grid search and everything she'd just learned from Alison.

Lisa *could* have had a breakdown. Prairie wasn't unfamiliar with the phenomenon. Hers had been a micro breakdown in the produce section of a grocery store after Maelynn was born. The therapist she'd started talking to afterward had told her that a breakdown was her body and brain enforcing a hard stop on what was going on so that the body and brain would get taken care of. Maybe Lisa's disappearance was a forced reset.

Lisa thrives when things get tough.

She's a big personality in a small package.

She must be doing something right with those kids.

You guys know what a crack-up she is.

Strong, funny people needed help with mental health, too, of course. Lisa had given Alison a ring, and possibly given Amber Jenkins a handbag. Expensive personal gifts. She had also given Alison the impression she didn't have any interest in or ownership of her new house.

Prairie had learned from Chris and Lisa's decorator that Chris had been gone since Friday. Was Lisa really waiting for him to return before she could approve Alison's layout changes, or did she need him to be there for her kids? He'd picked up the kids from school Monday afternoon, but the official story was that Lisa left after dinner, so she must have eaten with them. One last time?

Could Chris have followed Lisa when she left the house, or taken her away and done something after the kids were in bed? Would their kids have slept through his absence? Anabel could always tell when Prairie took a beer out to the patio at night. She had a sixth sense when there was no parent in the house, and every time, she would wake up and find Prairie.

Surely the police had talked to the kids. *There is no person of interest at this time.*

Prairie ordered her dulce de leche cookie. While the young man at the register fetched it from the case, she thought about Lisa's Kitty Blue Instagram account. Her twenty thousand followers. A few pictures from the cruises of Lisa in a bathing suit—always a one-piece with kimono cover-up, but more than enough to attract the Instagram vultures who believed that a woman living her life was inviting their attention.

Most of the women Prairie knew had had at least one run-in with a guy who wouldn't leave them alone, and even her own fairly boring social media accounts had caught the eye of gross dudes with grosser DM tactics. Something as innocent as a post-salon selfie could result in a dick pic.

And while the predator-stranger scenario seemed the least likely, a woman with a highly visible personal career, married to a bigwig in the community—a woman who was pretty and outgoing and who, to trash dudes, seemed "available"—might very well end up with a dangerous or difficult-to-shake stalker. Maybe Lisa, in the face of keeping everything running smoothly, hadn't taken it as seriously as would be best these days.

No piece really fit with another. Not yet.

She took her cookie to the back. She'd waited in line long enough that the women at the table had finished eating, and a few of them were gone. Rachel stood near the table, her purse hitched over her shoulder,

Homemaker

talking to the nursing mom, who was still trapped in her chair with her baby asleep on her lap.

Prairie hovered nearby until she managed to catch Rachel's attention. Then she took a deep breath and gave her a wave. *Oh, hi! Didn't see you there!*

Rachel acknowledged with a smile of recognition but didn't approach her or say a word.

Prairie took another deep breath. "Can I talk to you for a quick sec when you're done?" She put down her water glass and cookie on her table.

Rachel tipped her head to the side, then gave a small nod. "Let me finish up here."

Not enthusiastic, but she hadn't said no.

Rachel talked to the other woman for a few more minutes before she slid into the chair across from Prairie. She wore a sheer cream pintucked blouse with miniature mother-of-pearl buttons over black capris, with gold jewelry and Greek goddess sandals that must mean her feet were freezing during Wisconsin April. But they looked incredible.

Rachel gave her a reserved smile. "I haven't seen you in a long time, even though Ava's in two of Anabel's classes."

"It has been a long time." Prairie tried to let go of her discomfort. Finding Lisa was more important. "But I do have to get somewhere soon, and I'm on a bit of a mission that maybe you can help me with."

"What's up?" Rachel gathered her long, loose hair in a bundle around her wrist and smoothed it over one shoulder. She leaned forward, wary but listening.

Time to deploy the story lie.

"I got a message from a woman from Kitty Blue corporate this morning. She saw my name in the newspaper because I organized the vigil for Lisa."

Rachel was nodding. *Okay so far.*

"She reached out because everyone at Kitty Blue is worried about Lisa, and they wanted to do something for her. This woman who messaged me said they were hoping I might be able to pull together some quotes and pictures, maybe a little bit of video for them to use to make a tribute movie about Lisa to share on social media with a plea for information—just their way of doing their part to help."

Rachel's eyebrows furrowed. "Why do you need me?"

Prairie swallowed, trying to keep her tone light. "They gave me names to start with. People in Lisa's downline, and one of them was yours. I actually was going to call you later, but then I saw you here." Prairie hoped her face looked natural. The combination of dulce de leche cookie with the deployment of her story lie had resulted in intense nerves.

"Oh, you don't want to talk to me," Rachel said. "I don't really make money from Kitty Blue. It's more something I do for fun and to get my hands on the clothes."

"They're hoping for all kinds of different perspectives," Prairie reassured her. "I don't sell Kitty Blue, either. My take was they wanted to show how many people Lisa connected with."

Rachel took a deep breath. "I just saw her last week. I think it was Wednesday? No, Thursday. I had ordered new inventory, but I had to get it shipped to Lisa's because the city's tearing up my street, and the mail's getting held. My shipment got to Lisa, according to my delivery confirmation text, but Lisa wanted me to wait a couple days to go over and pick it up when Chris wasn't around."

Prairie must have had the question right on her face, because Rachel answered it.

"Husbands and their weird rules. Lisa loves to get in a coffee session with friends and Kitty Blue folks who stop by, and it annoys Chris when he's trying to work from home. I went over there, and Amber Jenkins was already there. She had been for a while. You should talk to her. They're close, and Lisa's been helping her a lot with her Kitty Blue."

"She's on my list to talk to." It was getting too easy to lie.

Rachel flipped her hair to her other shoulder. "Be kind, because Amber was really upset." She gave Prairie a look of warning that Prairie

Homemaker

didn't think was fair. Prairie had never been unkind. "She's been having a hard time lately. With a lot, which I could guess at, but it's not for me to tell. I hate to see it, because she's great. If I was half as organized as Amber, I would feel like I should be making money hand over fist, but her Kitty Blue business was struggling. Mine is, too, but I don't have the discipline to care."

Prairie wondered if it was less kind to ask people questions or to answer them with more information than was necessary—and private information at that. "What do you mean?"

"A lot of the distributors are struggling, especially since Kitty Blue changed up how it works. I don't understand half of it. Lisa's tried to sit me down to go over my numbers, because I think she's concerned about it. She takes everything seriously. I think she honestly expected every distributor in her downline would turn out to be as successful as she was. Some people are too good for this world."

"You don't think it was possible for everyone to do well?"

"How could they? They only put a few of the pieces everyone wants in every box. You don't get to choose your inventory, so if there's demand for something and you don't have it, you don't make money, but you're still out the price of the whole box."

"Which is expensive, I'm guessing."

"Very. It can be hard to sell the rest of your box because it's sizes and styles nobody really wants." Rachel flipped her hair again. "I hate selling it, but I like the events and the clothes. I order more boxes to get what I want and shove the stuff I don't want in the back corner of the garage. Aaron's not thrilled, but I told him, 'Look, I don't tell you how to spend your money, right?' I can always have a garage sale this summer."

Rachel leaned back in her chair, bouncing the heel of her sandal against the sole of her foot, and Prairie intuited that this was the end of the ride. "Maybe I could just record you saying something about Lisa to send to Kitty Blue?"

Rachel nodded, and when she leaned forward again, Prairie saw her eyes and neck had gotten red. Whatever was going on with Lisa, wherever she was, it was absolutely a fact that people really liked her, enjoyed her, loved her, and missed her. Prairie had been planning to fake record Rachel, but she went ahead and pushed the red button on the app.

"Lisa Radcliffe is one of the smartest, most dedicated, most generous people I know. She didn't have a bad word to say about anyone, and she was the first to shut down anyone else who did. It's no surprise she did so well in her business, because she built it with kindness and a real desire to see women do something exciting for themselves. She's great at business, great at making a home, great at raising kids, a wonderful friend, and we miss her like crazy." Rachel nodded and sniffed.

Prairie thought Rachel had delivered that so beautifully, she should consider a career in TV. "That was amazing. Thank you. I should have done a video."

Rachel looked at Prairie for a long moment, then seemed to decide something. "Here, let me text you some people you should talk to. Is your number still the same from back when the girls were in elementary?"

"Yep."

"Okay." She fussed with her phone for a minute before Prairie heard the whooshing sound of an outgoing message. "There you go," Rachel said. "That's everyone I know who might help. And I know you have to go, so I won't keep you, but I have one question that's a bit out of nowhere."

Prairie braced herself. "Hit me."

"What are you using on your skin?" Rachel finally offered her a real smile. A small one, but it was genuine.

Prairie might not have had gold Greek sandals, but she did love anything in a glass bottle or jar that overpromised and smelled good. "I'll text you my current routine."

"Yes. That would be good." Rachel stood up, and Prairie did, too. "I'm glad you said hello."

"Yeah, me too."

So that was nice.

After Rachel was gone, Prairie read through the list of names she'd sent. Then she grabbed her messenger bag, bused her dish, and headed for the door. She wanted to start working her way through these names as soon as possible. The sand in her mental hourglass of Time Left Before School Pickup was running out pretty quick.

But first things first. There was something more important she'd been neglecting.

She drove to the community center and found Megan in her office, bent over a sandwich and a bag of carrot sticks.

"The story lie thing is *magic*," she said.

Megan shrugged. She slid her hand to her computer mouse and clicked a few times, then picked up a spiral notebook on top of her desk and flipped it closed. "You want to sit?"

"I should have brought you a cookie from Delco." Prairie sat down. "But that place was starting to give me hives."

"You should have. Productive morning?"

Prairie, of course, desperately wanted to give Megan the full run-down, but she'd known her best friend for years now and could tell that she was either preoccupied with something important that she hadn't told Prairie about or she was more than a little irritated with her. Or both.

"Enough about me, already. What about you? I'm sorry I didn't get a chance to talk to you last night at the vigil."

Megan shrugged again. "I'm okay." She glanced at her notebook.

Prairie had never seen it before. It was one of the college-ruled kind with a cheap blue cover. "What's that?"

Megan put her hand on it. "Notes."

Prairie bit the inside of her cheek to keep herself from talking. This was a delicate moment.

"They're for an article I'm writing," Megan said after a lengthy silence. "A kind of long article. It was something that was . . . commissioned, actually. I turned down the commission a few years ago, but I started thinking about it more lately. I called the editor who had talked to me before and asked her if she'd still be interested in something, and she was. We talked for a couple of hours. It was good to talk with someone from my perspective about everything that's happened since Carmichael went to prison. My divorce, all of this." Megan gestured her hand to circle the center. "No one has bothered to talk to me about it like that, actually." She gave Prairie a long look.

Prairie kept her face neutral to remind her brain not to rush to an apology or try to get out of being checked. It wasn't easy. "I'm glad she could do that for you. You should have that. You deserve it. It's an important thing."

Megan nodded. "Yeah. And she wanted an article, but this time, she asked for something a lot longer. More in-depth and personal. She's actually introduced me to a literary agent, too. We're talking. About a book."

Prairie wanted to let out a whoop and hug Megan, but she sensed it was best to play it cool. "That's a lot that's been going on. Probably for a while."

"Yeah."

"Probably I'd know about it already if you could ever get a word in edgewise."

"Yeah, and if I didn't have three boys in a town house and a job that doesn't recognize a nine-to-five workday and an ex-husband who keeps sending his lawyer to talk to my lawyer to 'take another look' at the divorce settlement just because Mason told him I bought a new computer or, God forbid, new tires for the car and sprang for the nitrogen-filled ones."

Prairie couldn't stand it anymore. "I suck."

Megan narrowed her eyes. "Don't make me nurture your feelings in the middle of my calling you out."

"Damn it. Okay." Prairie closed her eyes and took a breath. "Please, please tell me about your agent."

"Maybe-agent."

Homemaker

"Your maybe-agent and your fancy article that's actually a book and your pathetic ex-husband. I promise I very desperately want to know."

Megan looked at her for another long moment, during which Prairie remained as still as possible. "I know you do. For the last few months, though, when all of this has been going on, we've slipped into that thing where I feel a little like I'm your sounding board and inspiration but not your friend. I knew I had to smack you, I just didn't have the energy to until this morning, when I accidentally ordered a triple instead of a double latte. Then I decided you were a complete waste and needed to be brought down like a dog who's been pooping in shoes."

"I do. I know, and it's not fair."

"It is not."

But then, to Prairie's great relief, Megan gave her a pass and told her everything, and Prairie successfully resisted the urge to offer help— whether by sending Deirdre to do free babysitting or by making it clear that she would be honored to read Megan's drafts, page by page or even paragraph by paragraph, the very moment Megan got the words down on her keyboard.

"That sounds amazing," she said instead. It filled Prairie with painful and wonderful pride to know someone like Megan, and also gave her the teeny-tiniest pang that Megan had such a clear and obvious shot at her *thing*.

"Thank you. It feels kind of amazing. Also terrifying, and way too hard. Today was the first time I started to feel like it might even have some kind of shape to it."

"If there's anything I could do to help, in any way whatsoever, please know that I'd love to."

Megan smiled, finally. "This is killing you."

"I am dead, yes. Completely dead, on the floor, from shame and an unfulfilled desire to make this up to you as quickly as possible."

Megan rolled her eyes. "You're a piece of work."

"This is not a fact I have ever been able to deny."

Megan propped her elbows on the desk. "I've only got ten more minutes on my lunch. Tell me what you found out at Delco."

"I don't have to. It will keep."

"I know, genius, but I want you to. I admit that I am also dying to know everything. You're entering the belly of the beast with this Kitty Blue thing. My envy is neon green."

Prairie filled Megan in on her brilliant story lie and her conversation with Rachel, then backed up to tell her about Alison and what Joyce had shown her with the map this morning.

Megan slumped in her chair, shaking her head. "I forgive you. That is some shit. There's way more up in the air than I ever would have guessed."

Prairie felt a spark of vindication. Driving over, she had nearly talked herself out of the idea she had learned much of anything, but walking through it with Megan made a few things stand out that she wanted to think more about later. "My plan now is to call as many of these people as possible before school pickup."

Megan got an evil look on her face that made Prairie sit up a little straighter. "You left something out."

"What?"

"I saw you talking to a *man* at the vigil, and you were doing that *thing* where you pretend there is no such thing as personal space and it's totally normal to stand six inches away from someone. I think your jacket was unbuttoning itself every time you made eye contact with him."

"No."

"No, you were not talking to a man, or no, you were not flirting with a man?" Megan picked up her phone. "I have your name and number in here. I can delete them right now."

"Yes, I was talking to a man." Prairie stopped. Megan wiggled her finger over the phone screen. "I couldn't have been flirting, though. Because he's FBI." Prairie leaned back in triumph.

"Oh my God."

"That's right."

Homemaker

"What did he tell you?"

"Nothing."

"Nothing? But it looked like you were giving him your best stuff. The only thing you didn't get to was that thing where you shove your hand in your back pocket and stick your boobs out."

"Possibly I made him match me on an app and go for a date with me tonight."

Megan put her phone down. "That's it. I can never delete you. I don't have time to watch Netflix. Even if I grow to hate you, I will hate-watch your life. Also, he's FBI. There was an actual, real FBI person scoping out the vigil. That must mean something."

"That's what I told Foster."

"Foster! Jaysus. He's hot, too. Like the character in a British movie who moves to the heroine's small town, where he wants nothing more than to be left alone after he's suffered a secret tragic event and is at first standoffish and then slowly is won over by the quirky town and then desperately frenches the heroine out of nowhere after only giving her long, silent looks for months."

"It's a strictly professional meeting," Prairie said, willing the heat from her cheeks. "I'm pretty sure."

"To be a fly on the wall." Megan looked away, lost in thought.

"That," Prairie said, standing up, "is my cue. If I'm going to get any calls in to these people before I have to pick up kids, I've got to go for real."

"You know what you should do first, though, is go talk to Shawna at my front desk. I checked this morning because I was pretty sure she was in with Kitty Blue, and not only does she sell it, she's also in Lisa's downline. And she's *pissed*."

"You're serious?"

"I was going to tell you if I decided to ever talk to you again. She has so much to spill. It's bad."

"You think she'll talk to me? Like for no real reason?"

"Oh, she'll talk to you. Just tell her you want to know everything, and she doesn't have to hold back."

Chapter 9

Shawna Lipton was a gold mine.

"You have to understand, I *move* this product." Shawna sat across from Prairie in one of the chairs she'd pulled from the front desk into the small room right behind it. She spoke quickly, with effortless confidence.

It turned out that Prairie knew Shawna—not by name, but enough to have said polite hellos to her before when she visited Megan at work or checked Maelynn in for Girls in STEAM workshops. She had long admired Shawna's lightning-fast efficiency with the center's outdated computer system, as well as her revolving wardrobe of colorful eyewear that always set off her light brown skin and its masses of freckles.

"I had money set aside with the intention of starting a business," Shawna said. "I didn't know if it would be a franchise or a direct marketing company or what, but I had a specific goal of finding a company that provided inventory and support, where I could build a sales income for myself. I went to a Kitty Blue party with my sister. I didn't expect much. I'd been to a lot of these things. But that party was the first time I really liked a product and could see building a market for it—and not just that, but a market Kitty Blue had overlooked."

"And what was that?"

Shawna glanced at the front desk. A kid was approaching with a basketball and a question in her eyes, but the other desk attendant swooped in to help, and Shawna turned her attention back to Prairie.

"You know Kitty Blue's based in Chicago? It was started by this already rich white woman who—well, the story is, anyway—wanted to offer the kind of stylish leisure wear she could find in boutiques and expensive chains but at a better price point, with the same quality, in a wider range of sizes. Obviously it took off, but all their marketing was the same kind of marketing that those boutiques and chains used. Real skinny and fit white ladies standing around in rooms filled with plants and candles and crystals, grinning at nothing."

Prairie laughed. She was familiar. "But you saw a different angle."

"Yeah. First I had a whole series of questions: What's the point of offering this stuff in every size if you're not going to actively make it clear in your advertising that it comes in every size? Why did it look like they were trying to market this stuff to the same people who could afford the more expensive version? And why weren't they showing more of how to mix up the pieces with the kinds of things ordinary women already had?"

"Right."

"I left that party *on fire*. I'm a CNA, and at the time I was picking up three shifts a week at a nursing home in order to stash extra into my savings. My mom is in an assisted living complex, but she's very active and has lots of friends. I had access to an untapped market."

"Older women with some disposable income who maybe didn't get out much to shop, and who wanted comfortable things to wear."

Shawna finger-gunned at Prairie. "Bingo. What's more, I have three sisters, and they're all in different big social groups. Church, community choir, Nigerian dance group. All kinds of women, all different sizes, who ranged from wanting to have an easy way to get new clothes without shopping to legit fashionable women who just wanted some new pieces to mix it up."

"Smart."

"Yeah, I *should* be smart. I'd been saving and researching for years by the time I got to that party. I called that distributor the next day and told her I was interested in hearing a presentation. I listened to her pitch. But then I took my time and looked at a bunch of other distributors' Facebook pages and websites. I wanted to find an active upline with lots of motivated distributors who seemed responsive. That's how I got into Lisa's downline."

"Did you know Lisa Radcliffe was in your upline?"

"Not then, but I liked the distributor who got me into it. It was a big commitment. Most direct marketing businesses have you buy what's essentially a demo kit. Maybe fifty to two hundred dollars. Then you have parties and events and take orders, which they fulfill, paying you a commission, as well as one to your upline. But Kitty Blue makes you buy all the inventory at once. Hang on a minute."

She got up and went to the desk, where some kind of drama was unfolding involving a woman's membership ID card and the other desk worker's inability to make it work in the scanner. Shawna had it sorted inside of fifteen seconds.

She sat back down. "Where was I at?"

"How much was your initial buy-in?"

"Ten thousand."

Prairie let out a huff of air. "Wow. That's a lot of joggers and tanks."

"At the time, I was reassured. It seemed like this meant Kitty Blue wanted distributors to build their own businesses. I prepped hard for that first shipment. When I got it, I was happy. There was a decent range of sizes, a lot of different pieces."

"But you didn't get to choose what came in your shipment, even after spending ten thousand dollars."

Shawna shook her head. "More on that in a minute. I got to work styling them and taking pictures, getting my friends to model. I made sure some of the pictures showed stylish people mixing up the pieces with street wear and other fads, but others showed my mom's old-lady friends wearing the clothes more with an emphasis on how they can be comfy and cute. See here, look." Shawna pulled out her phone, navigated to her Instagram, and handed the phone to Prairie.

Homemaker

Her account had an extensive link tree that took users to her website, her contact info, and a layout of her Instagram page where users could shop right from the pictures she had taken. It was different from any of the other Kitty Blue Instagram accounts Prairie had seen. She stopped on a picture of a tall Black girl wearing a Kitty Blue jacket with a FEMINIST ART WILL SAVE YOU T-shirt and a pair of battered jeans, and she found herself hovering her finger over the picture in sudden impulse-buying mode.

"That's impressive." Prairie handed the phone back.

"You want that jacket? You're a small in Kitty Blue. I've got it in a mustard and pink or a navy and light blue."

Prairie started to shake her head, then went with it. "Why the fuck not? Yeah. The navy, I think. I'll write you a check before I go, and you can give it to Megan to give to me."

"I can swipe you right here." Shawna pulled out a small, square card reader and plugged it into her phone. Prairie dug into her bag and handed her a card.

The woman was a force of nature.

"Done. Thanks. That will get me a few more millimeters out of this hole. Hang on again. Sorry." Shawna left, and Prairie watched her talk to a mom and two girls about what the schedule was for karate classes. She signed them up for memberships.

Prairie wondered what kind of fuckery was going on at Kitty Blue that someone like Shawna wasn't already a billionaire.

Shawna collapsed back into her plastic chair with a sigh. "You see what I'm doing. And like I said, selling isn't my problem. My problem is, first of all, I have no downline."

"Green Bay's an exhausted market."

Shawna snorted. "It wouldn't be if Kitty Blue didn't require that big initial buy-in. If they had some flexible options for new distributors, I could sign up a lot of folks. But they require that first inventory order at a minimum of right under five thousand dollars, and by the time you add in all the extra stuff that isn't really optional, you're looking closer to seven."

"Which is going to cut everyone out as a distributor except people who are already rich or people who have money saved, like you."

Shawna lifted a finger. "Or people with good credit."

The very idea made Prairie shudder. "Using credit to buy inventory when you don't know what you're getting or if you can sell it is a risky way to launch a business."

"Now you're talking my language. And from where I'm sitting, it's exploitation if the people telling you to take out that credit card are the same people selling you box after box of clothes, where most of that money goes right up the line, and what I can get back from my hustle is almost nothing. What does it mean if I have hundreds of consumers buying direct from me in a city like Green Bay and I haven't turned a profit?"

Prairie wrinkled her nose. "Something's wrong."

"Yeah, something's the fuck wrong, and I'll tell you what it is. You're going to love that jacket. No doubt in my mind. Say you come back and buy the mustard off me to give your sister, but then you want another one for yourself. Have I got another one? Hell no, I don't. Not unless I keep buying boxes, crossing my fingers with one hand and slashing them open with my box cutter in the other. I tell myself, I just need to build a bigger inventory. But every shipment I wheel into my garage is a little more off than the last one. A few more strange colors or pieces, or ninety percent of it's the same size and there's one thing in an extra-extra small." Shawna leaned in. "And they *know* it. They built it that way on purpose. Their business isn't structured on me selling clothes to people—it's structured on me buying giant useless boxes of their stuff, period."

"You're saying they're in the business of selling inventory to distributors."

"If they weren't, would they have rolled back their return policy a few months ago?"

Homemaker

"You can't return clothes anymore?"

She shook her head. "I never could—not in reality—but they used to *say* I could, then 'lose' my return shipments somewhere in the warehouse and tell me they were sorry but couldn't confirm they'd received them. Now they straight-up won't take returns. You get what you get."

"That's criminal."

Shawna glanced at the reception desk. "I'm not going down without a fight, though. I'm doing everything I can. I put together a whole report telling them what I'm doing and how much money they could be making off me and women like me. I showed them my marketing, my inventory database, financial projections. I sent that fucking thing straight up the line."

"What happened?"

"My upline acted like they were allergic to it. Briar Jorgensson, who got me into this, took a meeting with me and flat-out told me she was in the same situation as me, but worse. She's got four maxed-out credit cards and a husband who's so royally, hot-lightning, God-of-Thunder pissed off that she was afraid to let me call her on the phone in case he overheard. I went over Briar's head, up the chain, climbing over one nice white lady to get to the next one, until I got to the one person in all of Wisconsin who's as high as it goes."

"Lisa." Prairie had goose bumps all over her body. She put her hand on her phone in her pocket. Briar Jorgensson was the next person she had planned to call.

"That's right. And guess what happens less than two weeks after I contact her?"

"Wow. Yeah."

Shawna let her hands drop to her sides. She blew out a long breath. "I have five hundred dollars left in my business account. Five sixty-eight, with that deposit you just put in. And three hours down the road, on the north side of Chicago, there's a giant warehouse full of boxes of shit I could sell, only they won't give it to me. They'll give me exactly what they want to give me, if I send them seven hundred dollars to 'refresh my inventory,' but I've read the articles—they've got shipping containers they're letting get snowed and rained on in the loading dock. I don't want that shit. You tell me, what am I supposed to do now?"

Prairie didn't know. She willed herself to think of something, but if there genuinely had been a solution to find, Shawna would already have found it. "What about the lawsuits?"

"What about them? I've talked to a couple of the lawyers in Illinois getting together these filings. I won't get my investment back. They're not gonna buy my inventory. Doesn't help me now. Best case, I wait five years and get some half a percent of a class action settlement."

Prairie took a second to let the reality of that soak in. The hope and the loss, the criminal stupidity, the exploitation and impossible frustration. She wished she couldn't imagine it, but Shawna made it all too real. "Did Lisa ever get back to you?"

"Sure. She sent me an email. '*I understand what you're saying, you have some really interesting ideas, I'd love to explore them more, I'm thinking about what I can do to help you.*' Made me so angry, I couldn't bring myself to write back. She sent a few more, but I didn't read them. Just left them untouched in my inbox so I could burn them to a crisp with my eyeballs every time I open that app." Shawna had slid down in her chair. "I'm not afraid to admit I'm in a place of denial, trying to figure out my next step."

"That sounds like a rational response."

Shawna pulled her phone out again. "You want to see them, I'll forward them to you. Give me your email. Wait, no, I have it off your credit card, anyway." Her phone made a soft *zoop* noise. "There. Off my plate, onto yours. See what you make of them."

Prairie's phone buzzed. The buzz seemed heavier somehow. She had words, lots of words, direct from Lisa, on her phone. Right now.

And she had stories—Alison's story, Rachel's, and most of all Shawna's—pressing into her rib cage, making her chest feel tight with suppressed emotion.

After she left the community center, she used the remaining slice of time before she had to meet Anabel at the bus collecting as many more stories as she could get a hold of. She texted and direct messaged and emailed from her car, even managing to get a few women to pick up the phone. She asked questions and recorded more fake testimonials. She listened.

The women told Prairie variations on what she'd already heard. They loved the clothes. They liked the idea of the company. They'd signed on in a surge of optimism, but nothing had turned out the way they hoped—unless, like Rachel, they hadn't hoped for much more than to get first pick of some fun clothes and an excuse to socialize.

These women weren't pawns in a game or dumb moms who didn't know what they were getting into. Each of them had some reason she'd decided to sell Kitty Blue, some part of herself she wanted to nurture and grow. They were interesting women in many different ways.

They were eager to tell Prairie about Lisa. They all said how funny she was, and how unfailingly kind. Briar Jorgensson remembered the first time she'd needed to calculate a price sheet for an order, Lisa had sat beside her on her sofa, both of them leaning over the coffee table, and patiently walked her through the process for almost an hour before the light bulb finally came on. At least, that was what Briar recorded for Prairie to "share with Kitty Blue." Once Prairie told her she'd stopped recording, Briar explained that she'd mainly said that for Lisa, not for the company.

"Between you and me, I don't really care if Kitty Blue burns to the ground." Briar was on speaker, in the car just like Prairie, on her way to pick up a kid from school.

"Well, between you and me, you aren't the first one to say that."

"Did you talk to a woman named Shawna?"

Prairie's nape tingled. "I did. She mentioned you."

"Then I'm surprised you bothered to call me. I'm sure Shawna wasn't the nicest about me, and hey, I don't blame her."

"Like you, she seems more angry with the company." Prairie hesitated, then decided to go for it. "But she did say you were caught up in a bad situation with your husband over how the business turned out."

Briar filled the phone connection with a long fuzz of static, blowing out a breath. "The thing is, when Shawna contacted me, she was so mad, and I should have taken the time with her, but I just couldn't, emotionally, because I was dealing, on a daily basis, with Ethan's anger. I still am. And let me be clear, I'm not, absolutely not, in Shawna's situation. Technically, on paper, we can afford what I did. It'll mean very modest family trips with the kids for a couple of years, using the Y instead of a nanny, cashing out some shares of stock to take care of the highest-interest credit card, but world's tiniest violin, right?"

Prairie made a noise somewhere between agreement and clearing her throat.

"I really smashed Ethan's trust. I just kept wanting to make it work, and I hid how bad it had gotten. I rented a storage unit to hide the extra inventory. I opened a couple cards without telling him. I got into this wild spiral. I don't think I would've pulled up if it hadn't been for Lisa. She *understood*, you know? She didn't make me feel ashamed about the money, about hiding it from Ethan, maybe because she got it. Not everyone has some laid-back husband."

Prairie spotted Anabel's bus in the turn lane, about to arrive.

"Actually, there's a way that all of this has been good," Briar said, "because Ethan and I have gotten into counseling and understand each other so much better. And in the process of figuring out how far I'd gone under with Kitty Blue, with Lisa's help, I had a chance to help her, because she is really taking on a lot of accountability to bring these stories to the company and try to fix things. We had such a good talk, I don't know, end of the week before last? She gave me this beautiful Hermès scarf with a horse in bridles on it and told me that as I made things right, not to lose sight of when to be unbridled so I wouldn't be afraid of being passionate about something again. I really liked that."

Briar was the third person Prairie had talked to today, not including Alison, to tell her about an expensive gift Lisa had given her recently. There was Alison's ring, Briar's scarf, a designer sweater Lisa claimed looked better on the woman she gave it to, and a pair of emerald earrings meant to remind one of Lisa's friends that comparison was the thief of joy.

Amber's purse.

Prairie made herself table Amber again. She had to imagine that Amber—Lisa's *best friend*—must be completely gutted. It would be beyond insensitive to start asking her questions about her business problems.

But that didn't stop Prairie from wondering.

Briar was also the third woman after Alison and Rachel to mention Lisa's husband—and not the last. Chris's name popped up so often, Prairie started to doubt her reaction to it. Was it *normal* that none of these women could talk about a friend and her business without also talking about her husband?

She had that gorgeous boutique space on the main floor of her house, and I would have gone about every day, just to sit in her kitchen afterward and talk and drink her coffee, but she said Chris didn't want her to keep 'open house' hours, so it had to be strictly by appointment.

Chris was thrilled with the money. Oh, and he filled one of their garage bays with shelves for the inventory. Can you imagine? My husband doesn't notice when there's groceries on the counter to put away. He'll just pour himself a drink on the one tiny edge that doesn't have a bag on it.

We all went to the Chicago conference together. I'd been stuck at home with my kid for almost two years because I was breastfeeding, and I was dying to get some time with girlfriends and see something other than Green Bay. All of us were so happy to be there with no husbands. Except Lisa, of course, because Chris came with, and she spent all her time with him.

No one said they didn't like Chris or that they thought his behavior was a problem. But Prairie had been talking to friends about who they were married to for a long time, and in her experience, women didn't call out other women's husbands. They mildly complained about the dudes they'd married, or they laughed together at their husbands' ridiculous behavior, or one woman didn't participate in those conversations at all and everyone else noticed, but they never said, *Listen, honey, Jim needed to buy that second recycling bin from the city because he's a straight-up alcoholic. Stephen took off for a weekend with his buddies to Vegas for the third time this year because he's got an intense gambling problem. Tony's just a complete monster.*

Not until the divorce papers were filed. Then a woman would hear all of it—from all the friends who hadn't abandoned her, at least—and she'd think, *Well, why the hell didn't you say something before now? Wasn't my happiness worth more to you than my staying married?*

Prairie wished it didn't work that way. She wanted more for the women of her generation than for them to waste the best years of their mature adulthood on the wrong men, with no one who loved them telling them not to.

As she watched her daughter pick her way down the steps of the bus and emerge into the green spring day, Prairie said a prayer that her girls—her Anabel, her Maelynn—would never learn what it felt like to love someone who only knew how to give them control in return.

Chapter 10

Prairie stood on the corner across the street from Kettle's. It was damp, cool, and breezy, the daylight just faded enough that the bright fluorescents of the shop exposed the people inside through the plate glass windows across the front.

Foster sat at one of the tables close to the street. His back was to her. He wore a light blue sweater with a collared shirt. He had a jacket draped over the back of his chair. One of Kettle's pink teapots and a mug already sat on the table, so he must have been there awhile. It took forever to get a tea service after ordering.

For all her boldness and, yes, flirting, Prairie didn't know if this was a date. She'd gone back and forth about whether to wear her Thursday evening date outfit, which was a knee-length, well-made black wrap dress she'd bought from a high street shop in Grantham, Lincolnshire, when she and Greg had taken the girls to England eight years ago for a tour of gardens, petting zoos, and gentle history exhibits. In the end, she'd put it on.

A sensible black wrap dress that made her modest bust look nice was not, after all, any kind of invitation. That was why it was her Thursday night date dress.

Between homework and dinner, after she heard Joyce leave for her book club meeting and once Dierdre had arrived to hang out with Maelynn, she skim-read Lisa's emails to Shawna in one greedy gulp.

She wasn't sorry she'd done it. Lisa was, again, a surprise. But the day had left Prairie with only a scraping of resources. Her eyes, her muscles, a stretch of her body from the nape of her neck to her hips, were just plain *tired*.

She imagined breathing in all the rest of her resources into every part of herself and exhaling the Prairie who wanted to crawl under the covers and reset.

She crossed the street and entered Kettle's. A woman was setting up a microphone in one corner, near a flute laid across a performer's stool and a case big enough to hold what Prairie could only assume was some sort of obscure stringed instrument. Possibly Irish. *Oh no.*

Other than Foster, everyone seated at the tables had passed sixty long ago.

He turned and spotted her when the bell over the door rang. Prairie mimed that she wanted to order at the counter first. He started to stand, reaching for his back pocket as though he planned to follow her up there and pay. She put up her hand, palm out. *Let's not.*

Foster sat back down, his face impassive.

The smell of Lysol near the register was as intense as ever, the barista the same ageless woman who had stood behind the counter for years looking at her expectantly. Oh *God*, Prairie was hungry, and she kicked herself for skipping dinner, which was Beth's gorgeous glazed vegetable bruschetta, because Kettle's food offerings were as desultory as they had ever been.

"Can I get the black forest milk chocolate smoothie and one of those cheese plates?" She cast her eyes at the sad and dusty plexiglass bakery case perched on top of the counter. Experience had taught her that cheese plate preparation was a long process. ETA on the smoothie was anyone's guess. "And I'll take one of the turtle brownies"—*please don't be dry*—"and this." She waved a bagged sausage-and-cheese skewer from the cooler beside the counter.

The barista quoted her a total, which Prairie put on her card, with a tip.

Homemaker

"Okay, you're all set. It'll probably take fifteen, twenty minutes for me to get everything out to you."

Prairie repressed a sigh. "Sure."

She took her bagged-up meat-and-cheese stick and her shrink-wrapped brownie over to Foster's table. With his teapot, mug and saucer, spoon, and cream jug, there was barely room left to put her food down.

"Why, *why* this place?" She sat, pleased that his eyes flicked over her and warmed.

He leaned back. Close up, his sweater was nice. It had a faint pattern that made it look like something he'd bought in a European country no tourists ever visited. The collar of his shirt was pressed and had gray pinstripes. "The tea is good," he said. "They have a decent selection of used books. But mostly, I have never been here and run into someone I know, have interrogated, or have taken into custody."

"Fair enough. Although I'm going to stipulate that if we can't hear each other over the stylings of the soothing Celtic music, we're going to wrap this up on the park bench across the street." Prairie unbagged her very Wisconsin sausage-and-cheese stick and started pulling off the cubes onto a paper napkin she'd spread out on the table.

"You're not allowed in the park after sundown."

She popped a cheese cube in her mouth. It was oily. Gah. "Rule follower."

"Sometimes." A bare hint of a smile.

His game went with his look. Warm, unfamiliar, and interesting. His collar was undone, and his sweater was a V-neck, and that was warming, unfamiliar, and interesting in a different way. It forced Prairie to acknowledge that all the cockiness she'd been bringing to Thursday night app dates was a pretense and entirely due to the fact that not one of those men had a chance.

She wasn't sure if she was ready for a man who did.

Prairie took a deep breath. "Is a rule follower something you always wanted to be? I mean, I know you were in the military"—she picked up a cube of sausage and waved it in a circle as she talked—"but go ahead and unravel the whole yarn for me. I'd like to hear the Foster Rosemare story."

"That implies you haven't already cyberstalked me and learned everything there is to know." He lifted his tea mug. She noticed he had about fifteen empty sugar packets neatly stacked by the pot. Tea, no caffeine. Sugar fiend. He was vigilant against the nicotine demon.

Prairie toasted him with a sausage cube. "If I had, I wouldn't tell. I'd just listen to find out if what you told me matched my research. That way, I would know if you were a lying sociopath."

The flavor of the sausage was indistinguishable from the cheese. *Oof.* She wrapped the rest of the cubes up in her napkin and pushed it a few inches to one side.

"So you do this enough, the app thing, to have a strategy."

"I've been a woman since I was born. My whole existence is a strategy."

"Touché." He said the foreign word in a good French accent and sipped his tea afterward as though these were things men could do in Wisconsin without losing hold of their masculinity. "I was an officer in the army. I don't know if I always wanted to do this work. I was a good student in high school. Went to college. I liked psychology. Didn't know what I wanted to do with it. My dad had been in the military, so I did the same, joined up and went through officer training after graduation. From there, the FBI recruited me. And here we are."

"That is in no way a story. It's a series of factual statements, roughly in order, that I'm expected to make my own story from."

"I'm thinking you haven't known a lot of investigators." He glanced at her cheese and sausage. "You're not going to eat that."

Prairie shook her head.

He inched it closer. "The way I would tell a story isn't the same as how you might. Pretty much all I do is put together a series of factual statements—verifiable, is our strong preference—and roughly in order."

Homemaker

"Here's a series of statements for you." Prairie unwrapped her brownie. "A Green Bay mother of three left her home sometime after dinner on Monday night. She was driving a gray Chrysler Pacifica minivan with a red leather interior. She didn't come back. Police were notified she was missing at some point that evening. Late Tuesday, her van was found half-submerged in the bay at the end of a jetty with an access road few people know about or use. The woman's body was not in the van or nearby. The police have asked the public for information related to seeing the van or the woman herself, but they've provided no facts about where the woman was going, who she might have met up with, or whether they believe she may have been abducted and killed or taken her own life. Or if they think she's still alive. It's now Thursday night, about seventy-two hours later. No arrests have been made. No new information is available to the public."

Before, Foster's expression had been at least mildly warm. As Prairie laid out her take on the official story, she watched all temperature and light go out of it.

He'd done this a couple of times at the vigil. He was looking at her, making eye contact, but there was nothing. No thoughts, no feelings, no aggression, no cues. And yet it wasn't antisocial, somehow. Prairie found herself desperate to say words at him in order to get *something* back, even as his expression invited nothing.

"Whoa," she said, staring at his face. "Do you think you could, sometime, teach me how to do that? It would be so much more efficient than having to think up a story lie every time I wanted to get someone to talk to me."

"Do what. And what's a story lie."

She was getting used to his not-question questions. "That thing with your face where it makes itself into a black hole sprinkled with truth serum. And a story lie is a little made-up story to get someone to tell you something they wouldn't otherwise. Like if your teenage son is logging onto porn in the middle of the night but deleting his browser history, and you tell him you're going to buy a new data package, but

109

the internet company, as part of the process that helps you choose, will be giving you a report of your internet usage that includes every site your address has ever visited, and then he confesses."

"That's just a regular lie, but it's so masterful, it gives me chills."

"My best friend came up with it. She has three boys." Prairie discovered she was on the verge of boasting about Megan's article and her maybe-agent. She checked herself. First dates were not the time to start telling the guy across from you about your closest friends, your kids, or your ex-husband. "Have you been married?"

To her relief, his face returned to a very warm human state. "I have. We were married eight years. Louise. She died ten years ago, August. I met her when I had a few days' leave in Paris. She was finishing graduate school. Her parents were from Sierra Leone. She was genuinely remarkable. She died in a car accident." One side of his mouth smiled, though his eyes were a little sad. "Louise could do anything, but she was a truly terrible driver."

Prairie laughed, and for the first time since her divorce, something flared up, just a little, inside her. Foster's willingness to tell her about his wife, and his possession of emotional intelligence fine enough to make a small joke at his wife's expense, which he would not feel free to do unless he loved her, just so that Prairie could respond to his grief with a laugh, was . . . Well. It was different.

He was different.

"How did you end up *here?*"

"My dad lives in Door County. He's a big outdoorsman. He worked for the government. Took trips out west to go elk hunting, that kind of thing. He retired and moved to Sturgeon Bay to be close to my brother and his wife and kids. My brother's a doctor at the hospital. The first time I had the opportunity, I took a transfer here, because, yes, they do have an FBI office in Green Bay, Wisconsin."

"It must be so small, though. Like, barely any room for a photocopier. And you said you had nieces."

"Six of them."

"Wow. All from the one brother?"

"Yeah, surprised us, too. We're upstate Protestants. Heir-and-a-spare types. They kept trying for a boy, but I guess after the third or fourth girl, they were just in a groove."

"Do you have children?"

He shook his head. "Louise wanted to wait until I had a chance to do something more stable than the military and she'd gotten established in laboratory management. She trained as a microbiologist. We thought we had time."

Prairie glanced toward the counter. The barista had no customers. She was opening and closing the refrigerator, compiling Prairie's cheese plate from a collection of individual plastic tubs. No sign that she would be wrapping up the job anytime soon.

The woman with the flute tapped the microphone. The volume was turned up too high.

"Do you like it here?" Prairie had lived in Green Bay since right before Anabel was born, and she almost never met people who came from outside of Wisconsin. Everyone she talked to assumed she loved it here and would stay forever.

"I've lived all over. Every place has something to recommend it. People are mostly the same. Interesting people are rare, wherever you go." His eye contact deepened.

She looked down. As he'd been talking, she'd leaned forward, put her elbows on the table. She'd been resting her chin on the backs of her hands.

Prairie lowered her arms and sat up straight, embarrassed to find herself posed like a flirting young woman. "See, now that's *almost* a story. You could have saved me a lot of time and effort pulling it out of you."

Half his mouth smiled again. She was starting to understand that all Foster's small reactions were, in fact, his version of big reactions. Which meant that his big reactions, like when she'd made him laugh at the vigil, were some kind of fireworks display.

"I get the sense you like pulling stories out of people," he said.

"That's true, but there are limits. I like telling stories, too. For example, that series of connected and verifiable facts that I told you earlier—which was not a story—about the woman who drove away from home and didn't come back. Would you be interested in hearing a different version that is actually a story?"

The nape of her neck was tingling. She needed to get a grip.

"That depends."

"On what?"

"If the story you're going to tell is consistent with a woman who promised"—he checked his watch—"a little more than twenty-two hours ago not to do anything Harriet the Spy would do."

"I didn't climb into any dumbwaiters, if that's what you mean."

His nothing face came back, snapping the boundaries back into place. Then, without looking away from her, he reached into his pocket and pulled out a small black device, which he set down on the table. He pushed his finger against its side. A red LED light started blinking.

She looked at it, then back at him, raising an eyebrow.

"This is how I listen to stories."

"Were you recording this whole time?"

"I'm not in the habit of recording a *date*." He folded his arms on the table. If she had been a criminal, she was pretty sure she would have sung like a canary.

Desperate for a distraction, Prairie glanced at the barista again. She was loading frozen fruit into a blender. Progress of a sort. The flutist had begun blowing long notes so the other musician could carry out an interminable tuning process on her stringed instrument.

Okay. She could do this. "On Monday night, Lisa Radcliffe left home after dinner. Her three kids were home with their dad, her husband, Chris. I don't know what time she left or where she went. I don't know why. I don't even know how long Chris waited after she didn't come home before he called the police. But I know there's a lot more to Lisa's story than just those facts."

The red light kept blinking, snuggled up against the teapot. It turned the pink ceramic purple, then back to pink. Foster watched her. There were no questions in his eyes. Just nothing. FBI agent face.

Prairie laid it out for him—everything she'd learned about Kitty Blue and how much money Lisa made, how much money the women in her downline had lost, and how angry and desperate so many of them had become. The longer she spoke, the more the blinking red light spurred her on, and the more saying the things she'd heard and thought about Lisa made them seem vital to understanding what might have happened.

"So Lisa, who sells Kitty Blue, and who is missing, has a husband who is the kind of guy everyone says they like, but no one really does. He's controlling. He's always monitoring Lisa, making rules for her to follow that either limit how she's able to run her business or that put him squarely in the middle of that business. He's the kind of person who is constricting the ability of an outgoing, generous, and loving woman to navigate not just her business, but her own life."

Prairie leaned in, her hand curled into a fist on her lap. "And at least some part of Lisa knows it, because she and Chris are in the middle of building a huge, sixty-five-hundred-square-foot mansion, and she doesn't want it. Maybe she doesn't want to live even farther from town—she's told Chris she had a fantasy of living with the kids in a downtown penthouse apartment—or maybe she doesn't want to be tied down even more, because maybe Chris is the kind of husband who's going to use that big house like a prison."

Prairie's cheese plate and smoothie arrived. It took the barista a minute to work out a way to fit the food onto the top of the already crowded table. Prairie waited for her to finish and thanked her. She took a sip of the smoothie. It was delicious.

Then she started again.

"Either way you slice it, Lisa has stress in her life. Money stress, because the Kitty Blue train isn't going to be on the tracks much longer. Stress from her husband's expectations. Stress from the people in her downline she's worried about. She's looking at her mental health, and she's taking antidepressants to help. Maybe in this story we're starting to worry about Lisa. Is it all too much? Especially when we find out she's been giving her friends, in the last few weeks, expensive gifts, items that belong to her that she's telling them they'll have better use for or that she thinks will mean something to them. A quartz and diamond ring with a gold band. An Hermès scarf. A designer sweater. Emerald earrings."

Foster's face didn't change.

"You already knew about the gifts," she said.

Nothing.

"What about a nine-hundred-dollar purse?" Prairie watched him carefully.

He didn't know about the purse.

He had to know about Amber—there was no way he didn't, no way he or his team hadn't already questioned her about what she knew and where she thought Lisa might have gone—but he didn't know about the purse Lisa had given Amber, or that Amber had lied about it to Prairie, or that Amber had a cracked phone screen and a broken taillight and a kid whose shoes were too small. He didn't know Amber's husband was awful, or that Amber and her family used to live near Lisa but had moved to a less affluent part of town. He didn't know Amber had lost money in Kitty Blue or that Lisa was trying to help her.

Prairie told him.

She didn't feel great about it. She felt sick and a little sweaty, but she did it anyway because this was *information*. It was what law enforcement had asked for.

Then she stopped, a little breathless. The red light kept blinking.

"I wish I knew more," she said. "I wish I had a way to make a real story, with a beginning, a middle, and an end. But I don't have anything from you guys except that you want information, and you're looking for Lisa, and there isn't a person of interest. It could be you already know things I have no way to know. And it's possible the story I'm telling you only confirms what you seem to be implying and the public is starting to get, because you're not asking for volunteers to help search for Lisa Radcliffe. That might mean she took her own life—that it's the most likely story right now."

Prairie looked at his face. No change.

"Except." She took a deep breath. She felt like something was fraying that she wanted to keep hold of, but it was ripping out of her grasp in pieces. "Except I could tell that you knew about the gifts, everything but the purse, and a lot of the other things I said, but I know you haven't talked to anyone I talked to except Alison, and you guys only asked her if the Radcliffes owed money. That means you found out everything I found out a different way. From the family. From Chris."

She felt like she was missing something big. Prairie ordered herself to think. Think *hard*.

Her sudden realization set her brain on fire.

"You must have," she said. "You don't ask stuff like, 'Hey, was your wife giving away a bunch of expensive items, and was she generally overextended in addition to being depressed?'" Prairie leaned forward and put her palm flat on the table. "Because I've talked to you, and you don't ask anyone *anything*. You do what you're doing right this minute and let someone talk. Which means Chris volunteered that stuff. And tell me, *tell me*, Agent Rosemare, what husband is able to provide a detailed description of his wife's personal items that she decided to give to friends on her own time? If I gave my fucking kidney to a friend, my kids and my ex wouldn't be able to remember if it was the right or the left. Chris Radcliffe told you a story, just like I did. He told you a story about his stressed-out wife who took antidepressants and had been giving her friends pricey presents. And what I'm telling you is that you should seriously ask yourself why Chris had so much to say to you about Lisa when all the women I talked to wanted to tell me about *him*."

Prairie reached into her messenger bag and put her fingers around the stack of papers she'd put in there right before she left the house, hot off the printer. She hesitated, then pulled them out, shoved over her cheese plate until it threatened to fall off the table, and laid them in front of Foster. "Have you seen these?"

She watched his face. He hadn't seen them. Probably they were in a stack in his office, or on a thumb drive he was supposed to get to when he had an hour free, because once the police had done their initial sweep of the Radcliffes' finances and found no big red flags—once they had scanned Lisa's email and phone for affairs or scandals—what kind of time were they going to spend in the first few days on a mom's emails about selling clothes?

"These are emails Lisa sent to one of her distributors, a woman who has been busting her ass to sell Kitty Blue and is losing money for no good reason. What these are going to tell you, if you want to take the time to read them, is that Lisa hasn't been stressed out or sad about what was happening with Kitty Blue. She isn't mired in despair. She's *mad*, and she's been doing something about it. Lisa is trying hard to make things right, and before she disappeared, she was getting ready to put her own money on the line."

Prairie had the skirt of her dress gripped in her lap. Her palms were sweating. She made herself let go. "I don't know if Chris told you his wife made seven figures at Kitty Blue last year, but if he did, you might want to think about *how* he told you. And if he didn't, that's extra fucking super weird, and you'd better be thinking about why not, because I promise you, I heard about Lisa's money all day long. Nobody failed to mention it, and nobody failed to talk about it in a way that made it clear Lisa's money was wrapped up with her marriage and her husband and what *he* thought about everything."

Prairie sat back. "As far as the emails, though, I'm willing to bet Chris didn't say a word to you about that, because that's motive. A woman threatening a man's bottom line is always motive. The possibility of losing her Kitty Blue money, her *mom* money, was big enough to threaten his bottom line."

Long seconds passed as she waited for Foster to speak.

Nothing had prepared Prairie for the naked, terrible risk of telling him that story. It made her think of Megan walking into the police station all those years ago. Prairie had admired her so much, but she hadn't imagined what it must have been like for Megan to sit down at a desk or a table across from a detective and let everything spill out. Prairie had so little imagination, she hadn't pictured the man across from Megan. The way he would have looked while he listened.

A man with a closed-off face, unmoved by the thing that had rearranged Megan's whole life.

Foster reached out and turned off the recorder.

"342-VYN." He said the letters and numbers to her in a voice with nothing in it.

"What's that?" But the moment she asked, Prairie recognized it. Her license plate number.

"That's the number I am giving to everyone who is officially involved with this investigation and telling them if they see it on a black Accord anywhere it is not supposed to be—and I mean if it's parked at a grocery store you're not known to frequent—to hold you wherever you're at until I get there." His voice was even. He wasn't yelling. If anything, he'd lowered it enough that she had to strain her ears to hear him over the increasing din of Kettle's. "You and me"—he gestured between them—"are not Cagney and Lacey."

"They're both women."

Foster closed his eyes.

"You"—he opened his eyes, and his voice did get louder—"are not to speak, not one word, to Christopher Radcliffe."

"I can speak to whoever I want to speak to, as long as they're willing to talk to me."

"You can. My order was a courtesy. A courtesy that I hoped would remind you that the kind of conversations you're having are the kind that ruin lives. I will tell you that if you do speak to Chris Radcliffe, I will personally ensure you're arrested for obstruction."

Prairie held out her wrists, her fists bunched and tight against each other. *"Go ahead."*

Foster pushed back from the table. "I think we're done." He reached into his pocket and pulled out a fifty, which he swapped for the printed-off emails on the table. He shrugged into his jacket, a beautiful sports coat that flashed a glimpse of deep-green silk lining. Once it was on, he looked so handsome, Prairie felt a first stab of regret. He'd come here for a date, with a good game, dressed like a poem, and she'd ruined it.

"What's the money for?"

He started to walk away, but stopped, and Prairie noticed his shoulders were less squared off than usual. "Before you got here, I asked the woman behind the counter to bring me a muffin, and I hadn't paid yet. It's probably coming. I didn't want to stick you with it."

He turned around and left.

A jaunty Celtic tune started, led by a flute playing into a mic turned up way too loud.

A muffin landed in front of her on a plate. "That will be two thirty-six."

Prairie handed over the fifty. "Keep the change."

She got up, and for the first time in years, maybe ever, she didn't bus her table or even make it tidy so the server could pick everything up more easily. She abandoned the giant mess she and Foster had made, walked out of Kettle's, got into her car, and drove home, focusing only on one obvious automatic action after the next.

At home, she parked in her spot. Before she got out of the car, she looked at her phone. No notifications. She'd hardly been gone an hour. It hadn't taken her any time at all to get dressed up, get charmed, then get freaked out and drive a dump truck's worth of amateur gossip dressed up as *information* into her FBI agent date.

She thought about her voice getting recorded by that blinking red light and winced.

Walking to the door, she hoped Deirdre would have somewhere she wanted to go and not want to catch Prairie up in some long conversation about how her day had intersected with her horoscope. Prairie didn't have anything—not one thing—left.

When she walked from the kitchen into the living room, though, it wasn't Deirdre on the sofa. It was Greg, with Gingernut in his lap and Zipper on the farthest cushion wagging his tail madly, wanting to greet her but too scared to move in the event Gingernut would chase him.

Greg started to talk, probably to offer some convoluted explanation for why he was there in the first place. Prairie held up her hand to stop him. "Don't say one single word or ask me why, and don't think it means *anything*, but I need you to give me a hug."

He gently put Gingernut on the floor and stood. Prairie went to him.

Greg put his arms all the way around her. She bent her own arms up against his sides. She couldn't quite let herself fully embrace him. But she laid her face on his shirt, a shirt she had given him a few years ago for his thirty-ninth birthday, and closed her eyes, glad for a person who'd already seen her survive her worst days.

"Don't feel too bad," he said. "It's not easy. And he's an FBI agent. That's really leveling up."

Prairie snorted and stepped back. "Maybe it went amazing."

"I went out with this Green Bay Packers trainer, and she insisted on driving me to urgent care because I acted so drunk at the restaurant when I actually had a hundred-and-three-degree fever because I didn't know a grown man could get strep throat from his kid."

This was the first time Prairie was hearing about the Packers trainer date, though she'd known when Greg had strep. "We're amazing," she said. "All that suave charisma you learn not dating when you get married as children really comes in handy during the second act."

He laughed. "Wait until you give a guy a second date. Then you'll see how suave and charismatic you really are."

Right this minute, Prairie was happy to wait.

Chapter 11

"I just don't think I can sleep." Anabel was curled up under Prairie's arm, her voice rough from weeping that had finally eased.

"That's fine," Prairie said. "You don't have to try."

They were in Prairie's bed, the traditional location of nighttime emotional emergencies at 724 Maple. It turned out that Deirdre had left because her boyfriend was stranded at work and needed a ride home. Rather than inform him she was herself working and could not assist him—or call Prairie to come home from her date—or call Joyce, who was Prairie's backup—Deirdre had decided to take her emergency to Greg. Who'd come right over.

Post-hug, Greg had reluctantly revealed that Anabel was waiting up to talk to Prairie about "something horrible." He had not been able to get her to tell him what it was, although Deirdre had reported that Anabel had been cruel to Maelynn for no reason and had slammed so many doors, Deirdre seemed legitimately concerned the "noise bursts" breaking up the house's energy would call down demons or poltergeists.

"I never should've asked her out," Anabel said. "Having an unrequited crush wasn't even half as painful as being rejected."

What Prairie had gathered between Anabel's stormy tears was that the object of her unrequited crush was a senior girl named Emma. This was the same person who Anabel had been hanging around with at the vigil. They'd met at Gender and Sexuality Alliance meetings. Today at school, Anabel's months of private crushing had finally reached their limit, and she'd gathered the courage with the support of her best friend, Kai, to ask Emma on a date.

Apparently, Anabel had accepted Emma's rejection gracefully until she got home from hanging out with Kai after school and could safely burn the entire world to the ground with her feelings.

Everyone in the family knew that Anabel was gay because she had told them when she was in sixth grade, tossing the information over her shoulder on her way out the door to a swim class as though it were such an obvious part of herself, she was telling them her hair was getting a little long—but until now, the knowledge had been largely theoretical.

Anabel looked up at Prairie. "I shouldn't have asked her, right?"

Why did these conversations always have to take place at times when Prairie had absolutely no resources for them? She and Anabel had talked through what happened more than a few times at this point. She had heard a great deal about Emma Cornelius, who was accomplished and rebellious and produced her own true crime podcast, which interested Prairie for all the wrong reasons. Her heart hurt, her body needed rest, and her brain wouldn't stop obsessing over Lisa. But she was Anabel's mom, and Anabel needed her.

She reminded herself to tread lightly, lest her daughter sense her disrupted mental state and turn vicious. "Do you think it will help to dig into it some more?"

"Maybe. I don't know." Anabel took in a long, shuddering breath. "All the talking in the world won't change the fact that I'm fifteen."

"Fourteen."

"Fifteen in three weeks. And she's a senior." This had been Emma's primary point when she turned Anabel down, in a way that sounded remarkably kind, actually. She'd told Anabel that their age difference and differences in experiences made it more appropriate for them to be friends.

"True. You might—"

"I mean, it's so stupid. If I were eighteen and she was twenty-one, it wouldn't even matter, but just because we're in high school, it's

121

everything. The fact that I couldn't control the year I was born is going to make this impossible forever."

"It's more that the only life we can live is the one we're living right now, and right now is not the time for you and Emma."

"It never fucking will be!"

Strong words. Prairie couldn't think of anything to say. The child under her arm was entirely capable of having her heart broken.

Prairie knew that her job wasn't to prevent her children from feeling pain, only to help them know what to do when life was painful, but this was absolutely a moment she wished she could whisk away for Anabel. She, herself, was feeling the devastation that crushes could deliver in a brand-new way. Her terrible date with Foster hadn't devastated her, but Prairie couldn't pretend she wasn't reeling, or that she didn't wish it had gone differently.

She knew it meant she was interested in him. She didn't know if that was because she was interested in what she was doing with her time, thinking about what happened to Lisa, and Foster was caught up in those feelings, or if it was Foster himself and his handsomeness, his ability to keep up with her, his sly humor.

It made Prairie feel guilty to linger over thoughts of Foster. Lisa was missing. She could be in danger, trapped somewhere, hurt and alone in the dark. Prairie wanted to believe that capable people were doing everything they could to find her, but it was hard to resist the impulse to believe it was *her* job to find Lisa Radcliffe. Especially since she'd already managed to uncover information that seemed important to Foster.

Prairie felt obligated to this, and maybe some of those feelings of obligation weren't just her unique gifts or her understanding of Lisa's social circle. Maybe a lot of them were about proving to her old friends that she'd only ever been trying to help them and keep them safe.

Either way, she couldn't ignore the urgency of her feelings to look for Lisa. Before it was too late.

"I'm not stupid," Anabel said, her voice sleepy after they'd both been quiet for a few minutes. "I know I'll like someone again, but what

Homemaker

makes me so angry is that I can't just pound on my heart"—Anabel pushed her fist against her chest—"and make it completely reset. I want everything in my head to go back to before, when Emma was just someone really cool and not"—she hit her chest with her fist—"everything I think about."

Prairie pressed Anabel closer. "Oh, honey, my love, you're not wrong. I know this isn't what you want to hear, but I'm proud that you loved someone and were brave and took a chance, and I'm proud you accepted her answer gracefully, which is hard. It doesn't feel like it, but you've got this, you really do."

Anabel sniffed a little more. "Maelynn said it was all down to biological drives, and probably my pheromones don't attract Emma's pheromones. I think she was trying to help, but I was super mean. I feel bad."

It sounded like Maelynn *had* been trying to help. It might have been a thoughtless comment from someone else, but as an autistic person, Maelynn often showed her care and love by extending perspectives based on her special interests, which included science. Prairie knew that Anabel understood this, but even taking neurodivergence out of the equation, it would be a rare eleven-year-old who could comfort a teenager with a broken heart.

"There was probably no way in the moment for you to remember that her perspective would be very different. Apologize to her when you mean it, and explain it to her if you want to. But don't apologize for getting angry with her—"

"—apologize for how I expressed my anger. I know."

"Okay."

They lay in the dark, Zipper grunting with contentment over being allowed to be on the bed at their feet.

When Prairie and Greg were married, this room had been a guest room decorated with whatever bed linens and furniture everyone else had grown tired of. Some people might feel a California king was a bit too much mattress real estate for a single, average-size woman, but those people hadn't spent the majority of their adult lives sharing a queen with a six-foot, three-inch man with sharp elbows, scared or sick babies and children and toddlers, the random dog or cat who snuck their way in, and a spouse's wedge pillow for reflux.

It was nice to have the space to comfort a teenage daughter and warm her feet under the dog. More than nice, even if it tested Prairie's patience. Being here with her daughter, safe and warm, made Prairie's resolve to find Lisa burn bright and hot in her chest.

Just as Prairie was dropping off, she heard Anabel's voice. "I want you to meet her."

Prairie adjusted herself so she was sitting up a little and wouldn't fall asleep again. "Emma?"

"Yeah. I was going to introduce you to her after the vigil, but then you were busy talking to that man, and Grandma took us home. I think she could help you."

"Help me what?"

"Be a detective."

Detective. The word snuck up on her and set off an unexpected rush of feelings. "You think that's what I'm doing?"

"I mean, I could call it 'the thing you're not supposed to be doing, but totally are, trying to find Lisa Radcliffe,' but 'detective' is a lot easier to say. Emma's into it. Her podcast has a hundred thousand subscribers. She only covers cases where girls and marginalized kids or teenagers are the victims."

"That really is an amazing accomplishment."

Anabel sighed. "I'm aware." She turned to Prairie in the bed and propped herself up on her elbow. Prairie was glad to see that the grief was lifting from around her mouth and eyes. "The high school is always trying to discourage her now that it's popular, because whenever she drops an episode, they say it's disruptive. But she doesn't care. And, God, Mom, the research she does."

"It's good?"

Homemaker

"Not just, like, Wikipedia or whatever. She reads books and old newspapers and interviews people, and she's even had the family members of victims on her show. She says she's going to do this for a living, straight out of high school. She's the only one I know who never talks about college and has that holy-mission thing you're always talking about."

"Well, I'm not going to say I couldn't use some help." Prairie tucked a piece of Anabel's hair behind her ear. "Do you want to hear what I've been up to?"

"It's only fair. Mrs. Radcliffe going missing is, like, the only thing anyone can talk about."

Prairie felt a kick of misgiving. "Well, it would have to stay between us. And I can't tell you everything. Just the general highlights."

Anabel agreed, so Prairie told her a short-and-shallow version of what she was thinking about, making sure not to name names or suggest any of the theories going around in her head.

"Will you talk to Emma?" Anabel asked afterward.

Prairie really did kind of want to, but she worried. "I wouldn't want to confuse things. I wouldn't want your heart, because it's hurting, to suggest having me do this just so you can maintain some kind of connection to her."

"Yeah, but I wanted you to meet her anyway. And I kind of already told Emma she should meet you. She's interested. Plus, I didn't let on to her, at all, that she had shattered me, so she thinks everything's normal." Anabel flopped onto her back. "And what else is there to do but the same things I was going to do before? I mean, I can't *do* anything about my stupid heart, so I guess I just have to follow whatever my brain says to do for a while, until things get back to normal."

From the mouths of babes. "That seems like a good strategy."

Anabel huffed. "If I could count up the number of times you've said 'That seems like a good strategy' in my whole life, oh my God."

"I should get a mom badge."

"You should *not*. If someone started giving you mom badges, none of us would be able to live with you." Anabel rooted her hand around until it connected with Prairie's.

They were quiet for a moment. Prairie was feeling like she'd done pretty well, even though all she'd managed to do was give her daughter a sounding board. She thought about crushes, first loves, some of her own early stabs at romance, her date with Foster, and then she remembered something, all in a rush, that actually might help.

"You know, I read this thing once about crushes, and I thought it was smart."

"Mm?" Anabel murmured.

"It said that we always talk about having a crush like it's something silly girls do, as if it's shameful. But actually, when we have a crush, what we're doing is identifying in another person something we want for ourselves."

Prairie let herself sink into her pillow, staring at the ceiling. She thought of Lisa Radcliffe grinning on a cruise ship in a selfie with the founder of Kitty Blue. Of Lisa having custom glass shelves put up in her front parlor for a beautiful boutique she was only allowed to open at the margins of her husband's life.

She thought of Megan at her desk, closing her spiral-bound notebook so Prairie wouldn't read thoughts that felt too personal to share and too important to keep to herself. Of Shawna working at the community center, tapping her phone awake to answer questions from customers and post on her social media accounts and *sell* so she could bank money for a secure future.

And she thought of herself sitting at that too-crowded table at Kettle's across from Foster, spinning out a story so big, she hadn't even known it was inside her until she told it.

"It doesn't mean you don't have real feelings," Prairie said. "That's the point—they're *real* feelings. They're big and important. But the reason the crush feelings are so big is because of what they tell you about yourself. A crush is trying to show you what you most want to love about yourself, what you most *want* for yourself. Does that make sense?"

Anabel's hand squeezed hers, but she didn't answer. Prairie shifted, turning to face her daughter, and sensed in the weight of Anabel's body and the evenness of her breath that she'd fallen asleep.

That was okay. If Prairie had learned anything in not-quite-fifteen years of being a mom, it was that she couldn't get hung up on any one moment, any single bit of wisdom. You never knew what you might say to your kid that would be the wisdom to stick.

Sometimes, you were just talking to yourself.

Chapter 12

Prairie woke up to the sound of her phone vibrating. As she came into focus, she found herself on top of the covers, her dress rucked up around her legs.

Friday morning. It was Greg's day, which meant he came over early and got the girls up and ready for school and either took them there or Joyce did. Prairie had been vaguely aware of when Anabel's phone alarm went off and she stumbled from the bed. Zipper wasn't panting in her face, so Joyce must have given him breakfast and taken him for a walk. She liked to give Prairie the opportunity to sleep in on Fridays.

Prairie located her phone, having finally registered that a bunch of notifications in a row could actually be an emergency. She blinked at the screen.

It was not.

She elected to shower, followed by an extended skin care routine and a fresh pair of jeans that were nice and snug from the dryer and fit well, *thank you very much*. Then she was only one enormous cup of coffee away from being restored to full humanity.

"You're up!" Joyce greeted her from the mudroom entrance of the kitchen, unclipping Zipper's lead. "Pour me a cup and I'll sit with you for a second, but then I have to go back into the trenches. I'm hip-deep in a project."

Prairie pulled down a mug from one of the hooks over the coffee nook at the end of the breakfast bar. "You've been on fire since the conference. Maelynn told me how you learned the somebody-and-so-and-so algorithm that uses something-something math to model something I didn't understand whatsoever with DNA. She made it sound exciting."

"Wein and Ertürk. I showed her my conference materials, and she seemed to grasp the math immediately. Did Anabel get you? She was bursting with some kind of plan this morning. I had to tell her three times not to wake you up."

Prairie extended her home screen to Joyce, displaying the crowd of message notifications from her daughter. "I decided on coffee first, then firefighting."

"Wise woman." Joyce stood. "You probably need to focus. Real quick, though, sweetheart. Greg is coming with me today when I meet with my estate planner at twelve thirty. It's supposed to wrap up before he has to go get Anabel from the bus, but this guy always runs over. Would you be able to pick up the girls so Greg doesn't have to leave early?"

"I can do that." After Joyce gave her a squeeze and bustled off, Prairie swiped her calendar open and made a couple of changes. She made a mental note not to forget that she had a meeting with Anabel's online tutor, who liked to do check-ins with Prairie about Anabel's progress in the war against Algebra II.

The house went quiet. She pulled up the text thread with Anabel.

> so i realized emma is on spring break bc she does all her classes this semester at the community college

> they r on break. do you want me to txt her to meet w u. do it

Then:

> she sez she cld. she's doing research at one of those study rooms at the library until lunch. do you know which ones i mean. plz reply

Then:

> y are u still sleeping??? at the regular library not the one near us she's in one upstairs i just gave her your number. don't ignore her txts!!!!!!

Then a string of exploding brain emojis.

Prairie also had a new thread, with a text in green from an unknown number.

> Hi! My name's Emma Cornelius. I know your daughter from school, and she let me know that you may be interested in talking to me about amateur true crime research. She gave me your number and told me you'd be expecting to hear from me. You're welcome to catch me at the library this morning. I'm in the COM-002 study carrel upstairs of the main library branch on Oak.

Prairie read the text three times, agog. It was impossible that Anabel—whom Prairie had thought was growing up too quickly—would manage over the next three years to mature into this level of adult human poise.

Adolescence was miraculous.

Prairie put the phone down, tapping her bottom lip.

A good half-night's sleep had put her evening with Foster in perspective. Her intuition told her that he wasn't planning to ignore what she had told him last night, which meant that regardless of what he'd said at Kettle's, Prairie was in this. His threat of detainment was all theater. Probably. A threat like that was the only tool he had available to keep someone like her from getting hurt, which she could appreciate as a mother. She used threats, too.

Foster would learn soon enough why Chris had shared what he had with the investigation, as well as why he'd *not* shared what

Prairie had discovered about Lisa's business. How Prairie would find out what Foster learned was a question mark, since she didn't know if he would continue to talk to her about the case on the basis of her charm alone.

Which meant, of course, of *course*, that her best tactic now was to continue digging up everything she could that Foster could not.

Sipping her coffee, she thumbed her phone, flipping from text to email to Slack to QuickBooks to her calendar. She had plenty to do. There was a list in her notes app of things Maelynn needed for an online class she was taking for fun, an email from one of Anabel's teachers that Prairie had to address, parent-teacher conferences to sign up for, next week's grocery list to get ordered, and final bits and pieces to track down so her accountant could finish the tax filing.

Just a few days ago, the thought of working through a similar set of notifications had given Prairie a sense of satisfaction. Now, she couldn't muster any enthusiasm, and it occurred to her that she'd stolen the entirety of yesterday and a good chunk of Wednesday not for homemaking, but for Lisa. For being a detective?

Prairie flipped back to Emma's text. It gave her a sluice of tingles from the nape of her neck to the small of her back.

Interesting.

This Emma was young, obviously brilliant, and pissing everyone off with her true crime podcast, which were all excellent recommendations for a potential ally. Anabel had told Prairie the podcast was good, which meant Emma might have sources and methods Prairie could learn from. Maybe Emma Cornelius could open doors in this inquiry that Prairie wouldn't consider opening on her own. It was possible, even, that Emma was already looking at Lisa Radcliffe. Her disappearance was a local mystery, after all.

Prairie had just finished texting Emma and was writing back to Anabel when Joyce stuck her head in again. "Hey, I forgot to ask. How was your date?"

Shifting from thinking about Foster in the context of the case to thinking about him as *her date*, Prairie was briefly overcome by a confusing combination of feelings and images. Embarrassment, strong hands around a teacup, butterflies, a flash of green silk, and gray eyes that could be warm or inscrutable. "Not ready to talk about it."

Joyce's eyebrows shot up to meet the curls at her hairline, and she stepped into the room. "Because it was very bad or very good?"

No one in this house knew what *not ready to talk about it* meant. "A perplexing mosaic of both."

Joyce stepped in farther. "Really?" She tipped her head at Prairie and opened her mouth, then closed it again. *"Really?"*

Prairie put her phone down and turned around on the barstool. "Yes. Really. Make a note in your journal. 'It took quite a few rounds with the electric shock paddles, but Prairie appears to have revived her interest in men.'"

"*One* man, I assume." Joyce's blue eyes had started twinkling at Prairie. "I know you said you weren't ready to talk about it, but if you told me his name, you wouldn't have to, because I would privately look him up and sit with my own thoughts until you mentioned him again."

"Wow." Prairie shook her head. "You're blackmailing me with my own desire to have a private life."

"Was it the man involved with Lisa Radcliffe's investigation who Greg said you were talking to at the vigil?"

Prairie sighed. "It was. He's an FBI agent."

Joyce's sly smile and twinkling eyes went flat. "From here in Green Bay?"

"It's weird, but they actually have an office in town."

Joyce looked out the window. "I know." She looked back at Prairie. "Do you mind telling me—"

"Foster Rosemare." Now Prairie tipped her head at Joyce. "Is there a problem?"

Homemaker

Joyce's expression cleared, and she gave Prairie a small smile. "I haven't met him. Certainly, keep me posted."

With that, she was gone.

Prairie didn't often tell Joyce about her dates because Joyce knew everyone in the entire county. In the surrounding counties, too. Really, she knew everyone in Wisconsin, because her position with the DNR had been governor-appointed and statewide. She likely knew of Foster, even if they hadn't met.

And this was why Prairie Nightingale couldn't even pretend to have a private life.

⁂

Anabel's friend Emma turned out to be easy to identify. She was the only person occupying the library's glassed-in study rooms. Her head, with a long, black french braid bisecting shaved sides, was bent over a laptop. She had notebooks and papers spread around her, a thin leg hooked over the arm of the chair.

Prairie knocked on the door, her heart beating a little fast.

Emma looked up and smiled, waving her in. When Prairie opened the door, she heard a recording of someone talking coming from the laptop. "Hi!" Emma said. "There's another chair in the corner there. Hold on, let me turn this off. I was editing an episode."

Prairie dragged the chair over to the table and sat down.

"It's nice to meet you," Emma told her. "You look like Anabel. I like your name, *Prairie Nightingale*. Anabel told me you chose it."

"Just my last name, when I was thirteen. I grew up in a rural cohousing group outside Portland, Oregon, and I was homeschooled before it was really a thing. My parents named me Prairie, and I had their last name they had chosen together, Lovesummer, with the idea that I should research and pick my own name the year I was thirteen. I landed on Florence Nightingale to research, at first for obvious reasons, and then I learned all of this stuff about her work as the founder of modern statistics, and I fell in love with her refusal to live her life like she was supposed to as the daughter of a wealthy family."

"Huh." Emma tilted her head. "I think I like that, even if there are some appropriations there. Your parents were settlers on Indigenous land, naming themselves and their kids in a way that must have been at least partly inspired by what they thought they knew about our names and traditions."

Prairie nodded. "It's come up. Though not until much later."

"That's the way, right? I'm Oneida. My mom runs the center for Oneida and Menominee families on the west side."

"My friend Megan runs the Success Center and sometimes coordinates events with them. She probably knows your mom."

"Probably. My mom knows everyone." Emma said this with a proud glow.

Prairie smiled inside. It was good to see there was still a bit of girl nestled inside this obviously powerful young woman.

"Anabel tells me you're investigating the Lisa Radcliffe disappearance," Emma said. "Oh, by the way, I feel like I should tell you, Anabel asked me out. I turned her down, but I guess I don't want you to think I was, like, leading her to those conclusions or something. I'm an officer for East's LGBTQIA club, so that's how I met her."

"Oh. Well—"

"To be fair, it was about the nicest offer I've had in a long time. And Anabel's great, but I'm going to graduate in June, and she's got a lot ahead of her, you know, with the rest of high school. Plus, everyone knows it's exploitative and disgusting when senior boys date freshman girls. I don't see how it would be any less problematic for me to do the same thing, even if I wanted to." Emma wrinkled her nose. "Which I don't."

Prairie managed not to betray any surprise at this rather direct and unexpected speech. "Anabel told me you'd said as much. Not the part about it being exploitative and disgusting, but that you were on

Homemaker

different parts of your journey. Thanks, truly, for that. For your kindness and foresight."

"Yeah, of course. I'm pretty interested in what you've gotten into." Emma closed her laptop and crossed the leg that had been on the chair over her other. It was fascinating to watch her morph, minute to minute, from a teenager into someone very grown.

"Can this be confidential?" Prairie asked. "I don't know if you consider yourself a journalist or researcher, but—"

Emma circled her forefinger. "This room is a seal of silence. Lisa Radcliffe's not my usual beat, anyway. Sometimes I make an exception if a case has a strong local angle, and I've been fascinated, of course, but I focus mostly on kids and teenagers."

"It's been suggested," Prairie said, thinking of last night, "that I'm getting into something that's out of my league. And none of my business."

Emma's eyes narrowed. "By the cops."

"Yes. Well, by an FBI agent."

"FBI's still the cops. Cops work for the people. White people, at least. Did you know the police were originally created to deal with property crime, which included enslaved people seeking their freedom? They're still mostly concerned with property. Half the posts on the police department's Facebook page are stills from in-store surveillance cameras of shoplifters."

"I've noticed that."

"Somebody steals a dozen USB memory sticks at Walgreens and it's an emergency, but if a trans woman goes missing after getting drunk at a party on campus, that's a family matter until it's too late. The community gives power to the police, but that power is out of balance, because it isn't being used for justice for everyone. Law enforcement in this town is mostly white men. White men struggle with victimology when the crime doesn't involve people who look just like them."

135

Emma's dark eyes met Prairie's with a challenge. She clearly expected Prairie to object, but Prairie was intrigued by what she was hearing. "I'm listening," she said.

"What I do with my podcast is an attempt to get that power back into balance. The power of the community." Emma made a circle with her hand. "The power of law enforcement." Her second hand made a second circle. "If where they intersect in the middle is big enough, people are actually safe."

Community was something Prairie understood. She had been raised to believe community was the most important value. She hadn't wanted to live like her parents, but she was interested and had always been interested in people.

Pieces were fitting together, stray pieces inside her she'd never had a place for.

"You said the police struggle with victimology if the victim's not white and male," she said. "What's victimology?"

"Victimology tells us that if you learn everything you can about the victim, what you learn about them will lead you to the perpetrator."

Prairie thought about how easily, last night, she'd been able to extrapolate what Chris Radcliffe had likely said to law enforcement based on what she knew, as a woman, about husbands and what husbands bothered to know about their wives. "The perspective that law enforcement has on a victim is limited."

"Yes. They have systemic bias and personal prejudice that makes it harder to identify a suspect. That's why what the community is willing to do for themselves is a necessary piece. The community holds a diversity of experiences and identities that law enforcement can use to mitigate their own systemic bias."

Hoo. Emma Cornelius was not eighteen in the same way Prairie Nightingale had been eighteen, a commune-raised girl with no work experience and no college education who could only get a job securing cars on the car deck for the Washington ferry service and making coffee, and who spent most of her energy trying to have erotic experiences with boys.

Emma pulled out a notebook and clicked open a pen. "Tell me what you've been doing. If you think you can." She raised her eyebrows.

Prairie told her everything.

It was easy.

It was so easy, it made Prairie understand that with Foster, it hadn't been. She had wanted to know what he thought of what she'd found out, but she'd been too anxious—all because she'd failed to perceive Foster's authority and how it was affecting her.

When she reached the part of her story where she'd realized that Chris must have been the one to volunteer information to the police about the gifts Lisa had given her friends, Emma slid her laptop over and opened it. "Can I share with you some stuff that might help?"

"Absolutely."

"Okay, first, it's encouraging that the law enforcement you're talking to is FBI and has higher-level military experience. He's probably had more leeway in his approaches to investigation and been subject to more regulation about how he can treat people. My guess is that's why he's talking to you at all, other than the fact he's into you."

Prairie's heart stopped. "What?"

Emma rolled her eyes. "Cute." She turned her laptop around to show Prairie a web page. "I like this forum. There are a ton of them for true crime. This one has an active thread on Lisa. One thing you'll start to notice is the law enforcement who are on here, talking to civilians, are mostly retired guys who work cold cases, federal types, and former military police." Emma moved her finger around on the trackpad and clicked a forum link. "Here, this guy is saying he heard they'll be releasing CCTV photos today of Lisa. There's enough agreement that I bet they do. It would be right on time. Because"—Emma scrolled up in the forum posts—"they've had dive teams out a couple of times, the crime scene unit and dogs have searched near where they found her van, then the bigger grid search around the jetty and some other locations outside that area. A trailhead. The place where the Radcliffes are building their house."

Prairie made a note with her phone.

"The new build site is on Oneida land," Emma said. "My mom heard from an Oneida cop about the search they did out there. If they've found anything, they're holding it back so they can use it to confirm the validity of tips or confessions. They're going to have to reach out to the community for more. I bet what you gave that agent will heat something up."

"Yeah?"

"Not that you blew the case open, but it's always gratifying to do something good enough that the authorities start telling you to stop doing it."

That surprised a laugh out of Prairie. Emma smiled at her and kept scrolling down the list of forum posts. "It's really starting to bother them that they don't have a body. If somebody grabbed her, a stalker or a random bad guy, and killed her, then how do they explain where the van is, as a dump site, and why haven't they found her? Every day that goes by they can't find any trace of her makes it more likely they're never going to."

"Do you think it's possible someone could have been stalking Lisa, watched her leave her house, and abducted her?" Prairie thought about how desperate the upper echelons of Kitty Blue might be, given Lisa's emails to her downline.

"Did any of Lisa's friends bring it up? It's usually something women mention to other women. Sometimes there's even a common stalker in a community. Like, a guy who's harassing different people on the same loop."

Prairie shook her head, but she filed the idea away. She spotted a familiar name on the monitor and pressed her finger against the screen to stop Emma's scrolling. "That. What's that say?"

Homemaker

Emma leaned in and read the post. "That's somebody saying maybe Chris Radcliffe is going to turn out to be another Nathan Carmichael. 'They never look at the rich guys until the bodies start piling up.'"

"Carmichael," Prairie whispered.

Emma leaned back in her chair. "Anabel told me you figured that out. I never saw your name, though."

"No. I started looking at his money and doing background research because of something completely different that came up with the PTO. I ended up talking to one of his victims. Once she told her story, a lot of other women did."

"So you're doing this already. Give yourself credit."

"You're right. I should."

"But bear in mind that the crime scene techs, the investigative team, the computer guys, and the tip hotline folks all get credit, too. They are going to run everything down. The wacky stuff. The theories. Everything. That's why you don't go trying to spitball uneducated ideas like why haven't they had a forensic botanist look at the weeds stuck to a car. Take them something they can use that is within your actual skills to find out. Believe in the skills you have, like what you can get women to tell you. When they run it down, they're going to be one step closer to solving their case."

"Well, Emma Cornelius. Your mom did a good job."

"That's what I keep trying to tell her."

Emma's phone chimed. She picked it up and grinned. "Look at that, right on cue." She swiped and turned the screen toward Prairie.

It was a *Gazette* story with three pictures, all stills from CCTV. Emma turned it around again and scrolled. "They're from a camera that captured Lisa's van, with Lisa in it. The camera took motion-activated video of her inside the van, parked in a turnaround for a jogging trail in her neighborhood. The first capture is from nine fifty-five Monday night. The second is from nine minutes after ten, and the third is from eleven seventeen. The first two show her texting on her phone, and the last one is her pulling her car out, getting ready to leave. They say that's the last known visual of Lisa and the last time she communicated using her phone."

139

"Who was she texting?"

"It says her husband."

"Can I see it again?"

Emma passed her phone over. Prairie tapped on the photos, one by one, until they filled the screen. They were poor quality. Lisa must have turned her headlights off, because the only light source in the pictures was her phone, which lit up the bottom half of her face.

You couldn't see her hair well or what she was wearing. The grainy shadows surrounded her, and like Joyce had said, the camera captured the light. But you could see her small, pointed chin and jawline, her mouth set with concentration, her fingers wrapped around the back of her phone case as her thumbs typed.

Prairie looked again, flipping back and forth between the three pictures, pinching and stretching them bigger, trying to see the thing her brain kept telling her was there that she wasn't noticing.

Then she saw it. *Motherlover.*

"I have something, a not-spitball something, to take to the police."

Emma reached out and took her phone back. "Go."

Prairie got up and put her bag over her shoulder. "Thank you so much. This has been incredibly helpful—you have no idea."

"Good. Keep me posted, and say hi to Anabel."

Prairie waved over her shoulder, got to the main floor of the library, and sat down in the first empty chair in the reading section. She opened her phone, took a very deep breath, and sent her first ever text to Foster Rosemare, right under the one he'd sent her last night while she was driving to Kettle's to tell her he was there.

Probably also to give her his number.

First of all, I'm sorry about last night. Not for anything I did or said, but for not clarifying with you some boundaries about whether it was a date or about Lisa. Obviously, that didn't go well.

Foster texted back instantly.

I did no better.

Prairie waited for something else, for three dots to come up indicating he was composing, but there was nothing. Hm.

That's true, you didn't. Still, you'd think I hadn't had an interesting date since I got divorced.

(I haven't had an interesting date since I got divorced)

She bit her lip, because that was risky, right there, glowing back at her. She could see why Anabel and Kai had to get together to text people as a committee. This was hard.

Now the dots went up, and the dots went down.

Prairie smiled. She had won. Not that there was winning, but she *was* making him draft and edit.

I give.

She full-on grinned.

It's not a competition. Meet me at Dee's Diner at five. It's about the pictures that just released, so it's a Lisa conversation. But also I will share a meal with you. If there aren't enough boundaries with this request, you'll have to tell me.

Foster texted back with no hesitation.

Why not now?

She stood up, her body possibly responding to his text. She stopped at the circulation desk to unload the books Maelynn needed to return that she'd grabbed before she left home.

Very busy.

Got some homemaking to do first.

Chapter 13

Parking for pickup at Maelynn's school was an actual circus, complete with tigers, dancing elephants, and clowns. Prairie despised everything about the winner-takes-all jockeying for a spot. Eight hundred kids, most of whom weren't eligible to take a bus because the school served the whole city and had limited transportation routes, meant there were maybe three hundred parents trying to find somewhere to stick their car.

"There's one," Anabel said.

"I won't fit in there."

"You would, you just have to parallel park."

"Which I'm completely capable of doing."

"Right, you just never do it by *choice*." Anabel got out her AirPods. "When it's time for me to learn to drive next year, I'm going to have to do parking with Dad."

"Oh my God. Next year? Really? Are you sure you don't want to do your part for climate change and just not?"

Anabel made a face at her that translated to *cringe*. Good to know that their deep bonding from last night had expired. Prairie found a spot much farther away than she'd hoped and yanked the wheel to the right. The bell had already sounded. "Come on, we have to hustle."

"I'm going to stay in the car."

"Fine." No longer felt the love with her mother but was still scared of facing her wronged sister. Got it.

By the time Prairie reached the schoolyard, nine grades' worth of children had been released onto the blacktop, and she had to fight her way against the stream of bodies toward the place where Maelynn's class came outside. She'd just about punched through the thickest part of the mass, her messenger bag bumping into backpacks and cardboard trifold displays at every turn, when someone grabbed her elbow. Prairie turned, expecting to see a kid who had misidentified their mom.

It was Amber. She looked five years older and about twenty cranks more irritated than the last time Prairie had seen her in this same schoolyard three days ago. "Can I talk to you for a minute?"

Prairie craned her head toward where Maelynn was supposed to be. No sign. Her daughter extracted herself from school at turtle speed. "Yes."

"Over by the old playground entrance."

Oh no. That was where the moms took their kids when they needed to yell at them at pickup, even before they got them in the car.

Amber didn't drag Prairie to the naughty corner by the elbow, but psychically she might as well have. Prairie kept looking at the spot where the building would disgorge Maelynn, hoping for rescue. No Maelynn.

They reached the corner. Prairie noticed Amber was no longer carrying the fancy purse.

Amber saw her noticing. "What the fuck is wrong with you, Prairie?" She didn't yell, but her half-voiced whisper was much worse. There was no possible response to that opening, so Prairie just tried to keep the top of her head from floating away in panic.

"My friend, my fucking *best* friend, is missing. Gone. This has to be, full stop, the scariest thing that has ever happened to me. And I have been barely, barely"—Amber held up a shaking hand and pinched a small measurement into the air—"holding it together. The only thing that has been keeping me even a little bit okay is that I can be there for her kids. I can be someone familiar who's not quite as fucking shattered as Lisa's mom and sister, to give them some sense of normalcy and love. That is"—Amber took a deep breath, and tears started running down her face, but the anger didn't leave it—"*that is*, until this morning, when the cops came to my house and, in front of my kids, asked me and Noah to go with them so they could ask us some questions. And at first, I'm thinking it's regular. I had already talked to them in Lisa's living room, telling them everything I fucking could to help them find her, but then, *then*, they wouldn't let us leave together, in our own car, or make an appointment. They take Noah in their fucking police car, Prairie, right in front of the kids, and my little one is screaming and crying, but the cops insist they have to follow me in my car and won't even let me call my mom to be with the kids. One of them stays with my *kids*, Prairie! They separated me from my children."

Prairie felt tears burning in the corners of her eyes. "Amber, I—"

"No. Don't you fucking dare. I'm talking. You can keep your mouth shut for *once*. Can you do that? Do you even know how?"

Prairie put her arms to her sides. She had been protectively crossing them over her middle. She tried to keep her heart and her brain right here with Amber, because there was no point and no use in running away from this. *Amber's babies.*

"I was at the station all morning, out of my mind with worry, with no idea why they brought us in. I'm so confused by everything they're saying, trying to understand and answer their questions, until they want to talk about my purse, and I figure it out. The purse." Amber's voice broke. She took another breath and looked to the side. Prairie stood very still. "She's my best friend, Prairie. She's been there for me when—" Amber looked away again and shook her head. "And there you are, coming up on me to ask me questions about my *purse* on the day after I found out Lisa was *missing*. There you are, always getting into everybody's business, zeroing in on other people's problems. You know the cops talked to me about my taillight? About my son's fucking shoes being too small? Can you even understand what it's like to sit there and realize someone was looking at you like that, then running out and telling the cops about it?" Amber fisted her hands. "Your fucking Facebook invite, Prairie! When's the last time you talked to Lisa? What *was* that? You must have known that the police had already encouraged the family, *the family*, to have a vigil. But no. You have to do everything, fucking everything, your own way."

"Mom?" Maelynn's voice was behind her. Prairie turned around. Hardly anyone was in the schoolyard, and the parents who remained were hustling out their kids, trying not to look in Prairie's direction.

"Yeah, honey. I'm sorry. Mrs. Jenkins was just talking to me." But Prairie could tell Maelynn had heard at least some of it.

Amber swiped at her face and stepped close to Prairie. "Stay the fuck away from my family," she whispered.

She walked out of the yard in big strides, and Prairie realized she didn't have her kids with her.

Amber had come here for *her*.

She didn't even try to fight the self-doubt that rose up and started choking her. She deserved it. If she felt it, maybe she would learn from it.

"Come on, sweetheart. Let's get to the car."

Maelynn reached for Prairie's hand. She hadn't done that since the third grade.

Prairie drove home. Both girls were quiet. Anabel didn't ask what had kept them so long, because Prairie was pretty sure she'd had an angle on the schoolyard that would have given her a full view of the unfolding drama.

When she bumped over the curb into her driveway, she spotted Greg's car parked on the street, where it was supposed to be. The girls filed inside. Prairie took her time unloading her things in order to let them greet their dad and get settled into their homework.

It wasn't her night.

She wished it were. She wished she could escape her own thoughts and self-recrimination and occupy herself with motherhood.

She stood by the door, looking out at the street. Friday was garbage day. Greg must have put the bin out for her this morning. The truck

Homemaker

would have come and gone by now. She walked slowly to the curb and rolled the empty bin back to its spot beside the garage.

Greg opened the door. "Can I talk to you for a sec?"

"I don't think so."

He closed the door behind him and leaned against the house. "I got the weirdest phone call from Noah Jenkins."

Prairie closed her eyes. She stepped back and leaned against her car. Greg joined her. He put his hands in his jeans pockets. He was wearing one of his dress sweaters, probably because Joyce believed in dressing up to talk to financial people, and the sweater was his concession.

"Want to fill me in?" he asked.

She did not.

"Because it was pretty weird. I barely know this guy, and then he's yelling at me."

"I'm sorry."

"Did you snitch on him to the cops? Also, why? Or, more what I'm getting at, when did you manage to gather any information *to* snitch to the cops?"

"I've been really busy the last few days."

"I guess."

It was actually a nice afternoon. The galvanized tin planters Adam had put in on either side of the door were full of daffodils. Prairie remembered the therapist she'd gone to after her mini breakdown telling her that when she felt overwhelmed, she should identify two things she could see, two things she could hear, two things she could touch, and two things she could smell.

Yellow daffodils. Tin planters.

A cardinal. The sound of Maelynn playing with Zipper.

Her warm car behind her back. The strap on her bag digging into her shoulder.

Dinner for the girls and Greg, something with garlic. Greg's fabric softener.

She breathed in through her nose, felt her belly rise and fall, but didn't really feel like she'd taken in any air. "I've been talking to people about Lisa's disappearance," she said. "Mostly moms, people who knew Lisa. Asking questions."

He didn't say anything. He had learned some strategies from therapy, too.

"Kind of a lot of people. And to the FBI agent. Yesterday, I told him something I shouldn't have because I wanted him to take me seriously about other things I had found out. It was a mistake."

Greg was silent for a moment. He adjusted his position against the car and blew out a breath. "Only you know if you actually told this guy something you shouldn't have, something I'm assuming has burned Noah Jenkins's whiskers. But I listened to that guy for a while, and if he's not involved in what's happened to Lisa, he's sure as hell involved in *something*. I haven't been on the receiving end of that kind of puffed-up male violence since I reported that bug in the surgical robotics software code years ago and—you remember?—that investment guy found me in the parking garage of the MivvenTech Works campus."

"I remember."

"That guy ended up going down, if you remember that, too."

"That was scary. Like, *really* scary."

"I didn't know what to tell him. Noah. He wanted me to get you under control. He wanted me to make you stop inserting yourself in other people's business. He wanted me—and he didn't say it this nicely—to take you in hand. And Prairie, I honestly didn't know what to say, so I told him the only thing that was true." Greg turned his shoulder into the car and looked at her. The furrow between his eyebrows, which sank a little deeper every year, was as deep as she'd ever seen it. "I told him, 'She's not my wife.'"

Prairie looked at the daffodils. Swallowed past the knife in her throat.

Greg sighed. "I'm pretty sure one of those divorce books we read made it clear that I don't get to tell you I'm worried about you. And it's not like at any point even when we were married I could've told you what to do and you'd have listened." He shrugged. "Just to be clear, I don't have a problem with that. But I *am* worried about you."

Yellow daffodils. Galvanized tin. Cardinal.

Maelynn and Zipper. Garlic. Greg's fabric softener.

"Noah's wife cornered me at pickup," she said. "The cops talked to her, too. Maelynn heard some of it."

Greg's hands were fisted in his jeans pockets, but when he spoke, he sounded more baffled than angry. "What are you doing, Prayer?"

She thought of Emma at the library. All the smart things Emma had said about community and justice, and how Anabel had told Prairie that the school wanted Emma to stop making her podcast, but only because the administration thought it was disruptive. Not because Emma was doing anything wrong.

And Prairie was twice as old as Emma, learning the hard way how people felt about disruptive women.

"I found something," she said. "The police don't know about it yet. I'm supposed to talk to the FBI agent tonight."

"Is it going to put you in danger?"

She shook her head, but she didn't know.

Prairie genuinely didn't know.

"Greg?"

"Yeah."

She couldn't stand to see him look so concerned and worried. Like he wasn't sure about her judgment. She had to admit to herself that she had gotten used to Greg acting interested and delighted with her all the time. She expected him to be, even though he was right.

She wasn't his wife.

"I wish I wouldn't have stopped talking to Lisa, or I guess that she hadn't stopped talking to me. I liked her. I lost that friendship and a lot of others the last time I figured out something was really wrong. And then things weren't great with us. It would've been nice to have more people when I was going through all that. But I couldn't choose, could

I? I couldn't choose to ignore what I'd found out about Dr. Carmichael. I couldn't control what other people thought about me when I was getting a divorce. But right this minute, I feel like all of it, *all of it*, is my fault."

She turned and put her shoulder against the car to face Greg.

"I don't think I'm going to get to be friends with Lisa again. I'm pretty sure she's dead. And Greg." Prairie looked at him, but he was staring at the house, his jaw tight. "She's a mom. She has three kids. We *know* them."

"I'm having a hard time understanding why you are in the middle of this one, Prairie. To be clear, I do understand—I understood back then—why you got involved with the business with Carmichael. But when it comes to the Radcliffes, why does it have to be you?"

"Because if it *were* me? What if it were me instead of Lisa?"

The furrow between his eyebrows deepened, but he still wouldn't look at her.

"I wouldn't want anyone to stop looking for me," she said. "Not until they found out what happened, so they could make the best decisions possible for my girls and could give them everything they needed to cope. I wouldn't want my girls to grow up with the despair of never knowing what happened to their mama. And I don't think that if it was left up to the cops, they would understand enough about my life to find out what had happened to me."

Greg huffed out a half laugh. "Well, that's true."

Prairie touched his side. Finally, he met her eyes.

"If I can help, Greg. And I think I *can* help," she said. "I have to."

Chapter 14

Prairie made it to Dee's Diner first. She got a table by the window, assuming this was a federal agent thing that Foster would appreciate. She had originally picked Dee's because the fern-heavy, mauve-and-golden-oak family restaurant was close to her house and wouldn't be busy as early as this on a Friday, but now she was grateful for its uncoolness in her social set.

I have never been here and run into someone I know, have interrogated, or have taken into custody.

Or hurt, or made so angry she'd yell at her in front of kids.

Prairie didn't think she was hungry, but when the server came, her hindbrain ordered a mushroom Swiss burger, double waffle fries, a chocolate malt, and a starter of cheese curds with ranch dressing.

Foster walked in when she was dipping the last of the cheese curds into her malt two at a time. He carried a sleek leather document bag and had a gray suit jacket draped over his arm. His white oxford was still crisp this late in the day, though his tie was missing. He also wore a gun in a sidearm holster.

Because he was a federal agent, whose job was dangerous.

The closest Prairie had ever been to a gun was probably right this minute.

He slid in across from her and turned up a mug. The server came right over with a carafe of hot water. There were already tea bags in a caddy on the table. "Pecan pie?" she asked. "On the house, if you want it."

"That would be outstanding."

She bustled off, leaving Prairie to deal with Foster's intense gaze.

"You've got something you wanted to tell me." He adjusted a thin leather strap on his holster. Prairie wondered if that was intentional or habit. Either way, it was an effective reminder. So was the free pie.

Power.

She pictured Emma making two circles with her hand. Foster's gifts. Prairie's own. The intersection of the two.

Then she pictured Amber Jenkins getting into her car, driving to the police station behind the cruiser with her husband in the back.

"I do have something for you," Prairie said. "It's not a story this time. It's closer to a fact, although you're going to have to be the one to figure out if it's verifiable." She opened the flap of her messenger bag and found the stack of clipped-together printouts she'd made before she picked up the girls from school. She placed it on the table in front of Foster.

The server delivered his pie. Foster picked up his fork and took a bite, looking at the top page, where Prairie had printed out the best of the three CCTV photos.

"I'm not you, or trying to be you, but I know women," Prairie said. "I know my friends. I pick up on their habits, and I've never been able to help observing people closely. When I look at these pictures, all I can see is what's not there that should be."

Foster bent over the photo. When his eyes returned to her, he folded his arms on the table in a way that made Prairie see that before he'd been holding himself stiff, making sure she noticed his gun and his suit more than him.

"Tell me what you see."

"She's not wearing her ring." Prairie pointed to Lisa's left ring finger, clearly visible in the photo. "And I know some married people don't always wear their ring, but most married women I know wear at least

Homemaker

their band all the time. My handywoman, Barb, even has a silicone ring that she wears in place of her wedding set so she has something on that finger when she's working jobs where it's not safe to wear metal."

Foster picked up his fork and ate another bite of his pie. "I'm listening."

"What I know about Lisa in particular is two things. One, her ring had diamonds the size of garbanzo beans. It was a ring that on a sunny day would blind drivers as she turned her steering wheel and merged into traffic. If she's wearing it, no camera will fail to see it. Two, I never saw her without it. Ever. She had a ring holder at every sink in her house to hold it when she washed her hands, and she always put it right back on after. If she does take it off to sleep so she doesn't slice open her own face in the night, I'll bet she has another ring holder on her nightstand."

Foster's gaze had gone somewhere in the space between them. Thinking. When he looked back at her, his gray eyes were serious but warm. "What do you make of it."

It was the first time he'd asked her opinion as he might ask a colleague. An equal. Prairie took a breath. "My first thought is, check the ring stands, obviously. If she left it at home, that's that. But I don't think she would. Then I wonder, why is Lisa parked at a trailhead for an hour on her phone, after dinner on a school night, less than a mile from her house, texting her husband? The only reason I can think of that I would pull over to text my ex back when we were married is either he's asking me to pick up something quick at the store—in which case reading and answering his text takes two minutes, not seventy-plus—or because we had a big fight, and I got mad enough to leave the house. Maybe I got so mad, I took off my wedding ring and flung it at him. That is something I have done. Once. But either way I'm furious, so I get in the car and drive a little ways until either a text comes through from him or I start feeling a way that means I want to send him one. I pull in at a trailhead I know and sit there for an hour, yelling at him. Or apologizing. Or accepting his apologies."

Foster imperceptibly, hardly at all, shook his head.

For a moment, Prairie could not believe it had happened.

But it had. For sure. And Foster would not have almost-not-at-all shaken his head unless he wanted her to know that Lisa and Chris weren't fighting.

Okay. She flipped over to another page of her printouts. "The night she went missing, probably while she was sitting at that trailhead, Lisa put a 'like' on thirteen different Instagram posts that I could find, made by either women selling Kitty Blue or by friends. She commented on at least eight Instagram and Facebook posts, which, this one, minimally"—she turned the page and showed Foster a screenshot of a Facebook post—"*must* have happened during the window Lisa was at the trailhead. The post, her comment, and the two replies. All before eleven o'clock."

Foster maintained eye contact and waited for her to continue speaking.

Congenial eye contact from a grown man during an important conversation hadn't previously been on Prairie's Things That Make Me Horny bingo card, but she was going to have to add it. In her defense, she'd been on a great many Thursday night app dates, and she'd complained innumerable times to Megan in the aftermath that the single men of Northeastern Wisconsin—and the men who pretended to be single but decidedly weren't—did not know how to have a conversation in even the most basal definition of the term.

Eye contact, ironed oxford shirts, and a multisyllabic vocabulary were all it took for this man to clear a bar that Prairie had to admit she'd set much too low. To save herself, she needed to hoist that bar up ASAP, before she found herself caressing this man's leg under the table with her bright-pink errands-Hokas.

"Now I will be the first person to say that I don't know what any of this means," she said, "and your people probably have found even more. I *can* say that I wouldn't rule out that she simply wanted to leave the house and have some time to herself, and this was how she did that. But if I could talk to her or someone who knew her well, I'd want to know if this was something she did a lot. If the camera had seen her there before. What her social media habits were. And where, exactly, her ring went."

Foster put his arm along the back of the booth, momentarily short-circuiting her brain with an inexplicable and embarrassingly heterosexual vision of his strong wrist in french cuffs and the angle of his thumb. His *thumb*, for fuck's sake. He regarded Prairie for a moment. "Maybe she threw it out the van window."

"Why would she do that?" The server appeared with Prairie's mushroom Swiss burger and double order of waffle fries. Prairie had forgotten about them. She started mixing ketchup with mayonnaise for the fries, studying Foster closely. "Wait, you're saying she threw *something* out the window." Prairie flipped back to the photo. "This trailhead is the last place you have her using her phone."

Foster stole one of her fries.

"You're telling me she threw her *phone* out the window," Prairie said. "After this. It wasn't in the van, right?"

An imperceptible shake of his head.

"It wasn't in the van because she threw it out the window. These were her last known communications before she threw her phone out the window. You found it."

He reached for another fry.

"That doesn't make any sense. She has her phone right here but not her ring. That would mean that between her house and this trailhead she threw away her ring. Then between this trailhead and the jetty she tossed her phone. Like breadcrumbs?"

Another bare ghost of a shrug.

"Because, what, a bad guy is somewhere in the back of her van, a bad guy that managed his way into her van in the mile between her house and this trailhead, took her ring or she threw it away as a clue, and then what? Told her to park and act like everything was fine, text her husband, cruise social media, then trashed her phone, then did a horrible crime somewhere between the trailhead and the jetty?"

Prairie and Foster reached for the same waffle fry, the biggest one that was crisp and unbroken. She lifted an eyebrow midsnatch, and he took it from right under her fingers and dipped it in what was left of her malt.

She pretended she didn't watch him eat a fry covered in the dregs of her malt, but there was a part of her that had taken him in and was curled up around him with ridiculous heart eyes.

Prairie cleared her throat. "*Or* she had a fight with Chris and threw it at him before she left the house, but then calmed down inside of a mile and texted him ordinary texts and decided to check in with her Kitty Blue friends. *Or* she left it at home in one of her regular places because it was late when she left. *Or* she left it as one final gift to her children before she decided to end her life."

All these questions and suppositions, yet Foster hadn't stopped her or thrown up an inscrutable face. Prairie picked up her burger and took a huge bite, thinking.

"What matters is where that ring is right now and what Chris has to say about it, which is either, 'Oh my goodness, I can't believe I didn't notice my wife wasn't wearing her humongous trophy ring in that picture'—and mind you, after noticing precious little for years, my ex noticed the exact day, hour, and minute I took off my set after I asked for a divorce—and so Chris produces it, safe and sound. Or else he can't produce it, and didn't mention it, and you're dealing with his lies about what happened between them that night, or with a bad guy you don't know about."

"Or she tossed her ring between the house and the trailhead."

"Then you find it. It shouldn't be that hard. It won't look like the other rocks on the ground—it'll be bigger. Find it, and then you know it's bad guys, or else uncharacteristic behavior for a woman who was going out of her way to make sure the people she cared about had something of hers before she left."

"Those are a lot of different stories," Foster said. "Split your burger with me."

Homemaker

She cut it in half, took his little plate that held his tea bag, wiped it off and placed the burger on it, and put it in front of him.

"You do that just like my sister-in-law," he said.

"We learn how in mom school. At the mom parties, we learn things we can't tell anyone about."

Foster gave her one of his fractional smiles.

"It *is* a lot of stories," Prairie said, not looking at him, though she could feel her dimples sinking in, "but I think the missing ring merits them. There are two other things I can't stop thinking about."

"Which are. Oh, Jesus, mushrooms." He peeled open the burger and shoved them off with his pie fork.

She laughed and scooped his mushrooms onto her burger, which was easy to do because they were leaning toward each other, close enough that she noted where his eyelashes were thicker at the corners of his eyes. "First, we're back to Kitty Blue. I would have to assume you know all about it, even if that's not because of Lisa's case. Multistate fraud is your department, right?"

Foster wasn't smiling, but his pretty eyes were. "So is collaborating with law enforcement on potential capital crimes."

Prairie wasn't going to get near that one, at least not now. "I still care about Kitty Blue, because a lot of women in her life do. Also, where was Chris, like, this whole time? I mean, I know there's still no person of interest. I assume that means he was where he was supposed to be."

Foster dumped the rest of her malt in his teacup. "You're asking what makes a good alibi. Even an airtight one. Hypothetically."

Hypothetically. It was a window of opportunity, deliberately left open.

"I am," she said slowly. "Hypothetically. *Hypothetically*, if Chris has an airtight alibi, what does that look like?"

"Hypothetically, I can tell you the general features of an airtight alibi, though to be pedantic, if it's an alibi, it's already airtight. Everything else is just a story."

157

Prairie pointed her burger half at him. "Touché." She tried to say it how he had on their date, with the good French accent. He was not unaffected, judging by the way he looked at her mouth when she said it.

"Green Bay's not the biggest city, but it's big enough for the police to have digital forensics," Foster said. "Their job is to look at computers, personal devices, anything with a chip, and find evidence or coordinate information on those devices with information that is either volunteered or subpoenaed. Or compelled."

"Our phones know where we are all the time."

"Our phones know where *they* are. It takes more than the location of your phone to show that you were somewhere. Location gives us a start, though."

"Hypothetically, you're saying, Chris's phone spent the whole time that night at home, where it was supposed to be."

"Bringing Christopher Radcliffe into this does not make it hypothetical."

"Right. What's the other part of an alibi, if the tech is one part?"

"People. Or their proxies. And by 'proxies,' I mean cameras, receipts, mileage. That kind of thing." He half smiled at her. "Our breadcrumbs, falling behind us wherever we go."

"All right." Prairie put down her burger, wiped her fingers with her napkin, and leaned forward. "Let me give you a hypothetical."

"Permission granted."

"I'm picked up for a murder that happened sometime today. Then I tell you, today, I woke up, talked to my mother-in-law, texted my daughter and her friend, still from home, then went to the library, talked to someone, texted an FBI agent, picked up dog food and special weight-reduction cat food at Royal Pets, taking a moment to stalk a certain someone's social media, went home, talked to Beth, who makes our dinners and ordered groceries, did a couple hours in my office on my computer, mostly on taxes, and then drove to the bus stop, picked up my daughter, drove to my other daughter's school, and picked her up after getting yelled at by another mother. So. My breadcrumbs?"

Homemaker

Foster leaned back. "I seize your phone, your daughters' phones, and your computer. I subpoena the phone and internet company. I subpoena the library, Royal Pets, traffic and store cams on the route you give me, and the school for their CCTV footage. I ask you for the Royal Pets receipt. I interview your mother-in-law, anyone who saw you at the library, whoever you talked to there, anyone who saw you at Royal Pets, everyone at the bus stop, the bus driver, everyone at school pickup with a special interview for the mom who yelled at you, and then I check to see if your cat is actually fat. But I probably did that when I took all your stuff from your house."

Prairie laughed. "She is. She got fat during the divorce."

Foster laughed, too, and just like that, they were back in the place that had led Prairie to deliberately matching with him on the apps. "And I'm pretty happy," he said, "because I have tech, cameras, receipts, and both people who know you and strangers without a horse in the race who should've seen you. Which means after all that I can make a timeline. A series of facts, roughly in order, verifiable, that will tell me if at any point in your day you could have had enough time and enough privacy to do a murder." Foster finished his burger in one bite. "Also, I seriously can't believe you got all that done today."

"Homemaker. I left some things out, even."

"Impressive."

Prairie let what she'd learned from Foster marinate. The breeze from the open window of opportunity was not a thing to be wasted.

"The mom who yelled at you," he said after they'd sat in comfortable silence awhile.

"Amber Jenkins."

He didn't betray any surprise. "There wasn't any way to talk to her without her figuring it out."

"You guys came down on her pretty hard. You scared her kids. You scared the *shit* out of her. Her husband, too. He called my ex, Greg, and told him to force me into line."

"You and Greg can file a report."

"No."

"Why."

"She's a good person. I didn't think through what I was doing when I told you about her because I was trying to impress you with what a good detective I was. It's my fault."

"Maybe. But you saw something you thought might turn out to be important, and you reported it. It's always going to have consequences." He dragged a fragment of waffle fry through the wasteland of salt left at the bottom of the basket. Prairie could not recall where the rest of the fries had gone. "Like I said, there's a reason I like Kettle's."

Prairie wasn't sure what he meant until she remembered his explanation for why he wanted to meet with her at Kettle's. *I have never been here and run into someone I know, have interrogated, or have taken into custody.*

Investigation was the kind of work that made enemies. That was Foster's point.

He lifted the salty bit of waffle fry. "Could be something there with her husband."

Then Foster's hand stopped midway to delivering the fry to his mouth. He hadn't meant to say that out loud about Amber's husband.

"Noah."

No comment. But his eyes said yes.

"Even if that's true, even if all the breadcrumbs add up to that, I still feel awful for Amber. It didn't take much, looking around and talking to people, to figure out things aren't good with her, and it's probably her husband's fault. And obviously if he has no problem calling up my ex-husband on the phone and freaking him out, he probably has no problem calling Chris on the phone over money, or even Lisa." She glanced at Foster. "Maybe he's your bad guy. But that doesn't mean I'm not accountable."

"Well, no, it doesn't. I told you, this shit ruins lives. But if the breadcrumbs add up to someone who's angry," Foster said, "who's bad with money and keeps throwing his weight at people to intimidate them, and who is involved with Kitty Blue, understand that will be because you saw something and brought it to us. Something we didn't see, at least not at first. Not in these moments when the clock is ticking."

The clock. Prairie flipped through her papers to the timeline she'd put together. It was sparse. The police had released so little information. She turned it toward Foster. "Say you bring someone in for murder. He tells you, 'I didn't do it.' Earlier that day, he was at a conference. Seen by people he knew and people he didn't know. Tech. Cameras."

"We do like cameras, but we don't always have them. People known to the guy and not known are often just as good."

"No cameras?"

Nothing. He couldn't let her see if that was true or not true.

"Tech, anyway, and people. You're satisfied he was there. He tells you he left from his conference around, I don't know, the latest would be about two o'clock, two thirty, to pick up his kids."

"Some people would stop home first."

"Even if he did, Lisa's on a trail cam, alive, all the way to after eleven."

Prairie realized that somewhere in their conversation, some implication had snuck its way in between them that Lisa wasn't with them anymore. It unsettled her stomach.

"Then there's all the people and cameras at pickup. Plus Alison saw him there with the kids. She told me. From there, the kids are with their parents. *Three* kids. I have two, and they're on me all the time and everywhere."

"Unless you're not feeling well."

Prairie felt her nape prickle. "No. If I'm not feeling well, they need me for things they haven't needed me for in years. Or ever. I've tried telling Greg, or Joyce—that's my ex-mother-in-law who lives with me—or the sitter that I have to sit dinner out because I feel bad or I want to try to get something done. But nothing makes a kid more antsy to lay eyes on their mom than being told, 'Leave Mom alone.'"

Foster didn't say anything, but his silence felt like encouragement.

"There's tech and kids that put Chris at home, I assume all night until he calls you guys. There's a camera that puts Lisa at a trailhead until eleven and another cam"—she glanced at him—"that puts her at the jetty sometime in the early morning."

"Not that we've released."

"But if your ex-mother-in-law used to work for the DNR, sometimes you have a pretty good idea about where the cameras are and what they're pointed at." Prairie fished Joyce's map out of her messenger bag and laid it on the table.

"Jesus." Foster moved the dishes out of the way and leaned forward, smoothing out the map.

"It sounds like an airtight alibi. Or, as you said, a regular alibi, airtight by definition. I have a question, though."

"Shoot."

"Couldn't someone give you a story that they knew could be alibied, but there's another story that goes with the same set of verifiable facts but has the big, private, time-filled holes in it?"

"Sure, on TV. In books. But one of my general operating principles is that criminals are stupid. They always make mistakes."

"Right." Prairie pulled out the first paper she'd shown him. Pointed to Lisa's bare ring finger.

"Well." Foster sat up and stretched dramatically, his arms over his head like a frat guy. It didn't look like something he had ever done before in his life. She went still and breathless when she observed, through the fine fabric of his white shirt, the unmistakable outline of, well, *fitness*. "I'm going to go take a look at the pie case." He removed a manila file folder from his leather bag. "I'll keep these." He picked up her papers and put them in the back of the folder. Then he flipped through the pages that had already been in the folder. Selected out a few and put them on the top of the stack. Finally, he closed the folder and set the whole thing down on the table. "I'll be a bit. I think I saw they had French silk, but I need to double-check."

Homemaker

Foster disappeared behind an oak half wall topped with artificial ferns. The man who had already eaten a piece of pie, and had now left sensitive information on the table in front of her so he could go look at more pie.

Prairie stared at the folder like it was snarling.

It was just a folder. Card stock. Paper inside. She put one finger on it.

It didn't bite her, or alarm. She looked over to the half wall. How long did it take to look at a bunch of pies? One minute, maybe. If he asked for a piece, would he stand there and wait for it to be plated or order it and walk back over and catch her poking his folder?

She pulled the folder closer to her, then spun it around to face her and lifted the cover two inches. It was photocopies. Photocopies were not dangerous. She craned her head to look under the folder cover.

The photocopy on top was of a page from a Delwin and Corey day planner. Prairie used to buy them before she started putting everything into apps. They had a border of primroses around each page, which showed one day at a time, with a space to write for every hour of the day.

She could see Saturday's date in the day planner's distinctive font, as familiar to her as her own handwriting. It made opening the folder up feel easier, like she was only looking at one of her own calendar days. Not snooping at evidence.

The first entry was for 8:15 a.m. It read "Model UN check-in."

Beneath it, at 10:30, another entry read "meet w/Cait re: KB," and a third at 6:30 read "Field Museum behind-the-scenes!"

Tomorrow was Saturday, the day Lisa had planned to spend in Chicago for her oldest son's Model UN competition. After she checked him in, if her planner could be trusted, Lisa had intended to take a meeting about "KB" with "Cait." Prairie's best guess was that Cait must be Caitlin McClain of Kitty Blue. Prairie had seen photos of Lisa and Cait on Lisa's social media accompanied by effusive captions praising

163

Lisa's "boss babe bestie from waaaay back" who'd been the one to bring Lisa in on "the best business in the world." Prairie drew the open folder closer and forgot about the one-finger rule long enough to pull out her phone and take a picture.

There were more papers under that one, but her brain suddenly disassociated from itself and played back the moment she'd crunched her transmission speeding away from Lisa's house. She could imagine no way she wouldn't be caught if she didn't stop.

Gah.

She flipped the folder back around and tried to scooch it into the exact same place it was before, then leaned way back in her chair and started scrolling through her phone, her vision blurred and her heart pounding.

"They had it."

Prairie jumped. Hoped she hadn't accidentally yelped.

"Sorry, I startled you."

"Nope. Well, kind of. Just reading on my phone."

Foster slid back into the booth. He had an enormous piece of French silk pie and a glass of milk. Prairie didn't think she would ever eat again.

"Let me ask you something." Foster unwrapped a clean fork.

"Okay."

"Nathan Carmichael."

"You're going to have to add a who, what, when, why, or how to make that a question."

"Funny thing is, your name didn't even make it into the report. I looked you up in the system, first thing after the vigil."

"You did, huh?"

He gave her a fast, terrifyingly hot look. "No Prairie Nightingale in the system, other than some parking tickets outside the gifted school, from which I learn your middle name is Hawk. Compelling, but not relevant. Then I come to mention you in the case meeting, in the context of 'If you see this woman driving a black Honda Accord,' and one of the guys says, 'I know that name.' Turns out he worked the Carmichael case. The first victim to come forward mentioned you in her initial interview. I ask him to show me the case file. This victim said *you were* the one who came to her and got her story. She said you'd found out there were other victims, that there had to be others, because you'd looked into Carmichael after he didn't—and this was where my eyes crossed a little, because it was hard to make the connection—give you a check for the PTO. And she also said that learning about the other victims who hadn't gotten help was the thing that motivated her to come to the station."

"That's still not a question. But it is mostly accurate, as a series of facts, roughly in order." She tried to raise one eyebrow but suspected she only showed him her dimples.

"Here's what I've observed about you, Prairie Nightingale." He took a bite of pie and then used his napkin. "You ask good questions. You see things other people miss. You get people to tell you interesting stories."

Well. Prairie supposed that was the most effusive letter of recommendation she would ever get from this man.

"None of my guys noticed the missing ring. I didn't. It was a good catch."

"Yeah, because *victimology*," she said. "That's all I'm trying to do here, really, is help reduce your inherent bias and provide a fuller picture of a woman victim who you're just naturally going to see as an extension of her rich husband."

"'Victimology' is a big word."

"I'm learning the lingo." She shot him with her finger guns.

He laughed. Such a good laugh. "At any rate. Thank you."

"You're welcome. Please find Lisa."

The server came to their table and told Foster the bill was comped, and he thanked her while she tried, at the same time, to thank him for his service. Prairie wondered if the server even knew what service she was thanking him for or if she just saw a man with a barbered cut and gun and threw pie and comped bills at him.

He was a nice guy, was the thing, and when he was talking to regular people, he looked surprisingly boyish, his usual masks dropped. Because they were masks, not *him*.

She wondered if he'd ever drop all of them for her.

It was a thought she wouldn't have anticipated would be wildly exciting until it appeared in her mind.

"I have to go," he said. "I nearly didn't make it here, except I was forced to take a dinner break." He pulled out his wallet and left a twenty on the table for the server.

"Are you getting any sleep?" Prairie couldn't imagine what it must be like inside whatever bullpen they were working Lisa's case in.

"Here and there." He shrugged into his suit jacket, which Prairie couldn't help but notice was tailored to Foster Rosemare's last half inch. "Just so we're crystal clear, you're still not talking to Chris Radcliffe. Or anyone currently associated with this case."

"Yep." Prairie smartly tapped the manila folder. "Don't forget your stuff."

Foster picked it up and slid it into his bag. "You got plans this weekend."

A not-question delivered with the half smile. Prairie's stomach flipped like a teenager's. "Why, are you asking me out?"

"Nah, that's Thursdays. You're very busy. Homemaking."

"I am, but it so happens tomorrow is Greg's Saturday with the girls. The weather's supposed to be nice. I was thinking about maybe taking a day trip to Chicago." *I came into receipt of evidence that suggests a significant lead to follow in the big city.* "I like to watch them feed the penguins at the Shedd."

He buttoned his jacket and grabbed his bag. "Heard a lot of people like the Field Museum."

"Yeah. Good place to take your kid." Her eyes filled with tears.

Homemaker

Foster stopped. "We'll find her, Prairie. We're working on it. Those kids will know what happened to their mom." His voice had dropped another mask, and it was deep and kind and buzzed all the way through her.

After he left, she wondered who he meant by *we*.

Chapter 15

Prairie's Saturday-morning drive from Green Bay to the northern suburbs of Chicago was three hours of mostly empty interstate that she spent blasting one of Anabel's most obnoxious playlists in order to avoid her own spinning thoughts.

She found Caitlin McClain where she'd said she would be, outside the south entrance to the most upscale department store at the mall where Caitlin had asked to meet. Prairie was a little late due to a shortage of parking. Midday on a Saturday was maybe the worst time to meet at a mall.

Or the best, if you were looking for a crowded public place that was anonymous and safe.

As soon as Prairie introduced herself, Caitlin began walking away, gesturing for Prairie to follow her inside the department store. "I didn't think Lisa told anyone we were going to meet." Caitlin had taken off her sunglasses—designer, probably worth a car payment—but couldn't seem to commit to putting them away. Her eyes were big and green but red-rimmed. No eye makeup, despite having otherwise perfectly made-up skin and lips and brows that belonged in a magazine. She looked as though she might, at the slightest provocation, slip the sunglasses back on, slink into a rack of casual women's wear, and disappear.

"She didn't," Prairie said. "At least, I don't think so. Like I told you, I happened to run across her day planner." She flashed to a vision of Foster's folder, abandoned on the table when he went for pie, and reassured herself for the thousandth time that he had definitely meant for her to look at the papers inside it. He'd brought that folder to show it to her, effectively delegating this interview to Prairie. That meant Caitlin could have knowledge valuable to the investigation, and he trusted her to find out. "It said Lisa was supposed to meet with Cait this morning, and you're the only 'Cait' in the area who I could imagine her wanting to meet, given that she was trying to work with higher-ups in Kitty Blue to make things right."

"So you know Lisa." Caitlin reached up like she was going to run her fingers through her bright-red hair, then stopped. It was pulled back tight in an elastic at her nape. It made Prairie wonder if Caitlin was even wearing the kind of clothes she usually did or if she was trying for a disguise. No visible Kitty Blue logos.

Her clandestine behavior reminded Prairie to look up.

The cameras were everywhere, nooked tastefully along wooden beams, sconces, and boutique signs. Breadcrumbs.

"We used to be friends. Mom friends," Prairie clarified. Caitlin would understand what a mom friend was.

"Lisa and I went to college together," Caitlin said. "Back then, I would've told you we were best friends, but a lot of people might have said that about her. Lisa had incredible energy. No matter what she tried, it was like she was made for it. If you saw her in a play, you were sure she'd be a famous actress. She used to say, 'Life is not an audition.'"

"The more people I talk to, the more I wish I'd gotten to know her better."

"The Lisa I knew the last few years and the Lisa I knew back then weren't the same."

The comment made Prairie remember a night, long behind her now, when Greg was in the guest room after a big fight and she couldn't sleep. She'd called her mother in Oregon. She didn't get past saying, 'Hi, Mom,' before she started to cry. She told her mom she was certain she wasn't Prairie Nightingale anymore, she just wasn't, and she didn't know how to get that girl back.

169

Her mom had told her that she would always be Prairie Nightingale, no matter what. She would always be every girl she had ever been.

For a while, Prairie hadn't been so sure, but her mother's conviction had helped her find her way back to herself.

Caitlin led them through the department store, down the main corridor of the mall, and into a large, open space beneath a bank of skylights that formed a hub. She drifted to a stop, seemingly unsure of the right direction to take. "I'm sorry," she said. "I'm really not handling this very well."

"It's okay. You said the Lisa you know now wasn't the same as the Lisa you knew in college. Could you tell me about reconnecting with her?"

"Let's sit." Caitlin walked over to a bench along the border of the space, away from the flow of traffic. She perched on its edge, her purse on her lap, and carefully folded her sunglasses and put them away. "The summer after college, we lived together in the city. We had an apartment with some other girls from school. She wanted a job in a gallery. She majored in art history, but her minor was business because her dad always wanted her to keep her eye on something practical. She thought she could maybe run a gallery one day, but the only thing she could find that summer was in retail, and she got discouraged. She went home to Green Bay at the end of August and decided not to come back."

Caitlin put her purse beneath the bench, tight up against her shoes. She scanned the crowd as though she might see someone she knew.

"Her dad hired her to work office management at his financial management firm. She'd still come visit me here on the weekends a couple times a month. At first, she'd spend all day Saturday still looking for that gallery job or something like it, and we'd party at night. After a while, we'd just party. Then she met Chris. After that, I didn't see her anymore, and she hardly ever called." Caitlin looked at Prairie and shrugged. "But that was happening to everyone, all of us girls who went to college with these big goals. We graduated in ninety-nine. We assumed the world was ours. But if feminism had won, why is it that the last time we saw each other was when we were in each other's weddings?"

Prairie hadn't gone to college, but her own life and the lives of the women she'd known in her early twenties had followed the same pattern. "Were you in Lisa's wedding?"

"I was. It was in Door County at a winery. It was the only time I met Chris until he started coming to Kitty Blue events."

"You hadn't seen Chris since their wedding?"

"Until I recruited her, I hadn't seen *Lisa* since their wedding. I'd invite her to something, and she'd say yes but then not be able to make it at the last minute. Or she'd say no with some excuse that boiled down to being too busy or, if the get-together was down here, Chicago being too far to drive. But that was bullshit. Lisa loved to drive."

Prairie thought about Lisa's fantastic van with its cool red-leather interior.

"I fully expected her to say no when I asked her if I could come up and give her a presentation on Kitty Blue. It was a mercenary move on my part. I'm a single mom, and before Kitty Blue I'd spent years hustling, trying to put together enough money to make my bills. I was in the first tier of sellers recruited by Paige Leon." She glanced at Prairie with a question in her eyes. Did Prairie know the Kitty Blue world?

"Your upline is Paige, who's the founder, Indio Leon's, sister-in-law. Being in Paige's first tier makes you Kitty Blue royalty."

Caitlin's smile was sad. "It was funny, because Paige and Indio didn't recruit me. I wasn't the kind of person they were looking for, but a friend of mine was. She didn't want to do it. I went to the meeting in her place and turned over every penny I'd ever managed to sock away in savings to buy inventory. My business took off fast. Pretty soon, Paige was telling me they wanted to expand into Wisconsin, Indiana, Ohio, and I thought of Lisa."

"Was she interested right off the bat?"

"Not at all. She clearly didn't want me to come up to Green Bay to give her the pitch, but I'd just finished writing a check for my kid to go to private school, *the* private school. I'd paid off my student loans and bought a place that meant I was never going to have to deal with a scary Chicago landlord ever again. I needed to keep growing to make bills and keep the Leons happy. I wanted that downline bad."

"How did you convince her?"

"The way everyone in Kitty Blue is convinced. I brought her a box of clothes." Caitlin turned her body toward Prairie on the bench, tucking her foot under her knee. "I wasn't part of a con. I believed in Kitty Blue. I believed in its potential to transform a woman's life. I felt like I was part of a family, of a group of the best girlfriends I'd ever had, and for a long time, it felt amazing. Now?" Caitlin shook her head. "Paige Leon was supposed to be at the meeting with Lisa and me today."

"Whoa."

Caitlin gave her a faint smile. "I wasn't sure about taking Paige into confidence about what Lisa had been sharing with me, but then I thought, 'Paige is supposed to be one of my best friends. A sister. Why aren't I talking to her?' I was afraid I would lose everything. That's not a good reason, is it? I told Paige I wanted her to meet with me and Lisa when Lisa was supposed to be in town." Caitlin pressed her lips together so tightly, they went white around the edges. "When the news hit that Lisa was missing, the first call I got was from Paige. But it wasn't to commiserate. It was to ask me if we still had a problem or if everything was good."

Prairie let that settle between them. This information was *intense*. She didn't want to push Caitlin, who seemed more brittle and grieved with every word. "I can help you get any information you want to share to the right people," she said.

"Thank you." Caitlin looked like she could cry, but her eyes just got more red. Probably she didn't have tears left. "Today's meeting with Lisa was her last one before meetings she had scheduled with the attorneys generals' offices in Wisconsin and Illinois. She had already given them financial documents demonstrating that there was no way for anyone in Kitty Blue to make money except from distributors in their downline

Homemaker

buying inventory from the company. She wanted me and Paige to sign off. She was preparing to pay personal restitution to the worst affected in her downline."

"I knew some of that." Lisa had mentioned restitution in her emails to Shawna.

"You might also know that Chris had met with Indio Leon herself, going over my head and Paige's, too, and told the founder of the company that he and Lisa had a good talk, and reassured her nothing like this would happen." Caitlin shot a glance at Prairie. "This was some time ago. He didn't get involved in Kitty Blue until Lisa was making a lot of money. Then he came to our mega-meetings, the Celebrity Blue cruises. He acted as her manager. Indio loved him."

"What did she love about him?"

"He was a factory-made version of the ideal Kitty Blue husband, like how Indio wanted every distributor to polish and present their husband on social media to give the impression that being a distributor made every part of your life better. He backed up Indio. He told Lisa and others in the inner circle that her job wasn't scrabbling for customers who wanted jackets and running tights. It was signing on more distributors to grow the company. Lisa did it his way, Indio's way, for a while, but that wasn't what had interested her about Kitty Blue. She tried to push back. She made her home boutique. But Chris is a big developer. He doesn't make money building individual houses. He makes money signing on investors, and then he takes his cut. Kitty Blue made sense to him."

"Lisa told you this?"

"Some of it. A couple of months ago, I got an email from her from a new email address, sharing her documents and what she wanted to do. She had thought about trying to turn Kitty Blue around from the top down, leading a restructure that would make everything fair. But I think she saw that with such a tiny executive group, people who were mostly related to each other and had chaotic family dynamics, it would never happen. I know she had someone on the inside giving her information.

Probably one of the Leons' nonfamily hires. A lot of those people are gone now, ousted by the Leons. That's why shipments and communication and refunds have been so shit."

Prairie's brain didn't know what to fire on first. "You said she was using a new email?"

"She bought a computer that Chris didn't know about."

Prairie pulled out her phone. "What was Lisa's company email?"

Caitlin told her.

"Was this her secret one?" She showed Caitlin the header from one of the emails Shawna had forwarded to her.

"Yes."

That explained why Foster hadn't seen Lisa's emails to Shawna. They hadn't been in a neglected pile on his desk. They'd been sent from a computer he didn't know existed—a computer full of potential evidence that law enforcement didn't have.

"What do you think her goal was for the meeting you were supposed to have today?" Prairie asked.

"To give Paige and I one last chance. She didn't want to ruin or humiliate or destroy anyone. She wanted people to do the right thing." Caitlin pressed her fingers to her temples. "She's a good person."

Caitlin couldn't settle on whether to talk about Lisa in the present tense or the past. Lisa was her friend. Someone she loved and admired.

"Do you think anyone—Chris or anyone at Kitty Blue—could be capable of doing something that prevented Lisa from going forward with her plans?" Prairie asked.

Caitlin was so still that Prairie eventually realized she was holding her breath.

She exhaled with a shudder. "I've been asking and asking myself, but I don't *want* the answer." Caitlin pushed her hand against her middle. "I thought I was doing something my kid could be proud of." She turned to Prairie, broken open so completely it was hard to look into her face. All her color had gone, and the lines around her eyes were like delicate, otherworldly webs. "There has not been one word from any official Kitty Blue channel about Lisa's disappearance. The downlines are posting candles and prayers on the forums. The Leons have said nothing."

"You're Lisa's upline. I know she's supposed to bring you any problems. Can you remember anyone who was really angry? Anyone who lost money, who had a spouse who was upset over his wife losing money? Someone who stands out?"

"A lot of distributors are angry." Caitlin looked away, considering something. She turned back to Prairie. "I'll pull the whole list off the company database and send it to you." Prairie could only nod, though her heart had skipped at least two beats. "She was most worried about a close friend, someone who she brought in first and who initially made a lot of money."

"Was her name Amber?"

"Yes. Her husband blamed Lisa for everything his wife lost. Lisa felt responsible because Amber had wanted in to make a living. Her husband had lost everything they had with his business. He's called the office and harassed people. He wanted to talk to Indio herself. I don't know if he managed to."

"I see."

What if Noah Jenkins had found out that Lisa was trying to take Kitty Blue apart? He'd talked to Greg in a way Greg described as violent. What would he do to someone he thought was taking away any hope he had to get what he felt he was owed?

What if Kitty Blue, threatened by Lisa's actions, would *use* Noah? Aid or abet him or, minimally, just let his anger take its natural course?

Lisa Radcliffe was one of their top sellers, as close as a non-Leon could be to the highest echelon of the company, right on the brink of taking it down and almost certainly taking down the Leons with it. What would someone like Indio or Paige Leon, people with *chaotic family dynamics*, do when they found out what Lisa had planned?

Who else knew, besides Paige Leon, what Lisa was planning to do in Chicago today?

If she had managed to get here.

Criminals are stupid, Foster had said. *They make mistakes.*

Prairie didn't know what mistakes had been made, but she felt—she *knew*—she was getting close.

"Caitlin, what would you most like me to do?"

"I want her to be found safe. But if that can't happen, I want what she wanted. I'm all in on what Lisa wanted."

"I think," Prairie said carefully, "that Lisa would have also wanted you to forgive yourself. To live every day like it's not an audition."

"She would. I can try."

Prairie had never been more grateful for fresh air than the moment she walked out of that mall. She looked out over the cars, listened to the highway humming in the distance. It was almost four o'clock.

She remembered Lisa's day planner and realized something. Lisa had planned to go straight from her meeting bringing down a multimillion-dollar company to taking her kid to the freaking Field Museum for their special experience with behind-the-scenes tickets.

Prairie really, truly would have liked to have known this home-maker better.

Hats off, Lisa Radcliffe. You were always you. You never stopped being you.

I promise, I'm going to make sure to figure out if the bastard who hurt you made even one single mistake.

Chapter 16

It was 6:00 a.m. when Prairie's house of cards started to collapse, forcing her to ask herself if she had any business making promises to a missing woman.

Through a fuzz of interrupted sleep after she'd collapsed into bed at ten after fighting north Chicago, Milwaukee, and I-43 traffic on the way home, she heard Greg yelling at Joyce, his voice so uncharacteristically panicked that Prairie's whole body went to ice as she stumble-ran downstairs.

Greg was covered in blood—or, at least, one arm and the side of his white sleep shirt were—and at first she thought he was holding baby Maelynn in his arms, her orange-fuzz infant hair matted with blood, and so Prairie screamed, rushing to Greg.

"I know, I know. Mom is calling for help. I think Gingernut's okay, just in shock."

It took Prairie's instincts some time to catch up with reality. His hands were not covered in Maelynn's precious baby blood. In fact, Maelynn was eleven years old, not a baby. It was the cat in Greg's arms, missing half an ear. When Greg had stayed over last night in the Annex, he'd left the sliding glass door open a crack to admit some spring air. Unfortunately, Gingernut's weight-reduction diet had been working well enough that she managed to slip through the crack and get in her first catfight in seven years, presumably as the victor.

Joyce drove Greg and Gingernut to the urgent care vet, and Prairie assumed parenting duty three hours early, already wondering when she'd be freed up for Lisa's case again. Valuable time was slipping away. She'd texted Foster before she returned from Chicago to tell him to look for a second, secret computer. He'd seen her message but hadn't replied. The only update Prairie had on the case was a short article in the paper reporting that the police took Lisa's husband in for an interview—to ask about the ring, she hoped.

She wanted to *do* something, and the something she wanted to do was not to spend an hour cleaning up cat blood in four different rooms from six different surfaces while trying vainly to prevent Zipper from licking it up. She'd just started pancakes from a box mix for the girls when she got a long email from Anabel's math tutor, which reminded her she'd forgotten about the meeting they were supposed to have on Friday in the whirlwind of going to the library to see Emma, doing errands, and sharing a mushroom burger with Foster. The news from the math tutor was so distractingly bad, Prairie forgot about the pancakes, burning them so badly on the griddle that two smoke detectors had gone off at once.

She gave the girls cereal and told them to eat in their rooms.

Now she put her head down and pressed her hot cheek directly onto the Iconic White Silestone countertop of her breakfast bar, willing it to cool the blood that had risen to the surface of her skin and return it to her body, where it might freeze the rage in her heart.

"It stinks in here." Maelynn climbed up on a stool next to Prairie. It might have been cute in some other reality, but not in this reality, wherein Maelynn had already come downstairs to interrupt Prairie several times.

"I opened the windows. It will take a while for the burned smell to go away."

Maelynn put her head down on the counter so her face was close to Prairie's. "I think the cereal you gave me must have red dye in it," she said. "I have those hives on my stomach again."

Homemaker

"There's hydrocortisone cream in the upstairs bathroom cabinet."

"I looked. It's expired."

"It's not like milk, it won't curdle."

"But what if after a certain date it transforms into something toxic, and then I use it and die?"

Prairie sat up and looked at her daughter. She wore pants so small the snap at the top didn't come together and a T-shirt that was so big it fell off her shoulder. Prairie usually did the laundry on Wednesdays. The day of the vigil. She herself was wearing a novelty thong she'd purchased eight years ago. "I guess we can run to the drugstore."

Her phone rang. Joyce. "Hey," she answered. "How's Gingernut?"

"She'll be fine. She's on antibiotics and a painkiller, and she'll have to wear one of those collars. They're going to keep her for observation until five because of the sedation, and they want to do a metabolic workup. I guess her blood sugar's too high. With the recent weight loss, they want to make sure she doesn't have diabetes."

"Lord."

"Greg says he'll pick her up, so you don't have to worry about it, which is good because I want you for something else. Do you think you could get the girls organized in about fifteen minutes and the three of you could come with me on a little field trip? It's about Lisa. I've been doing some research."

Prairie looked down at her hoodie, which had pancake grease stains. She'd pulled it out of the dirty laundry. "Do we have to look presentable?"

"Not for this."

"All right, but what kind of research?" One never knew with Joyce.

"I'll explain on the way," she said. "See you in a bit."

❧

Joyce honked twice as Prairie was yelling at Anabel for the third time to get off video chat and put on her shoes. Anabel stomped down the

179

stairs. An hour ago, at breakfast, she'd been in one of Greg's old Stanford sweatshirts with leggings covered in animal hair. Apparently, while on video chat with Kai, she'd decided to experiment with a look Prairie could only pin down as *pastel goth*. She had cut open the sleeve of a T-shirt and re-closed it with about twenty snap barrettes.

"What?" Anabel asked ferociously.

"I didn't say anything," Prairie protested.

"You're looking at my outfit."

"Your grandma is waiting in the driveway. Can you put on whatever shoes go with that so we can leave?"

Anabel stared at Prairie with an expression Prairie could only describe as Anabel's pupils vomiting out her soul. So it was going to be that kind of almost-fifteen today. Awesome.

"I'm sitting in front." Prairie passed Anabel on the way out the door. "You sit behind your grandmother so I can see you when I turn around to lecture you about Algebra II."

She very much enjoyed watching the fear enter Anabel's eyes. But, like everything else that morning, the Algebra II lecture—which Prairie had imagined as brief, killing, and resulting in Anabel's remorse and spontaneous offer of strategy and rededication—did not go to plan. By the time Joyce pulled into the Walgreens parking lot, Prairie had completely lost her shit, Anabel had threatened to move into Greg's riverside loft, Maelynn had cried, and Joyce's shoulders had gotten stiffer.

Joyce snapped off the ignition. "I'm going in to get the hydrocortisone Maelynn wants. When I get back, the three of you will love each other." She left the car.

Prairie wished she could leave, too. She would walk the quarter mile down to Pancake Heaven, order a stuffed french toast and a pound of extra-crispy bacon with an XXL Bloody Mary, and never, ever go home.

"I'm sorry I lied." Anabel said this at a fraction of a decibel, as if Prairie's heart could be opened by submissive remorse.

"Not ready."

"*Fine.* But I did have cramps."

Homemaker

Prairie whipped around, recharged. "Twice a week for a month? You lied to your dad, you lied to me, you lied to your math tutor and wasted his time and our money. How many lies was that, Anabel? Oh, wait, you don't know, because you're failing math!"

Then, the worst. Anabel started to cry.

Prairie felt more than horrible. She felt guilty and stubborn and *stingy*. There wasn't anything left in her to be kind with.

"But it's going to be okay," Maelynn whispered. "Right, Anabel? Because of our project."

"Shut up," Anabel said.

"No, I think it's time. It's been going on a whole week. And it's *working*."

"What's been going on for a whole week?" Prairie asked.

Not only did she not know, she didn't have the faintest whiff of a guess. This week, she'd gone on two maybe-dates with an FBI agent. She'd talked to a million people and organized a vigil. She'd gotten her name in the paper and met a podcaster. She'd driven to Chicago and back to clandestinely liaise with a high-level associate of a dirty company on the brink of exploding into scandal. She'd even spotted important clues everyone else had missed, all in the service of finding Lisa Radcliffe.

Prairie had tried to be a detective—a word she couldn't even call herself out loud—and it had immediately, spectacularly tornadoed her work as a homemaker and a mother, burning through her resources until she was an ill-tempered husk in a dirty hoodie and an ancient pair of thong panties, which were currently buried so deep in her crack, they were cutting off the circulation to her taint.

"Anabel and I are doing math together." Maelynn sounded proud.

"What do you mean?" Prairie took off her seat belt, adjusted her underwear into a more bearable position, and turned all the way around.

Maelynn looked at Anabel a little nervously. "On Monday night—"

Prairie couldn't help it, her thoughts went right to *the night Lisa disappeared*.

"I couldn't sleep, and I heard Anabel crying in her room. She was trying to study for her Algebra II test. I was just going to give her a hug, but then I saw the practice problems that were up on her classroom website, and I just knew how to do them. When I showed her, she got it. It was fun. After Anabel didn't want to keep going because it was late and she was tired, I took her textbook to bed to read it."

"You read her Algebra II textbook."

"Yeah. It wasn't hard. She didn't get a good grade on the test, because we only had a little time and she's been failing for a while, but I looked at it, and the ones she got right were the things I taught her. So we did it again, every night this week. I'm setting an alarm to get up and go to her room."

Prairie looked at Anabel. She nodded, with a very small smile on her face when she glanced at Maelynn.

God, the love, sometimes.

"That's a kind thing to do for your sister," she said. "But you shouldn't be getting out of bed. You need to sleep. I have a question, though."

"What is it?"

"What's going on in your math class at school that Anabel's is so simple for you?"

"I've been trying to tell my teacher that everything we're doing is too easy, but he just makes me help the other kids," Maelynn said. "I don't want to do sixth grade math anymore. I meant to tell you, but I forgot, but I did remember to tell Dad. Then he showed up at the school on Friday and told me he yelled at everyone. I'm going to take a special test on Tuesday to see what would be the right math for me. Dad says they have to put me in the correct math class, even if it's via videoconference at the high school or even college."

"Oh."

Prairie's throat felt tight. She pulled out her phone, chasing a thought. On Friday morning, Marian had messaged her and assured her she would take care of everything. There it was. Marian had pulled

Homemaker

down messages that would normally go to Prairie, and there was a whole set of them from Greg about math.

Prairie had never checked or responded, but Greg had done everything with the school exactly how she would have done it.

She couldn't think of a single other time in her history with him that he'd handled this kind of parenting without her explicit instructions and emotional support. Even as he'd agreed to Prairie's plan to rearrange their coparenting life more equitably, he'd never taken the lead.

Not until Prairie simply took herself out of the equation.

She didn't know how to feel about that. On the one hand, it was good to know she could count on Greg to step up and do the work when she had other things on her plate. On the other hand, why had nothing she'd ever had on her plate before been important enough to prompt Greg to step up?

Joyce opened her car door. She pushed an overfilled Walgreens bag into the space next to her seat and climbed in after it. "Do we love each other again?"

"We do," Maelynn said. "We had a good talk."

"Great!" Joyce pulled several boxes out of the bag. "I couldn't figure out which hydrocortisone cream was the one you like, so I got all of them."

"Let me see."

Joyce handed them back to her, and Maelynn investigated them carefully while Joyce buckled her seat belt. "They had a sale on leftover Easter candy," Joyce said. "I bought everything they had. Have at it, girls."

Prairie claimed a bag of truffles. As they pulled out of the parking lot, she looked out the window and ate her candy and felt okay. Not good, not like Supermom, but okay. Okay Mom.

They passed the football field at the big Catholic high school. "This is the first spot on my research in the Lisa Radcliffe tour," Joyce said.

"That's where Lisa and Chris Radcliffe went to high school. They graduated together."

Prairie craned her neck to look at the building disappearing behind them. "Chris and Lisa went to high school together? I thought they met after Lisa was out of college."

Joyce took one hand off the wheel to point her finger in the air dramatically. "I found so much interesting stuff for you. Look under the Walgreens bag."

Prairie rummaged beneath the bag and extracted a dark-brown expanding file with an elastic band around it. "This?"

"Start in the first pocket."

Prairie whipped the elastic off and pulled out Joyce's papers. More photocopies. On top was a yearbook page, *1999 Seniors* in script across the header, black-and-white photos in a grid. There was Lisa, right in the middle of the page.

Lisa Jankowski.

She had remained fundamentally the same, in the way that some beautiful girls become beautiful women without passing through any awkwardness. Her hair was brown back then, and curly-wavy-wild, which suggested adult Lisa achieved her signature blond style through regular visits to the salon for color and blowouts. Her face had been a bit fuller, but Prairie thought Lisa at eighteen looked just like the girl Caitlin had described—vibrant, smiling, fun. "She must have been popular."

"Oh, she was. Keep flipping," Joyce said.

Prairie slid the yearbook photo to the bottom of the stack and looked through the next few pages. Majorette. The lead in *Our Town.* Art club. Young Catholic Leaders. Science Olympiad. There were candids from the cafeteria, Lisa outdoors in a human pyramid with a bunch of other girls, on top because she was the smallest. There was even one of her holding a piglet for the softball coach to kiss after a fundraiser, her head thrown back in laughter. She'd won academic awards in two

Homemaker

subjects and a student body vote for Best Personality and Most Likely To Succeed.

"You found this at the school?"

"The librarian was very helpful. They keep all the old yearbooks and the school newspaper, which came out monthly back then. The next few pages are from the newspaper."

The one on top featured a photo of Lisa in a pageant dress, accepting first-runner-up flowers and a modest scholarship. Her ambition was to become a school principal. Then, a stack of music reviews written by Lisa herself, in her sophomore year, when she must have tried her hand on the newspaper staff.

Lisa looked like the kind of girl who would star in an after-school special as the sweet-natured best friend of the girl who tried drinking. Loving parents and ordinary problems. A crew of wholesome friends and a set of ordinary, completely achievable ambitions.

Although she hadn't become a school principal. Or worked in a gallery. Or even regularly had a group of cheerful women browsing athleisure wear in her former dining room while she encouraged them to "just try it on" and made plans for a night out.

"Where's the stuff about Chris?" Prairie dug into the next pocket in the file.

Joyce put her hand over Prairie's to stop her. "Be patient. We're almost there."

She turned into a neighborhood on the west side, close to downtown. The houses were a size no one built anymore, comfortably medium two-story homes with mature trees. Joyce pulled over in front of a pointy middle-class version of a Tudor, stucco in a traditional brown and cream that looked a bit tired.

"It's been sitting empty awhile," Joyce said. "My Realtor friend says it's in limbo because there's enough back taxes owed on it to make it unattractive to flippers, and it needs a new roof."

"Are you moving, Grandma?" Maelynn craned her body toward her window to get a better view of the house. "It looks like a witch's house."

185

"How could I possibly survive if I didn't live with you girls?" Joyce got out of the car, and Prairie followed suit.

"You couldn't," decided Maelynn. She got out and ran up the little walk lined with large concrete pavers, dark with age.

Looking at the house made all the baby hairs stand up along the back of Prairie's neck. She studied the blank front windows and the sharp peak of the roof. The cedar trees along the front had grown up too tall, too close to the windows.

Joyce stood next to Prairie while the girls poked around, already heading toward the backyard. "This place was built in 1931." She strolled up the walk and knelt down by one of the pavers. "What does that say?"

Prairie dutifully followed, dropping to one knee to read the inscription pressed into the concrete. "Big *V*, little *d*, big *B*." The letters were worn around the edges, with blobby stars stamped between each one. She thought that Foster should really meet Joyce if he thought Prairie liked to draw out basic information. Except he was probably one of those guys who was delighted by older women and whom older women adored.

She pulled her phone out and checked it. He hadn't texted her back yet. No downline list from Caitlin, either.

Joyce pulled back the flap of her folder and extracted two pages, then handed Prairie the first. It was another set of yearbook photos. Prairie didn't recognize any of the faces. "What am I looking at?"

Joyce tapped a photo near the bottom. *Christopher Van der Beke.*

"Van der Beke?" She glanced at the concrete slab. *VdB.*

"This house is where Lisa's husband, Chris, grew up," Joyce said. "It was built by his great-grandfather, Arthur Van der Beke."

Prairie stared at the yearbook photo. She could see a bit of Chris in the breadth of his shoulders stretching out his black jacket and his angled jaw, but comparing this photo to any photo of Chris today would be like comparing a tree stump to an Ethan Allen dining room

Homemaker

table. Same raw material, completely different level of polish. "He changed his name?"

"He did indeed. Arthur emigrated from Belgium. He brought a bride with him and invested money from his parents into a concrete business that his older brother had already started here in Green Bay. It did quite well. Within two years he bought this lot and started building. He purchased everything outright, and if you peek inside, you'll see there was plenty of money left over. The finishes are lovely."

The front door was dark oak inset with panels of leaded glass. Prairie had to stand on her tiptoes to peer into the entryway. Her view was the bottom of a narrow staircase to the second floor. Under the dust and broken curtain rods and weird paint color choices, you could appreciate it was one of those houses people said had good bones.

"Those stairs are a little tricky," Joyce said. "Up to code, my Realtor friend told me, but I felt uncertain going up and down them."

"You've been busy."

"I like an interesting project, and what you've been doing is interesting." Joyce handed Prairie the remaining paper. It was from the same yearbook, a page listing all of the graduates in alphabetical order, with Christopher Van der Beke down at the bottom. The only names that were offset were those of the valedictorian and salutatorian. The salutatorian was Lisa Jankowski.

"This is the only place Chris appears in the yearbook, other than his photo," Joyce said. "I checked every issue of the newspaper from the four years he was in high school."

"Not a social butterfly, then. I feel like you're about to tell me why."

Joyce smiled. "What I can tell you is that Chris's grandfather, Edward, was the youngest of Arthur's children and the only boy. He inherited the business. He did fine with it. It got no bigger, but it kept going. When his mother died, he moved into this house with his wife. It must have been a tight fit. They already had five children when they brought Richard, Chris's dad, home from the hospital. I'm thinking that with such a big family, Edward wouldn't have settled on this house if he had better options—and, like I said, the business wasn't growing, even though in the fifties and sixties there was a lot of construction going on. I couldn't find out why, which in genealogy usually means it's a hidden 'why'—a story that didn't get written down. My guess is alcoholism. Chris's father took the business over a few years before Edward died."

"Chris's dad must have done well, though. Chris is loaded."

"That's what you'd think, isn't it? But he only just managed to hang on to it. And, just like his father, he moved his wife into this house after everyone else had scattered. Chris would have been five years old."

Prairie stood on her tiptoes and looked in the window again. History started so far back in the past, it felt like make believe, and then abruptly it spit you out in the present day at an abandoned house that, she realized, shouldn't be abandoned. Chris's parents were Joyce's age. "What happened to them?"

"It took some digging, but I did find Chris's father, Richard. He's at a memory care assisted living facility out near Luxemburg, although rumor has it he killed off most of his brain cells a long time ago. Another drinker. Chris took over paying the property taxes on this house in the early 2000s. He sold it, and since then it's been through a bunch of different owners until the last one defaulted and the house went back to the bank."

"What about his mom?"

"Well. What about her? Gina Radcliffe, then Gina Van der Beke. The newspaper ran one of those courtesy obituaries for her that the funeral home submits—you know, just a few lines listing birth and death dates, surviving relatives, and the time of the service. But there's also a death certificate that documents an accidental death from an injury. She had a subarachnoid hemorrhage—that's bleeding on her brain from a skull fracture. In the blank where the certifying physician had to describe how the injury occurred, he wrote 'fell down the stairs at home.'"

"Oh, God. These stairs?"

"The very same."

Homemaker

Prairie pressed her hands against the door. Falling down those hard, steep wooden stairs to the oak floors in the entryway would be a fast and brutal way to die.

"There's a copy of her death certificate in the file. She was forty years old."

"He took his mom's maiden name. How old was he when the accident happened?"

"Fifteen. Of course, accidental death is another one of those things that genealogists look at and wonder. Death certificates don't tell you if there were witnesses, for example, or a police investigation. The coroner didn't do an autopsy, and I didn't find anything in the paper about it. If there'd been an official inquiry, I would have. But I can't get my hands on things like reports of police being called to the address, or if there were any questions internally about how accidental the fall was. If her husband's breath smelled like liquor when the ambulance showed up, the records wouldn't say."

Prairie thought about this. "Even if his mom dying wasn't anything more than a fall, his dad doesn't sound like a prize. It could be that he changed his name to honor his mom. He lost her at a hard age."

Could the loss of his mother be why Chris had sought to control Lisa—because some part of him was still a teenage boy who couldn't control the circumstances of a fatal accident that had taken his mom away?

Or maybe the long story of the Van der Beke men was one of those that, once it took a turn into failure and darkness and violence, wouldn't end until justice had been served.

Joyce touched her elbow. "Come on. Let's get the girls. I thought we could grab lunch at the pizza buffet place."

Prairie followed Joyce around the side of the house and into the overgrown yard behind it. "Mom, look!" Maelynn said as they rounded the garage and spotted the girls hunkered down near the back corner of the property. "We found a dead crow!" She was pink-cheeked with excitement.

"Don't touch it," Prairie said automatically.

"We didn't. Anabel moved it with a stick so I could see it better."

Prairie and Joyce walked closer, joining the girls to make a circle around the small, untidy pile of lost life in the grass.

"Wow," Prairie said. "That is a super dead crow."

"It makes me sad," Anabel said.

"It could be that it was just the crow's time," Joyce suggested.

"Corvids are really smart," Maelynn told them. Animals were one of her longest-enduring special interests. "That's the proper name for the family crows belong to. If a crow comes to an untimely death, by electrocution or murder, the other crows have an inquiry. Mom, you'll like this. This is what you're doing." Maelynn touched Prairie's arm to get her attention. Prairie could not stop looking at the pile of blue-black crow feathers. "If it's determined to be an accident, then all the other crows avoid what killed it forever. Like a particular cat or an electric line. If it's murder, they execute the murderer among them who did it." Maelynn said this in a breathless rush. "Corvids are amazing."

This is what you're doing. Prairie felt a little breathless herself in the presence of death, standing in the backyard of the house where a mother's blood had been spilled and the loss had forever altered the course of her son's life—possibly contributing in some way to the disappearance of his own wife. To the end of everything that Lisa Jankowski had been and wanted to be.

Had Lisa known she was in danger? Had Chris Radcliffe's mother? Or had the knowledge come only when it was too late to do anything about it?

Prairie had lost friends when she pursued the truth about Nathan Carmichael. This time, more than friendship was at stake, and she still didn't have an answer to Greg's question about whether she was putting herself at risk.

Her phone buzzed. She pulled it out.

No ring. No laptop. Can you meet?

She shoved it into her back pocket without responding, then put her arms around her girls. "Grandma said she'll take us out to pizza. Sound good?"

It did sound good. They sounded good, chattering through lunch and on the way back home.

Prairie watched them tumble through the door, kick off their shoes and leave them right in the middle of the floor, even though she was forever reminding them not to, and disappear into the kitchen. She kicked off her own shoes. Left them where they fell.

Her phone stayed silent in her pocket, but she could feel the urgent pressure of Foster's question. *No ring. No laptop. Can you meet?*

She wanted to text him back. She would. Soon.

But first, she needed this. A few hours of stolen Sunday for herself, and her kids, and home.

Chapter 17

"You know what I think the key is? Exposure." Megan tucked her leg underneath her thigh and took a long draw on her twenty-four-ounce blended coffee with extra vanilla, dragging the straw out to suck up the whipped cream. It was Monday morning, and Prairie and Megan were sitting in the front seats of Megan's SUV in the community center parking lot.

"Tell me what you mean by 'exposure.'" Prairie played with the zipper on her new Kitty Blue jacket, which Megan had just turned over to her and she'd immediately put on. She *adored* it. It had a tiny peplum hem in the back that she just knew made the most of her butt.

"Chris changed his name," Megan said. "He walked away from his whole life after his mom died. His dad is stashed in assisted living. His past is buried under a ton of rubble, and he doesn't talk about it. It's a secret."

Prairie had filled Megan in on all the latest case news last night. Having chased the high of enjoying an afternoon at home with her kids until it wore off in a screaming fight between Anabel and Maelynn over the theft of Maelynn's favorite charging brick and cord, Prairie had retreated to bed with her laptop and spent hours digging through Chris Radcliffe's professional life online—corporate website, puff pieces in the newspaper, a video of a talk he'd given to the Rotary years earlier. The deep dive confirmed for Prairie that, at least professionally, Chris didn't talk about his roots or his family's concrete business. Instead, he talked about the city's potential. Its future.

Everything Chris said faced forward, which struck Prairie as significant.

This morning, after Greg left with the girls for school and Prairie was in the shower, Megan had texted that she had some thoughts about Lisa, and they needed to do a car break. A car break was something Megan had invented: Prairie met her when Megan's work break began, with sugar, and they would sit in Megan's car to visit without kids as much as they could in fifteen minutes without Megan technically leaving the premises of the community center.

"I mean, I can't definitively confirm Chris *doesn't* talk about his early years," Prairie said. "But everything I'm seeing points to that conclusion."

Megan put her drink in the cup holder. "What I am in a position to understand better than most," she said, "is how hard it is to expose a man who has done bad things. When we came forward about Nathan Carmichael, you will remember that I had to tell my story over and over to the *same people*. So did the other victims. The resistance of most of our society to expose the bad deeds of men protects him even now. The reason my brand-new agent is excited about my book"—Megan grinned, and Prairie shimmied and silent-clapped—"is because, even with Carmichael's ass in prison, what he did was never *really* brought to light beyond a brief media flurry and dry court proceedings. And if this book is published—"

"When."

"—*when* it is, I'll have to keep talking about it and proving my credibility."

"Right. So stupid. But yes, that is reality."

"This thing with Chris is the same."

"Is it?" Prairie's question was genuine. "Even though there's been so much publicity about this case?"

Yesterday, while Prairie was looking at a dead crow with her kids, the police department had issued a press release asking for anyone who sold Kitty Blue for Lisa to please come forward to answer some questions. Prairie assumed the request was part of an effort to learn more about Lisa's business dealings and locate her missing laptop, but the statement had also made it clear that Lisa Radcliffe had not had any confirmed contact with anyone since her disappearance, nor had she used her credit cards or bank accounts, and she was believed to be in serious danger.

Immediately afterward, Emma Cornelius had dropped an episode of her podcast featuring Lisa's case that went deep into the chaos that was Kitty Blue, Lisa's involvement with the company, and how much money Lisa was making. The result was that the story had quickly begun to spread beyond regional media to national outlets.

"The media is tripping over itself to run stories about the perfect wife and mother that ask, *Did Lisa harbor a dark secret about her involvement in the failing Kitty Blue empire?*" Megan dropped her voice to make it sound like she was narrating a particularly scandalous episode of *Dateline*. "But those stories expose *Lisa*. There isn't a single goddamned thing about Chris, other than as a handsome community savior and father of three, even though the police brought him in for questioning just yesterday. Nothing." She dropped her hands to her lap. "And if you and a grandma can figure out he *changed his name* and his mom died under mysterious circumstances, why can't someone in the media? They *can*, but they won't. And Chris has worked hard to protect himself beyond how the world protects him."

"He doesn't want anything exposed that he can't control."

Megan picked up her drink and pointed the cup at Prairie. "You got it."

"You're saying the question might not be what happened to Lisa, but what happened to threaten Chris with exposure before Lisa disappeared, or threatened to expose someone else, maybe at Kitty Blue, in a way that Lisa ended up paying for it. Is that right?"

Homemaker

"That was my brilliant insight in the shower this morning, yes. At this point, we've thrown away the idea that Lisa's disappearance was some kind of impulsive thing or breakdown, or that she drove her van into the lake and, I guess, swam out into the bay until exhaustion took over."

"I hate that," Prairie said.

"Agreed. But it's off the table for me because of what you've found out. The police statement also doesn't give the impression they're looking at those possibilities anymore. I haven't heard of another search being organized. That leaves whether someone who is not Chris came for Lisa—"

"The Kitty Blue theory, currently very exciting to every mainstream news affiliate in the country."

"—or did Chris kill her," Megan concluded. "And why."

"Or both," Prairie suggested.

"If we assume the police are already working pretty dang hard to run down the Leons, either to implicate them or exonerate them, doesn't that leave you to figure out any kind of why, and especially fucking *how*, for Chris?"

"I guess so." Prairie felt cold, even in her new jacket. The media's interest in Kitty Blue—interest that she had introduced into the equation—had made her feel mostly terrified. What if she was getting this wrong and taking the focus off the "real" investigation? She could hurt someone.

But so could Chris. If he'd already hurt Lisa, he could hurt someone else. Prairie thought again of Lisa's van sinking into the cold water of the bay. The steep staircase at Chris's childhood home. How furious Amber Jenkins had been in the schoolyard, and Greg's description of the intimidating phone call he'd received from Amber's husband.

"I don't know if I can pull it off," she admitted. "I am up to my neck in something here."

"You are. But you've got this." Megan reached across the front seat to give Prairie's denim-covered knee a quick squeeze. "You know

195

yourself, Prairie. That's a gift. When you try to help people, there are always going to be consequences, but you do this thing where you take on guilt and responsibility that doesn't belong to you. That's when you start getting in your own way."

"Oh no. You're still talking about Carmichael." Prairie knew how much Megan's life had changed since she showed up to talk to her that day and ended up driving her to the police station. She did worry about it. "Do you think we're only friends because I feel responsible for what I did to you? Because I promise that's not it."

"Oh, Prairie." Megan smiled. "You didn't do anything to me. He did. I made my own choices about how to handle it. You were part of them, but they were mine. You didn't make all your friends stop talking to you, either."

"I was never sure if it was me going after Carmichael or divorcing Greg that was the real issue."

"It was neither," Megan said. "That's my point. Those women didn't want to think about how close we all live to being hurt by a kind, trustworthy man who's made himself a pillar of the community. Rather than think about it, they put it on you, and that wasn't fair. Do you understand that?"

"I guess. My head understands better than my heart." Prairie's eyes started to well up.

"You don't have to balance the scales of anybody else's behavior. That's one of the things I'm trying to write about in my book. You only have to think about how your own life is changed. The entire goal is to get to where all you want is more of the good stuff you already have."

"And you want more of your good stuff?"

Megan grinned. "I do. But I have a question for you. You've done a great thing with your 724 Maple Project, at least from the outside, for yourself and your girls and even for Greg. I wonder, though, did you really change your life enough? Right now, what do *you* want more of?"

Prairie felt her voice lock up tight.

Megan gave her a brisk nod. "You can put a pin in it, but as your best friend and someone who loves you, I have to ask. Now before you start spiraling on me, I'm going to jet. Car-break time is over, and your phone is blowing up."

Prairie gave Megan a grateful smile. "Foster and I are playing phone tag. I was supposed to meet him for breakfast, but he canceled. At least, I hope it's him. If it's school calling to tell me Maelynn threw up or Anabel got suspended, I will politely let them know that Mondays belong to Greg."

Megan raised an eyebrow. "Breakfast? Like, *we're not dating but we're trying out a meetup in the morning* sort of breakfast, or *we're sharing case tips in a clandestine location* breakfast? Although, honestly, both sound interesting."

"Both? And?"

Megan took one last long drag on her drink and opened her car door. Prairie followed her out into the parking lot.

"I want an update after you see him." Megan started to walk back toward the building, and Prairie's phone came alive with frantic buzzing again. Megan turned back. "Keep me in the loop."

"I will." Prairie climbed into her car. She found three new messages from Foster in her notifications.

10:02.
Sorry again about breakfast.

10:11.
When are you free? I should be able to get out of here in an hour.

10:17.
Never mind. Something came up. Will catch up with you later.

Prairie let the phone drop. She closed her eyes and rested her head against the seat back and listened to her ears ring in the sudden silence.

She couldn't think about what Megan had said about *her* yet. Megan was right—she would spiral if she tried to. She'd done all the laundry in the house yesterday, folded it and put it away, trying to soothe the fear that something important was getting away from her.

It was easier to think about Lisa in the terms Megan had used. Whether Lisa, by marrying Chris, had gotten more of what she wanted, a life full of good things.

In high school, Lisa Jankowski had power. It was the kind of fleeting power the system gave girls that led them to believe they could do whatever they wanted, but Lisa had owned it.

Would Lisa Jankowski have known Chris Van der Beke in high school? There were about four hundred graduates in their class. Chris hadn't participated in any activities. He likely worked for his dad when he wasn't at school. Prairie found it hard to believe their paths would have crossed.

By the time Lisa met Chris, she would have met Chris *Radcliffe*, not Chris Van der Beke. It was possible Lisa hadn't recognized him from high school, if she would even have known him. How impenetrably had Chris protected himself? As they got to know each other, how much did Lisa learn?

In twenty years, Lisa's life had become more and more tightly circumscribed. As Chris's wife, she didn't have the adult woman's version of her high school life. Her social media was interesting for what *wasn't* there—no spa weekends at Kohler or quick vacations in Door County with girlfriends, no big family birthday get-togethers, no backyard barbecues or dinner parties, even though those things were an ordinary part of the lives of women in her social set.

Prairie was inclined to think that Lisa hadn't known Chris in high school. He'd been anonymous. Disconnected. But Prairie was willing to bet that Chris had known Lisa. He'd seen her strength and charisma and wanted it for himself. Then, once he had her, he'd systematically taken Lisa's power away.

It would be a horror story if it weren't so completely ordinary.

It was also still just a story, and not one that necessarily ended in murder. Megan had said Prairie would have to figure out the why and the how. What might Chris have been willing to do, or let happen, to protect himself from exposure?

Prairie wanted to meet with Foster to give him Caitlin's list of Lisa's downline, which Caitlin had finally sent early this morning. She was digging it out of her bag when her phone buzzed again. Foster, surely.

"Hello?"

"I need to talk to you. Can you meet up with me at the park by the school?"

Prairie held the phone away from her face, shocked. "I can. What time?"

"Twenty minutes."

"I'll see you there."

The call disconnected. Before she could lower the phone, a text popped up from Foster.

I can meet now. Kettle's?

Impossible. I'm held up. I'll check back in an hour.

Make it sooner if you can. I'm swamped, but I know we should talk.

I want to, Prairie wrote. Her thumbs hovered to say more, but that's all she had. *I want to.*

She shoved the list back into her bag and pulled out of the center's parking lot, reassuring herself that at least this meeting would be in a public space in full view of the windows of the principal's office and the cameras mounted to the school building.

Would that be enough breadcrumbs if Amber Jenkins decided to smoke her in a public park?

❦

There was only one parking spot available anywhere close to the park where Amber had asked her to meet, which sat on the perimeter of the lot that served as overflow parking for the staff of the gifted school. It was a parallel space exactly the size of Prairie's Accord.

"Shit." She idled at the corner and then saw Amber, sitting on a bench with a tote bag next to her, six feet away from the empty bit of curb.

She pulled up even with the first car, in front of the space. "You can do this, Prairie Nightingale. You can totally, totally, do this."

She turned her wheel, shifted into reverse. Checked her mirror.

"Fuck. Wrong way." She pulled up alongside the first car again and turned the steering wheel the other way. She crept backward at a sharp angle to the street, trying to remember how far she needed to be into the space before she started cutting the wheel back. Not yet. Not yet. She braked hard.

"Mother*lover*." The Accord was at a ninety-degree angle to the curb. She'd waited much too long.

Prairie cranked the wheel, put the car in gear, and pulled out of the spot so fast, her tires screeched. She kept going, braked at the stop sign, hung a right, and lapped the entire park with her cheeks burning. By the time she arrived at the spot again, she'd managed five square breaths and was ready for a third attempt.

She held her breath.

Her back end was more or less in the right place. Her front end jutted out halfway. She was not doing that again, she was *not*.

Prairie tried to keep it breezy as she extracted herself from her car. "Hey!"

Homemaker

Amber had her hand over her mouth, shaking her head. Laughing at her. "I guess you can't do everything."

"The spot was kind of tricky." Prairie stopped in front of Amber.

"Not even a little. I've gotten into smaller in the Escalade."

"Yeah." Prairie pulled on her new jacket hem. "So, what did you need?"

Amber's laughter and smile faded. "We're not friends." She looked away in the direction of the playground equipment.

"No," said Prairie softly. "We're not. I'm sorry. I didn't handle—"

"Don't," Amber interrupted. "Absolutely do not. I'm going to be dealing with the fear my kids felt on that day for *years*, and every single time I do, I'm going to think of you."

The punch of pain in Prairie's chest reminded her of how much she'd hurt in the friendless aftermath of Carmichael's arrest. "That's fair."

Amber quickly looked away again, her mouth tight. "I have something for you, but after I give it to you, I'll tell everyone who asks that you're a liar if you say it was me you got it from."

Prairie glanced over at the cameras mounted to the school building. "Are you sure you want to give it to me, whatever it is?"

"No. But I'm not going to give it to the police. I don't ever want to see or talk to the police again." Amber looked up at Prairie. "Listen. Don't interrupt me."

"I won't."

It took a long, silent minute for Amber to find her words. "When Noah and I started fighting a couple of years ago, I thought it was just stress. He's always been a passionate person. I thought we'd get some counseling, it would be fine. But the more things he tried that didn't work, the worse the fighting got, until it was just this"—Amber cleared her throat—"wildfire. In our house. I knew I had to leave, but I didn't have anything. Then Lisa got me into Kitty Blue, and for a while, it was better. Noah was so excited. Our marriage and family were good."

Prairie knew this part of the story. The part where everything was new, and the woman felt capable and hopeful.

"But I'm sure you've guessed by now how that worked out."

When Amber looked at her, Prairie pressed her lips together.

"He blamed Lisa," Amber said. "And, because of you, the cops figured out he'd even called her a few times and cussed her out. The wildfire started back up. That's when I started turning on our home security cameras when we fought. I never meant for those fights to go *anywhere*"—she jutted her chin at Prairie—"but to a lawyer, so I could figure out the best thing to do for my kids. Instead, the cops watched them. All of them. They watched the one where Lisa had come over and Noah was there. Do you know, do you have any idea, what it's like to realize they are looking at your husband for murder?"

Prairie made herself meet Amber's hurt and angry stare. "I don't."

"Do you have any idea, at all, what it's like to provide the alibi for your own husband in the form of another video of your husband yelling and berating you during the night your best friend disappeared off the face of the earth?"

Prairie shook her head.

"So many times, when I could tell Noah was getting bad, I'd call Lisa. Or I would sit and text her, and she'd stay with me. Keep me company. That night, the night she didn't come home, I could tell that Noah was getting bad, but I didn't call her, because Noah had made me feel ashamed. He'd found out Lisa was paying the lease on my car." Amber glared at Prairie. "I didn't fix the stupid taillight because I didn't want her to get stuck with the fee, but what if I could've saved Lisa because she would have been on the phone with me? This is the kind of stuff I think about. On repeat. So I am never talking to the cops again, and you can do some dirty work for me. You owe me that much."

Amber picked up the tote bag between her feet. It was a Girl Scout cookie sales bag. Even though Prairie had guessed what might be inside, she was still a little shaky when the top of the bag flopped over and she saw the silver edge of a laptop sticking out.

202

Homemaker

"She gave it to me about a month ago. She didn't want Chris to find it, because he didn't support what she was trying to do with Kitty Blue. That's all she said about it. I don't know the password."

"It doesn't matter. I'll give it to the police."

"So they can find her."

"That's all any of this has been about." Prairie hadn't wanted those words to sound like an apology—she hadn't earned the right to apologize to Amber and likely never would—but they did.

Amber got up, leaving the bag behind for Prairie. "Lisa didn't want to be married anymore. I didn't tell the cops that, either. They didn't even ask me—not anything like that. Who cares what a wife and mother wants, right? They mostly were interested in the money Lisa was giving me to help me get by and get what I needed for my kids, and in Noah's involvement and what I knew about it, and if I was angry."

Prairie wanted to apologize again, but it wasn't the time.

Amber walked away, headed toward the far corner of the park. Prairie turned to go, and then Amber called out. "Prairie!"

"Yeah?" They were at least twenty feet apart. The wind caught Amber's hair and revealed the bright-red waves under the conservative blond.

"What she actually said was, 'If I could get a divorce and do it like Prairie Nightingale did, I would file tomorrow.' I wasn't going to say, but Lisa liked you. She stood up for you when other people . . . Anyway. I think she would have wanted you to know."

Mostly, Prairie heard the past tense. Her eyes burned as she watched Amber leave with her shoulders back and her arms swinging. Like something was free already.

For a long while, the cameras watched Prairie cry.

A city vehicle drove by and ticketed her car.

Her phone vibrated in the pocket of her new jacket.

> Six o'clock. Kettle's. Be there, or I'll send a cruiser to pick you up.

Wouldn't miss it, she wrote back. But you don't have to impress me with a driver. Save your game for other things.

She watched his three dots cue up and disappear until it was clear he didn't have a comeback for that.

Prairie got in her car, shoving the ticket in the glove box, trying to think about what the next right thing was to do until she had to meet Foster. She set the Girl Scout cookie bag on her passenger seat and considered the silver corner of the computer inside it. She didn't have any urge to open its lid. She'd never be able to guess Lisa's password, and she couldn't risk leaving fingerprints or contaminating whatever evidence might be there for the authorities to find.

She knew that she ought to text Foster back and tell him to come take it from her. She was supposed to feel that it would be wrong to sit on anything, even for another few hours, that the investigation might be able to use to bring Lisa home.

But Prairie didn't think Lisa was coming home.

Right or wrong, when she saw Foster later today, Prairie wanted to be able to tell him a story that would put all the pieces of Lisa's case together and explain how and why her life had ended.

Any consequences of *that* decision, she knew, would be hers and hers alone.

She picked up the list from Caitlin. Skimming over the pages, she willed her brain to make sense of what was a fairly complicated spreadsheet with columns of names, codes, inventory numbers, and contract information. She saw the names of a few women she'd talked to.

Then one name jumped out so dramatically, it might as well have been traced with radium paint.

She fumbled for her phone, her heart nearly breaking her eardrums with its pounding.

"Yes, honey! How are you doing?"

"Joyce. I need you to fire up your witchy genealogy machines and find out everything you can about someone the way you did for Chris and Lisa, their past and what they were like and their old pictures. I'm going to need everything you can get."

For what she wanted to do next, she needed to track down Greg. Prairie signaled and pulled her car away from the curb.

"Of course," Joyce said. "I was on my way to my Learning in Retirement class on Jung, but that might be fun to get started on this afternoon."

"No, you'll have to skip the Jung, and I'm really sorry, but I need it by the time I leave for an appointment at five thirty. Especially if you find anything along the lines of 'a history that no one wanted to write down.'" Prairie sent a silent thank-you to Megan for putting her on this path. "I think that's going to be the thing that finds Lisa."

Chapter 18

Greg was easy to locate. Mondays were his custody days, and he liked to "work from home" at Prairie's dining room table. She'd considered making a rule to prevent this intrusion and fence him off into his own area, but she'd decided instead to give herself permission to interrupt him whenever she liked. It was an arrangement that worked well for them most of the time.

It was not working at the moment, however. Joyce had taken off for a meeting at a library archive just as Prairie arrived home, promising that she had all her monitors firing in service to Prairie's research project, and Prairie had spent the last several minutes prying Greg's attention away from an email in order to explain that she urgently needed his help.

Now, she crossed her arms. "You *told* me to be safe."

"How is it safe to take my ex-wife on a mysterious field trip in the middle of the day ten minutes before I have a videoconference?" Greg took off his glasses and leaned back in his chair. He had a new haircut that was shockingly stylish. She was trying not to comment on it.

"How many videoconferences have you been a part of, Greg? Will the world tip off its axis if you miss this one about"—Prairie looked over his shoulder at his laptop, displaying a screen with a waiting for host to arrive message—"neuroinformatics intersections with AI, current applications and innovations?"

Homemaker

"Possibly. My missing the videoconference would be but one flutter of the butterfly's wings."

Prairie pressed her palm against her forehead. "Please do not. Please just take me in your anonymous car where I want to go."

"Wait, you want to go wherever we're going in my car because it's *anonymous*? Because your car would be picked up by the fuzz?"

"Full disclosure," Prairie said. "It is true that the police have made a note of my Accord. But also, second full disclosure, I probably shouldn't go by myself anywhere at the moment."

"For danger reasons."

"Not exactly. But yes."

Greg pinched the bridge of his nose. "I have to pick the girls up in a few hours."

"I already called Megan. She'll keep them until you get home."

He shut the lid of his laptop gently. "I feel I have done an excellent job lately of respecting boundaries and generally upholding the harmony of our unconventional but *potentially* healthy arrangement."

"Agreed. Will this take a really long time?"

"Will what?"

"The speech I have to listen to before we leave."

"Prairie Nightingale."

She took a deep breath and made a gesture. *Continue.*

"However, I would venture to remark that this request is out of bounds of coparenting or cohomemaking. It is, in fact, the request of one friend to another."

"Indeed," she said.

"But we are not friends."

"I've heard that today already." Prairie thought again of Amber and the bag with Lisa's computer in it—now tucked away inside the safe in Prairie's conference room. Amber had trusted Prairie to do something important, and Prairie intended to honor that gesture with her best effort. She had to know more about Chris Radcliffe. Because she was a mom, she also had to be careful and smart about how she did her digging.

"I think we can explore the *potential* of our friendship," she said to Greg. "Don't you?"

"I'm good with that. Is this how you really want to start, though? Because I was thinking more along the lines of reading the same book and talking about it."

"This is how I want to start. By you driving me around Green Bay and then to an address I will specify later while you are six-feet-plus tall and male."

Greg stood. "Get your stuff and get in the car."

"Yeah?" Prairie jumped up. "Thank you! Oh, and we need to bring Zipper."

"Why, though?"

"It's better if you don't ask a lot of questions."

"Yeah, but it's too weird if you just sit in my car while I drive you around with no clue what's happening."

"Maybe just trust me." Prairie rounded up the dog and hustled to the car. Greg opened the back, and Zipper jumped in, so excited that his sides were heaving while he whined low in his throat and scampered wildly around the back seat.

Greg got into the driver's seat and pushed a button somewhere in the array of LED controls, starting the vehicle with a refined purr. "Where to?"

"Head toward that Kwik Trip you think has the best doughnuts."

"It does have the best doughnuts."

"But you know all the Kwik Trip doughnuts come from the same place, right, Greg? That they're not baking them at the individual stores?"

"Agree to disagree."

Prairie spent most of the drive shoving Zipper away from her ear. He was a terrible car dog. Either he got too excited, loping back and

Homemaker

forth across the rear seat, or he got too anxious and threw up. Prairie was grateful that Zipper seemed to be going with option A.

They stopped at a red light close to where Prairie wanted Greg to turn. "Let me show you where we're going from here." She held her phone out so he could see the screen.

He glanced at the route on Prairie's phone. "No."

"Please. It's important." Prairie stared at the red pin she'd dropped in the location where Lisa and Chris Radcliffe were building their new house.

"I don't think we'll even be able to get close."

"I just want to see. I figured out a place we can park that's out of the way, and then from there, well. We're just walking our dog."

Greg blew out a breath. "You're going to have to tell me how you got to this point." He looked at her and turned onto a curving two-lane road with lots of trees. "I want to know what you've been doing this week."

Prairie told him most everything. Roughly in order, with verifiable facts where she had them. She danced around the subject of Foster somewhat. She and Greg weren't friends quite yet, even if he'd teased her about Foster after the vigil.

He pulled the car into the place she'd found on the map, and Prairie clipped Zipper into his lead and let him out of the car. Greg didn't say anything as they walked to the building site. He was like Maelynn that way. When he had big thoughts or strong feelings, he kept them close.

"See?" she said as the site came into view. "We don't even have to duck under the police tape. They've got that all draped up there."

"I don't think sneaking around the back side of it is going to make us look better when they show up to arrest us."

"We're on a walk."

"Yep. Me and my ex-wife and the family dog, out for an innocent afternoon stroll on an empty piece of private property that may be associated with a crime that's all over the media. Couldn't be more believable."

The trees broke where they had been cleared for the site. Prairie knew they were standing in what would be the home's backyard, but she was disappointed not to be able to make sense of what she was seeing. To her, it mostly looked like mud, graded up to a rise until it met the road, with regular arrangements of holes and concrete squares and rectangles, plus the giant piles of dirt that were ubiquitous at all building sites.

Greg whistled, low. "Wow. I thought I was doing pretty well in the silicon game, but I got into the wrong field."

"It doesn't look like anything. Not at all like a house."

"The deck alone is the size of Montana. I wonder how many stories this is going to be."

"What deck?"

Greg drew with his fingers as if he were connecting some of the holes together like dots. "That deck."

Prairie shook her head. She was reminded of when she and Greg built the addition onto their house for Joyce. They'd just moved to Green Bay and were doing half a dozen remodeling projects at once. Prairie had been pregnant and overwhelmed. She hadn't understood anything about the build—not the blueprints, not what the builders were doing, not how anything they were doing was going to end up being like Greg said it would.

Greg pulled out his phone. He tapped a couple of things and moved next to her so she could see the screen. He had a drawing app up. Though Greg had gone into tech, Anabel came by her skills as an artist honestly. After looking at the site for a few seconds, he sketched in the road with his fingertip, followed by a footprint of a house, drawing rectangles and squares to correspond with what was on the ground. Then he drew circles, like the holes that were closest to them, some with concrete in them, and connected them in a large trapezoid, with diagonal lines across it like deck boards.

"*Oh.*" Prairie looked at the build site and back to Greg's drawing. She could see it now.

Homemaker

"And, for reference, this is about the size of the footprint of the house on Maple." In a different color, he drew a shape that she recognized as the outline of the first floor of her house inside of the outline of the Radcliffes' deck. There was a lot of Radcliffe house left over all the way around.

"Dang." Prairie wandered closer. She wanted to be in the space, to put herself somewhere Lisa would have been and try to feel what Lisa would have felt. Zipper did his name proud, zipping back and forth at the end of his lead, smelling everything. "These huge deck holes, they're for the posts?"

"Footers. All of this is footers."

What had Alison, the decorator, said? *They were still pouring footers last time I was at the site.* "They hold up the deck."

Greg crouched down next to one of the concrete-filled ones. It was a big circle with a cap that stuck up out of the ground. "See this fitting?" He pointed at a fabricated metal piece embedded in the concrete. "That's where the post goes. The post takes the weight of the joists, which take the weight of the deck. You sink the concrete down below the frost line, which gives you stability. Stable concrete, strong post, joists that spread weight out over the posts, decking on top."

"And there's so many of them because it's such a huge deck."

"You got it."

Prairie looked up at the site again. "Are they done with this part? The holes and soil engineering and footers part?"

"I think just about. It won't take long for it to start to resemble a house from this point. There's still some of these footers left to pour on the deck, but since that's less critical, they may finish when they get started on the next phase, or even before they start laying the joists. If it ever gets finished."

Zipper suddenly started pacing and sniffing faster, back and forth, back and forth. "Zipper! Do *not*," Prairie said. He hunched and wiggled his butt, leaving a giant breadcrumb three feet from where she and Greg were standing.

"You have a bag?" Prairie asked.

"In the car." Greg started moving in that direction, then stopped. "No. I hadn't used them in months, so I brought them in and put them next to his leash in the mudroom."

Prairie kicked some dirt over Zipper's offering. "Maybe they would think it was from a wild animal."

"Sure, but just in case they have some kind of a breed-specific dog shit concordance, maybe we should go."

On the way back to the car, he was quiet again. Then, when Zipper stopped to lift his leg on a tree, Greg turned to her. "You told me what you know, what you've found out, and what the police are probably looking for, but not what you think happened."

That was why Prairie had wanted to see the building site. She didn't know every part of the story she was trying to put together—not just yet—but she could feel the pieces starting to move into place somewhere in the back of her mind. She knew she was close. She'd felt the same way driving to Megan's house on the day she'd gone there to ask her about Dr. Carmichael.

"Do you remember when we lived in Seattle, in the second apartment, we had Jerry and Linda across the hall?" she asked Greg.

"They had four full-size tropical birds in that apartment."

"Right, and they fought all the time. Like, *all* the time."

"Linda said couples are supposed to fight, because it clears the air and keeps good communication flowing." Greg pulled on Zipper's lead, and they started back toward the car.

"She also used to say that in a marriage, if you're not fighting and clearing the air, then you're colluding to never talk about everything you should, which is much worse. Then she'd raise her eyebrows at me, like, *Make sure you never collude with your brand-new husband, young lady, or you'll end up divorced.*"

"Prophetic."

"Just nosy, I think. But she was right about colluding. If things aren't going well in a marriage, you're either fighting or you're colluding.

Homemaker

When you're fighting, everything you're unhappy about with the other person is out in the open. When you're colluding, you're still fighting, but silently."

"Give me an example."

"When Maelynn was a baby, we divided up our schedules so that we both had time to do different activities, and we agreed you would make dinner on Monday nights."

Greg's nose wrinkled. "I remember."

"The first week, or the first few weeks, you made dinner. But then the third week, and the fourth week, it got to be about five o'clock, and I could tell you weren't going to make anything, so I stepped in and did it."

He winced. "I never made Monday night dinner again."

"It went back to being my job. You knew you weren't making dinner. I knew you weren't making dinner. You knew I was annoyed with you for not making dinner, and *we* knew I didn't want to point out that you weren't making dinner in case it would open up some bigger fight about what you weren't doing, what you wanted me to be doing, or what I wanted you to do. We colluded to never mention Monday dinner. Or any of the other things we didn't want to fight about."

"But eventually we fought," Greg said, with a frown that made her heart hurt.

"We sure did."

"We never learned how to share the labor, though," he said. "We fought the love right out of our marriage."

Prairie swallowed over unexpected grief. She had loved Greg for a long, long time.

She'd loved him when he accepted a job in Wisconsin, over the phone, while she was in the shower after throwing up all night, newly pregnant with Anabel, even after they had just discussed how great it would be to raise a kid in Seattle. She'd loved him when he worked long hours and couldn't get up with the baby. Not once. She'd loved him all the while as new parts of her brain and body were recruited to make *his* life more comfortable and easy.

But the kind of love that made it possible for them to stay married had been choked by the collective fiery, painful, burning stings of a million tiny cuts.

In the end, her body had decided for her, breaking down in tears, headaches, insomnia. She'd known if she stopped moving through the motions of meals and soothing hands and who needed to be where and when with what, it would all fall apart. Everything. Greg and Anabel and Maelynn would fall apart. Prairie, too. And that was terrifying. She'd thought she was making a home, not holding on to something broken with both hands.

One night after Prairie had been racing away from tears all day, Greg came home late. The girls were in bed. He found her in the dark, vacuuming, clearly distressed, and asked her what she had made him for dinner.

That was the night Prairie started to fight.

The blood from all those cuts that she had willed to scab over came pouring out and blocked up her heart, and she couldn't love this good man anymore. Not unless Greg could look at her with desire unencumbered by what he wanted to take for himself.

They didn't get there.

He grabbed the nape of his neck. "Yeah. But what were Lisa and Chris doing?"

"Chris wanted the house," she said. "He wanted to move Lisa into a giant symbol of their successful, permanent marriage. Lisa didn't want that because she wanted a divorce, not to be stashed away forever in the middle of nowhere. But she wouldn't have been working with Alison on the interior design if at any point she'd decided to come right out and tell Chris the truth. They didn't fight about this house. They colluded. You collude because what you're *afraid* of is a fight. You're afraid to fight because it's scary, potentially even violent."

"Okay."

Homemaker

"But what happens if your collusion is so monumental, Greg, that it's got a deck the size of Montana and a buried past where maybe your wife doesn't even know your real identity? What are you trying to keep from happening when you're colluding at that level?"

Greg's brows knit together, and he let out a breath. When their eyes met, he looked stricken.

"I think what happened is that Lisa decided to go ahead and have the fight," Prairie said solemnly. "She asked for a divorce. Then Chris killed her."

"God."

Cold grief rushed through her. "Lisa was brave. But maybe she didn't know how brave, because she didn't know how big Chris's secrets were and how much shame he was carrying around. I think he was more dangerous than she'd calculated."

Greg thought for a moment. "You don't think Kitty Blue has anything to do with it? They seem pretty damn shady and highly motivated."

"Kitty Blue intersects, but after everything I've learned about Kitty Blue from the bottom up, my main impression is that the Leons are disorganized. If they can't get it together to send orders correctly to people, how are they going to murder or kidnap a housewife in another state right under the nose of her family?"

"That's reasonable. But you told me Chris has a confirmed alibi. He made a really gutting statement just this morning at a press conference that convinced me and seems to have convinced the media. Given everything you've told me so far, *how?*"

Prairie shook her head. "I don't know. But I have a hunch. We need to get back to the house so I can talk to your mom."

Chapter 19

Prairie sat crisscross applesauce in the back seat of her Accord, using Maelynn's car organizer to sort the papers Joyce had given her. She made notes on them with her laptop balanced on her knees.

Lisa's laptop was in the wheel well between her feet, safely tucked inside its bag. Prairie glanced at it every few moments. Her mind wouldn't truly be at rest until she turned it over to Foster, but he wasn't due to arrive for another thirty minutes. She'd parked in Kettle's lot an hour ago. She had so many things she wanted to tell him, she was going to have to prevent herself from tackling him to the ground as soon as she saw him.

Because of the *information*, of course.

Joyce had pulled out the stops, handing Prairie a fat stack of website printouts, property tax records, *Gazette* articles, and more. It was all gold, but Prairie kept going back to two photocopies from East High's 2007 yearbook. One was a professional photographer's shot of kids who'd painted a mural on one of the school's interior walls, the other an amateur snapshot of kids on spring break that was part of a collage. Both pictures showed a pair of girls, their arms around each other, sporting matching knit black beanies, skinny legs in tight jeans, and black Vans. They could have been twins, though the girl Prairie was interested in had hair to her waist and a smaller smile.

Dawn Mitchell. Chris Radcliffe's office manager. The woman Foster had been watching at the vigil.

Homemaker

Her senior portrait was in the book, too. In 2007, they were still using a black photographer's drape that gave the girls a modest V-neck under their collarbones, but Dawn had defied the conservatism of the drape with a thin leather choker that held a silver anarchist charm—quite the statement alongside her captured-ball septum ring and her unpolished, wild mane of hair. She wasn't smiling, which made her appear far younger than her age. The precision black eyeliner and spiky mascara gave her the look of a kid who'd gotten into her mother's makeup.

Each senior was provided a small box to add a personal message under their picture. Hers said, *Never let them tell you that what saves your life is a hobby. —Raven*

The second girl was identified in the mural photo as Jayme Yaeger. Joyce had found her, one class year behind, among the seniors of 2006.

Prairie grabbed her phone and pulled up Facebook. The profile picture for the first result matched the photos so closely that it appeared Jayme hadn't aged one bit since high school. She wore battered jeans and a black T-shirt, and she'd looped her arms around the neck of a handsome bearded man with a guitar. Jayme had her own nail art and massage therapy business, its phone number listed in her public profile information.

Prairie called the number. A woman's voice picked up on the second ring. "Jayme Yaeger?"

"That's me! Are you looking for an appointment? I'm booked out the rest of this month unless you have a wedding party that needs nails done on a weekend morning."

"Actually, I'm calling with the Green Bay Business Incubator." The story lie came so easily, Prairie was a little ashamed of herself. "We've started doing profile slideshows about our mentors to show at our monthly luncheons, and we always include a 'throwback' series of slides featuring our mentor just for fun, so everyone can see how far the person's come. I'm putting together one for Dawn Mitchell, and someone gave me your number as an old friend who might have a cute story or picture."

Jayme went so quiet, Prairie checked her phone screen to make sure the call hadn't dropped. "Hello? Sorry if this isn't a good time."

"No, it's okay. It just took me a minute. No one I knew called her Dawn. We all called her Raven. But I haven't heard from her for years."

"Oh, okay. If this wouldn't be something you'd want to do, I understand." Prairie crossed her fingers.

"No, it's all right. Do you know who gave you my name and number?"

Prairie's mouth started talking before her brain caught up. "The receptionist at the incubator did, but she isn't the person who knows you. And I'm just a volunteer. I think she said she got it from someone who gets massage from you?"

"Oh, I bet it was Katie," Jayme said. "She does a business class, maybe with you guys? I trade massage with her for hair color."

"That sounds right!" Prairie quickly pressed onward. "We mostly want to get a sense of what Dawn—Raven—was like back then. If you had a quick story or two, and any pictures to text me or email?"

"I've got pictures, I guess. They're mostly crappy cell phone shots from way back. I probably used to have better ones, but I have no idea where to look. I don't know if you'll want them in your inspirational slideshow."

"I do have some yearbook pictures already. There's one in front of a mural at your high school."

Jayme laughed. "Oh, jeez. Well. Raven and I were pretty inseparable for a while. She was a year ahead of me, and I met her because I was dating a guy who was stepbrothers with the guy in her class who she had a massive crush on. He had a band, Nowhere Fast. They had a few okay songs but mostly were all talk. Raven was an amazing guitarist and singer. Not just high-school good. The summer after she graduated, she started doing YouTube videos before YouTube was big. Some of it was covers, but she was also writing and recording her own songs. Maybe the videos are still up. She used 'Ravenell' for her name on the account."

"After high school, did you guys stay friends?"

"For a few years. Her dad made her do those Microsoft certificates at the technical college. She liked computers. She would talk about recording software and making her own album, but she never seemed to get around to it. We partied, we were dumb kids. I finished massage therapy school and was working at Clarity Massage at the mall, and she hooked up with a temp agency, so we saw each other less and less. You know how it goes."

"I do. Everything changes so fast."

"Right? I kept after her to do something with her music, and for a while she had a regular gig at that bar, the tiki-themed one with good live music." Jayme paused. "Key West."

"I've driven past that place."

"They loved her. She drew crowds. Then the nine-to-five sucked her in. That contractor guy she got a job with. I saw her sometimes after that, and we'd party, but then I got pregnant with my daughter, so I wasn't going out as much. The last time I really talked to Raven was for my baby shower. I didn't even recognize her at first. She looked like Pam on *The Office*, and she was going by Dawn. But for your slide show you should say that she was talented. She should've been the person at our high school who got famous. Even our teachers wanted her to go for it."

Prairie looked out the car window. The sky was pretty. She felt tired. "I will. I'm curious. Did she ever get together with the guy in the band?"

Jayme laughed. "God, no. I mean, tons of them were half in love with her at any given moment. Girls, too, honestly, but she never seemed to realize it. She always went for the guy who was never going to give her the time of day."

There was a human screech in the background on Jayme's end of the call, followed by a wail, and Jayme told Prairie she had to go. As the connection dropped, Prairie watched Foster round the corner and open the door to Kettle's.

He was early. Some inconvenient part of her heart gave a small thud.

It would be nice if she'd had a few more minutes to try to sort out what she thought about Jayme Yaeger and Dawn Mitchell before she went inside, but Prairie didn't feel like her exhausted brain was likely to spit out anything brilliant. She'd heard too many stories that sounded like eulogies for women's potential. She was carrying too many broken pieces inside her heart.

As she started gathering her stuff for her meeting, the photocopy with Dawn's senior picture slid into the footwell. Prairie reached for it. It was folded in half.

A distant chime in her head rang, connected to no particular thought. She smoothed it out and stared at the crease, trying to figure out what she was looking at.

Then she saw it.

"Oh, shit." Prairie felt the blood drain from the part in her hair, icy, all the way to the back of her neck. She reached up, hands shaking, and turned on the interior light.

She looked at all her papers again.

Then she scooped everything up as quickly as she could and scrambled out of the car and into Kettle's.

She sat down at what must've been Foster's regular table, leaning over to gently liberate the files and papers from her full arms onto the tabletop. Foster nodded a greeting from the counter, where he was second in line. He raised his scar-bisected eyebrow and pointed at the menu. Did she want anything?

She shook her head. She couldn't eat. Thinking was using up her available resources.

Prairie tapped open YouTube on her phone and put in the profile name Jayme had given her, guessing at the spelling. Ravenell. It came up with a cover photo of a guitar on its side, a flowered strap draped over the strings. The menu of videos below only showed one. She clicked on the "About" page, and it said Ravenell had joined in June 2005 and had a hundred and sixty thousand views. The lone video left on her channel had been uploaded in 2011. Prairie dug through her bag to find her AirPods and pushed play.

In the video, Dawn's hair was shorter than it had been in high school, though not quite as short and salon-mussed as at the vigil. She wore an oversize, soft top that fell off her shoulder, and her arms were bare, revealing a colorful half sleeve, a collarbone tattoo of a flock of birds in silhouette, and a wrist tattoo designed to look like a bracelet of ivy. Instead of facing the camera, she was turned in profile to her fingers on the frets.

It only took a few bars of Dawn playing and singing for Prairie to understand why Jayme had been so complimentary. Dawn's voice was smooth and light, with the kind of gravel on the low notes that made people want to turn something up and sing along. Prairie didn't recognize the song. She would bet money it was an original.

"What's that." Foster watched over her shoulder as Dawn played the last few notes.

Prairie pulled out her AirPods. "That's Dawn Mitchell."

He sat down and rubbed a hand over his eyes. "Chris's office manager at Bay View Development."

"Yeah. Back then, people called her Raven."

"She looks different."

"Let's start there, actually." Prairie started shuffling through her papers. "With how she looked then and how she looks now."

"Hi, by the way."

Prairie glanced at him. Foster had that almost-smile she now knew was reserved for her and was not just his general smile for anyone. It cut right through the wild cacophony the day had whipped up inside her.

"Hi," she said, into the quiet space between them.

She was a mother, and an age where she paid particular attention to skincare and always wanted more sleep but never got it. But she'd gone on the apps for a reason. She recognized the ache she felt as want, as something that had snuck in after healing from the end of her marriage.

Prairie wanted. She wasn't sure if what she wanted was companionship or sex or some other unimaginable thing that might happen on a date, but she'd wanted it enough to risk dating.

She hadn't known how much she'd wanted someone to like her. To notice her. To laugh at her wit and look at her like she was hot, and take her seriously enough for her to need to make boundaries.

She didn't know Foster. Not yet. But she did know she liked how he made her feel when she saw him and when her phone buzzed with one of his stern little texts. She liked that she hadn't met him on the apps. She'd met Foster doing exactly what it was she wanted to be doing.

Prairie had never met a man that way before.

"It's not Thursday," he finally said. "But I don't care."

"I don't care, either."

Color slashed across the top of his cheekbones, and he smiled at her again.

That was enough for now.

"Here." Prairie gave him the yearbook photo.

Foster cleared his throat and sat down across from her. "Raven, I presume."

"Yes. Now hold on." She pulled out the other photocopy and handed it to him. When he looked at it, his FBI agent face snapped immediately into place.

Prairie leaned across the table and folded the yearbook photo along the crease.

"No," he said, his voice flat.

"Look, I'm aware that you're really busy. I'm sorry. I'm not telling you how to do your job, but also I can't unsee that resemblance." She pointed at the papers in his hands. "I can't. And despite the fact that I am woefully undercaffeinated and have only eaten a handful of miniature Snickers I found in my bag on the way over here, I don't think I'm hallucinating."

Homemaker

Foster put down the papers and scrubbed both hands over his face. He extracted the Tic Tacs from his pocket and shook four out into his hand. "I've had a long day."

"I imagine."

"I'm up to my neck in chaos. Tomorrow's more than a week since she disappeared."

He was looking at her the same way Maelynn did when she was certain, by virtue of Prairie being her mother, that Prairie was responsible for whatever physical or emotional discomforts Maelynn was experiencing. For this reason, Prairie knew it was best just to let him unspool these complaints at her feet, where she could gather them up sympathetically like they were a mewling baby animal she would take care of. "That must put even more pressure on you," she said.

One corner of his mouth hitched up in a smirk. He'd caught her placating tone. He shook his head slightly, then sat up straight and adjusted his sleeves. "Should I stop?"

"No, you go ahead. I have about two minutes' leftover listening capacity, and I've decided to give it to you."

"Lucky for me." He sounded amused. This was a man who could laugh at himself. Who didn't expect her to solve his problems. "The police chief's starting to lose it. The media's a full-on circus, and he wants to know why they were a step ahead of us with Kitty Blue. He asked me specifically how a high school student with a podcast had access to interviews we didn't, and did I know who the source might be. Of course, I can't tell him that, because that's technically FBI knowledge, because it's *my* knowledge, and my inability to be of assistance in the way he wants is not helping to smooth over the rough spot in our interagency cooperation."

"A *lot* of pressure." Prairie put her hand on top of the bag with the laptop in it. She hoped she hadn't made a mistake when she'd decided not to give it to Foster hours ago.

"Kitty Blue is a nightmare."

"I'll bet."

"They're out of state, which means coordinating additional layers of cooperation, not to mention lawyers are crawling out of the woodwork. The Leons are in the wind, no one seems to know where. They have a literal compound in Arkansas, of all places, and a ranch—who has a ranch, besides Harrison Ford?—over by Grand Junction, Colorado."

"I think Harrison Ford's ranch is in Wyoming." Prairie decided to try another strategy that worked with Maelynn. "You should have a hot beverage."

"I ordered tea, but who knows how long that's going to be."

"I'm going to check on it," Prairie said. "While I do, why don't I give you this for you to take a look at? It belonged to Lisa." She handed him the tote bag, careful to keep the fabric over the computer's shiny surface so he wouldn't touch it accidentally. "It was turned over to me anonymously, and we don't know the password, but I hope it still might be helpful."

It took her several long minutes at the counter. She almost had to pry the teapot from the barista's reluctant hands.

"Here you go." She put the pot down in front of Foster. "I grabbed the entire sugar butler from the coffee station."

He'd lifted the bag away from the laptop and used the fabric to slide the computer partway out without touching it. Prairie watched him push it carefully back into the bag and place it between his feet. "You turned over what might be vital evidence to a missing persons investigation in a Girl Scout cookie bag."

"I hope it's vital. I don't think the bag will contaminate the evidence in any way. I didn't touch it, only the bag." She slid into her seat.

"Given to you anonymously."

"Let's say by a tipster."

"That'll be one more fun thing for me to explain." Foster poured himself a tea and dumped in five sugars and all the cream from the miniature pitcher.

"Have you ever heard of a work wife?"

"A what wife."

Homemaker

"A work wife. Or husband. A work spouse. It's someone you connect with at work. You share jokes and bitch about work with them so you don't have to take your issues home to your real spouse. A friend told me about it."

"Okay."

"But I got to thinking about if it was reversed. Say you're a man—"

"I am."

"—you have problems at home, and you start taking home problems to your work wife."

"I wouldn't do that."

Prairie smiled. "I believe you. Because if you did that, all the friendly, collegial support between you and your work wife would start to look like something more. From the outside, it would look like emotional enmeshment, say, or even an emotional affair. Intimacy that could lead to a physical affair."

"Could look that way from the inside, too, if I wasn't careful."

"Yes."

He steepled his hands. "You're suggesting Dawn is Chris's work wife. You're implying she might know something more than anyone who's talked to her has given her credit for." Foster poured himself another cup of tea. Dumped in five sugars. Prairie waited for him to get a refill on his tiny pitcher of cream before she could continue.

"What I found out, or really, what Joyce found out—"

"Joyce, your ex-mother-in-law."

"Yeah, the one who's retired from the DNR. She's also an experienced genealogist."

"Right, obviously. Your amateur sleuthing buddy who is your ex-mother-in-law. Sometimes my late wife's second cousin, who's a chef, gives me a hand investigating a capital case here and there."

He smiled, and she realized he wasn't making fun of her. He was approving of her.

"Genealogy is a very exciting new forensics field. She recently got back from a conference."

225

"Tell me what she found out."

"I'll show you. That way you don't have to sit through one of my stories." Prairie handed him Joyce's report, which included the information she had discovered about Van der Beke Concrete and Gravel and its generation-by-generation disintegration into obscurity, Chris's family history and his name change, the yearbook photos, and his mother's brief obituary and death certificate.

He flipped through the pages slowly, forgetting about his tea, rereading some parts. Taking it seriously.

When he was finished, Prairie gave him the pages with everything she'd found out about Chris's business, including her marginal notes and highlights about how Chris never mentioned his background. She included her handwritten notes about when Lisa and Chris had met and her attempts to put that on Chris's timeline as a businessman. Finally, she handed him the fax from Caitlin McClain listing her full downline, on which Prairie had highlighted Dawn's name. "Do you want me to get you more tea or anything while you're reading?"

He flipped to the second page of her papers. "Thank you. A cookie."

"One cookie, coming up."

She got herself one, too. Counter service for two cookies took a thousand years. But when Prairie put more cream for his tea and a cookie in front of him and sank back into her seat with her own, he was still reading. "What do you think?"

He turned to the last page and put down the sheaf of papers, looking at her with his interested gray eyes. "Tell me the story, Prairie."

This time, she was ready.

"Chris Radcliffe concealed the difficulty and pain of his early life, and maybe even the violence of that life, behind a new name. He wanted the most popular girl in high school. He had to wait, but he pulled it off. He married a bright, outgoing, educated, well-connected woman and then made her disappear. He was a man who couldn't keep hold of this woman—a woman he fundamentally didn't understand—except by controlling her."

Foster leaned forward, listening.

"He needed his wife's collusion for it to work," Prairie said. "He needed her to pretend with him that their marriage was enviable and their lives were privileged and rare. He needed her to pretend that her happiness depended on raising children and caring for her husband alone in a huge house far from everyone else. He needed it because other people's admiration and envy of that life was the foundation of Chris Radcliffe's self-image, and that self-image was the only thing keeping Chris Van der Beke and everything that had happened to him at bay."

Foster thought about that for a moment. "But his wife stopped colluding when she decided to go after Kitty Blue."

"Yes, and that threatened Chris with exposure."

"Exposure of a less-than-perfect life. Something ugly that would tarnish his image."

"He'd figured out how to control Kitty Blue by charming the Leons and telling Lisa how to run her business. How to make money and manage Lisa's brand. When the Leons started losing control, he thought he had Lisa under his, and that she would walk away from Kitty Blue with her bag of cash and let the chips fall for the Leons."

"But she had a different plan."

"She had a conscience. She wanted to put things right. And maybe, *maybe*, Chris would still have found a way to manage her and what she was trying to do if she hadn't stopped colluding in the biggest and most absolute way she could."

Foster's posture perfected itself. His eyes were bright.

"She asked him for a divorce," Prairie said.

He hadn't known that. "Verifiable."

"I can verify she *wanted* to," she confirmed. "And do you remember what I said to you about divorce the first time we met?"

"Statistically, it's dangerous for a woman to get married to a man. Even more dangerous to get divorced."

"You're a good listener."

"You're hard to ignore." Minuscule half smile.

"So that's the *why*. It answers the question of what Lisa could have done that threatened Chris so utterly, he would be willing to repeat a violent pattern in his own history."

"You don't think Chris's mom just fell down the stairs."

Prairie shook her head. "And I'm hoping that my *why* is confirmed somewhere on that computer," she added, "because my source is somewhat reluctant to come forward to corroborate that Lisa wanted out."

"We'll pull the computer apart tonight, is my guess. Don't worry. But if we can't, or nothing's there about your why . . ."

"I'll talk to her. She loved Lisa, so I don't actually think it will be that hard." Prairie broke off a piece of her cookie. "The *how* part was trickier—at least until I remembered about work spouses. For most people, a work spouse is a positive relationship, right? They have your back, they listen to you, they help you blow off steam and put things in perspective. Unless you're the kind of guy who only knows how to offer people control. It's going to suck to be that guy's work wife. I had to figure out why someone would accept that role anyway."

"You had to figure out Dawn."

"I put Joyce on it." Prairie ate her bite of cookie so she had something to swallow past the very sad feelings about Dawn. "Joyce found Raven. Another talented, well-loved, interesting woman who, according to an old, close friend who I found and talked to, had a thing for unavailable men, and who completely changed after she started working for Chris."

"Remind me when that was."

"About seven years ago. If you look at how lean his permanent staff is, given the projects he's got going and the size of his firm, it's likely she does more than an office manager's job. I think Dawn makes everything work. Probably she makes everything work so well that Chris has much less control over that office than he thinks, but the important thing is that what Chris has with Dawn is perfect, unthreatened collusion. Chris picked the best woman he could think of to be his wife, and he relied on her competence while he limited and controlled her. That's not a

Homemaker

man who's only going to do this at home. He's going to do it at work, too, if he can, and he's going to find a woman like his wife to do it to."

"I'm following."

"What if Chris Radcliffe is forced by events unfolding at home to ask Dawn for her help—the kind of help that's so dark, and so exposed, that maybe it's irresistible to a woman with a thing for unavailable men who's been waiting for this one man to break in her direction for a long time?"

Foster looked out the window. "Seven years."

"Seven years, and her life is all work."

"It's a big jump from an unhealthy and unrequited relationship with your boss to conspiracy to murder." Foster looked back at Prairie. "If I'm understanding you correctly."

"You are."

"There's nothing in it for Dawn." Prairie was about to interrupt, but Foster held up a hand. "No, bear with me a moment. I understand your feeling, but we've already agreed, a story's just a story until you've got verifiable facts. If we go back to statistics, you're suggesting something rare. Both conspiracy and a woman perpetrator. What's more, my people have talked to Dawn. We've also talked to people who know Chris, who minimally know his routines and schedules and have been able to verify, within our very important window, his whereabouts. There has not been one single whiff of an affair."

Foster's voice was low and fluent, focused. He was inviting her into confidences about his case that Prairie was sure he wasn't strictly supposed to. He was offering her trust. He believed what she'd told him, that she wanted to know where Lisa was. She wanted to know what happened to her, same as him.

Same as him.

Foster put his elbows on the table and gave her his full attention. "But let's set statistics aside and cross the streams. Dawn is somehow involved with Kitty Blue and was conspiring with them, and Chris was letting it happen to protect himself from the fallout of what Lisa had uncovered. This at least gives Dawn a financial motive, possibly. Although the FBI dug pretty deep into Kitty Blue, and I'm telling you, that scenario is speculative fiction."

Prairie wanted to say, *I need to talk to her. I know what questions to ask.* But she was worried he'd tell her not to.

She did not need permission.

Foster reached into his pocket for his Tic Tacs. He opened the lid in a practiced gesture with his thumb and shook a few out. He stared at the little white mints in his hand. "Tell me what you're thinking."

"For a change, why don't you tell me what *you're* thinking?"

He tapped the photocopies she'd put in front of him. "This will get examined to its bones, along with everything else you've shared. We have ways we can verify what you have here."

"You think it's good. It's worth looking at." Prairie glanced at his hand on the picture on top of the stack. The one folded in half. She hoped they *could* verify what she'd seen. Or disprove it.

"I do. It is."

"Okay." She closed her eyes. "Okay." She stood up and hitched her bag over her shoulder. "Thank you, then, Agent Rosemare, for listening."

One of his eyebrows lifted by a millimeter. "You're taking off."

"I should get home. I ran out on Joyce, so I owe her an update. Plus, my ex's cat had half her ear ripped off and maybe has diabetes. I need to check in."

The eyebrow hitched a little higher. "I have a little time to stay and talk. For you."

Foster let her see then. He let her see that if she stayed, he would want to know more, but about her. He would answer all her questions, but about him. He would walk her to her car.

He'd kiss her before she got in and drove away, and when he did, every bit of his serious, stern focus would be in that kiss.

230

Homemaker

"Again," Prairie said, hoping he couldn't tell she'd been holding her breath, "it appears that I need to remind you, I am very busy." But her dimples were irrepressible.

"Homemaking."

"Yes."

"It's interesting, though," Foster said, "how priorities start to shift when you're working a case."

"Is that what we're doing?" She pointed back and forth between them. "You and me, we're working a case, like Cagney and Lacey?"

Foster didn't answer.

He smiled, though. All the way.

Whoa.

"Keep in touch," he said.

"Oh, you'll be hearing from me soon."

She started toward the door. As she pushed it open, he called out to her, "Hey, nice jacket."

Prairie turned around. He had not been looking at her jacket.

"It's definitely *not* Thursday, Agent."

She walked out into the evening, her own smile entirely for herself.

Chapter 20

Dawn's house was white and small, set between a small cream house and a small beige house. It was part of an inexpensive neighborhood built for working-class families in the late seventies or early eighties, the kind of neighborhood that so embodied Green Bay, with its tasteful Madonna and Child creches and tidy landscaping, that it made Prairie feel like an outsider even though she'd lived here for fifteen years.

Cars were parked along the street. She had to go a couple of blocks away to find a spot she could drive into. The walk gave her a chance to breathe, listening to the last birdcalls of the day and the kids yelling at each other in their yards on a pretty spring evening growing dark.

It would be nice to see her kids when she got home.

Dawn's tiny front yard was as perfect as her neighbors', with plastic solar lights staked in the ground on either side of the walk leading to her front door. Standing on the porch, Prairie could hear the television and see its blue-flickering lights through the sheers over the picture window to her right.

There was no doorbell, but as Prairie knocked, she spotted a camera mounted where the awning over the front door met the house. Breadcrumbs.

She stepped back so Dawn could look at her through the camera on what Prairie guessed would be her phone. Just a nice lady with a polite smile.

Homemaker

The volume on the TV went down. The main door opened, and Dawn stood on the other side of the storm door. She was still in work clothes, a cute A-line skirt with a bird on the pocket and a pink, long-sleeved crewneck sweater. The big, dark curls of her messy bob drooped attractively over one side of her face.

"Hi!" Prairie gave a little wave. "My name's Prairie. We haven't met, but my kid goes to school with Lisa's kids, and I organized her vigil. I'm really sorry to drop by unannounced."

"Hi," said Dawn. To her credit, she hid any confusion she must have been feeling with a pretty smile. "Um, it's okay. I'm sorry I don't remember you, though." She unlocked the door and opened it, leaning on it so it stayed open. Prairie noticed a tortoiseshell cat flicking her tail, watching from the back of a cute duck cloth sofa. "Can I help you?"

"I was actually wondering if you had time to talk. I know this must be a really difficult and hard-to-manage time at work and with Mr. Radcliffe. I'm sure the police have had all the usual conversations with you—and who knows how many other people, like the media—but I thought you could use someone neutral to listen."

The truth was a gamble, and not socially usual, but Prairie was trying to speak to the part of Dawn who must be incredibly alone right now. She believed Dawn deserved a chance to tell her story, just for herself, at least once.

Dawn's brows knit together. "Well. That's very sweet, but I'm okay. It *has* been pretty distracting. I had to get a new phone number, for one, once the media discovered mine. We all did at the office. They were trying to get a hold of us to talk about Mrs. Radcliffe. No one has come to my door, though." She raised her eyebrows, indicating the outrageousness of Prairie's behavior, though her expression was friendly.

"I was homeschooled and don't have a good handle on social norms."

Dawn laughed, surprised. "For real?"

"Yep, in Oregon. Where I grew up wasn't *technically* a commune, but we had a community kitchen and had to sign up for our time to make meals, and one time my mom bartered a blanket she crocheted for a pair of Guess jeans to give me for my birthday."

"Oh my God. Was there a cult leader?" Dawn relaxed her body and stuck her hand in her bird pocket.

"No, but I would definitely know what to do to get that gig going."

Dawn laughed again. "Well, I am doing mostly okay, but it was nice of you to think of me." The cat appeared and rubbed its face against Dawn's bare leg, surveying Prairie with friendly imperialism. "That's Tillie."

Prairie knelt down and held out her hand. Tillie ventured a few steps onto the porch and allowed Prairie to pet the top of her head and scratch gently behind her ears. "I talked to an old friend of yours today."

"Oh, really? Who?"

"Jayme Yaeger."

For a second, Dawn's expression went eerily blank, and then color flooded her cheeks. "Wow. There's a name I haven't heard in a long time." She grabbed the cuffs of her sweater and pulled them up, then shoved them back down. It looked like something she did when she felt uncomfortable.

"Your tattoos are beautiful. You don't have to cover them up, if that's what you're doing." Tillie arched and flopped onto the concrete porch. She batted at Prairie's hand until Prairie began to stroke her side.

Dawn shrugged. "It's a little bit conservative at work for them. I'm actually thinking about getting them removed."

"They go with being a singer, though. You used to play at Key West, that's what Jayme said? When you were Raven."

"Whoa. *Ha.*" Dawn yanked her sweater to her elbows again. Prairie recognized the ivy-circlet tattoo right away, and the bottom tendrils of Dawn's half sleeve. There was an outline of a raven on the soft underside of her other forearm that reminded Prairie of the crow in the backyard of Chris Radcliffe's childhood home. Maelynn's corvids, gathering around their dead to find out what had gone wrong and put it right.

That's what you're doing, she'd said.

But sometimes what went wrong wasn't anything a woman could protect herself from.

"That was a long time ago," Dawn said. "I don't play anymore."

"Jayme told me you were good. That you could've done it professionally, and she wasn't the only person to think so."

"She was always super encouraging." Dawn picked at the bird on her pocket and then glanced behind her as though looking for a way to wrap up the conversation. Prairie needed to think of a way to make Dawn invite her in, and fast. "But what I ended up doing—it's a good job. Chris has given me a lot of responsibility, and I'm good at it. Honestly, I wasn't ever going to make it as a musician. It was fun, and hey, I liked the parties, but I'm happy where I'm at."

"It must feel good to have a job where your boss depends on you."

Dawn shrugged and reached up to tuck a big curl behind her ear. A solid silver bangle that Prairie hadn't noticed before unhooked from the knob of her wristbone and slid partway up her forearm. Prairie recognized it. She had a very similar one at home that Greg had bought years ago from Tiffany after she told him she was pregnant with Maelynn.

"That's pretty." Prairie pointed to her own wrist.

Dawn touched the bangle. "Thank you. It was a nice surprise."

"I bet. He did a good job." A Tiffany bracelet from a husband to mark an important occasion—a minor anniversary, a second pregnancy—was the sort of present a wife found sweet. But a Tiffany bracelet from the man you were having an affair with would be a bigger deal by several orders of magnitude.

"He did." Dawn's smile was small and private.

"Did Lisa find out?" Prairie asked this gamble of a question in the same voice she used to talk to her girls when they were upset.

She heard Dawn's breath rush from her body.

Prairie felt like she'd lost and won at the same time. She liked Dawn. She wished Dawn could have listened to Jayme, her teachers, or those first fans in that crowded bar. Surely among her fans there had been at least one ordinary and good man who recognized her talent but didn't want to collect it or diminish her. Prairie hated that Dawn had never met that man. Although she might have met and rejected him. Sometimes that was how it went.

"Why don't you come inside." Dawn held the door and moved out of Prairie's way.

With the cat at her heels, Prairie stepped into the house. The entry opened right into the living room, which gave way to a small eat-in kitchen in one corner and to a narrow hallway with three doors facing it on the other side—probably two bedrooms and a bath. For all its limitations of space, the house had refinished wood floors and the nice duck-cloth-covered furniture Prairie had noticed from the doorway. Everything was spare and neutral without feeling empty, like a spa waiting room. The place looking so nice, so *carefully* nice, made Prairie's heart hurt. Dawn was a woman who wanted things for herself. A good home and a good job.

Dawn turned off the flickering TV as she sat on the arm of one of her chairs, not yet committing to a social visit. She didn't offer Prairie anything.

That was okay. Prairie would have felt guilty accepting hospitality from her. She sat across from Dawn on the edge of the lone unupholstered chair, an extra from the kitchen set. "I'm not here to judge or to start something," Prairie said. "But I need to show you this." She reached into her bag and pulled out the photocopies of the three photos she'd presented to Foster at Kettle's. She put them down in a row on the raw-edge coffee table. Tillie jumped up and stretched out beside them.

Dawn slid off the arm of the chair into the seat. She scanned the papers Prairie had arranged on the table and brought her hands to her mouth. Her eyes filled with tears, spilling over instantly.

Prairie put her finger on the trail cam picture, where the woman's face was lit from underneath by her phone, her eyes and brow and hair in shadow. Next to it, Prairie had laid Dawn's senior portrait, the unsmiling mouth and neck and smooth chin so precisely the same as

Homemaker

the features in the trail cam photo that it had given Prairie chills to look at them together.

The third picture was Lisa's senior portrait, laid next to Dawn's. They weren't twins, but they could be mistaken for sisters. They had similar fine, petite features and the same mouth that seemed ready to smile even when it wasn't.

Tears kept spilling over Dawn's hands, pressed against her lips like they were trying to keep her silent. Her hair came loose from behind her ear and bounced over one eye. "Where did you get these?"

"Different places," Prairie said. "I had help from my mother-in-law and what the police have released to the public. I've talked to a lot of people this week, trying to put together what happened to Lisa."

"Are you friends with her?" Dawn's lips were wet, her cheeks pink.

"Once, a little bit. I would have liked to be better friends. It didn't work out, but I'm a homemaker, too. Like I said, our kids go to school together. And I'm someone who, when I feel like there's an injustice, has a hard time letting it go." Prairie gathered up the photocopies. "Dawn, I really did come here tonight because I thought you might need someone to listen. That's the truth. Nothing's going to be the same after tonight, and even if you don't talk to me now, someone else will come knocking pretty soon. The people you talk to next are going to be focused on getting justice for Lisa. I want to hear *your* story. I get the impression that no one's been looking at you or paying attention to you except Chris Radcliffe for a long time. I wonder if, in the days since Lisa disappeared, your world's gotten quieter and darker than you had any way to anticipate."

Dawn put her hands down. Her head was shaking no, like some other part of her brain was still trying to keep her from talking.

"Will you tell me?" Prairie asked. "If you do, I will make sure that whenever anyone asks me what you said, no matter how many times or under what circumstances, I will tell *your* story without adding or taking out or speculating. And I'll also say that what I want for you is a good lawyer to be with you before you tell your story to them. The very best one. I just need to know, to start with, if that's you in Lisa's van."

Dawn wiped the tears off her cheeks, first one side, then the other. She watched Prairie put the photocopies away and let out a long sigh that dropped her shoulders from her ears.

"I didn't hurt Lisa," she said. "But you're right. That's me in Lisa's van."

Chapter 21

When Prairie first met Foster at the vigil, he'd told her, *I don't know anything until I know it.* Prairie had thought she understood what he meant.

She couldn't possibly guess what Dawn was about to say, but Prairie knew that whatever it was, it would be a story that changed lives— rippling out from this room and washing through the entire city of Green Bay.

It would be the truth.

"Tell me what happened," she said.

Dawn grimaced. "The last time I talked to Lisa, she was herself in every way, and that was almost two weeks before the day she disappeared." She spoke slowly, each word rasping from her throat. "I didn't hurt her. I didn't even see her."

Dawn was not denying being involved in what had happened to Lisa. She meant, Prairie was certain, that Chris had been the one who hurt Lisa. Chris had been the one who did something with Lisa's remains. But she had to be sure. "When you say that you didn't see her, do you mean that you didn't see her after she had passed away? You didn't see her body?"

Dawn squeezed her eyes tight, the tears still coming. She was shaking. "He didn't even *say* 'b-body.'" Dawn hardly could, either. "He told me she had gone away. Just gone away forever. He was crying. He said he put her to bed. I had never seen him like that. He didn't know what to do, so he came to me."

"But when he said she had gone away, you understood he meant that she'd died."

Dawn nodded. Prairie's lungs felt as though they'd been crushed in a fist. "Where did Chris come to you?" She said his name deliberately, wanting to give Dawn permission to say it, too.

"I was in his room at the conference hotel. Not because . . . It was work. He had to go home to talk to Lisa. She'd called him home before the conference even ended to talk, but he was supposed to be doing a software demo on his laptop at the time she wanted him at home, so I said I would do it. I ate lunch in his room and did the training, waiting for him to come back. I didn't know any of it was going to happen." Dawn dropped her head into her hands.

"What did Chris ask you to do?"

"Nothing. He came back to the hotel after running home to talk to Lisa and cried at my feet, holding on to my legs, saying that she had gone away, that he had put her to bed. He'd never cried before. His arms were so tight around my legs. He'd never held me so tight." Dawn gathered her cat into her arms.

Prairie understood. "You had to fix it. That's what you do. Especially because he couldn't even ask you, and he couldn't go to anyone but you."

"Everyone believed he was in his hotel room the whole time he'd been gone because I had been doing his live software demo with the rep on screen grab, and he'd left his phone in the room. Sometime last month, he gave up using a belt holder for it because some of the guys he golfs with were teasing him. But he'd been carrying it like that so long, he wasn't used to having to remember it. He kept leaving it places. None of it was on purpose, but my taking over the demo and him leaving his phone is why the police believed he was at the hotel." She spoke more rapidly now, in a no-nonsense tone that Prairie imagined she would use on the phone for business calls.

Homemaker

"Okay."

"It seemed like he just wanted me to help him erase what had happened at home, or rewind it—not hurt anyone. The opposite of that, to help. Really, really *help*. Like I'd be helping Lisa."

"You wanted to help him."

"Yes. I wanted to help him. I remember thinking that helping him was helping Lisa's kids. Her kids were everything to her. She would go in and change the schedules I made for him so that he would spend time with the kids. So they would see their dad and feel like he cared about them and all their events."

Prairie thought of all the work she'd done to make sure Anabel and Maelynn not only spent time with their dad but believed that he wanted to and that he had made the time to do so. She knew Greg loved his girls, but the truth was he didn't know how to prioritize them when he knew Prairie would always put them first.

Lisa was a good mom.

Dawn sucked in a shaky breath. "He was supposed to go to a mixer after the software training. I told him to go ahead and go, and to say hi to a few people so they'd see him. And then he suddenly was fine."

"What do you mean?"

Dawn pressed her face to Tillie. "He was calm. He told me that was a good idea. He said how good I was, that I took such good care of him. I started *retelling* him what happened, the same way I would do to prepare him for a meeting he isn't ready for. I said, 'When Lisa called earlier, she wanted to see you at home, but you couldn't leave until after you did the software demo and dropped by the mixer.' He told me, 'Yes, Lisa wanted me to leave early because she has a migraine and wanted to go to bed, but I told her I couldn't leave until after the mixer, but that I'd be able to stop by home before I picked up the kids.'"

"Is that the only thing he said about Lisa, or did he tell you what happened between them?"

Dawn shook her head. "He didn't tell me anything like that. He only told me that he was going to get his kids from school and eat dinner with them, but later, after they went to bed, he wanted me to come over."

"How would you know when and where to come?" No way had Chris used his cell phone to call Dawn in the window when Lisa had disappeared—not without the police finding the call record.

"We had phones. Throwaway phones, with private numbers. Last year, when things started between us, he gave one to me." Dawn looked down at her cat, cradled in her arms. "I never wanted to get involved with a married man."

Prairie had friends who'd cheated and been cheated on. She didn't judge. Judgment didn't make a whole lot of sense to her as a way to process human behavior. "It's pretty easy to say you wouldn't do something when you're not doing it. It treats it like it's one decision that you make all at once. It's not, though. There are a lot of decisions you make that don't seem like they're hurting anyone until they all add up and they do."

"I was trying to figure out a way to stop it. I found a therapist. I would text her when I wanted to be with him, or if I wanted to reach out to him. She would help me make plans to end it, help me make a script to use with him. One time, I even used it, finally. My script."

"What happened?"

Dawn looked away, toward the door, seeming to search for an explanation. "Chris doesn't have patience to listen. Like, he can't sit in a meeting for any length of time. I always felt like I was grabbing onto his sleeve to get him to stay in the room. If he can think of any reason to, he'll leave a room when people are still talking. It was ten times that bad when we were . . . together. I'd get a text on the phone he gave me, then go to the house."

"What house?"

"The model home. In his neighborhood."

"Good lord." Prairie closed her eyes. She hadn't meant to say that out loud, but sometimes. Some things.

Homemaker

"I know. How stupid am I? It's an almost twenty-minute drive for me! From work or my house. It's four *blocks* from his place." Dawn pushed her fingertips into her eyelids. "But that's what I'm trying to explain. I always feel like I'm trying to get him to stay in one spot for long enough to hear ten of my own words stuck together in a sentence. So then I would do abnormal things whenever he asked me to come to him. Without even thinking."

"But you tried to stop it, you said. You tried to use the script."

"It was one of the times he called me to meet him at the model home. I would park in a turnaround." Dawn looked at her lap. No doubt she was ashamed to say this to Prairie. A stranger.

"By the trail. Where that trail cam is set up."

"I didn't know a camera was there, not until I saw the pictures in the *Gazette*." She let go of the cat to push her hair behind her ear. "But that's where I would park, then walk to the model home. He always had on running clothes, because I think he told Lisa he was going for a run. Then, after . . . he would. Go for a run."

Jesus. Of course he did.

"A month ago is when I decided to end it. He'd started taking my clothes off, but I told him I needed to talk. He made it clear he was stressed. I could tell he was. I knew him. But I did it. I broke up with him. Then, he laughed."

"He laughed?"

Dawn let out a long, shuddering breath. "I was in Lisa's downline. I couldn't afford it, but Chris told me to take out a credit card and invest, and he'd pay the bill via my paycheck. He was stacking Lisa's downline for Kitty Blue. I felt weird about it. He kept making me buy inventory with the card, but the paycheck money stopped coming. He wouldn't talk about it. Lisa was the one who talked to me. She told me she was in the process of fixing things with Kitty Blue. She wanted to help me, but she didn't know Chris was the one losing my money. I held her off. That's where it was left until he laughed at me."

"Then what?"

"He asked me how I was going to pay my twenty-two-thousand-dollar credit card bill if we broke up. He told me there was always going to be a me and him, no matter what."

Every muscle in Prairie's body locked up in anger.

Dawn put her nose against the top of Tillie's head. She closed her eyes. "The other times, we would go upstairs, but that time, he backed me up against the kitchen counter. He kissed me. He had never kissed me before, so I was surprised, and I kissed him back. But he pulled up my skirt. I tried to sit down on one of the kitchen chairs to slow him down, but he—he held me up."

That was all it took, then. A boundary, offered without malice, had given this man permission to be angry and violent. Prairie kept her voice steady as she looked right at Dawn, leaning forward. "I understand. I am sorry. I am very sorry that happened to you. It was wrong that it happened to you. He hurt you."

"I didn't end it after that."

"It's okay." Prairie started to take deep breaths. It was what she did when her children were confused or upset, because they would often mimic her without realizing, calming down in the process. "It's okay."

"I didn't know how to. I ghosted my therapist. I just do what he says. This week, I haven't talked to him or seen him except at the vigil. He hasn't come to work. I know what I'm supposed to do and what I'm supposed to say. I know how I'm supposed to feel, even, how Chris probably thinks I feel. I feel a lot of things."

Prairie gave her a moment before she spoke again. "I want you to know that I gave those pictures to law enforcement. I told someone that I thought it was you at the trailhead in Lisa's car. I did that with full awareness that Chris likely had all the power, and there was no way he hadn't hurt you. But I agree with you that you're accountable to Lisa's children, and so am I."

Dawn turned her cheek against the cat's head to look at Prairie. "I'm scared. I'm so scared, but I knew when you said you were friends

Homemaker

with Lisa that you must have. I would do the same. It's probably impossible to believe, but I do think women should take care of each other."

"It's not impossible to believe, Dawn. You're doing the right thing by telling me what happened. Now I can keep your story safe in case you get scared. Telling your story means you are going to give up a lot, for a long time, and be afraid, but I also hope you'll be able to be free of things that hurt you and that led to you hurting other people. I hope you can ask for help to process how you've been hurt, and I'll ask for you to have that, too. You'll need it to heal and do better."

"You think we should go to the police station," Dawn asked. "He killed Lisa, and I helped him hide it, so you think I have to confess."

"Yes. I think it would be better to volunteer what you know than to wait for them to find you. And telling the truth will help keep you safe from Chris."

Dawn sat up. Her face was drained of color. "Will you make sure Tillie's okay?"

Prairie swallowed down her own tears. "I will. Right now, put in my phone where you take her to the vet, what kind of food she eats, and anything else important." Prairie pulled out her phone, opened her notes app, and handed it to Dawn as Tillie jumped down from her lap. Dawn started typing, her mouth and jaw tight with resolution. She looked so much like the trail cam picture, it took Prairie's breath away.

"Here. Thank you." Dawn gave the phone back. "He texted me on the throwaway to park in the model home's garage and come by foot to his backyard, where the carport was. He said he would give me Lisa's van keys and phone through the back slider. I did that. When I got in Lisa's van and turned it on, I saw his son's bedroom light come on, and maybe he looked out, but I didn't worry because Chris told me he would tell the kids that Lisa was going to the store."

Prairie thought about the blinking light on Foster's recorder and her own phone in her back pocket. If she were a real detective, she would probably get her phone out and record everything Dawn was saying, but she didn't feel like a real detective. She felt a lot more like a woman who understood how easy it was to layer every part of your life with the life of a man. She remembered the mental gymnastics she'd performed to feel powerful while also feeling ashamed that she had a husband she regularly covered for when he forgot something important about their kids or his mom. Prairie had experienced the unsettling anxiety that her relationship wasn't altogether honest, but instead a happy fiction she was creating every day with her hypervigilance, emotional labor, and social marketing.

Nothing in what Dawn had told her was a confession the police had known to ask for. Prairie's own experiences had led her to Dawn's door. It had taken her years to fully confess everything she had done, Greg had done, *life* had done to kill their marriage, and she hadn't had to stare at a piece of plastic recording everything she said.

The first time she'd uncovered a crime, Prairie had connected with one of its victims and become her best friend. This time, she was connecting to a woman who was both victim and conspirator. She wasn't a detective yet. She was a woman who noticed what didn't fit and who knew how to listen to what women didn't or couldn't say.

Maybe she would be a perfect detective someday, but not tonight. Not yet.

"I thought Lisa's kids were told she was in bed with a migraine?" she asked.

"I'm not sure. He told me that if they heard her van, he would tell them their mom was going to the store. He had come up with the migraine story before he left the conference, but I don't know if that story was for the kids or . . . other people."

The cops, she meant. Prairie remembered Foster at Dee's Diner, hinting that Lisa's kids had left her alone that night after Chris would have picked them up because she didn't feel well. Not an airtight alibi, if the investigators had looked harder—except that Dawn using Lisa's phone and driving Lisa's van had convinced them there was no need for Chris to even *have* an alibi before Dawn drove Lisa's van off the property. The trail cam picture and Lisa's phone established she was alive well after Chris came home from the conference.

"I went to the turnaround place by the trail in Lisa's van," Dawn said. "Chris texted me on my phone what to do, which was to pretend to be Lisa on *her* phone. Posting to social media and everything else. Then he told me to smash Lisa's phone and park Lisa's van in the model home's garage and come back on foot again. He had me sit in the garage bay where Lisa's van had been and handed me *his* phone, his real phone. He told me he'd already started texting with Lisa's sister about how worried he was Lisa wasn't home, and I should keep it up. He needed ninety minutes. That's what he said. Stay in the garage on his phone and give him ninety minutes. I had done that kind of thing for him before, when he was late from a site and was supposed to meet with an investor or something. I bought him time."

Tillie was at the front window, looking up at the sheer curtains that obscured the view of the street. Dawn crossed the living room to stand beside her.

"He left the van bay and went out to the other bay where he parks his truck. I heard him in there, but not for very long. Maybe he loaded something in his truck bed. I'm not sure. Then I heard him start up his truck and leave. I felt strange sitting in the dark garage, pretending to be Lisa, like I wasn't even there. I wanted to leave. There was part of my body that wanted to go in the house and get the kids and go far away with them. But I couldn't. I was frozen doing what he asked me to do."

She twitched the curtain open to look outside.

"He got back in ninety minutes. He told me to get the fuck out of there. I knew he must have gotten rid of her, even though he didn't say it. I knew. I told him Lisa's sister was on her way. I held her off for a while, but she hadn't been able to get Lisa since before lunch, and she was worried. He took my throwaway. He told me to make sure no one saw me and to take care of Lisa's van."

Take care of Lisa's van. The words made Prairie feel hollow. "What made you think of the jetty?"

"I like birds. I use an app to identify birds at the nature preserve there. I was just going to park her van, but I got upset. I started to cry and freak out. I miscalculated where the road drops off into the bay. It was so incredibly scary. I kept thinking, *I've been in a car accident*, but I couldn't tell anybody."

Dawn rested her balled fist against the window sash. "I almost didn't get the door open. There was water everywhere. The engine was still running. I was afraid to be in front of the van, but I had to swim in front of it, because there wasn't a place to climb up the jetty near the door. I started to think I was going to die. I finally found a place I could get out of the water, but it took forever, climbing up the rocks. I walked home from there. I couldn't get my car at the model home because I thought maybe Chris or his sister had called the police."

Prairie mentally plotted where Dawn's house was onto the map Joyce had drawn for her with the jetty on it. Miles, even as the crow flies. She pictured Dawn hauling herself out of the water and walking home in the dark, alone. Soaking wet. In April. Probably wearing her work clothes.

Prairie had never had to do anything like what Dawn was describing, but she understood how Dawn had ended up in that situation, in the dark, all alone. At first, she'd trusted Chris, admired him, maybe even loved him. Over the years they worked together, Chris had drawn her into collusion, just like he'd done with Lisa. Just like Amber had found herself colluding to keep her marriage with Noah working.

The only difference between the collusion of Prairie's marriage to Greg and the collusion between Chris and Lisa, Chris and Dawn, was that when Prairie finally decided to fight with Greg, he hadn't responded with violence.

She'd been lucky. That was all.

"Oh my God." Dawn's voice was alarmed.

"What?" Prairie sat up straight. She couldn't see what Dawn was looking at.

Homemaker

"Go out the slider in the kitchen. Right now." Dawn ran over and grabbed Prairie's bag, then shoved it into her hands. "Just go out. Just go."

Prairie couldn't get her feet to decide what to do. Later, she would recognize that was because she had never exited someplace clandestinely, in fear, in her entire life. Her body simply didn't know how to follow those directions.

It meant she couldn't process the fact that someone had knocked on the door and was opening it without waiting for an answer. Which meant Prairie was sitting there on a chair with a bag in her lap when Chris Radcliffe walked into the room.

Chapter 22

Dawn immediately put herself between Prairie and Chris. "Hey! Wow! I didn't expect you," she told him. "Did I miss a call?"

Chris craned his neck a bit to see beyond Dawn. It didn't take much effort. He was considerably taller than her, and broader, too. Bigger than Lisa. Bigger than Prairie. Prairie's chest felt full, like there was too much happening for her body to deal with, and she knew she was afraid. She *knew* it. But she didn't feel it.

She was too angry.

He was *so much bigger* than Dawn. He was *so much bigger* than Lisa. Not better. Not smarter. Not more worthy. No one had ever told Prairie that Chris Radcliffe was funny or considerate or thoughtful or intelligent or kind—none of the things they'd told her about Lisa. No one had told her how much he adored his kids or how much effort and energy he put into raising them right. He didn't know how to do *anything*, as far as Prairie could tell, except manipulate women into giving him what he wanted.

"Hey, Chris!" Prairie stood up. "It's me, Prairie Nightingale, Anabel and Maelynn's mom." She deliberately identified herself by the role society had given her—mom—to defuse any threat. "I'm so sorry I haven't had the chance to talk to you personally or bring something by for the kids. I talked to Dawn to help set up the vigil, of course. We were almost done closing some loops from that. It's good to see you.

I'm devastated for your family." The tears in Prairie's eyes were real. "I'm sure there will be developments soon."

Chris's gaze jumped around the room, from her to Dawn to the four corners, then to the cat and back to Prairie. The grooves on either side of his mouth were deeper than Prairie remembered from recent media coverage, his upper lip a bit thinner. Habitual dissatisfaction. He was dissatisfied with her existence.

Fine with her. Because, after all, why was he even here? He certainly hadn't come to tell Dawn he was sorry and ask for forgiveness before he turned himself in. There hadn't been anything in the news that Prairie had seen that would have tipped him off to the precariousness of his position, and unless he'd bugged Dawn's home, he couldn't know what Dawn had just told Prairie.

More than likely, he was here at Dawn's house to get her to do something else for him.

As far as Prairie was concerned, he could fucking wait.

"We haven't got the chance to catch up in such a long time," she continued. "Bryce and Caroline go to school with Maelynn now."

He looked at Dawn. Prairie realized he was waiting for Dawn to take care of him. To fix this situation so he didn't have to deal with it.

"I need to grab a few things for Tillie before my ride gets here," Dawn told him. Her eyes darted to Prairie, and her determined expression told Prairie everything. Dawn was a smart woman. Prairie needed to buy Dawn time to call the police. "Excuse me." Dawn left the room.

Chris started to go after her, ignoring Prairie as if his very existence as a man meant he was not obligated to respect social niceties.

"Our talk's been pretty emotional," Prairie said, "and I've stayed longer than I meant to, knowing Dawn actually had to leave." She looked down the hallway where Dawn had gone. "We've been really pulling for your family, Chris. Praying and hoping there will be something we can do to help."

He halted almost comically, one foot in front of the other headed toward the hallway, his arm in midswing. He didn't turn in the direction of Prairie's voice, but he couldn't ignore her completely. He didn't know what was going on here. He didn't know if this was actually a mild social visit and Dawn really needed to get ready and go somewhere or if it was an insurrection.

Because he hadn't talked to Dawn. He'd assumed his control was utter.

It was clear that Chris hadn't planned to offer Prairie the simplest social exchange. His total dismissal was so indicative of his belief that Prairie wasn't even *real* that it made it easy for her to think up something to say that would keep him from leaving the room. "I guess I should be honest and say that I'm not really pulling for *you*, personally." Her heart was so enormous in her throat that she could hardly breathe. "Chris Van der Beke, I think you're a dick."

She watched his neck get red, throwing the stubble of his close shave into relief against his white shirt collar. He didn't look as handsome close up. Prairie hoped Dawn had definitely called the cops and hadn't heaved herself out of a bedroom window, because baiting a murderer was objectively a terrible idea, even when he was ten feet away and didn't appear to have a weapon on his person.

If he got too close, Prairie would scramble behind the back of the couch. Then he couldn't grab her without chasing her down first.

"You need to go." Chris's voice, when he spoke, was surprisingly reasonable. Soft, even. Like possibly she didn't understand the situation, and that was sad, but he had to keep in mind that their children went to school together and probably she was overwrought, and he would forgive her later.

Nope. "I'm not going anywhere. I'm not going to leave Dawn alone with you, and my guess is the police will be here soon."

He did that thing that men and athletes on the field do where they open their mouths and wipe the corners. He managed to combine it with an extra-loud man sigh. "That's good. My family has, unfortunately, had problems with people harassing us. Even people we've trusted in the past. I was going to call the police myself."

Homemaker

"You know, I doubt that. Did Amber call you?"

Prairie watched his fake mild expression freeze and his red throat go white. "What are you— How did you know that?"

"Lucky guess. The last time I saw her, she seemed to be in a field-salting mood. Probably you think you need to get some things straight with Dawn now. You know, make sure you're on the same page with how to explain your affair. Like, 'It was only one time, I was under a lot of stress, Lisa and I were actually already looking at counseling and had put it behind us.' In case anyone asks."

Chris almost imperceptibly crinkled his nose, the same way Zipper crinkled his nose at Gingernut when he wanted to snarl at her but couldn't because she was too scary.

"Huh," Prairie said, as though he'd spoken. "Well, I'm sure there's nothing to worry about on your missing wife's super-secret computer. Those are usually full of viruses from all the coupon downloading."

"I got all of her stuff." Dawn appeared in the doorway holding a big grocery tote and a small pink cat carrier with Tillie's nose poking out of the grate. "Thank you for taking care of her."

Dawn's face was gray, but her expression was serene. Prairie was incredibly proud of her, even as she really fucking hoped the police were on their way.

"You can use any kind of litter," Dawn added. "Sorry to stick you with buying it, but I figured you wouldn't want to take a used litter box."

"I have a few, including a fancy robot one I control with an app. Tillie will poop luxuriously." Prairie adjusted her messenger bag and reached to take Tillie and the tote, keeping her eyes glued to Chris and her senses on alert.

"Dawn," Chris growled.

Dawn didn't look right at him. Prairie was afraid she might faint, but Dawn was in charge here. "Prairie's going to take care of my cat, because I'm probably going to be arrested."

253

"Wait until you have a lawyer before you answer questions," Prairie reminded her. "I'll talk to them first. It might take some time, so just hang in there."

Dawn nodded, her eyes red.

Suddenly, Chris closed the gap between him and Dawn, and then he had her arm above the elbow gripped in his huge hand. She let her arm drop heavily to the side, an instinctual move to get him to let go. He didn't, though. Instead, he forcibly pulled up on her arm and shoulder, trying to turn Dawn's body toward him, out of the room. It was distressing to see.

"Don't touch her," Prairie said, had to say. She was a mother.

"Chris." Dawn's voice strangled. Chris pulled her harder.

"I'm going to make an educated guess at your plan." Prairie pitched her voice loud and steady as she set the cat carrier and Dawn's tote on the ground beside her. "You want me to leave, but I won't. You've got Dawn by the arm, and you're going to take her somewhere private. You want her alone, because if you can get her alone, you get your control back. Her attention won't be divided, and she'll have no choice but to do what you want her to. Here's the problem. Having even one other woman here who isn't in your power messes everything up."

Chris didn't look at her. Dawn lifted her chin. *"Let go."*

He didn't.

"I mean, how is it going to work?" Prairie asked. "You're going to drag her out of here while I go into stasis? I am not cooperating. Dawn is not cooperating. Your plan sucks, because the only kind of plan you know how to make is the kind where a woman does what you want her to. As soon as she stops—the *instant* your wife takes action on her own against Kitty Blue, or asks you for a divorce, or your employee tells you she doesn't want to have a physical relationship anymore—your plans fall to pieces, and all you've got left is what you learned in the first place, from your dad."

Later, Prairie wasn't sure what she'd thought would happen next, or even precisely what did happen. But she *thought*, in the last moment before the room chaotically lit up in red and blue moving lights and filled with the sudden noise of sirens, that she saw Chris turn his body away from Dawn's. Prairie knew his eyes met hers like he'd finally noticed her, because she'd finally said something he could hear. *All you've got left is what you learned in the first place, from your dad.*

It looked like he let go of Dawn's arm.

Then it was loud and bright, with fists pounding on the door and the door opening to admit the full blast of noise and light, and Dawn said something, but Prairie missed it. When she turned to ask what it was, Chris had disappeared.

He tried to run out through the back slider. *His* body knew how to escape.

But there was a cop there. Then there was a cop next to Prairie. He started to put his hands on her, and she sat down and pulled the cat carrier onto her lap so he wouldn't. She didn't want to be touched.

She held on tight to the cat and the tote, waiting for Foster. The cop didn't move away from her, but he didn't bother her, either. Because she had followed the power and seen how Dawn telling her own story, in her own words, had broken up that power, regathered it, and put it back where it belonged.

Inside of Dawn, Prairie hoped.

Inside of *her*, too.

Chapter 23

"Why did she give her to us?" Maelynn sat on the big sofa between Prairie and Anabel. Tillie spread her sleek body out across their laps, purring like a diesel engine. To Zipper's delight, Tillie loved dogs, so he was welcome to sit right next to the four of them, getting scratches from the girls and occasional soft and playful bats from Tillie.

Gingernut was still convalescing with Greg.

"Because Dawn has a big journey to go on." Prairie thought about how to explain the very gray area that was Dawn Mitchell to Maelynn. It was hard when the judicial and carceral system made justice and healing almost impossible. "Think about it like a quest. She'll have to go to battle in order to save her best self and figure out how to have a productive life. Dawn will have to learn a lot of things she didn't learn before, and she will have to go through trials."

Anabel snorted. "Yeah, like a criminal trial, for starters."

Prairie sighed. "That's true. That's how the system is structured, at least for now. But Anabel, do you think, given everything I've told you, that Dawn deserves to be incarcerated for murder or accessory to murder for a long time, or even the rest of her life? Do you think her removal from society would heal our community? There's no right answer here. I'm interested to know what you think, because you're a kid, between the ages of Lisa's kids, who lost their mom."

"She died," said Maelynn. "She wasn't lost."

Homemaker

"Yes," Prairie agreed. Maelynn disliked euphemisms. "She died. Lisa died."

Prairie had reached out to Alison and talked to her briefly. She'd messaged Amber. She'd told Shawna she should read her emails from Lisa if she hadn't already, and she'd left a very sad voicemail for Caitlin. She was wrestling with loss and accountability, at the end of her own journey—a journey back down a road she'd traveled before, revisiting people and places she'd felt rejected from, or had genuinely been rejected by. She'd learned that fewer bridges had burned than she would've guessed, but there were many ways she was on her own.

She had also learned that all the ways she was on her own were ways she had chosen.

She wouldn't have guessed that, though maybe she should have. Maybe she should have known that if she didn't want to raise her girls like she had been raised, and if how she had chosen to live her life had started to chafe, she needed the option to travel some roads alone to understand who she was.

Prairie loved mothering. She loved making a home for her children. But she had channeled who she was into her husband so he could have more and more, and she'd never asked herself why. She'd never asked Greg if that was what he most wanted her to do, while he also never made her feel as though he was in love with *Prairie*, rather than in love with being loved by her.

But she hadn't loved Prairie, either. Not like she might have. Not like she wanted to.

Anabel rubbed the little patch of velvet between Tillie's eyes and took in a long breath. "If someone killed you, and someone else helped hide what they did, I would hate both of them and want them to rot in jail forever. Mr. Radcliffe didn't force Dawn Mitchell to do it. She could've bailed at any time and gone to the police and told them Mr. Radcliffe probably killed his wife and where to find him."

"You said Mr. Radcliffe hurt Dawn Mitchell, too." Maelynn squeezed Tillie's toes, one by one. Prairie was starting to worry Tillie might actually die from pleasure. Surely she couldn't breathe through all that purring.

"That's right."

"Once, I put Calvin Mallory's name on his Google Slides set for him when he turned it into the digital group box, because Ms. Deeling takes off a full letter grade if you don't put your name in the file name, and when Calvin gets upset, he scream-whispers the F-word, and I hate it."

"That's not the same," Anabel said. "You were trying to help."

"Not really. If I wasn't worried about him getting mad, I wouldn't have helped him. He wouldn't do it for me." Maelynn looked at Prairie. "I didn't like that I did it. It's cheating. I'm sorry I didn't tell you."

"That's okay," Prairie said. "I understand, and I'm not upset."

She'd kept them home from school yesterday because she was tired and rattled, and she'd wanted them nearby. She'd kept them home again this morning because Lisa Radcliffe's case had exploded into an actual media frenzy, prompting an email from Maelynn's school principal with information about how the school would handle drop-off and pickup in the midst of all the trucks and reporters circling the schoolyard, hoping for a glimpse of the Radcliffe kids with Lisa's parents or her sister—anyone connected to the case who they might be able to get on camera.

Maelynn said Bryce and Caroline hadn't been back to school since Lisa disappeared.

"What I think is that you're both right," Prairie told her daughters. "Anabel, because Dawn definitely has to answer to Bryce, Caroline, and Davey's feelings. And Maelynn, because Dawn's behavior was altered by her very scary relationship with a powerful man. My thought, for your consideration, is that we don't have a system that really knows how to look at both of those things at the same time."

"Maybe you should go to law school," Maelynn said. "Or run for office."

"I haven't ever been interested in having more school or being a part of politics other than voting and protesting."

Homemaker

"You never went to school at all. You're worse than a dropout." Anabel said this with one of her new looks that Prairie had to ignore unless she decided to love the sound of doors slamming and teenagers yelling.

"You call up your grandma Anabel and tell her that. Here." Prairie pulled up her mother's contact and handed Anabel her phone. "Seriously. Push that call button and tell Anabel Lovesummer that the work she did on behalf of her only daughter's education amounted to less than a public high school dropout's."

Anabel's smug expression collapsed. "Oh my God, no. I take it back. But you know what I mean."

"I assume you mean that my unconventional education has contributed to the flourishing of my unique intellect. But I can't possibly know what you mean, if not that."

"That's what I meant." Anabel said this and didn't even roll her eyes.

Prairie smiled. "It just so happens that I *was* thinking about what I might want to do next, given that I've had this important experience."

"You want to be a detective," Anabel said.

"Wait, I thought you already were." Maelynn turned her body toward Prairie. "You're not?"

"I do, and yeah, I am. Maybe. I'm thinking about whether I would like to be a detective in a way where I had an office. And I went to the office to do this work. And I was here less. What do you think about that?"

"You sound like that divorce education movie," Anabel said. "The one where the mom has to tell her kids that their lives are going to change because she has to go to work now that Daddy's left, and they yell at her like, 'You're not even a real mom anymore!' and slam doors."

"*Preparing for Transitions*," Maelynn said. "I didn't find that one helpful at all."

Prairie laughed.

"You'd still live here and work in town, right?" Anabel asked.

"If I do anything, which isn't for sure yet. I'm more interested in hearing what you guys think."

"Will your office have better snacks than here?" Maelynn asked. "Thecia's mom has an office at the hospital where Thecia does her homework after school, and she has her own snack fridge."

"You can be a detective. I don't care." Possibly Anabel had the very smallest of smiles. "But if Maelynn gets a snack fridge, I get one, too."

"That's it, then? You're willing to sell off fifteen years of quality stay-at-home mom for a couple of snack fridges?"

They both nodded.

"It's not a problem," Anabel said. "I don't need a stay-at-home mom anymore. Anyway, you didn't even notice I was failing math."

"Wow," Prairie said. "Wow."

"I think I just need a mom," said Maelynn. "Even if I didn't get fifteen years in like Anabel. I don't think I needed as much parenting as she has."

Maelynn rarely, if ever, told jokes, especially at anyone else's expense, and Prairie had to guffaw at the surprise of that one.

"Hey!" Anabel said. "I mean, true, but hey!"

"Well. Good talk, girls. Follow up with me later if you want to, if you have more thoughts you need to share. But right now I have to get ready for my meeting."

"Why are you having a homemaker meeting?" Maelynn said. "I thought you said you were a detective now. You should just have Dad do it."

Prairie held her breath at that, if only because talking out loud about starting a detective office to her girls felt big, and when anything felt big, it was hard not to also feel like it was foolish. She didn't know the first thing about opening a detective office, including if there was a class or license required. She didn't even know if Green Bay, Wisconsin, *needed* a detective's office. Right this moment, when she imagined it, all she could see was the inside of a white box, floating in space, with a snack fridge inside it. There was no way she would buy two.

Homemaker

"Maybe I should have your dad do it," she told Maelynn. "But I'm going to take this one step at a time. For now, you two have to scram."

Maelynn scooped up Tillie and carried her with her to her room, with Anabel following.

Prairie went to her old bedroom suite–slash–conference room and started turning on the lights. She opened the french doors to the patio, where everyone usually came in when the weather was good. The morning was overcast but warmer than it had been. The grass had begun to look more green than brown, although there was snow in the forecast at the end of the week. Spring in Wisconsin.

On her phone, Prairie toggled to the agenda that Marian had posted to Slack yesterday afternoon without Prairie having to ask. For most of the week, Marian had been monitoring, updating, and managing all the Slack threads that Prairie usually handled. No one had complained. Prairie wasn't positive anyone had even noticed.

Which made her feel, just a tiny bit, as though she'd been playing at something. Or fooling herself. *Did you really change your life enough?*

She got a notification from her printer app. Marian had sent through the agendas to print, but the printer needed to be turned on. Prairie did that. She put water in the coffee machine and poured a few more sleeves of espresso pods into the hopper. Her phone buzzed again to tell her someone had come to her front door.

She checked the camera. There was a man on her doorstep. Short hair, trim pants, crisp oxford with the sleeves rolled up, and an honest-to-God Fair Isle sweater vest. Foster.

He'd been at Dawn's, arriving with the second wave of police. He'd told an officer he would escort Prairie's vehicle to the station. She'd followed his black sedan. He'd taken her into the station, explaining plainly what would happen, offering to help her call anyone she needed. She'd answered questions from the FBI, too. A woman agent interviewed her, Cathy Simmons. She seemed to know Prairie had been sharing information with Foster.

261

After, he'd checked in with her over text. He hadn't once expressed any frustration with her for leaving their meeting to talk to Dawn. He'd introduced her to people at the police station respectfully.

She got a call or text from Foster every time he knew she would be called with follow-up questions. He said it was a "professional courtesy."

None of this was the reason why she'd had the courage to talk to her girls about being a detective, but it was connected. Foster's respect had cast their interactions as collaborative, and her as important.

Important *professionally*. She had only recently regained enough bandwidth for it to occur to her Foster had been *exceedingly* professional in the aftermath of what happened at Dawn's house and ended in Chris's capture and arrest. *Solely* professional. In fact, Prairie had enough bandwidth at this point that she had kept herself up the night before feeling somewhat peeved at Foster for not so much as sending a stern text in her direction. She'd composed and deleted a few texts of her own, peeved with herself, and then had to talk herself out of impulsively sending him a thirst trap at three in the morning.

She hadn't done it, because she was afraid. Personally. Professionally. Change was scarier than Prairie ever gave it credit for. Even good change.

"Come around the side," she told him through the app that connected to the front door speaker. "There's a patio."

"This looks like a party."

"What?" The sound on her front door camera was terrible.

"Lot of cars pulling up."

"It's not a party, it's my staff meeting. Just come around."

He arrived on the patio at the same time as Marian, who had an armful of pastry boxes, and Beth, Prairie's chef, who dodged around Prairie to disappear inside the house. Prairie stepped out of the doorway just as Marian turned to Foster.

"Foster, this is Marian Banks," Prairie said, "who is my logistics genius. Marian, this is Agent Foster Rosemare. He works in the Green Bay FBI office."

Marian didn't even raise one of her perfect eyebrows. Her face was a study in serenity, excellent bone structure, and the power of winged eyeliner. Her hair was perfectly waved, and when she put the pastry boxes down on a table, her coral boho dress was the last word in why people had been carving boobs and ass into stone for tens of thousands of years. She held out her hand. "Nice to meet you, Foster."

He shook her hand with an expression that was devastatingly charming and handsome. He had directed this charm at Prairie more than once, but Foster-to-Marian charm was friendly and pleasant, whereas Foster-to-Prairie charm was *friendly*.

She would take that.

"It's nice to meet you," he said. "Your name was on the permit for the vigil. I'm impressed you were able to get that processed in such a short period of time. You must really be a logistics genius."

Marian tipped her head, and Prairie knew she was assessing Foster much more closely than he could possibly perceive. "I am, but that's not why I was able to get it. I've lived here my entire life. The Bankses are a big family. I know a lot of people. Everywhere."

Marian delivered this warning to Foster to check himself in a way that was so sweet and winning, most people would not have caught it. Most *men*, anyway.

But Foster only nodded. "I understand, and I'm glad I've met you." He looked at the pastry boxes. "Can I help you with those."

Marian smiled and picked them up. "Nope. I've got it. Take your time, Prairie." She disappeared through the slider.

"I can let you get to your meeting," he said.

Prairie took a minute to look at Foster and think about what she wanted. "Did I miss your call or text that you were coming over?"

He shook his head. "You didn't. I should've. I'm working at home today and went to call you with an update but impulsively decided to come here instead."

Impulsively. "If I hadn't been home?"

Foster grinned, a powerful move on his part. "Then I would have called you."

She grinned back. "I'll allow it. Is this a visit about Lisa Radcliffe or is it primarily . . . impulsive?"

"I thought about that on the way over. There are details about Lisa and her death I could share with you before you hear from the media. I feel you should know what I know. But I could've called you with that story." This time, his half smile was vulnerable.

Prairie could feel the back of her neck heating. She knew that no man had ever been this honest with her at this stage, and even thinking of these moments, of the time they'd spent together as a *stage*, made her stomach flip right over. He was here, in part, to talk again about Lisa, but Prairie understood it wasn't because he needed an excuse. It was because he genuinely wanted to share his work with her, his thoughts with her, and he was interested in hers.

He wasn't splitting her in two. She was splitting *herself* in two, as if she were, on the one hand, a baby detective, and on the other, a woman and a mother.

To Foster, Prairie very much suspected that she was simply *Prairie*.

She took a deep breath, trying not to be too self-conscious. "Walk around this trellis on those stepping stones to the other side. There's a tiny patio with a couple of chairs and a table. Sit down, and I'll bring you a coffee and a pastry."

"Thank you." He smiled and strode away.

Prairie opened the slider. Everyone was still milling around as Prairie made a coffee with lots of cream and sugar. Marian sidled up to her. "So, he's hot."

"You think?" Prairie took a napkin and a pastry.

"I don't have to think about it. He's solidly a newly blossoming silver fox."

"His hair is dark!" But Prairie laughed.

Homemaker

"That's why I said he was blossoming. You can tell that's where he's headed." Marian made a sinuous motion with her hands, splaying them outward. "Blossoming. Maturing on the vine."

"Marian Banks." Prairie tried for a scolding tone, but she was laughing.

"You're talking to him now?" Marian indicated the coffee Prairie was making.

"Yes. If you're willing to start the meeting without me."

"Yes. Do you have two minutes for me first?"

There was a shift in Marian's tone that arrested Prairie. Her brain anxiously zoomed over everything she'd dropped since she started looking into what had happened to Lisa, everything Marian had picked up and taken care of that might have made her feel undervalued or like it was time to move on. And why shouldn't Marian have those feelings? She'd been doing the 724 Maple Project since the girls were small. She'd had a front-row seat to the end of Prairie's marriage and the adjustment that followed, and now she likely was seeing the writing on the wall about where Prairie's interests had shifted.

Prairie didn't want to panic as she followed Marian into her living room and Marian closed the conference room door behind her, but she was panicking anyway. There were changes in her life that Prairie didn't want. Losses she didn't want to bear. Marian was one of them.

"Listen," Marian said. Then her brows furrowed. "Jesus, Prairie, you need to breathe."

Prairie gasped for air. "Sorry."

"Quit freaking out. I don't know what you're going to talk to the FBI agent about, and maybe he's only here to hold you against the next available wall, based on how he was looking at you—"

"What?" Prairie took a big breath again. Now her brain was manufacturing a series of intrusively horny scenes of Foster backing her against the side of her house, and her central nervous system was not prepared for that onslaught.

"Stay with me. My point is that if you're at all going to talk to him about this detective idea you have—"

"Wait, how did you hear about the detective idea?"

"Stop interrupting me. My entire job is knowing what's going on with you, and that's my point. I answered your bananapants ad for this position at a moment when I had a lot of options, but every single one of them bored me. I thought this job wouldn't bore me and wouldn't underestimate me, and I was right. Are you listening?"

Prairie widened her eyes. "I am listening."

"I was right. It's been fun. But, Prairie, this job is starting to underestimate *you*. And that's how it's supposed to be. You're supposed to grow and outgrow things. I wanted to have a chance to say that whatever it is you're doing next, if there is any way, take me with you. I want in."

Prairie looked at Marian, beautiful and smart Marian, unflappable under every circumstance, who had made this homemaker project and Prairie's life make sense at a time when nothing in Prairie's life was working, and she felt horrifically rotten that she hadn't made it to this conclusion before Marian did, and hadn't brought her into her thoughts the moment she'd started having them.

"Yes," Prairie said. "Of course, yes."

"I can tell you want to apologize to me. Don't. For now, I only wanted to secure my 'yes' before you got any farther down the road." Marian smiled. "Get the coffee and get yourself to the patio where you sent that man. We'll talk later." Marian leaned forward and gathered Prairie's long hair to drape it over her shoulders. "This is a good top."

"It was my mom's." Prairie looked down at the peasant blouse, soft with age, the neck ties undone. It had a row of simple red embroidery across the yoke. Prairie had stolen this shirt from her mom when she was a teenager, wanting something different to wear to a party. Now she wore it when she was thinking of her mom.

Prairie grabbed the coffees, her mind spinning and her heart racing.

Homemaker

Foster looked surprisingly comfortable in one of the small, vintage chaises she had bought for the outdoor patio after the divorce. He even had his ankles crossed, resting an elbow on the curlicue white-painted wrought iron while he looked at his phone.

Prairie put down the coffee and pastries on the little glass-topped table. "You know what? I just remembered you don't drink coffee. I can go back in and make you a tea."

"Don't you dare." Foster grabbed it and took a long drink, reaching for a doughnut at the same time. "God, that's really fucking good."

Prairie caught herself watching the way he leaned up from the chaise to drink his coffee, surprisingly spare and fit. The chaise suited him like it would have suited a similarly old-timey handsome man like Clark Gable, or one of the ones who danced.

"Do you need anything else?"

"A bed. A cigarette. But no, thank you."

"My friend Megan keeps a pack of Virginia Slims menthols in that gardening cabinet for when she's over here ranting and needs to secretly angry-smoke." Prairie pointed to the galvanized cabinet.

"Yes, please. But no. Absolutely not." He smiled at her.

They weren't on neutral territory. She couldn't believe she was actually longing for Kettle's. She could hear Marian and Beth talking inside, their voices muted. Foster didn't look uncomfortable cradled in Prairie's pink-and-orange-cushioned chaise, but she felt like a humming electric rod had been roughly jammed into her backbone. She was sitting up straight on the end of her own chaise with her feet neatly together.

Foster put his coffee down and sat up to face her, his knees centimeters from hers. The last time she'd been this close to him was at the vigil. "Chris confessed."

Prairie closed her eyes. "Oh, thank God."

"I didn't want you to hear it somewhere else. But if you don't want to hear everything, that's okay."

Foster let her take a moment in the silence, watching chickadees bounce on and off the trellis that made this patio private. "I'd like to hear what you can tell me," she said, when she was certain.

"A team is at Chris and Lisa's build site right now. The new house. Recovering Lisa."

Prairie's mouth went claggy and dry.

"We had Chris's build managers at all his properties go over them under a microscope and look for anything out of place in case we missed something. There was one concrete deck footer at the new house that shouldn't have been there. The crew had poured twelve before they had to quit for the day. But there were thirteen."

She felt her eyes fill. She'd been at that build site with Greg and Zipper. She'd seen the concrete caps sticking out of the ground.

"I took that fact into the interview room. Thirteen concrete footers where there should be twelve. And, from you, I took what we'd learned about his background, his family business in concrete. I told him I'd seen the portable mixer in his garage. I told him we'd checked with the build manager on how deep those holes were and how much concrete it would take. We'd looked at the corner of Chris's garage and seen dust where it looked like bags used to be stacked up. I told him we were going to take apart the site no matter what, so he should tell me."

"Dawn said he needed ninety minutes. It must be fifteen from their current house to the new site. That's thirty round trip, maybe a little less because it was late and there wouldn't be any traffic, but still, an hour to mix up who knows how much concrete—"

"Nine sixty-pound bags."

"He loaded nine sixty-bound bags of concrete and a portable mixer into his truck, drove to the site, mixed it with water from, what, some spigot, poured the concrete, and loaded everything back up in *ninety minutes?*"

"We got his truck on camera. Thanks to Dawn and his resulting confession, we knew to look for it. To the site with the bags in the bed, back to the house with nothing but the mixer. Guess you learn a few things when you grow up pouring concrete."

Her heart wanted out of her body. Her skin felt bare and exposed. Her girls were upstairs. Her kids.

"You don't have to hear this, Prairie."

She shook her head. "I know. Tell me, though."

His gray eyes met hers, and his brow knit. "Dawn's story corroborated everything. Lisa called Chris at nine forty-five in the morning on Monday. She wanted him to come home to talk. We learned from Lisa's computer that she planned on telling him she was going to file for divorce. She wanted to tell him after he'd had a nice conference—according to Lisa's digital diary, he was always in a good mood after those things—and before she had to pick the kids up from school."

"She planned herself a natural exit in case he was upset. If he didn't get home from Manitowoc until about lunchtime after she called in the morning, they couldn't talk—or fight—for longer than a couple hours before she had to leave and get a spot to park at her kids' school."

"I didn't think of that."

"You haven't had to get a divorce and organize fights around the children."

Foster looked into his empty coffee mug. "Chris left the conference about eleven. It took him an hour and five minutes to get home."

"No breadcrumbs there? Why didn't you guys figure out he left so much earlier than he said?"

"The hotel has some hallway and lobby cameras up, but the coverage is limited. We got Chris in the vendor fair in the morning and on the lobby camera right before the mixer. It seemed to line up."

"The breadcrumbs fit his story, but it wasn't the real story."

Foster tipped his head toward her, acknowledging she'd been right about that. "He parked behind the hotel where the cameras couldn't see him and took back roads to and from Green Bay, which was his regular habit. No breadcrumbs there, either. Not that we were looking too hard. Dawn's alibi, plus the people who'd seen him at the conference, plus our thinking it was Lisa in the van on the trail cam, meant we hadn't dug in as far as we might have."

"What happened when Chris got home?"

"He won't talk about what she said. Claims he doesn't remember. But we know Lisa had seen a burner phone Chris was using to text with another woman, and she pieced together he was having an affair with Dawn when she stopped at the office and saw the same type of phone on the corner of Dawn's desk. We think she must have confronted him with that, or else that Kitty Blue might have come back in. Lisa had diverted three months' worth of estimated tax money out of her Kitty Blue account, which Chris monitored, to fund her lawsuit and start making payments to her downline. She'd put down a deposit and first month's rent on a nice house for her to move into with the kids, right around the same time she started giving expensive gifts to her friends as a way to let them know she cared. She said all this in her diary, journal, whatever you want to call it. She told Chris she'd sent the money to the IRS for the taxes and started spending it behind his back."

"That's smart. As big as Lisa's business was, her quarterly taxes must have been huge checks."

"It could be that was what set him off. He might have known from Lisa that she hadn't talked to her mom or sister yet and that she hadn't actually hired a divorce lawyer. Or he might have acted without knowing any of it, just because she said the word 'divorce.' That kind of thing—how much premeditation was involved—the prosecutor's team will tease out."

"How did he . . ." Prairie took a deep breath. "How did Chris kill her?"

"He won't say. My guess is manual strangulation, given they were fighting and the forensic team didn't find blood at the house, but we're going to be waiting on the medical examiner's report awhile. They're still up there at the house site working. They set up a tent last night and a bank of lights. They have to go slow."

Homemaker

"He didn't take her to the build site until nighttime. Where did he put her in the meantime? I mean, Dawn said he put her to bed. He drove back to Manitowoc, alibied himself, and then went home again before he picked up his kids."

Foster hesitated. "He wrapped her in the fetal position with the top bedsheet, tight—" He made a circle with his hands, and to Prairie's horror, she realized he meant to show her the size of the bundle Lisa had been made into. She was such a small woman. "—and stored her in the locking tool chest in the back of his truck."

Prairie covered her mouth with her hand.

"Then he picked his kids up from school with Lisa's body in the back. He left her there until Dawn came and he went up to the house site to put her body in the hole for the footer and then pour around and over top of it."

"Oh, *Jesus*."

Prairie didn't try to stop the tears. She let herself cry.

She cried for what Lisa had wanted, and how close she'd come to getting it, and how stupid and unworthy her death was when she'd deserved so much better.

Prairie cried for Davey and his lost trip to Chicago, for all three kids having to grow up without their mom and dad, and she cried for everything Dawn Mitchell had been through and everything still ahead of her.

She leaned on her knees and let the tears fall down her nose and drip to the patio stones. The soft cloth of her mother's shirt stretched tight across her back as she let the hurt come up and out of her body the way her mom had taught her to in all those years she didn't send Prairie to school. Everyone alive was born to feel their feelings—that was what Anabel Lovesummer said. Avoiding them, denying them, or stuffing them down made people sick. Prairie cried until her throat was raw and her diaphragm settled down. Without a tissue, she had to wipe her face on her shirt.

When she finished, Foster was still there. He didn't look uncomfortable. He did look sad. This close, she noticed the rims of his eyes were red, and he had shadows underneath them. He smelled good. It was a faint Christmas tree smell, mixed with coffee and the early spring breeze.

There were forget-me-nots in the flower bed behind him, not blooming yet but almost ready to start. The sun had come out.

Prairie thought of her white box with a snack fridge inside, but it felt foolish to imagine putting herself up against the kind of senseless violence that had ended Lisa's life. "I don't know how to do this," she whispered.

She thought she meant how to be a detective, but maybe she meant all of it. Foster. All of it.

"What you already did was critical. What you did gave Lisa's children and her family a safe place to start building their lives again."

"But the whole way, you were there. Doing fancy FBI things. Verifying. Investigating. And everything you did, you had a right to do. It's your job."

"I'm not you, Prairie. That means I can't do what you can do." Foster had dark glitter in his gray eyes. "My experience is so different from yours that, I could not, even with all of my resources, have gotten to here so quickly, or possibly at all, without your help. The kinds of questions you ask. The things people are willing to share with you. *You.*" He tapped her knee with one finger, softly. "And the people you have on your side. Forensic genealogy *is* an important new field. Logistics geniuses who know everyone in town are rare. So is a connection to an irreverent viral podcaster. I might have fancy FBI things, but you have resources you're not crediting."

He hadn't moved his finger. Prairie wanted to make a joke or reach for her coffee, but the extraordinary validation he offered her meant she *had* to be as honest with him as he had been with her. Not about the work she wanted to do, but about the two of them. "There are stakes to this that you have to be aware of."

Homemaker

"You're a mother," he said. His voice was low. He wasn't looking away.

"Yes. And they know about Thursday nights, but I've never told them anything about what I thought I was looking for or what I wanted. They don't have any way to need less from me or a reason to be asked to accept less."

"You can't be sure any relationship wouldn't ask for more than you can offer."

"No."

"And you haven't had the experience of more leading to more. When it comes to this." He gave her his half smile, the one that she was beginning to understand was only for her.

"I haven't. And you've already guessed I'm thinking about changing my business cards. I don't know what that will take. From me. From my family. I've never done anything like this. I want more, but I don't know yet where the more would come from."

She wanted him to understand and to provide reassurance for every fear she had and even the ones she hadn't anticipated yet. That wasn't fair, but she liked him. She *liked* Foster. He made her feel something completely new that was breathless and beautiful.

He just held the warm weight of that one finger against her knee. "I had a very good marriage," he said. "I can't speak for Louise, but I loved every minute I had with her. Every conversation, every laugh, every time we went out dancing, even every argument. I loved her. She was my best friend. I thought I would spend my entire life with her and die happy. For a long time, I felt like I didn't need any more, ever, than what I had with her."

Prairie wondered if Greg would have, at any point, said this about her. She hadn't thought she would have wanted him to. She used to tell people how he proposed to her, in his car on the way to dropping her off at the coffee shop where she worked, as if it were endearingly, nerdily funny, when really it had always stung. *If we were married, I could put you on my health insurance.*

"And now?" she asked.

"At first it was theoretical. It was just my realizing that I couldn't really say Louise had taught me about love, shown me what it was and what it felt like, only for me to pack it in mothballs and never share those things with anyone else."

Prairie laid her hand down on her thigh, her own finger sliding alongside Foster's but not quite touching. "When did it stop being a theory?"

That was when Foster broke eye contact, smiling at the ground, shifting the tension so that Prairie could feel the entire spectrum of two people who might be willing to try if they had some guarantee they wouldn't fuck it up.

She laughed. "Oh no. All of those moves, Rosemare, and you didn't know what you were doing."

"Me!" He started laughing, too. "You matched with me on an app after less than ten minutes of knowing you. I thought I might have to politely excuse myself to have a coronary."

"It's the suits," Prairie said. "Possibly they're a thing for me."

Foster got closer, moving one of his knees between hers. She knew now the risk he was taking, how afraid he must be even as he put himself inside her space—and the way he was looking at her, at her face, at her mouth, making an entirely new space, an *us* space—unexpectedly dissolved Prairie into hot bonelessness.

She wasn't afraid. She wasn't.

"Can I kiss you?"

It was the first goddamned time he had ever asked her a question, and he'd asked it against her mouth because she'd already reached for him. As she breathed her "yes" to his lips, he put a hand on her face in a way that was so final, it made her wonder how long he'd been thinking of touching her like this.

He pressed his thumb under her bottom lip, communicating to her that his mouth would follow.

Homemaker

His mouth. Prairie didn't know if she'd ever liked anything as much as his mouth, if she'd ever felt so urgent and yielding at the same time. She didn't have enough time to take everything she wanted from the heat of Foster's body, from his mouth, or to give him everything she wanted to give of herself. One of her hands was restless over his short hair, down his neck, while the other had found its way under the hem of his sweater vest to press itself against hot cotton.

But, at the same time, she felt patient, like this kiss could be endless. Like she could give him everything he wanted when his mouth traveled down her neck and then back to her lips, when his fingers dug into her hip. Foster really, really knew how to kiss. There wasn't anything to worry about. He kissed her like he wanted to do nothing else and like she was easy to kiss, like she felt and tasted good. His kiss made her feel strong and very, very beautiful.

It had been a long time since she'd kissed anyone. Prairie couldn't be sure if she'd ever kissed anyone like this. All of her was in this kiss. It was easy.

She broke the kiss with more kissing, deep kisses she replaced with soft bites and softer kisses. He kept his face near hers, then tightened his hands on her one more time before letting her go. But he stayed close.

"Prairie Nightingale."

"Foster Rosemare."

"I have a question."

She smiled. "No, you don't."

He smiled back, ignoring her joke. "What are we going to do now?"

She wanted to be able to tell him. And he had asked, so she understood that he didn't know, either. Despite the fact that they'd just had one of the most paradigm-shifting make-out sessions of her life, Prairie found that reassuring.

"I don't know. We don't. We have no idea."

Foster moved back a little. "We don't. It's a mystery."

She laughed. "What a terrible joke."

"Yes." Foster smiled. "It is, but I'd collaborate with you to solve it."

"That's good news. It would be awkward if you wanted to solve this one with someone else."

Foster was still smiling, but his eyes were very serious. "I don't."

A phone buzzed, and Prairie reached into her pocket. It wasn't hers.

"It's me." Foster looked at it. "I have to go."

"Okay." Prairie stood up. Her knees were wobbly. Foster's hand found her elbow. He slid it away over her upper arm, and that last touch gave her goose bumps under her thin blouse.

"I'll keep you in the loop." He started around the trellis to leave, then stopped. "Maybe I can text you Thursday and see what's up."

Prairie smiled, nervous and uncertain with the enormity of everything they'd told each other filling her chest with feeling. "That's tomorrow, and you can."

She watched him go, thinking about how she'd said to Anabel that the reason crush feelings were so big and important was because of what they told you about yourself. They were about what your heart wanted you to have in order to fall in love with yourself.

She imagined the white room inside her head where a detective office might be. Instead of seeing it empty, she saw a desk with Marian sitting at it, managing everything with style and patience and ease.

She saw another desk with curved monitors and a lot of tabletop space for Joyce to do forensic genealogy.

A desk with Emma, working on her podcast.

Prairie realized that the two minutes she'd spent with Marian in her living room before she talked to Foster had been their first official meeting.

If she had any doubts, she would have to remember that she'd known far less when she became a mother, a homemaker, and she was very, very good at that.

Chapter 24

"That's where it's at right now. Some of that hasn't been released to the public yet, so if you did a podcast on Lisa's case, you'd have to stick to research you find yourself." Prairie was sitting at the kitchen table at Emma's house, eating one of the most delicious cookies she'd ever had—tahini and butterscotch—that Emma's mom, Alice Cornelius, had made.

"That's some good stuff, Emma. Did you take notes?" Alice dunked a cookie in a cup of coffee and looked pointedly at her daughter.

"I recorded it." Emma grabbed what had to be her third cookie from the plate in the middle.

"You and that phone. Record it, but write something down. You can't rely on those things one hundred percent. The file fails, then what?"

"Then I freaking call Prairie, that's what."

Emma lost some of her famous poise around her mom. It gave Prairie hope that her own children behaved better with other people than they did with her.

"Hmpf." Alice rolled her eyes. "How many daughters do you have, Prairie?"

"Two. Anabel's just turned fifteen, and Maelynn's eleven."

"I just have this one." Alice pointed at her. "But she has what I call a 'High Child Index.' Like the heat index. It's really eighty-five degrees, but all the other factors make it feel like it's ninety-eight. Emma. One child with a High Child Index." Alice sipped her coffee. "Lot of other factors."

"Yeah, you like to say that, but what are you going to do without me, huh? You'll miss me."

"I won't have to miss you. Where're you going to go without money? You leased an apartment by the river with your imaginary money? You have someone lined up to do your laundry? You come with me right now to the basement and tell me which one is the washer and which one is the dryer, then I'll help you pack your things."

"I could have money."

"From those sponsorship people? Like painting billboards all over your art."

Emma looked at Prairie. "She was supposed to let me start accepting sponsorship on my podcast once I turned eighteen, but that was months ago. Now it's 'when you don't record in my garage.'"

"Well," said Prairie, "that's maybe a good segue into talking about the proposal I sent you."

"I read it over," Alice said. "Here's what I think." She said this to Emma. "She's offering you a job, and you don't have one, and you graduate soon. Take it."

Emma shot her mother a death look so potent, it gave Prairie proximity chills. "I can make my own decisions."

"With your AA degree in, what was it? *New Media.*"

"Graduating with a high school diploma and an AA degree and a successful podcast is not good enough?" Emma's voice was light, but Prairie could hear the hurt of an old argument in her tone. Enough hurt that Alice shook her head and sighed but didn't say anything else.

Emma Cornelius knew what she wanted and what she was willing to do to make it happen. She understood things about how the everyday world intersected with justice. She knew things about the community Prairie couldn't. Prairie didn't want to leave talent like Emma's on the table if she was going to do this.

Homemaker

Emma turned the phone so Prairie could see her own proposal file on the screen.

"I like this part," Emma said. "It's a strong mission, and I like that you've at least taken a stab at market analysis and the financials. But here"—she indicated a heading, INCOME PROJECTIONS—"things get mushy. You don't know if it's going to work, because you're wanting to do something nobody else is doing. That's a risk."

Prairie did not disagree.

"You might have just got lucky with Lisa Radcliffe. I don't know for sure you can do it again, especially because with Lisa the only people you had to talk to were people like you."

Prairie could not disagree with that, either.

"You might not be able to make it work with anyone else. There's going to be folks who walk through the door of a business like this who are really hurting, really in trouble. Folks who haven't had success with any other method or system. I can't be sure you can talk to those people or help them," Emma said.

Prairie's throat was tight. "Maybe not."

"But on the other hand, you might."

"That's my hope."

"Also, the mushy financials make me think you haven't figured out for yourself yet how you're going to charge people who are hurting when they walk through your door. For example, in Lisa's case, who would you have invoiced?"

Prairie tried to come up with an answer. She couldn't. There wasn't anyone involved in Lisa's case who she could have sent a bill to except maybe law enforcement, who hadn't asked for her help and were unlikely to bring her on as a consultant in the future.

Emma put her phone down. "I don't want to work for you," she said. "I don't want to be your employee in another one of your experiments. No offense."

"None taken." This was a lie.

"If you want to do this, we do it as equal partners," Emma said.

279

"Partners." Alice sounded skeptical.

"My time is valuable," Emma said. "I'm already busy with my podcast. If I give my time to Prairie and this project fails, I've lost progress I could have made on my own venture."

"She's offering to pay you," Alice pointed out. "The smart move would be to take her money."

"I think the smarter move is to have my own stake. That way, I have a say in decision-making, and when the business succeeds, I get a share." Emma narrowed her eyes at Prairie. "I'd like you to front my stake. As an act of restorative justice."

Alice let out a sound somewhere between a laugh and a yelp.

Prairie opened her mouth. Closed it again. She had been about to say something careful, like that she would need to think about it and get back to Emma, but Emma was one hundred percent right to want a stake of her own. And Prairie one hundred percent owed Emma the opportunity to participate as a full partner.

She mentally put a big *X* through her original business plan and spoke her new one out loud. "If you're okay with owning twenty-five percent, and a quarter is mine, and Joyce and Marian own the other half."

"I'd like to participate in authoring final negotiated contracts and to be paid for my time at the rate you offered in the proposal. If that works for you, I can offer my soft verbal agreement." Emma said this with no expression other than one eyebrow raised, but then she met Prairie's eyes, and they both grinned. And laughed.

"Praise the Lord, you have a job," said Alice. "I think."

"She has a job," Prairie confirmed.

❦

Later, in her car, Prairie turned on her music a lot louder than usual. She wanted a break from thinking, and loud music was the only thing that

Homemaker

worked reliably these days. Ever since Chris's arrest, the media stories had been constant.

Whenever she could, she'd been hanging out with Megan, because every time they met, it was about her book. Prairie loved that Megan trusted her to help work out tricky problems, listen to Megan complain about writing, and read aloud the really amazing parts.

She parked in the underground garage in the guest spot and took the elevator to Greg's floor. He answered the door in his fake-vintage Nirvana T-shirt, cradling Gingernut to his chest.

"Hey, you." He moved to the side so she could walk past him. "You can sit at the counter there if you want. Just move those things to the side."

A series of clear Pyrex bowls was lined up on the reclaimed wood bar, each of them with different amounts of chopped vegetables, liquids, and spices. "What's this?"

Greg put down Gingernut, who Prairie thought looked pretty sleek. Her missing half ear actually gave her a dashing appearance. "Yeah, that's dinner. It's salmon that'll be baked on a salt slab with a lime and cane sugar sauce, with spicy fried plantains on the side. Maybe a salad, too. I haven't decided."

"Dang. Am I in the right apartment?"

Greg shrugged and gave a little laugh. "It was about time, right? It's embarrassing I haven't navigated my way around the kitchen triangle"—he swooped his hands between the range, fridge, and sink—"before now. The girls really like these plantains. They're Beth's recipe. I've been scheduling her to teach me to cook, and she insisted I was ready to take over now that she's moving to LA. I think, on my nights, I'm going to take that on with the girls instead of finding someone new or doing takeout."

"Are you worried I'm having a midlife crisis?" Prairie trusted Greg with this question because he'd known her for so long and he had every reason to tell the truth.

"If you are, I am, too. And if I am, then maybe having a midlife crisis is important so a person doesn't fossilize into an insufferable human."

He'd asked Prairie to come over this afternoon to talk about the 724 Maple Project and his part in their family life.

"Let's not start with me, though," Prairie said. "Where do you want to start? I was really glad that you wanted to take time and talk about all of this, since I won't be available as much."

Greg put his hands on his knees. "You don't have to gold star me when we both know I am way, way behind on this stuff. I'd have to do about a hundred more school meetings and a couple thousand meals before I was even approaching a sensitive-working-dad amount. You know my mom's been giving me books and articles to read for years, things I'd scan so that I could tell myself that the inequities described in them didn't describe me? At the risk of admitting that I'm that asshat who had to do the work to get it, that's exactly the asshat I was when you were working on finding Lisa. The number of items Marian was bringing to me on an hourly basis, the number of fires I had to put out."

"The stuff with Maelynn and her math teacher—"

"What a prize tool that guy is. Like, he has her fucking test scores right in front of him. What does he think? I like that principal, though, she's smart."

"That's what I mean. You handled that beautifully. I didn't need to take over or monitor it. Honestly, I wouldn't have done as good a job."

Greg laughed. "No gold stars, remember? I read about that, finally—how moms end up over-rewarding their partners in the hope they'll feel validated enough to do one goddamned thing. Maybe you would've handled the math differently. But isn't that the point? Our girls have only had the benefit of your parenting, for the most part, which means you've had to learn and handle things that, you're right, have given you the skills of a CEO. But what if I had applied my CEO skills equally from the beginning? What could our girls have learned about what to demand for themselves in the world? How much more might they know about alternative rock? And maybe, maybe, Prairie,

Homemaker

you wouldn't think you were having a midlife crisis when all you want to do is work outside the home."

Prairie wasn't sure what thought to land on first. She'd had a few hints of how Greg was feeling lately, and he had applied a fuller presence, but she also didn't want him to think she was simply handing off a baton. "I love the 724 Maple Project. It's given me so much. There's still a lot I want to accomplish as the mother of our girls."

Greg pulled one of the bowls toward himself and circled it around on the bar. "You need to understand that I wouldn't have stepped up. I didn't get it. I knew it was important to you. I knew it was related to how things had gone wrong between us and how you wanted to reframe that for the girls. But it *had* to be the 724 Maple Project. You had to do everything you did with the lawyers. You had to hire people and make business cards, and honestly, even then, I didn't get it. The last year or so, I've started to have moments with the girls where what I see in them reminds me viscerally of some of the best women I've worked with and known. Of you, Prayer. So much you. And then I'm fucking terrified because, Jesus Christ, it took me this long to understand I was parenting *women*? That they were *watching* me, how I treated women, how I really regarded them? I looked back on some stuff I did and said, and I—" Greg shook his head. "It's not good. There were plenty of reasons I should have known better."

If he had told her these things years ago, after a fight or in a counselor's office, Prairie would've been able, maybe, to clear out a spot in her heart for them to start again. But what she was feeling now was that Greg's saying all this made a very, very big space not for Greg, or for her and Greg together, but for their children. It made Prairie excited for what they could have instead of worried about what she might take away from them. "Let's make a new project."

"I would like that." Greg looked around the loft. "It's time I get a house. This loft is ridiculous, and Gingernut has not come around."

"A house is a great idea." Prairie sniffed back a tear. "That sounds good."

"And I'm looking forward to getting a set of those cards." Greg smiled. "I've always been pretty jealous."

"My homemaker business cards?"

"Yeah. Greg Ozmanski, Homemaker."

"You got it. I'll have Marian order them up as her last punch list item before she leaves and hooks her wagon to my new folly."

"Don't fucking do that. I can take care of it. Look, I'm going to fuck this up. You know that, right? I'm anticipating a lot of irritation and callouts. Gemma is very, very skeptical that I'm capable."

Greg's business partner suffered no fools. "You know that all I do is fuck up and then fix the fuckups, right?" Prairie asked. "That I wasn't somehow *born* to be a mother who knew how to make doctor's appointments while I ordered new school clothes on my phone on a tour of the backyard to clean up dog shit? I learned those things. Now you get to learn them, and you'll have the benefit of me and your mom and even the girls to help you and check you." Prairie smiled. "That's supposed to be a pep talk, by the way."

He laughed, even as he did look terrified after he'd been so smug about the salmon and plantains. But Prairie was starting to understand that "terrified" was where a lot of good things started.

They talked until it was time for Greg to pick up the girls from school. A little, Prairie wanted to stick around and see how he would get Maelynn to eat salmon, but that was, thank goodness, none of her business.

"Hey," Greg called out before she got on the elevator.

"Yeah?"

"What are you going to call it?"

"What, my detective agency?"

"Yeah."

"I haven't thought of a name yet."

"Well, I think you should call it Prairie Hawk Investigations." He made an arc with his hands like the name was on a marquee. "That sounds so badass. I would order the T-shirt in a hot minute."

Homemaker

"Huh. Prairie Hawk. I like that."

Greg tapped his temple. "Think it over."

"I will. But I already know I like it."

She more than liked it. She recognized it. Prairie Hawk Investigations was the name of a real thing, a name that put flesh on the spirit of the idea she'd been kicking around since she started investigating Lisa's disappearance.

Prairie Hawk Investigations made the white box want something more.

Prairie didn't have anywhere to go after she left Greg's, which was rare. This wasn't garbage time, she realized. It was *her* time.

She made loops around downtown, passing back and forth between the east and west side. She thought she was admiring the light on the river, the difference between the smaller Victorian brick buildings on the west side of downtown versus the taller, more muscular art deco buildings on the east side. But then she recognized that she was *looking* at the buildings, trying to superimpose one of them over the white box in her head. She was noticing signs for leasing offices in the windows of buildings, and some part of her was asking, *This one?*

She kept looping back to idle in front of the same building. The Baylor Building. It was the tallest structure near the river on the east side, sturdy and clad in stylish, early-twentieth-century bright-white ceramic tiles that shone in the sun—a literal white box, if not for all the exquisite moldings.

She'd been inside this building when she and Greg were going to marriage counseling. There were floors and floors of offices along parquet hallways, and office doors with the wavy glass windows and gilt letters. At least half of them were unoccupied because people generally preferred more modern amenities for their business over wood floors and gilt and unbearable, covetable charm.

Prairie pulled up into a parking spot, considering the building. On the street level, it had a restaurant, the kind of place you took a date after going to live theater—a place with atmosphere and a well-stocked bar. There was also a coffee shop. Directly across the street was a newer parking garage with free parking for tenants.

She took in the way the light reflected off the glass. The vibrations of cars going over the metal bridge across the river. The boats on the water a person would be able to see from the building's windows. The east side of downtown was where the newspaper was, all the courthouse and city buildings, law enforcement.

She imagined PRAIRIE HAWK INVESTIGATIONS spelled out in gilt letters on wavy glass. Then she called Marian.

"Let me see." Prairie could hear her typing on her laptop. "The seventh floor has a vacancy with the biggest square footage. There used to be a law office in the space." Marian gave Prairie the lease price.

"Jesus! That's so cheap. What's wrong with it?"

"It's an old building. The bathrooms are the shared public bathrooms on the floor. We'd have to get our own tech connected. Security is only provided during business hours, and entry is keyed, not digital. On top of rent, we'd have to pay our portion of utilities to keep a drafty, century-old office on the seventh floor heated and cooled, which will take a significant chunk out of our operating budget. It's a terrible idea."

"But also the very best, coolest idea?"

"Ordinarily, I would begin a slow campaign of steering your whim into a better idea that you ultimately believed you'd thought of yourself, but—"

"Wait." Prairie reared back from her phone. "How often do you need to do that? How often *are* you doing that?"

"Focus on the 'but,' Prairie."

Prairie remembered there was a reason she was making Marian a partner, and it was probably at least in part so someone kept her in hand. "But?"

Homemaker

"My mom plays bunco with the building owner's wife's sister, and I happen to know that he's good for maintenance, has an excellent building super, is generous with tenant remodels, and keeps his mouth shut and his head down about the businesses in his building. I think all of that, and maybe especially the last part, would be a good thing."

Marian's connections had connections. Good lord. "Will you—"

"I've already drafted an email to the leasing office. I'll leave a voicemail after we get off the phone. You know you can go inside and take the elevator up to the seventh floor and poke around."

Prairie grinned. "I'll leave you to it. Talk to Joyce and Emma."

"You got Emma?" Prairie could hear Marian's excitement in the question.

After they hung up, Prairie fed the meter and sprinted across the street. Up close, she could see the wear on the old building, but when she opened one of the heavy glass doors to the lobby, she was greeted with the smell of coffee and the beginning of the dinner service. There were people with laptops in the seating area by the plate glass windows in the coffee shop, as well as a few people at the beautiful bar in the restaurant. The wide staircase to the second floor had marble treads, and the lobby's two elevators featured gold-painted ironwork. She hadn't noticed many of these details when she was going to marital counseling. Most of the time, she was already crying or bickering with Greg on their way into the building.

The elevator was small and old-fashioned. It deposited her on the seventh floor with a soft ding. As she looked around, the white box in her head faded away, replaced with parquet hallways with deep moldings, wavy glass, and stained marble windowsills on windows that looked out on the river.

It was perfect.

Looking at the place where her detective agency would have its office, Prairie remembered waiting to start her first shift at her first job, as crew on the Seattle–Bainbridge Island ferry. She'd been homesick for rural Oregon, and she hadn't had the faintest fucking clue what she was doing. But halfway through the crossing, she'd just finished wrapping a huge rope around a cleat on the foredeck, something she'd done only in training, when she looked out at the ocean—big and deep and exciting.

The endless possibility of the ocean swept away Prairie's self-doubt in the salt air, and she knew she didn't have to worry. Change was just change. If she'd believed in herself enough to leave home, to find herself on the sea, everything from this point on would only get bigger.

She'd been right, too. It was a moment that had led her, after all, to her girls, and from there to this previously unimaginable but interesting moment.

Prairie pulled out her phone and sent a text.

What if we shared a meal and only had ourselves to talk about? Do you think we could do it?

If we can't, I would propose we keep trying. Ilow's that?

Foster found her in her cozy booth in the restaurant on the ground floor, at the stylishly tweedy bar-restaurant. The drinks were delicious and expensive. Prairie was halfway through one served in a coupe glass with rose-scented foam. She'd also ordered a flight of desserts.

"Prairie Nightingale." Foster slid out of a deep-green suit jacket that was almost black and hung it up on one of the brass hooks on the wooden booth. To Prairie's surprise, he sat down and unknotted a very pretty tie, folded it into a neat square he tucked into the jacket's pocket, and unbuttoned the top *two* buttons of a perfect white shirt.

"Dinner *and* a show," she said, proud of herself for flirting with this man so well.

Foster smiled. "I've always liked this bar, but I've never had a drink here."

"Let's fix that." Prairie caught the eye of the server. "My *date* would like to order."

Homemaker

"Sure thing." The server turned to Foster, pad ready. Foster sent Prairie a quick grin that she had never seen before.

He ordered a drink and shared the dessert flight with her. Then they both ordered fries, and all the while, they talked and talked.

About themselves. About each other. Not about anything in particular.

Acknowledgments

We have written more than twenty books together, but this is the one that changed everything. Prairie Nightingale, Foster Rosemare, and the family and friends who surround them have carved out an oversize niche for themselves in our hearts. Our gratitude to these characters—for the stories, the inspiration, the confidence, and the company—is utter.

Sometimes the Green Bay in this book closely resembles the city where we live. Other times, it's the city where we *wish* we lived. But there are definitely a few instances where the Green Bay depicted here has been fictionalized for convenience to our plot. As outsiders who have spent many years living as "fish out of water," we want to thank our adoptive city and beg its forgiveness for the liberties we've taken.

This series found its first readers at the manuscript stage, and their avid reading and supportive comments encouraged us in more ways than we can count. Thank you, Susan, Barry, Barbara, Bridget, and Julie, for your tangible and emotional support, which bolstered our faith in our vision for this series. It made such a difference.

Thank you to our team, Tara and Pamela, for your creativity, care, and tireless support. We told you we wanted to reach as many readers as possible, and every day you're making it happen. Our editor, Liz Pearsons, along with Megha Parekh, recognized our vision for this book and offered us the opportunity to work with Thomas and Mercer to make it a reality, and we are beyond grateful for the understanding, enthusiasm, and support we have received. The editorial work of Andrea Hurst, Tara Whitaker, and Kellie Osborne made the book stronger and provided welcome encouragement as we got close to the finish line.

Our children, August and James, are our inspiration, joy, and motivation every day. Thank you for caring less if the dining table never returns to its original purpose and instead is where we keep writing stories, at the very heart of our home together. Prairie would approve.

About the Authors

Photos © 2023 a. lentz photography

Ruthie Knox and Annie Mare are authors of more than a dozen romance novels between them. Together they write contemporary queer romance as Mae Marvel. Ruthie and Annie live in a very old house with a garden in Green Bay, Wisconsin, with two teenagers, two dogs, multiple fish, three cats, four hermit crabs, and a bazillion plants. For more information, visit www.ruthieknox.com and www.anniemare.com.